A Window Away

A Novel by
Margaret A Youhana

PART 1

*Our mission is to efficiently provide the world's finest, most
comprehensive book publishing service, enabling every author to
experience success. To find out how to publish your book, your way,
and have it available worldwide, visit us online at www.trafford.com*

Trafford rev. 2/4/2010

www.trafford.com

North America & international
toll-free: 1 888 232 4444 (USA & Canada)
phone: 250 383 6864 ♦ fax: 812 355 4082

Acknowledgments

I would like to thank:
- My son Ramses for his support and trust in me.
- My daughter Rebecca for her practical assistance, encouragement and the confidence she gave me throughout the period of writing the work.
- Doctors Sanjeev Relan and Lorna Benedicto for answering my medical questions.
- James, the balloon pilot from Balloon Aloft Australia Proprietary Limited, for the useful information he gave me on the subject of a balloon ride.
- The gentleman at the Russian club and the lady at the Russian nursing home for letting me know how the Russians came to Australia from Manchuria.
- The staff member at the University of Sydney for telling me about the everyday routine of a medical student.
- The gentleman at Gladesville Psychiatric Hospital who told me about the location, history and type of patients who were admitted there.
- Christopher Tabakof for filling me in about the situation on board the ships that used to bring the displaced postwar people to Australia.
- Most of all, I would like to thank John Drake for editing my manuscript and telling me all about the publishing business.

Preface

D r Julius Varda took his glasses off his tired eyes and placed them carefully on his leather-topped desk. He rubbed his eyelids for a while then leaned back in his deep swivel chair, taking a keen delight in the comfort that can only be expected from a state of the art, high-class upholstery item. His last patient had cancelled earlier and he couldn't be happier about it. A few minutes earlier, he had heard his assistant's car roar out of the driveway and turn into the main street. The whole place was his now.

Julius tried to take this opportunity to unwind and enjoy the quiet, before heading home. All day long, he had seen nothing but frustrated and worried parents who used every trick they knew of, to calm their kicking and screaming children, children with feverish faces, runny noses and nasty coughs. Some sort of an epidemic flu was going around and the surgery had been unusually crowded that day.

Outside a torrential rain was raging. Julius lifted his arms, locked his fingers together and placed them at the back of his neck. Raising his head, his gaze became fixed on a colour-faded tennis racquet that was still hanging from the initial nail his grandfather Jonathan had hammered in, on the opposite wall, a long time ago.

When the young doctor was remodelling his grandparents' house to turn it into his surgery he had decided to let that particular item stay where it was. Obviously clashing with the rest of the décor, that link between him and his troubled past had aroused the curiosity of many who entered the room. Amazingly, one look at that old thing, that cherished relic from the long gone days, still had the power to take his mind away. Once again he let his thoughts wander away to an enchanted world, where pain was a little more bearable and memories didn't hurt as much as they used to. Instinctively, Julius stood up and walked over to the window. Pulling the curtains attentively aside, he glanced at the closed window facing his, in the house next door. A hint of a smile lighting up his features, he blew a tender kiss from the tip of his fingers to an imaginary person standing there and curiously staring at him.

Julius often found himself doing that and every time he did it, this simple act worked its magic. It restored his faith in life, inspired him with confidence and helped him acknowledge that there is some sort of harmony in the scheme of things. He had come to believe that nothing happens on this earth without a reason, without a purpose. In the years gone by, that window had played such a significant part in his life. Sometimes, he really believed he could hear the sweet voice of a little girl calling him, "Yul! Yul! Aren't you ready yet? You'd better get cracking or we will be late for school." Other times, her tantalising voice would be heard, as she yelled out, "Get off your bum, you lazy one. Last one to the park is a rotten egg."

The house next door was let to a team of dentists these days, but to Julius, it would always be grandma Goddard's home. Millie, her grandmother Martha and their talkative parrot Tooty, used to live there. Occasionally Millie's journalist dad stayed there too, when he was in Sydney and not in some foreign country, covering a story worth printing in the papers.

Julius returned to his chair and decided to wait for the rain to ease a little, before venturing out. Behind his desk, a sudden idea popped in his head. Furtively he opened a side drawer and rummaged trough his papers, looking for an ancient notebook he believed was still lying in there. To his relief, he found it. Flicking through it, he came across a tatty old sheet of paper left between the pages. Eagerly holding it to his eyes, he realised he wasn't wearing his spectacles. After putting his glasses back on, he began reading a poem he had written, more than a decade ago.

There was a time, when love kept us together,
We were from two windows, facing each other.
Every day we exchanged a hello and how are you,
Everyday, we talked about whatever was new.
Now, my lips are silent, my heart is broken,
Now, one of the windows is no longer open.
I don't think it was any fault of mine,
It's not like the moon moved in the wrong sign.
It was.....

Half way through the poem, Julius stopped reading. He put the paper on the table and swirled his chair around. Dropping his eyelids down, a mysterious smile lifted his facial muscles giving him a mesmerised look, as he began whispering tenderly, "Millie, my beautiful, adorable Millie. If only you knew what you meant to me. If only you knew ..."

Julius returned to his poem and, with the nostalgia of a love lost, he went on reading.

It was your sudden trip that took you away,
Brought tears to my eyes and darkened my day.
That metallic monster, with silvery wings,
Changed altogether, the system of things.

Chapter 1

Liuba was only fourteen years old when her father died. He was a truck driver and was on one of his usual runs. He was transporting wheat from Tabriz, a city in Azerbaijan, to Tehran, when he became aware of a puncture in one of the tyres. Strangely, this happened just before reaching Shibly, the notorious precipice. Notorious because, over the years, that perilously steep faced mountain had in fact claimed the lives of many truck drivers and bus passengers. Apparently he had stopped to change the offending tyre and, in the process of doing that, the tragedy must have taken place. For the next passing-by drivers who had found him frozen stiff in the snow, it wasn't hard to imagine what had happened. It was the same old story, the same dreaded mishap that had killed so many of their colleagues before. The metal ring that holds the tube, snapping out of its place, must have hit him in the chest. Whether he had died instantly from the impact or he just had fallen unconscious and eventually had frozen to death in the subzero temperature, was anyone's guess.

Liuba was an only child. After the terrible event, she and her mother had a hard time coping with the loss of a dear father and a loving husband who unfortunately was the sole breadwinner in the family. Luckily, as they say, as a door closed another opened and Liuba's mother found herself a job in a nearby hospital. It was a part time cleaning job but she was making enough to pay the rent

1

and put food on the table. When summer came and, in the gardens of Tabriz, the snow was replaced by lots of colourful flowers, Liuba started to go to Tamara's workroom. Tamara was an Armenian lady dressmaker, a friend of her mother's. She had agreed to keep the girl under her wing. For a little pocket money, Liuba was supposed to do some finishing work on garments, do the false basting on the pieces of cut materials, make tea or coffee for the customers as well as tidy up the workroom at the end of the day. Young Liuba was happy with the arrangement. She was earning money while learning a few tricks of the trade. Keeping herself busy during the school holiday was also taking her mind off her father's death, because she was still missing him a great deal.

That afternoon, after a hard day's work, Liuba left Tamara's place, a bit tired, but she was proudly feeling her hard earned pay and bonus in her cardigan pocket. She couldn't wait to give the money to her mother, unaware of what was awaiting her at home. Once she got to their front door, she knocked and waited a while before deciding to open it with her own key. Stepping inside, she couldn't help noticing a strong aroma of barbequed chicken, floating in the air. She went straight to the kitchen to see to the food. Lifting the lid of the pot, she stared, with disgust, at an unsightly solidified substance, sitting at the bottom of it. A minute later and the whole kitchen would have been filled with the smoke of burnt soup. She took the piping hot pot off the burner, put it carefully in the sink and called, "Mum, mum, where are you? Your soup is about to turn to charcoal."

Liuba turned towards the doorway that led to the corridor and the bedrooms, when she saw one of her mother's slippers on the floor. Her instinct told her that something was not right. Cautiously she tiptoed to investigate the other side of the doorway when she found her mother's frail body crumpled on the floor, one hand clutching to her chest, the other trying to grab onto something.

When the neighbours arrived, after hearing Liuba's hysterical screams, they didn't have any idea how to calm down the wretched girl. Looking at each other's faces, they unanimously agreed that the poor woman's heart must have given up. It seemed that she could no longer withstand the pain of not having her husband around. After a long period of screaming and weeping, Liuba went quiet, all of a sudden. In a catatonic like state, her gaze fixed at nowhere in particular, she sat motionless in a corner, looking completely detached from the rest of the world. For two whole days, religiously she kept pressing her mother's slippers to her heart. Unable to bring her back to reality, neighbours and friends had no choice but to wait for her aunt to come over from Tehran and decide her fate.

Aunt Sophie was the only relative Liuba had left in the whole world. Sophie was a kind-hearted person who was always ready to lend a hand to people in distress, always there when she was needed. Besides being a remarkable human being, Sophie had an ability to communicate with young people. Trustworthy as a friend, she was well educated, serene yet vivacious and full of beans. People who came to know her often wondered why she had never been married, as she was also a pleasant looking lady with whom everyone felt at ease to go to with their problems. Only five months had passed since Liuba's neighbours had met her for the first time. That was when she had come to Tabriz to participate in her only brother's burial ceremony. Aunt Sophie was the Headmaster's assistant, in the primary school where she used to teach, in her younger days. She had managed to take time off work and arrived precisely on the third day after her sister-in-law's death, just in time to take part in her funeral.

It was only when Liuba's eyes met with her aunt's that things changed in her behaviour. Suddenly, as if somewhere inside her subconscious mind, something had snapped, there was an explosion of suppressed emotions, a kind of release from restriction. It seemed like Liuba's knotted throat had burst open. As if a blocking gate was lifted off a dam, because only then her dry eyes miraculously filled with soothing tears. She cried and cried, loudly at first, then gradually, devoid of energy, her sobbing dropped to a lower volume, until it was only a soft wail. Occasionally, raising her head, she gave aunt Sophie a despairing look. Wiping her eyes, she at once asked her, with a broken voice, "What am I going to do auntie, what am I going to do without them?"

"You'll be all right," cried Sophie, holding her in her arms and patting her dark brown hair, affectionately. Throughout this ordeal, Liuba never let go of her mother's slippers. No one could lure them out of her hands, even if they tried to do so. That was her way of clinging on to something that was representing her mother's last moments of being alive. It took a lot of pleading and reasoning from aunt Sophie to finally placate and persuade her to go to sleep. Still clutching the worn out slippers in her tight fist, she agreed to go to bed.

The funeral, then the wake that followed the seventh day after the burial was out of the way. As soon as all the attendants had left, Sophie wrapped her arms around Liuba's petite body and began talking to her, as gently as she possibly could, "Now listen to me carefully, my dear, dear girl. Life goes on, whether you want it or not. Believe me, I have been there and I know how much you are hurting. It is understandable and I sympathise with you. I am aware of the extent of your grief. You have lost a great deal, but it's time you thought about yourself, about your future. I am here now and I assure you, you will never be alone, if I can help it. You know I never had any children of my own, but if the good Lord was to bless me with one, a daughter perhaps, I would have liked her to be just like you. So start packing your bags, because I am taking you to Tehran to live with me."

Out of breath, Sophie paused for a while. She held her niece a bit away from herself in order to look her in the eyes then she went on with her talk, "I am sure you will like it there and I promise you, on my newly departed brother's grave, that you won't need for anything, as long as I live."

Pale faced and hollow cheeked, Liuba kissed her aunt and nodded, praising the Lord that, although heartache had come to her by the bucketful, she still had someone to lean on, in her darkest days.

Sophie and Liuba placed their flowers on the two graves and lit up candles all around. Together they cried and prayed a lot. Finally, after saying goodbye to their dear departed, they left the cemetery and headed home. Half an hour later, they were on a bus and on their way to Tehran. Two days later the pair unpacked, had a light dinner and went to bed. They had a big day ahead of them and only two weeks to prepare for the school's opening.

The next day, Sophie took her niece to various shops and bought her all the necessary gear a young girl of her age would need. She even had her own dressmaker design her a new wardrobe, one that, under different circumstances, would have made Liuba jump for joy. She was grateful though and she thanked her aunt loads of times for her generosity. The following Saturday, Sophie was back to work and her niece found herself on the grounds of her new high school that was just a few blocks from the primary school were Sophie worked.

Liuba used to get home almost an hour before her aunt, so she had time to start the dinner before attending to her homework. As time passed the two became so attached to one another, they looked more and more like a mother and daughter. More time slid away and Liuba's grief seemed to have lessened. Nevertheless, whenever something was bothering her, like the time a schoolmate was giving her a hard time, jealousy being the main instigator, she couldn't help but go back to her old habit of pairing shoes that were at a distance from one another. In serious cases, she even took her mother's slippers out of their hiding place and pressed them to her heart. She kept on biting her lips, with a vague look on her face. In Liuba's mind, when shoes were sitting next to each other, things were in harmony. It made her believe that wounds would find a way to heal, but if they were apart, it meant chaos, alarm bells would go off and the ugly face of sadness would come back to haunt her again.

Chapter 2

When the Second World War ended in Europe and other countries affected by it, people all over the world eagerly read the papers or kept up with the news through the wireless that was constantly broadcasting the latest reports about it. They wanted to absorb every minute detail the media could impart to them. They learned, in disbelief, all about the atrocities that had gone on in the occupied countries during the reign of the Third Reich and the Nazi regime. Everyone was somehow touched by the horrific discoveries. Everyone, in a different way was trying to come to terms with it. All over Europe, nobody was left unscathed by the war. Those who were in the eye of the storm had died or suffered tremendously. Many families had lost one or more of their members. Ordinary people either perished by the hands of the Gestapo and the S.S. or saw their friends and loved ones die a slow, agonising death, in captivity, if not in the gas chambers.

After the Holocaust, for some survivors, it was as if the war had never ended. They just couldn't muster enough strength to overcome their ordeal. Their souls ravaged beyond hope, they found it hard to live with the memories that kept haunting them, day in and day out. Others barely found in themselves the courage to put the pieces of their shattered lives together and went on with their troubled existence, an existence often tainted by recurring nightmares and glimpses of the heartrending events they had witnessed or endured.

In times of war, apart from the pain and sufferings, there is a financial factor to consider too. As they say, "you can catch more fish in troubled waters." It was unfortunate that the majority of citizens who were trapped in the middle of it had lost most of their belongings or found a big dent in their financial situation. However, somehow a small group of people, mainly those in power, managed to gather considerable amounts of money or precious objects and got away with it. In the meantime, while the war was raging, some very ordinary people became lucky too. They were perhaps in the right job, in the right place, at the right time or they were just smart and resourceful. In the Middle East, one such individual who made a bundle during the war was Malcolm Yonan, an Assyrian businessman residing in Iran.

Rumours were that the Iranian King had a penchant towards the Nazi regime. In fact, it was his pro-Axis tendencies that forced him to abdicate in favour of his son Mohamad-Reza Pahlavi, in the year 1941. Allegedly being there for business undertakings, German entrepreneurs were already stationed in Iran, from way before the war. Their influence was felt all over the country. Supposedly executing their contracts, constructing train stations, building bridges or erecting other impressive monuments, they were gradually tightening their grip on the Persian Empire. During the war, there were a few skirmishes here and there, a few bombs were detonated, as the country was experiencing civil unrest. Some bloodshed had occurred in the Azerbaijan region as well as other places. Things could have been worse if Allied forces didn't intervene when they did. Germans would have stayed to dig their claws into the core of the six thousand year old Persian civilization. Anyhow the Germans left the Iranian soil in time before Russian, British and American troops poured in.

Not everyone, especially not the common people, knew what the presence of the Allies in their country would mean in the long run, but for the time being, their stay provided a lot of much needed jobs for those who were willing to work. Convoy trucks had to be driven from places to places, so a great deal of drivers found steady employment. So too, skilled people were hired to help with building schools, hospitals and factories, as well as constructing roads and bridges.

Frances Malik took a sip from his tea then carefully placed the cup on the table, wondering why it was so cold. He was so engrossed in the news he was reading in Ettelaat, the Iranian daily newspaper that he couldn't recall how much time had passed since his wife had brought him his tea. His dark eyes filled with sadness, he went on reading. From time to time, he shook his head in disbelief, mumbling under his breath, "Incredible! Absolutely incredible! How can something so atrocious, something of this magnitude happen in this time and era? This should never happen again, it should not happen at all."

Frances was a literature and history teacher in one of Tehran's prestigious high schools. He was also doing some translating jobs for the government, as he could speak French fluently. He was from a Christian minority, living in Iran. To be precise, he was of an Assyrian origin. Residing in a big house with a big garden, he was living comfortably with his wife and three children. There was a printing place at the other end of the garden. It was let to a group of people from another religious minority who used it to publish their own newspaper. With his income and the rent he was collecting, one could say that the Maliks were doing fine.

Reading some more startling news about the plight of the Jewish population in Europe, Frances couldn't stop his thoughts from turning towards his own people.

After losing the war to the Medes and Babylonians, some six hundred years before Christ, Assyrians were eventually left to live in Iran. For centuries they had considered Iran to be their motherland, and they were accepted and mostly respected for their skills and their loyalty to the authorities. Nevertheless, at times when they were subjected to bigotry by their peers, they couldn't help but feel like aliens, in a place they were resigned to call their own. Being singled out made them feel like strangers in the very house they had been born in. Scattered all over the world, the number of Assyrian speaking families was gradually dwindling down. Their tradition was running the risk of being overlooked in the process.

Frances went on thinking about the Jewish population, Hitler and his followers were set to wipe out from the face of the earth. "It is madness to even think they could exterminate a whole nation, just madness," he went on mumbling, anger sending blood to his cheeks. Once again his mind drifted on to a pet project, he was keeping to himself. It was more like an idea, a dream he was nurturing for quite a while. Like a dormant volcano that wakes up and becomes active, all of a sudden, he began searching for a way to put his plan into action.

Was it the war and what had happened to the Jews in Germany or the need to see his people reunite and be counted that gave him the incentive? Whatever it was, it made him all the more determined to get up and put a step forward towards his goal. A sentence he had heard or read somewhere suddenly popped in his mind. "A journey of a thousand miles starts with a single step," he quoted as he scratched his head then, smiling optimistically, 'Well! At least I can't say that I didn't try,' he thought.

Frances took his teacup to the kitchen. Myriam, his wife was busy placing a piece of lavash bread in the buttered bottom of a big pot. She smiled as she found him watching her cook. She took a colander filled with steaming half cooked rice from the sink and emptied the content in the pot, on top of the lavash bread and turned down the knob on the stove.

"I see you are making tahdig."

"Yes dear, the children love the crispy bread under the rice. Do you want another cup of tea darling?" she asked, as she generously dribbled some melted butter all over the rice.

"Yes, but I'll get it myself," he answered, looking visibly preoccupied with something. He waited a bit then added without preamble, "Can I, I mean can we invite a few people over, one of these days? I want to discuss the matter of starting an association of a kind with them. What do you say Myriam?"

Knowing exactly what he meant, Myriam nodded approvingly. "I don't see why not, dear. You can invite whoever you think is more suitable for the job. Will next weekend be a good time? The children will be out. I'll prepare something nice to serve the guests."

The following Thursday night, after having a scrumptious meal, Frances and Myriam, together with the seven guests they had invited, retired to the lounge room. Once they were sitting comfortably and the compliments to the cook were out of the way, nibbling on seeds, pistachio nuts and dried fruits, they began talking about the subject at hand. They discussed every facet of Frances' proposed plan and finally they came to an agreeable conclusion. Instinctively bending down to the bowl of seeds Myriam had placed on the table in front of him, Frances took a handful of the plump and seasoned watermelon seeds. He quickly hulled and ate them one by one, with the skill he had learned as a child, like all the Middle Eastern people did. Then, holding the list he had come up with, Frances gave the group a short but ceremonious speech that finished with, "So, you see my friends, it's up to us to do something to preserve our glorious culture. All that people know about us are a few references in some encyclopaedias. Thanks to a few Hollywood style movies, they may have heard of our Queen Semiramis and one or two of our kings who had reigned all those years ago, somewhere in the Middle East, but this is not enough. Our aim is to make the world realise that we, the descendents of a nation, once so powerful, are still living amongst them."

He paused for a while then, looking at the paper, he read, "We all agreed that the printing and dispatching of pamphlets to the future members will be my responsibility. I will also be locating venues suitable to hold our parties. While doing some research about legal matters, I will try to liase with the council and find out about any possible problem we may come across, regarding the law."

Stretching his open hand towards one of the guests, he continued, "Avrahim will be in charge of organising the parties and get togethers. These parties will give members the opportunity to meet each other on a social level. Sophie, with her exceptional dancing skills, will teach the young dance enthusiasts, all the steps of the Sheikhani and other Assyrian dances. Nathaniel will be in charge of bookkeeping and other money matters. As for Shimoon, he will tell members and their children, a bit about our history and teach them the Assyrian language as well as some English."

Excitedly, they all nodded then began talking amongst themselves.

Myriam entered the room carrying a tray of tea served in small glass cups. A bowl of quince jam to be consumed with the tea, together with little plates and spoons, were also placed in front of the guests by Shimoon's wife Seraphima who had been helping Myriam in the kitchen.

After thanking Seraphima, Myriam added, "don't forget that Seraphima and I, and hopefully other volunteering ladies, will be doing the catering for the parties."

The group also consented that, being the original founders of the Association, they would have to put some money in the coffer for the preliminary expenses. They were convinced they would be reimbursed once the project got off the ground and actually started to show profits, from the entry tickets, raffles and other activities, they would have to come up with later. They were all hell bent to make their endeavour pay off and, with a bit of luck help them reach their goal.

"I will ask my brother Malcolm for a donation too. Lord knows he can afford it now, with all the money he is about to make from his movie theatre," said Shimoon.

"I heard it's always jam packed with people, I am sure he will be willing to help our cause," Avrahim added.

Sophie Guilliana took her job so seriously that, way before the due time for the first party to be held, she had a group of youngsters ready and willing to dance. Amongst them were three young men she had chosen for a special dance. Conveniently, Jonathan Varda, Adam Yonan and Saul Aziz had the same build and height and were good friends too. This was important, since they had to spend a lot of time together rehearsing their steps. They used to meet every afternoon in the local primary school, where Sophie was working. Being the schoolmaster's assistant helped her get the permission to use the premises. There, in the huge gym room, tirelessly she made the trio practice and practice all the different steps of the authentic folkloric Assyrian dances. After the preliminary stretching and breathing techniques, a sequence of precise movements were to be learned. Then they had to master the art of dancing in unison, which meant making the same motions and gestures with a fastidious accuracy, as if they were one.

Sophie was very pleased with their achievement, she kept telling it to her niece Liuba about their progress. Although Liuba was preparing herself for her high school exams, Sophie urged her to go and see the group dance, before the launching party of the Association.

Her head buried in the textbook she had brought with her, Liuba was quietly reading and taking notes. When the rehearsal began, she put the book away and, from the inconspicuous corner where she was sitting, she watched the three young men perform their incredible act. Mesmerised by the spectacle, her eyes got stuck on Jonathan, the one who was first in the line, in other words the one who was waving the special handkerchief, as he was leading the group.

Her heart racing, her palms sweaty, Liuba couldn't take her eyes off the man's tall and slender figure. She just couldn't stop herself staring at his freshly shaved, faultless face and his high forehead. There was something about Jonathan's features that reminded her so much of Tyrone Power, the handsome actor she had seen and admired in a movie that Sophie had taken her to, a few weeks ago. From time to time, a strand of hair would fall over the young man's face, as he moved his head from side to side. He would then toss it aside with a swift move, making his performance all the more exciting and characteristic. It was no wonder that Liuba's heart was beating at a rate that was new to her and this worried her, since it was the first time she had felt that way for someone of the opposite sex.

Chapter 3

M alcolm Yonan learned the art of trading the hard way, starting from the first rung of the ladder, so to speak. After getting his year nine diploma, since he wasn't so keen on furthering his studies, his next option was to find himself a job. His father urged him to change his mind. "At least do another three years, get your matriculation papers, you'll need them some day, son," he pleaded with him, but Malcolm had other ideas in his head.

For some unknown reason Malcolm was eager to start work and gain a certain degree of financial independence. Unfortunately his plan didn't pan out, at least not the way he had hoped. After a few weeks of knocking on doors, disappointed and tired of rejections, he decided to accept his father's job offer. It had been a long time since he had been in his dad's fabric shop. He couldn't believe his eyes when he saw the appalling state it was kept in.

From his first day at work, Malcolm proved everyone, including himself, that he wasn't a quitter. Grabbing a broom and dustpan, he began sweeping, dusting, scrubbing and rearranging things. In no time, the place looked so different, his father couldn't recognise it. His second task was to find a better way to display their merchandise and make the materials look more appealing to the clients. The last thing that needed to go through a drastic change was the prehis-toric filing system. The account keeping books had to be updated too. When everything was to his satisfaction, young Malcolm put a couple of signs outside on the footpath, inviting people to come and visit the revamped fabric and haberdashery shop.

Malcolm's hard work payed off and his father couldn't be happier for the good reason that the cost of the transformation was almost next to nothing. Clients poured in from all around the area. Two weeks later they had to hire an extra salesperson to assist in the rush hours. With his innovative ways of dealing with the day-to-day problems, things couldn't have gone any better when, all of a sudden, to everyone's disbelief, Malcolm declared his decision of leaving his job and moving out of his family home, as well.

"Why do you want to throw everything away now," asked his father, visibly worried about his son's recent change in behaviour. Lately it seemed that the young man was going through a rough patch. His parental instincts were telling him that something serious was definitely amiss in his son's private life, but he just couldn't put his finger on it. 'Maybe he has girl problems,' was his best guess.

"Don't worry dad, I know what I am doing, I want to explore new horizons. Please, don't go thinking that I wasn't happy here. I have learned a lot while I was working for you," Malcolm said before his dad interrupted him.

"But son, you did so much in the shop, without you my business would have been left in the same rut. After your mother died, God bless her soul, I lost interest in everything. I neglected my work. You gave it a new lease of life," his dad said, trying hard not to show his disappointment.

"Oh Dad! I wish I could have done more but I feel it's time I moved on. I need to go away and discover what's there for me, what is it that I want to do with my life. Trust me dad, I will do my best to make you proud of me," he said, giving his father a big hug.

"I have no doubt about that and if this is what you want, God be with you. I hope you find what you are after, son. I will surely miss you here but I'll be all right. Don't be a stranger though, drop me a few lines once in a while," said his father, not hiding his sadness too well. His mind turned to his elder son Shimoon, the studious one in the family. Three weeks ago, he had also moved out of home after his wedding to Saraphima, so it was understandable that the old man wasn't looking forward to living by himself.

At the shop no one was happy with Malcolm's departure, except for the boy servant who was sick of emptying his ashtrays, even though he didn't mind the smell of his cigarettes from afar.

Before the end of the month, Malcolm was settled in Khoram-shahr, an industrial city in the south of Iran. He was due to start work the week after, as a bookkeeper for a company that was importing various household items from Europe and Asia. In his new office, Malcolm soon found out all about chinaware, statuettes, crystal vases and all sorts of ornamental objects, as well as mirrors, bathtubs, sinks, tap fittings and doorknobs.

While doing the routine tasks expected of him, Malcolm kept his eyes and ears open. He did a lot of research, gathered a great deal of information. His tenacity to learn took him to the point that, in a rather short time, he knew the whereabouts of all the over-seas companies from where his bosses were buying the colourful merchandise. He knew every item's wholesale price, the shipping cost, tax and custom fees and names of retail outlets the goods were sold to. Malcolm's knack for absorbing minute details came to him so naturally, it seemed that he was born a businessman. He worked hard and long hours, putting aside all the cash he could spare.

Impatiently Malcolm waited to collect enough money to start his own little company. He had been in Khoramshahr for only two years when he received a telegram informing him of his father's stroke. Pained with the bad news, Malcolm felt the need to go back home. He also took this as a sign that the time had come for him to go solo, work wise. He was almost sure his father wanted him back to take over his business, since Shimoon had never shown any interest in managing the shop. Leaving his job rather abruptly, he returned to Tehran, armed with a lot of experience and stacks of information crammed in his head. More or less expecting it, he came back to an ill managed business, waiting to be rescued once again, but this time he was determined to turn it into a bigger success, with a new insight on things. Unfortunately his father died soon after his arrival. Malcolm knew all along that he would not be happy, trading fabrics for the rest of his days. He had serious dreams for his future. After a few months, when the shop was back to the way it was before he had left, he sold it for a good price. In his absence, Shimoon and Saraphima had a son they called Adam. The thought never occurred to Shimoon that he should have a share from the sale of the shop, since he knew it was his brother who had turned it into such a lucrative business. Malcolm surprised him though, when he presented him with a generous cheque and let him have the two Kerman carpets from their father's house.

"No, you keep the carpets," he objected.

"It's all right. I am never home, besides your little one needs to crawl on something softer," Malcolm said, ruffling the toddler's hair affectionately.

It didn't take Malcolm too long to find a suitable place to set up his office. Praying for God's blessing and for a bit of luck, he decided to take the risk and hope for the best. His dedication and confidence paid off indeed, because in a short period, he managed to make himself known in the business world. To buy at the right time, for the right price and sell with huge profits when the goods were most needed became his trait. He could smell a good bargain from miles away. In Tehran's Market centre, he was soon referred to, as the business mogul of the time.

Travelling back and forth to the European countries, Malcolm was constantly looking for luxury items, with a keen eye for quality as well as good appearance. His ladies' laced satin lingerie, high-class knitwear, makeup products, raincoats, umbrellas, wallets and nail grooming kits were in great demand in Lalezar and Nadery Street's most prestigious shops, as well as the main stores in other major cities. The exotic cigars and cigarettes that came in handsome packaging were also selling like hot cakes. His office, in the heart of Tehran's famous Bazaar area, was always inundated with traders sniffing for novelties to fill their boutiques. French fabrics, Italian silks, Spanish laces as well as English woollen underwear and all sorts of little trinkets were snatched off his hands as soon as the shipments arrived. He made himself quite a reputation and a lot of money in just a few years.

Malcolm was in London wrapping up a deal with some tweed suit and overcoat manufacturers when the subject of Australia and its fine wool industry came about. Back home, he had heard a few things about the big continent on the other side of the globe. At least he knew about kangaroos and merino sheep and the soft yarn made from its fleece, he also knew about the angora wool. After checking his calendar, there and then, he decided to book himself on the next boat due to sail towards the land down under and inspect its market closely. He barely had time to inform his people in Iran of his intentions, before going on board.

A couple of months later, Malcolm found himself walking on the streets of Sydney. Without wasting precious time, his curiosity at its peak, he made the necessary inquiries and went on a round of visits to some wool corporations and acquired the knowledge he needed about the industry. He also looked in on some textile screen printing places and was impressed by the vibrant and warm colours used on the fabrics. A few days before Christmas 1937, after closing a temporary deal with the fabric merchants, while Australians were wrapping presents and decorating their Christmas trees, Malcolm finally permitted himself to go sightseeing. Overwhelmed by the sun , the sceneries, the beautiful flowering trees and shrubs, the friendliness of the people there, not to mention the clean and wholesome life one could have in this land of plenty, he decided that this sun kissed country was the place where he wouldn't mind spending the rest of his life.

When Malcolm returned home, he didn't stop expressing his admiration for Australia. He just couldn't help himself resounding the praises and recommending the advantages of living in such a country. Unfortunately, it all fell on deaf ears. His family and friends, too attached to their particular little lives, didn't show any interest in uprooting themselves for some supposed dreamland. If it wasn't for their vine plantations in Rezayeh or their money making trucks that carried goods from city to city, it was maybe a well paying job they didn't see the sense of leaving. At least not just yet.

Malcolm was born in Shamsejahan, a village in Azerbaijan, thus his love for big open spaces ran deep in him and it was no wonder that the vastness of Australia was so appealing to him. Anyhow, the subject of migration had to be closed as, a few months later, the war broke out in Europe and to his sorrow, Malcolm heard that Australia was also involved in the battle and was threatened by a Japanese invasion.

While the war was raging, Malcolm thought it was safer to stay put and keep well away from the occupied countries. He had no choice but to put his import-export deals on the back burner and search for a worthwhile project that would fill his days in Iran. Still wondering about his next move, one evening he took his nephew Adam to see a movie. Adam, now a teenager, loved the western films so that day, instead of Fernandel's film "Mankind's Enemy Number One", Malcolm took him to see featuring John Wayne and Lola Montez. It was in the pitch dark of the theatre that the idea popped into his head.

At that time, there were only a few cinemas in Tehran and hardly any in other cities, so Malcolm thought about trying his luck in the entertainment industry for a change. After kicking the idea around for a rather short while, he decided to put his money in a cinema, one that would be more inviting to the public than the existing ones. Two weeks later, he heard of someone who had started the building of such a venue but had trouble coming up with the rest of the money needed for its completion. Malcolm rushed to see the man and offered to buy it from him, the way it was. After some haggling they came to agree on a price that would be acceptable to both of them.

As soon as the deal was legally concluded, with the help of a group of professional tradesmen and artists, Malcolm put the last touches on his elegant theatre. On the opening night, he went as far as handing out a small bag of colourful lollies with every ticket purchased, and that marked the beginning of his success. It so happened that the majority of the Iranian people were crazy about American movies and it didn't matter to them whether they were watching a musical, a comedy or a western. They just loved to take all the family to a movie palace, with a supply of seeds, nuts or lollies and a few bottles of lemonade, retreat for a couple of hours into a fantasy world and watch their favourite stars on the big screen. In those exotic surroundings they found it easy to forget life's daily grind.

Malcolm struck gold with his first cinema, as it was the cheapest entertainment the average person could afford. In fact, for less than a toman, one could be entertained in such a relaxed atmosphere.

Within a year Malcolm bought and renovated a second cinema, and installed a refreshments stand at both venues. Not only did he make money selling tickets, he also sold tons of roasted watermelon, sunflower and pumpkin seeds, plus nuts and soft drinks, on the side. Years later, eating seeds and pistashio nuts in the cinemas was prohibited because of all the noise and rubbish it generated, but by that time, Malcolm couldn't care less. He had sold both of his cinemas and had walked away with a truck load of cash to go back to his previous passion.

The war was finally over and Malcolm was ready and willing to return to his entrepreneurial business. He had missed being on the road and finding new markets to explore. After studying the state of the world's economy and treading carefully, he set up shop again and began negotiating with several companies. Europeans had started rebuilding their lives and their ruined countries. After the crippling recession, Australia also seemed to be back on track. Malcolm made another trip to Australia, the country he had been so fascinated with before the war. He just wanted to see if it would have the same effect on him as it had done the last time. He liked it even more and, once again, he fell in love with the breathtaking charm of Sydney. So much so that he decided to make it his home.

Malcolm returned home to make the necessary applications and liquidate his assets, leaving a much smaller office still operating in Iran. He appointed one of his top aides to run it, giving the man the responsibility of keeping him well informed with the latest developments. In a meeting to inform his workers, he pointed to Australia on the world map, and announced that he intended to open another office in his new country. After Malcolm left the meeting, one of the workers sarcastically uttered, "I give you my word that he will not succeed and will be back with his tail between his legs."

Chapter 4

L iuba sat at Aunt Sophie's dressing table and finished combing her newly trimmed black hair while biting on her lower lip, until it turned plum red. To her disappointment the colour didn't last for too long and the mirror reflected back her original pale face and equally colourless lips, a telltale sign of the stress and nervous state she was in. She rummaged through her aunt's scanty make-up bag and found a nearly finished lipstick. Liuba managed to get some of it on one index finger and rubbed her other index finger on it. She then dabbed a little on her lips and cheeks, hoping nobody would suspect she had make-up on. Satisfied with her looks, she grabbed the nice patented leather bag that Sophie had given her for her seventeenth birthday and called, "I am ready, auntie."

Aunt Sophie and Liuba were both going to Adam's graduation party. Looking forward to seeing Jonathan brought a tingling sensation to Liuba's heart, a sensation that left her abashed. She was distressed to admit to herself that his features had been stuck in her mind since the day she had seen him on the dance floor. Despite being aware of the unlikelihood of him ever noticing her, she couldn't think of anything else but him and his captivating chiselled face. She tried to convince herself that she wouldn't let her feelings go to her head but that was easier said than done. She closed her eyes to whisper a prayer, "I only want to see him, that's all. Is there any harm in that? Can't a girl have a wish, dear Lord?"

Since the untimely deaths of her parents, Liuba had turned to God and her religion, for solace. There wasn't a day that she didn't find herself talking to "Alaha", meaning God in her native Assyrian language. Since she had come to live with Aunt Sophie three years ago, Liuba was pampered and loved beyond her expectations, but she was still bearing the scars of past events. There was an empty space in her heart, a space left unoccupied since she had suddenly become an orphan. There wasn't a moment she didn't feel the need to fill that void and Aunt Sophie's kindness just wasn't doing the trick. She needed more. Now that she'd seen Jonathan, the thought of him had given her a glimmer of hope that he was the one who could heal her wounds and make her whole again. Every night, after saying her prayers she imagined herself walking with him in an enchanting setting, where a fresh breeze would be sweeping her hair. He would stop to pick a flower and, looking amorously into her eyes, he would offer it to her. Being the only way she could let go of her fears, these thoughts would almost always help her drift into a restful sleep.

Adam's graduation party was being held in the courtyard of his parents' house. It was a fine evening, just the right sort of weather for an outdoor gathering. As soon as Sophie and Liuba arrived, Liuba's eyes began scanning the crowd to find Jonathan. At last she spotted him talking to Adam and felt blood rushing to her cheeks. To her apprehension and delight, Aunt Sophie walked towards them, tagging her along. When they got closer, Adam saw them first. "Hello Aunt Sophie, and this must be your niece, glad to meet you," he said. Jonathan turned his head and stopped abruptly, a surprised look widening his brown eyes, which became fixed on the girl who was standing next to Sophie. Trying to regain his composure but still staring at Liuba, he blurted, "Hello. I can see that beauty runs in the family." Blushing with embarrassment, Liuba looked down and averted her eyes, sensing how much faster her heart was beating. Fortunately someone called the boys who excused themselves and walked away, before they could detect the uneasiness that came over her. "See you around," Jonathan said before disappearing.

Later on, after the food had been served, a few of the young members of the association who were good with musical instruments began playing an authentic tune. Francis Malik, acting as master of ceremonies, asked Adam and his friends to show the guests the fruits of their hard work, right after he thanked Sophie for making that possible. The guests stood back forming a circle that would give the dancers enough space to move around. Nicknamed 'the terrific trio', the three young men made their way inside the circle and joyously tapped their feet according to the rhythm of the music. They danced the 'Three Kicks', a famous and complicated folkloric dance. They performed with such a staggering precision and synchronised steps that it seemed as though they were sharing the same mind. "You taught them well, aunty. They truly give the word discipline a new meaning," Liuba whispered to her aunt.

"Yes, aren't they amazing," Sophie replied proudly.

An army of helpers started to bring big bowls of fruit. "I feel a little cold, I left my jacket inside, can you bring it for me, dear," Sophie asked Liuba.

"Certainly," said the girl, as she got up to get inside the house. She reached the living room and walked towards the sofa to grab the jacket when she heard voices coming from a bedroom situated right opposite the living room's wide doorway. Feeling she may be intruding on a private conversation, she stood there behind an ornamental Ficus growing in a big pot.

"Thank you very much uncle," she heard Adam say.

"This is only to tide you over during your university studies but anything else you need, just write to me and I'll send it to you, providing you keep on studying hard. This world is not a good place for idle people. So, make sure you don't squander any of your precious time. Now go and join your guests."

Liuba saw Adam stash an envelope in his breast pocket as he stepped out into the corridor. Liuba waited a while until he was out of sight then ventured towards the doorway and that's when she saw them. She saw the man whom Adam called uncle, and Seraphima, Adam's mother, embracing each other.

"You will take good care of yourself while I am away, won't you? And don't forget to write if I am needed for anything. No matter how far away my trip takes me, I will be there for you. Remember you will always be in my thoughts."

Liuba couldn't help noticing a surge of emotions disfiguring the man's features, as he uttered those words. At that time Malcolm saw the young girl staring at them and let go of his sister-in-law. Liuba ran off but she had already seen the tenderness in the man's eyes. She had seen how he shut them tightly, savouring the intensity of those brief but significant moments. In her innocent mind, there was nothing to it. She didn't make a big deal of what went on there. She knew Adam's uncle was on his way to Australia and it was only natural that he would feel emotional, saying goodbye to members of his family. What she didn't know was that she had just witnessed the side of Malcolm no one, including Seraphima, knew existed. She had heard about his reputation of being a hardened, dried up bachelor, without any of the deeper human feelings. To others, Malcolm was only viewed as a cold, dispassionate money making machine.

The musicians were playing La Paloma, a tango, for a change. Almost all the young people and some young at heart walked to the dance floor to participate in a much slower kind of dance. Liuba was having an idle chat with a girl from her school when the girl's eyes lit up, as her gaze became fixed on something beyond Liuba's shoulders. Before Liuba found out what was happening she was whisked away, her hand firmly clutched in Jonathan's hand. She kept objecting and he kept pulling her away.

"I can't, I can't, I don't know how to dance," she was pleading.

"I'll teach you, don't worry, it's easy, you'll see."

Held rather closely against his chest, Liuba wished those next few minutes could go on forever. It felt as though she had died and saw herself floating in heaven. The sensation was so overwhelming it took her breath away.

That night Liuba found it hard to fall asleep, with Jonathan's face and the tone of his voice invading her thoughts. She kept wondering if all that had really happened. She went on torturing herself with thoughts like, 'He knows that I exist, but with all those beautiful girls parading in front of him, what chance do I have, what if he was just being nice to me for Aunt Sophie's sake?' When at last she fell asleep, Jonathan's image haunted her dreams. He was holding her hand, urging her to follow him somewhere. Suddenly she found the two of them on a vast prairie, she could feel the warmth of the sun on her face and her shoulders, as they were running, chasing each other amongst the tall grass and wild flowers that swayed by the breeze and undulated like a sea of colours.

A group of schoolgirls, including Liuba, were assembled in front of the superb Assyrian church that was still under construction but fine enough to hold a mass in. When their supervisor gave the go-ahead signal, the girls marched through the big and impressive mahogany door, walked all the length of the aisle and found the pew they were supposed to occupy. It was Easter day and they had been preparing to sing during the mass that was to be conducted by Mon Signor Sheikho. The parishioners, who had come in droves, were making a buzzing noise with their whispers but that stopped when, all of a sudden, the big organ resounded.

Love stricken Liuba had trouble keeping her mind from drifting away. She sang automatically with the other girls but the chain of her concentration was repeatedly broken by thoughts of Jonathan. At one stage everyone knelt and, head down, eyes shut, they prayed in silence. Instead, Liuba lifted her head and looked at the golden statue of the Lord Jesus Christ embossed on a wooden cross. She stared at the crucifix for a while before she found the courage to pray, to really pray and mean it. With all the faith and devotion she felt in her heart, she asked God to grant her, her only wish. 'All I am asking you, dear Lord, is Jonathan and nothing else. I don't care if I live in poverty and if I have to work hard for the rest of my life, I'll do anything, as long as I always have him by my side.'

When the mass ended, the girls were the last to step out of the church. Outside, as soon as Liuba's eyes got used to the garish light of the sun, she saw him. He was standing next to a pillar at the right hand side of the door and was in deep conversation with two young women. Liuba's heart sank when she noticed how the two were devouring him with their eyes. 'Dear God, please, don't forget what I have asked from you,' she murmured with a sigh. Minutes later, it seemed that her prayer was getting answered because, like magic, she heard Jonathan's voice calling her name and when she felt his warm hand touching her bare arm, something reassured her that she wasn't dreaming.

"We have another rehearsal tomorrow afternoon, why don't you come and practise with us, that is, if you want to learn dancing," Jonathan said earnestly.

"I don't know. I'll ask auntie, if she thinks it's a good idea then I'll be there," she said, batting her eyelashes in nervous anticipation.

Was it Liuba's sweet innocent smile or the childish glow in her eyes that had become so irresistible to Jonathan, because every time he set eyes on her, he could sense something flip in his heart. The twiggy girl had made such a big impression on him that he couldn't think of anything else but her delicate face when she wasn't around.

"It depends on why he wants you to learn dancing, in the first place. Maybe he is more interested in you than your dancing ability," Sophie said, when Liuba mentioned Jonathan's suggestion and asked her opinion about the matter.

"Why do you say that auntie, what makes you think he could be interested in me?" Liuba inquired, hoping to find out what Jonathan's feelings were for her.

"I wasn't born yesterday, my dear. I know a thing or two about the affairs of the heart. You can go to the classes if you wish, but my advice to you is, don't fall for the first guy who crosses your path, you have your whole future ahead of you," Sophie said with a concerned tone.

"I know auntie, you don't have to worry."

The following day Liuba met Sophie after school. They walked to the rehearsal hall and small talked casually. When everyone was there, Liuba practiced with the others, making sure she looked genuinely interested in the dance routines. Before dismissing the class though, Sophie managed to approach Jonathan and, with a stern look in her eyes, "Young man, we have to talk, alone, it's important," she told him. The next day, nerves on edge, expecting to hear harsh words from his teacher, Jonathan went to see her during her lunch hour, as she had requested. Sophie went straight to the point and asked him his real motive for encouraging Liuba to learn dancing.

"Nothing in particular, I assure you," he mumbled like a little boy caught with his hands in the cookie jar.

"The truth Jonathan," she said, looking him straight in the eyes.

"All right, I confess, I am guilty in a way. I only wanted to see her more often, to hear her voice when she giggles. She looks so good when she smiles. That's all, honest," he said, then looking suddenly distressed, he added, "I swear on my mother's grave I would never...."

"I know, I know. It's not your decency I am worried about. It's just that I don't want Liuba to end up hurt. She is so sensitive, so vulnerable and she has suffered enough in her life. I only want to protect her from possible heartaches but, should she decide to be serious about a man, I wouldn't mind seeing her with someone as trustworthy as you."

"The trouble is that I am as broke as anyone can be. I feel painfully embarrassed by my present financial situation. My biggest wish though, is to one day marry Liuba and make her happy, but my hands are tied at the moment. I wish I was able to give her everything she needs and deserves, in addition to my love and devotion, of course, because I do love her," he said. With a desolate look in his dreamy eyes, he then added, "I promise, auntie, I won't bother her any more, I can see that I am not the right person for her."

"Money is not the most important thing in life, you are young and healthy. Also, the future is unpredictable, things can change and problems have a way of sorting themselves out, if you give them time. Anyway, I'll talk to you later."

For some unknown reason, Sophie's philosophical words generated a glimmer of hope in Jonathan's heart. They met again and had another discussion about Liuba. Sophie told him about the painful days Liuba had gone through, after the death of her parents. At the end, they reached a compromise. Sophie agreed to let Jonathan and her niece practice in her house, obviously intending to keep a close eye on them. The idea was for them to get to know each other a bit better. "And we will see what comes later," Sophie had concluded.

Three lessons down the track and the two youngsters were unable to keep their eyes off each other. It was undoubtedly clear that they were seriously in love and with their hormones raging, Sophie didn't think it was wise to let that arrangement go on any longer. Time had come for her to move to the second phase of her plan.

Not enjoying the best of health, Jonathan's father had a bit of difficulty managing his small auto repair shop. In the meantime, to his biggest disappointment, Jonathan had learned that he hadn't been capable of making the grades required to enter Tehran's University.

"Don't be hard on yourself, you can try again next year," Adam had told him, to elevate his mood.

"Sure I will, but now the best thing for me to do is to go and help my father and see what the future has in store. Who knows, I may end up liking being a mechanic," Jonathan had answered, sarcasm and discontentment altering the tone of his voice.

Working together, father and son were making enough money to live on, but for Jonathan, to get married and start a family was an unthinkable subject. Sophie was aware of it too. Nevertheless, there was something about Jonathan that was making her believe he was the man her niece needed, even though he was not financially well off.

Next evening, Sophie showed up at the repair shop. Pulling Jonathan to a corner, and without mincing her words, she stated, "I will not object to your marriage to my niece. I believe she loves you as much as you love her, but there are two conditions to my decision."

"What are those conditions?" Jonathan asked with worry.

"Firstly, you have to let me pay for the wedding reception, the attires, the cars, the lot, even though in our custom, all the above expenses are the groom's responsibility. It will give me the greatest pleasure to do this for Liuba. Secondly, after the wedding, I absolutely insist that you come and live with me, until the day you can afford a house of your own. I don't want to see the two of you move from one rented apartment to another."

Jonathan couldn't have asked for a better solution to his problem, especially since Sophie was making it sound like he would be doing her a favour by giving in to her demands.

"Whatever will make you and Liuba happy is fine with me, as long as I get to marry the girl I love," he said, eagerly kissing her hand.

After inviting him for Friday's lunch, Sophie left the place.

Surprising his father by telling him the good news, Jonathan ambled out, a renewed spring in his step. Deciding to buy himself a new shirt, he began walking towards the shops, a happier man. As he turned around the corner, he heard the familiar cry of Paganini's violin. The busker was playing a sad tune, as usual. Jonathan wouldn't know the name of the piece, since he had never studied classical music, but he always enjoyed the sound of whatever the old soldier used to play on his instrument. Barefooted, hair tousled, he was a tall, well built man, wearing a tattered army general's uniform. Tight lipped at all times, he had an expressionless face and a certain detached look in his eyes. In fact, his whole persona was telling volumes about his possibly tormented soul. There were rumours that he had come from a once wealthy family, and that currently he was living somewhere around there, with a sibling of his. What had happened to him, no one really knew. Whatever it was, it must have been horrific enough to turn him into the zombie like creature that he had become. Nobody knew his real name, but since he played classical music with such expertise, the street kids had nicknamed him Paganini, after the renowned composer.

As he got closer to the man, feeling particularly benevolent, Jonathan took a one toman bill out of his pocket, rolled it neatly and pushed it in one of Paganini's button holes. Sensing something gay in Jonathan's composure, the raggedy busker pressed his violin a little closer to his cheek and played the famous Russian piece "Casatschok", with a newly found energy.

The new tune made Jonathan so elated, he couldn't help himself but to react to it. Right there, in the middle of the street, his arms crossed in front of his chest he tried his best to imitate the steps of the popular Russian dance that he used to see little girls perform in parties. Light footedly he kept jumping up and down for a good while. Watching his spontaneous act, a group of schoolgirls in their grey public school uniform burst into giggles, then rushed away.

"I have heard that the violinist gives all the money he collects to a mosque, for poor people," one of the girls commented, as she kept on chewing her gum.

"Yes, my mother thinks that his wife and three children were all killed in the war, that's why he is like this," another girl added casually, without realising the magnitude of the tragedy she was talking about.

A few metres away, a little boy standing outside his house witnessed the whole incident with sheer amazement too, before he was asked to get in.

"Matthew, your soup is getting cold," his mother was saying.

A peculiarly funny smile creasing his rounded face, the boy went in, eager to tell his story in full detail to whoever was interested enough to hear it.

Sophie heard the doorbell and, knowing it was the door-to-door bread salesman, she stepped out and bought a freshly baked Turkish bread called barbari. She wrapped it in a towel, brought it in and placed it in the basket on the breakfast table. The rich aroma of the tealeaves brewing in the little teapot on top of the Samovar was wafting in the air. Liuba arrived and, after saying good morning, she poured a bit of dark tea in two cups. She then held each cup under the little tap of the Samovar and, turning the tap on, she topped them up with boiling water to dilute the brew. She added sugar to her cup and began stirring her tea, a bit noisily. Sophie was buttering pieces of the bread. She spread some fig jam on one of the pieces and handed it to Liuba. "By the way, I saw Jonathan yesterday," she began to talk. "We had a bit of a chat from which I gathered he is interested in you. In fact he expressed his wish to marry you and asked for my permission," she continued.

It seemed that the world had suddenly stood still for Liuba. Eyes enlarged, she stared at her aunt, her features transformed by a mixture of surprise and disbelief. Seconds later, a big smile spread across her face but soon faded as she asked worriedly. "Oh auntie, I hope you didn't object, please tell me you didn't, because, you know, I like him too."

A frown tracing two tiny lines between her eyebrows, she waited for a reply that mercifully came in time to appease her.

"I have already said yes. I don't have to be a clairvoyant to know how you feel about him, my girl."

"Am I so transparent auntie?"

"Yes, you are!" Sophie said rather loudly, opening her arms to her overjoyed niece.

"You are an angel auntie, you truly are."

In a flurry of excitement, the two women started making plans, delirious about the prospect of happy days ahead. At times, Liuba stopped to catch her breath, her temples throbbing, her heart racing with joy.

"By the way, he is coming here tomorrow, I have invited him for lunch," Sophie said, kissing Liuba on the forehead.

Flowers in hand, Jonathan knocked at the door, the next day. During lunch, the three of them had a casual conversation but after dessert, in order to give the young ones some time alone, Sophie kept making herself scarce by going to the kitchen, more often than required.

As soon as the talks of a wedding had come about, the subject of furthering their studies had flown right out of both Jonathan and Liuba's minds and oddly enough, nobody had tried to remind them of it either. They had Sophie's blessing and that was all they wished for. Before leaving, Jonathan asked Sophie what was the next step he had to take. "According to tradition, you and your father and any other family members you wish to bring along, have to come and officially ask for Liuba's hand in marriage from me, since I am her only relative," Sophie said, amused by Jonathan's selfless question.

On the evening they had planned to do that, Jonathan and his father Raphael left home, wearing their best suits. They were carrying a big bunch of flowers, a bottle of cognac, a large box of chocolates and a piece of jewellery for Liuba. The trinket was a brooch that used to belong to the late Mrs Varda. Sophie's house wasn't so far, so they decided to walk the distance. As they turned into Khayam Street, Raphael slowed down and stopped in front of Vlodia's Bar. "What would you say if we had a nip of something," he asked cautiously. "I am a bit unsettled, this is a woman's job, for heaven's sake. I need something to calm my nerves," he added.

"It'll be all right dad, don't worry, but if you think it will help, go ahead, just don't take too long."

They entered the Bar and came face to face with Adam's father Shimoon. Pointing to the flowers and chocolates, "Where are you going with all this?" Shimoon came to ask, raising an eyebrow, but suddenly it dawned on him, "Don't tell me it is happening, this can only mean one thing," he said, nodding a few times. Then tapping on Jonathan's shoulders, he added, "Congratulations my son, you two will make such a handsome couple. Adam has told me a thing or two about you and young Liuba. She is a charming girl, I must say."

"Yes, cried Raphael. I am very happy for my son, but I can't help it, my stomach is churning, we really need a woman's presence, in times like this."

"My wife is away but I can go with you, if it will make a difference. Sophie is a dear friend of mine and I have a great respect for her, but let's soothe those nerves of yours first."

As they approached the Bar area, they saw Mr Vlodia involved in a disagreement with Maroussia, the Russian woman who used to sing at night in the restaurant. "I have to pay rent, electricity, food and all sorts of things," she was telling her boss, in their native language. Despite her obesity, Maroussia had a beautiful face. Under her golden fringe, one could see a pair of big blue eyes, pencil thin eyebrows, a full mouth and a soft rose coloured skin. She had been a renowned opera singer back in Russia, but at present, in Iran, she had to be grateful for having a job. In fact, if it hadn't been for Vlodia's support, she would certainly be struggling on the streets, just to survive. Granted, she had a roof over her head, but apparently, her pay being insufficient for her needs; she had been caught taking hand picked clients to her place after work. Judging by his reaction, it seemed that Vlodia was a tad peeved when the lid had been taken off her extra activities. Maroussia didn't even have a clue to what the fuss was about, since after work, her life was her own to live it, the way it suited her.

"What is eating him, she is not his property," Raphael exclaimed, as he spoke a bit of Russian and understood fragments of the conversation.

"What is the matter?" Shimoon inquired.

In a few words, Raphael tried to explain the situation, not noticing the cryptic look Maroussia gave Jonathan, nor seeing him drop his head and blush slightly.

On that important day, Jonathan couldn't help feeling a little sheepish and uneasy, remembering the few visits he himself had made to the talented girl. In his mind, for a fleeting moment, he tried to blame Adam for enticing him to go there. "We have to start somewhere, man. How can we go through life, not knowing the first thing about sex? This is the only way we can get any experience in that regard," Adam had pleaded with Jonathan and had him convinced. Despite his short lived embarrassment, Jonathan was glad to have followed his friend's advice. He was mostly grateful to Maroussia for having been helpful and understanding, as she had guided him and shaped him into the confident man, he believed he had become.

Eventually, the three men arrived at Sophie's place in a better frame of mind. After exchanging the usual polite banalities, they had their dinner. Shimoon told a few anecdotes, as for the lovebirds, they kept glancing at each other and smiled every now and then. The evening was progressing brilliantly. A relaxed Raphael made the suitable speech, starting with the outdated but traditional and somewhat corny phrase, "We have come to you, bearing flowers and would like to ask your permission to pick a flower from your garden." To that Sophie was expected to say, "It's fine with me, but we have to see if Liuba agrees and believes that her parents would have been happy with her decision, should they have been still with us today." Customarily the girl should refrain from answering straight away but Liuba was so exited that, as soon as they asked her her opinion, she said yes, and they all cheered. Fired up with enthusiasm, Jonathan opened the bottle of cognac and his father suggested they name the day. A bit of whispering followed but at the end they all consented on the twenty second of the coming month.

From then on everything went as smoothly as it could. Spring was nudging winter out and, on a fine day in February 1945, it all came together when, in the newly completed Assyrian Church in Forsat Street, Tehran, Jonathan and Liuba's lives were joined in holy matrimony.

Being Liuba's sole relative, Sophie didn't let any detail go unchecked to make the wedding reception as perfect and traditionally accurate as possible. At home, the largest room was furnished for the newlyweds. Sophie had moved her things to the bedroom at the end of the corridor. Liuba was on a roller coaster ride of emotional thrills. She couldn't believe that a person can be so happy and not die from it. Every time she looked in Jonathan's deep brown eyes, all the sad memories that had marred her teenage years just faded away, as if they had happened to someone else. She was convinced that Jonathan had been hand picked for her by some heavenly force. Not a day passed that she didn't thank that celestial being for coming through for her and grant her her most intimate wish. Truthfully, her union with Jonathan seemed to be a match made in heaven. Filled with sweet surprises, their lives had blended together harmoniously. The warmth of Jonathan's love for her had totally changed her mental attitude. She looked constantly radiant and full of joie de vivre. Seeing them so in love, friends and relatives believed nothing could ever come between them. The pair's happiness became more complete when Liuba found out she was going to have a baby.

It was a cold November night when Sophie grabbed the prepacked valise and followed the expectant couple. Soon the three were on their way to the maternity ward at Baher Hospital. Sophie was feeling extremely clucky and exited by the notion of having a baby in the house. In the wee hours of the next day, severing the umbilical cord, the midwife congratulated Liuba for giving birth to a healthy baby boy.

Minutes later, beaming from ear to ear, Jonathan couldn't decide between squeezing his wife's hand, kissing her sweaty forehead or caressing his son's tiny little toes and cute little fingers.

"Jonathan, how do you like the name Marcus?" Liuba asked, all of a sudden.

"If you like it, then Marcus it is," he said, blinking back tears of joy.

Chapter 5

From the first day he arrived in Sydney, Australia, Malcolm started looking, searching, studying and taking everything into consideration. In his search for a place to reside, he came across a comfortable house to rent. Located in a quiet street in the suburb of Cameray, the house was a deceased estate with that particular old world charm and was ideal for him to live in as well as take care of his future enterprises, while the next of kin were deciding what to do with it. While he was busy settling in, Malcolm didn't mind eating fruit, bread and butter and the occasional fried eggs, and more fruit. Even though he loved fruit, soon he grew sick of them. He continued with that regimen until he began feeling like he was stranded on a deserted island and had to survive on bananas and pineapples. Even the sandwiches he made for himself didn't seem to be an answer to his cravings. Always wondering what he would have for his next meal, he was yearning for a decent home cooked meal, like one of his favourite Assyrian or Iranian dishes.

On his quest to find a good place to eat out, he stumbled upon an Italian restaurant and struck up a friendship with the podgy and good-natured proprietor, Giuseppe di Marco. Giuseppe wasn't a stranger to that homesick feeling Malcolm was having from time to time, but he had migrated to Australia with his wife and that was a bit different. Often, over the noise of the coffee machine and the idle chatter of other customers, they managed to exchange a few

39

friendly words or tell stories about their lives in the country they had left behind.

The minute his application for permanent residency was accepted, Malcolm looked for an adequate office space and began hiring the personnel he needed. Stretching his wings further afield, he continued using his know-how for buying and selling different ranges of products and making daring deals with Eastern countries as well as Europeans. Within a year, well established as an Australian business personality, he tried to have a crack at the international market. He exchanged his old Holden for a brand new Morris Oxford and made the arrangement to buy the house he lived in, as it was up for sale. Once the deeds were signed, Malcolm decided to get some repairs done here and there, since the old house was in great need of a radical facelift, both inside and out. Starting in the kitchen, he had the tiles and cabinets changed, the old "kooka" was replaced by a new stove, and a few electrical appliances were added to make cooking easier.

His fiftieth birthday fast approaching, Malcolm was at a stage of his life when it became obvious to him that money and power were not the only things that mattered to a man. He needed stability and purpose in his everyday living. He needed more. The proverbial 'Home Sweet Home' to go to, at the end of a hard working day, seemed to have a good ring to it suddenly, and suddenly, loneliness became the most outstanding issue to him. The infrequent and short-lived relationships he had with women in the past never meant a thing to him. They had all left him feeling empty and unfulfilled. With the renovations out of the way, he often found himself walking from room to room in that spacious house thinking how nice it would be to have a wife and one or two children to pass his wealth on to.

Unexpectedly one day, Malcolm met the woman who matched the image he had in his mind of the perfect wife. Nadejda caught his attention from the day she came to work for him as a tea lady. She was an interesting girl who had indeed every attribute he was looking for in a woman. Malcolm was greatly impressed by the clarity of her skin, her lovely red cheeks and sensuous mouth, in addition to the soft curves, all in the right places. In fact, Nadejda could make heads turn. Often Malcolm saw her wearing the same clingy floral dress that revealed quite a bit of cleavage. Even though, on a few occasions, his secretary commented that the girl's head was always in the clouds, Malcolm found her lack of concentration harmless, even amusing. After hearing her talk, he also became besotted by her cute accent, a dead give away of her Russian origins. The only sore point was their age difference and that could make Malcolm's plans undone. Together with her mother Tatiana, Nadejda had come to Australia from Manchuria China, only eight months earlier. She had told everyone at the office that her mother was living in Bathurst with a group of Russian co-travellers. As for herself, she was in Sydney because that was the only place the people from the Australian Council of Churches were able to find her a job.

Malcolm called Nadejda to his office one afternoon and told her he had something to tell her. Thinking she was in trouble, the girl lost her colours. He reassured her that everything was all right then, using simple sentences, he let her in on his wish to marry her. "You don't have to answer me now," he started to say, but she interrupted him, "Can I think couple days then give answer?" She asked.

"Of course you can, dear. One thing though, please don't tell a word of this to anyone in here, they don't have to know, at least not yet."

"I understand," she said before disappearing.

The next day, she knocked at his office door and entered without waiting to be called in.

"I decided, I will marry you," she declared, with a nervous giggle.

He was taken aback by her speedy answer. "I am glad, you have made me really happy," Malcolm said.

"Me too," she said, smiling.

"How about we go out for dinner, so we can talk about this some more?"

"All right," she said, with the same pleasant tone that left Malcolm wondering if she had really comprehended whatever she was hastily agreeing to. At least, he thought, she would have had to discuss the matter with her mother. He couldn't help wondering if it wasn't his wealth that had tipped the scale in his favour.

Malcolm wasn't a particularly handsome man, but his silvery temples were giving him a certain middle age charm. Even his piercing eyes and his slightly aquiline nose didn't make him less of a catch. In a way, glad to have been spared the suspense, he gave Nadejda the address of the place they were to meet and let her leave.

Given the hectic pace of his life, Malcolm could only allow himself a few hours every other day to court his young fiancé. Nevertheless, he had ample time to take her around the city for spending sprees and show her the advantages of being wrapped over the arms of a winner. As much as he could, he introduced her to the good life. There were a few reasonably posh restaurants and high-class shops in that postwar era where he could take her and buy her extravagant presents, without worrying about the prices. Judging by what she was wearing over and over at work, Malcolm had a fair idea that she didn't have many personal possessions and needed a lot of clothes and accessories.

Christmas was around the corner and, conscious of what her life would have been otherwise, Nadejda was over the moon with the direction her life was taking her. She was growing fond of Malcolm and was thankful for the amiable way he was treating her. By the time they exchanged their vows in front of Malcolm's friends, including Giuseppe and his wife, and a few of his top employees and business acquaintances, Nadejda had turned from a naïve, modestly attired woman into a well groomed, almost confident lady. The wedding took place in the Catholic Church in Cremorne, and afterwards, the small party gathered in Malcolm's house for the wedding reception.

Being legally called Mrs Yonan, Nadejda's job was to keep looking pretty and do what was expected of her as the boss's wife. She had been warned and had accepted to get used to her husband's way of life and to cope with the hassles and late hours that were part of his work. In other words, she was supposed to be a homemaker. Their marriage had more than a decent chance of working and their life together to be a pleasant one, providing they put their hearts into it. Malcolm was an old fashioned kind of man so he thought he would bring in the money and she would spend it wisely on their home and the upbringing of the children he was planning to have soon. They had decided that during the day, Nadejda would go to adult classes to better her English. Meanwhile she could participate in other classes where she could learn cooking as well as any other skills she wished to gain command of.

Five whole months passed by without a hitch. Calling twice a week, as usual, the cleaning lady kept the rooms tidy. Too preoccupied with work, it escaped Malcolm's eyes that the interior of his house hadn't yet started to reflect that characteristic woman's touch. Nevertheless, all seemed right on the home front except that for one excuse or another, Nadejda never cooked, not even the simplest meal. They either ate out or bought a few things from a delicatessen so, for Malcolm, life turned out to be pretty much the same as it had been before he got married.

Remaining confident, Malcolm trusted that his wife would gradually fit cooking into her daily schedule. Besides his wife's lack of culinary expertise, there was another more important matter that was nagging at Malcolm. Day after day he eagerly waited for Nadejda to come to him with news of her pregnancy but that dream didn't seem to be about to materialise. Some nights, he would lay awake in bed mulling over the subject, asking himself if it would ever happen, mainly because having children was the predominant reason that drove him to marry Nadejda. He liked her, he liked her a lot, but he never admitted to himself or anyone else that he was actually in love with her. Maybe it was her name Nadejda, meaning hope in Russian, that had put the first spark in his heart and got him interested in her, and not so much her physical attractiveness. He had hoped that she would eventually give him a child and, maybe in the long run, he would somehow learn to love her, if only he could be able to wipe a certain memory out of his mind. Disheartened, recently he had begun doubting the likelihood of that ever occurring.

For so long he had the secret of his first love stashed away in his chest. Over the years, no one knew how hard he had tried to forget about it and let it rest. He wishfully speculated that his wife and consequently his children would help him blot out the memory of that face he so adored. Now, the spectre of that forbidden love was once again tearing away from its hiding place like a captive creature would. He could feel that monster grow invisible tentacles that would reach, grab and twist his heart around, squishing it ferociously until he felt it bleed.

'Will I ever be free of you, my dear, dear love?' he kept bemoaning, every time her big brown eyes and her long curly lashes crept into his thoughts, making him agonise in silence and feel lonelier than ever.

Malcolm was lounging in his big chair at the office and smoking cigarette after cigarette. He was so deep in thought about his wish to be a father that the news about the Australian troops advancing across the 38th parallel into North Korea, broadcasted on his wireless, couldn't snap him out of his daydreaming. He was waiting for an important call which came through as he felt a long yawn rising. Suppressing it with one hand, he picked up the phone with the other and was soon immersed in a big-buck discussion with his sales person. "Is it absolutely necessary that I should be there?" he was saying after a lengthy debate.

"Yes," a voice said at the other end of the line.

"All right then, I'll leave as soon as I can," his secretary heard him say, before he replaced the receiver.

Malcolm reflected long and hard whether he should take his wife on that trip but at the end he voted against it. 'She will be bored,' he thought, since he would be too busy going from one meeting to another, talking business. 'I wouldn't have enough time to spend with her, I'll take her on a holiday some day though,' he decided.

As he was packing his bags at home, Malcolm tried to make his wife understand the reason he had to leave her alone, for almost two months. "Nadejda dear, this will give you the opportunity to do some shopping for the house, you know, cushions, towels, bed sheets, and anything you need for your studies. Oh! Yes, curtains for the kitchen. Make a decision on the colour scheme and buy whatever you like and if you need money, drop in at the office and ask Lucas for it. I will instruct him to give you some for the housekeeping too."

"All right," she said, without displaying any enthusiasm. The fact that he trusted her taste in buying things for their home didn't have any effect on her. It seemed that she couldn't care less what colour curtains were hanging in their kitchen.

The next morning, after ringing Lucas, Malcolm was on his way, leaving his house in his wife's care for the first time. What Malcolm couldn't have suspected in a million years was that Lucas, his trusted accountant, had recently developed an addiction for betting on horses. In fact, Lucas's compulsive gambling had landed him in big debts, debts he couldn't possibly pay back on his salary. He had already borrowed a little fortune from the till to cover his last losses, but he needed more. His presumed ace of a strategy had failed dramatically, and had let him sink even deeper into debt. Had Lady Luck smiled on him, just this once, he would probably have put back what he had taken from the company coffer.

Malcolm's carte blanche to give Nadejda all the money she wanted couldn't have come at a better time for Lucas. And in this crucial time, he had to act fast if he didn't wish to have a visit from the loan shark heavies. Nadejda, as he remembered her for being a little bit of a harebrained female, would serve his purpose brilliantly. He just had to get her to sign a few papers, pay her small amounts of cash and later add a digit at the beginning of the sum, making it a much bigger figure and keep the difference for himself. This way Lucas got his debtors off his back. He felt momentarily safe, but conscious that his disloyalty would be discovered, sooner or later, he decided to put his hands on a sizable amount of cash and run before dirt had time to hit the fan. So he took the payroll money and disappeared just before payday.

For the first couple of weeks of her husband's absence, Nadejda felt as though she had grown wings. Overwhelmed by a strange sense of relief, she couldn't wait to savour that feeling of liberty to the fullest. She had money in her hands and she was free to enjoy herself the way she was becoming accustomed to. The carefree existence she had as a newlywed, had her convinced that she was on easy street and could continue living the very same dizzy life for as long as she wanted to. Every day, after her class, she jumped in a taxi that took her to the heart of the city where her favourite shops were located. After a light lunch she ambled from one shop to another, browsing and touching any merchandise that caught her eye. In every trip, she managed to purchase bagfuls of strange knick-knacks, which she brought back home. At home, the items that filled those bags quickly vanished in her bedroom drawers, under the bed and in the linen closet. Soon there was no room for any more things to stash away.

Only once a week, Nadejda's outing had a different pattern. On that day she used to wear the most inconspicuous attire, throw a scarf over her head and hide her face behind big dark glasses. Carrying a bag filled with some of those goodies she had bought, she used to leave home for a destination she preferred no one knew about. On the other days though, she liked to look her best and, thanks to Malcolm's generosity, she could dress to kill. While she was shopping, Nadejda met a lot of people, a lot of men. Attracted to her flamboyant looks and friendly disposition, all sorts of men tried to chat her up, wherever she went. Although she was never interested in them in an improper manner, Nadejda enjoyed the attention she was getting from them. The excitement of being complimented made her feel good about herself. Unknowingly she let that irresponsible attitude damage her clean and innocent image, to the point that to onlookers her naivety was interpreted as floosiness. People who knew who she was saw her talking and giggling with men and soon tongues started wagging. She became the subject of office gossip when Edith the stenographer came to work one day after a visit to her dentist. Edith told the girls that she had seen Mrs Yonan sitting in a café with a young man. She also said that she saw them hug and kiss before parting.

"Are you sure it was the boss's wife you saw?" Beryl asked.

"My tooth was hurting at the time but nothing was wrong with my eyesight," she replied, then pursing her lips she added, "and I can tell a slut, when I see one."

Malcolm came back home two days sooner than he was supposed to. He entered the house, put his luggage in the hallway and hung up his raincoat. Anticipating some sort of change in the décor, the only thing he noticed, once he stepped into the living room, was dust covering every surface. Their bedroom was in a deplorable mess too. In a state of big disappointment, he ventured in the kitchen and wished he hadn't, when he saw dirt and grime everywhere. In the sink, he found ants having a get together on unwashed dishes. He opened the square fridge he had bought before his wedding and was confronted with a foul stench. There wasn't any food on the shelves except for some mouldy cheese and decaying fruit that explained the unpleasant smell. 'What the hell,' he muttered, turning his face away in disgust.

Judging from the state his house was in, Malcolm realised that Nadejda was not going to be domesticated in a hurry. 'There must be a reason for all this,' he thought optimistically. Despite his tiredness, he decided to make a dash to the office. At least he could count on his faithful staff for running the place smoothly. Unfortunately things were not any different there either. When his secretary saw him, she said with a sigh of relief, "Oh! Mr Yonan, I am so glad to see you."

He sat down at his desk. "What is going on? What have I missed? Is something the matter?" he asked, seeing her so agitated.

"Oh! Mr Yonan, we are so sorry. Who would have believed that Lucas, of all people, could be a dishonest man?"

In a few words, Beryl explained the situation to Malcolm while he was fiddling with his lighter to light up his cigarette.

"We just found out two days ago and we couldn't contact you, so Franc called some auditors for assistance."

Taking a puff at his cigarette Malcolm coughed a bit as smoke hit his lungs.

"Are you absolutely sure he is the culprit?" he asked.

"Well, he is missing and so is the money, besides who else had access to the books and could withdraw money?"

"We will get to the bottom of this soon enough," he interrupted her. A few minutes later, lighting another cigarette, he inhaled deeply as he began browsing through the papers that Beryl had left on his desk.

In a meeting organised by Franc, Malcolm asked everyone to come forward with any information they had about the Lucas affair. He also wanted them to fill him in with details of other important matters that needed to be addressed, when Nadejda's name came up.

"Did my wife come to see Lucas for money?" he asked.

"Yes, I believe she came at least four times," said Franc.

After some frustrating hours trying to sort out things and keep abreast of the situation, exhausted Malcolm decided to go home, his mind cluttered with various questions. 'What did Nadejda do with all the money she took from Lucas and if she had neglected the house so much, what had she been doing all this time. Could she have been in cahoots with Lucas, then again, why would she steal from her own money,' he kept wondering. When he entered their home, Nadejda was there. He found her sprawled on the sofa, still in her going out clothes, and could swear she had been crying.

"You are back," she said, without making an effort to get up or display some kind of joy for seeing him.

"Yes, I am back, and we have to talk, but now I am tired and hungry. I also know that there is nothing to eat in this house."

"I know, I ate out, I didn't know you were coming today."

"What, what would you have done if you knew and where were you all day?" he blurted out, surprised by his sudden burst of anger.

"I went to school, you know that."

"After school, where did you go after school?" he asked with the same angry voice.

"I went for a walk, I don't know, I went shopping."

"Walk, shopping.... Nadejda, can't you see the state of this house? How can you live in this pigsty and what did you buy, may I ask?" Malcolm paused a while to clear his throat, then went on with his interrogation.

"I am waiting. What did you buy with the five hundred and thirty pounds that you took from Lucas? I don't see any new curtains in the kitchen."

"I didn't take five hundred and thirty pounds, all he gave me was three times thirty pounds and once forty pounds, that will be... hundred and...," she began counting on her fingers pensively.

Malcolm's face turned ashen. "Are you sure?" he asked.

"Yes, and I have some money left in my purse. Do you want it back?"

"So the rascal embezzled even more."

"Who is rascal? What is embezz...?" She muttered nervously.

"Nothing for you to worry about, just tell me why is the house in such a mess and what happened to the decorating you were supposed to do?"

"Cleaner didn't show up and I bought some things for myself."

"What things? Show me, damn it."

"Don't shout at me, you are scaring me."

Malcolm sensed something odd in the way she was acting. Her reluctance to come clean with her acquisitions made him a little suspicious. Holding one hand on his mouth to prevent himself from coughing, he walked to the main bedroom and began opening wardrobe doors, although in normal circumstances he wouldn't care less what she spent her money on.

Malcolm figured he would know more about his wife by the items she needed to buy for herself. He pulled out all the drawers and, in a state of disbelief, apart from the good dresses, hats and shoes that he gave her, he saw loads of bags filled with the most useless little trinkets and tacky imitations of old fashioned jewellery. Flimsy chiffon scarves, vials of cheap perfume and a diamante tiara were also found in a separate box. In his rage, he threw all the bags she had stashed in the nooks of the wardrobes on their bed. His biggest shock came when he pulled down a bag from the top shelf and a flood of colourful fake marabou feather scarves fell out and flew around, snaking gently in the air before hitting the floor. Malcolm stopped abruptly, nostrils flaring. Turning to Nadejda, he yelled as he asked her with indignation.

"Were you planning to open a costume shop or start a brothel behind my back?"

Nadejda looked like a child caught smudging lipstick on the walls. She was whimpering softly, her cheeks flushed. Feeling trapped, she wondered if there was a way out of that jam. Finally, darting her widened blue eyes at Malcolm, she blurted out.

"You want to know? I will tell you, I can't hide this anymore."

"Tell me what? What sordid secret have you been keeping from me? Were you a prostitute or something?"

Nadejda gave her husband a look of concentrated puzzlement, not quite understanding why he thought she could have been a prostitute.

"No, of course not," she cried, "but if you really want to know the truth, I have to take you somewhere. First buy yourself something to eat then I will tell you where to go, but promise me you won't say a word until we are there and when you know everything, you decide. Decide if you still want me.

"Now don't be ridiculous, for heaven's sake," was all that Malcolm could say, not knowing what was there to uncover.

While wiping her eyes and blowing her nose, Nadejda grabbed and pushed some of those feather boas and the tiara into a shopping bag. With a wry amusement, Malcolm looked at her, hoping there was an explanation to all that. He was determined to find out about her recent activities mainly to have a clear view of where his marriage was heading. The earlier discovery of his accountant dipping his hand into the company till seemed a minor setback, he thought. All the money that Lucas had gouged out of him was nothing that he couldn't replace but this crisis with his wife had a potential of putting a damper on everything sacred to him.

Malcolm's hopes of having a normal conjugal life and the chance of starting a family were at stake. For some unknown reason he felt he was in for a major shock, one that could change his future. They both left home and walked silently to the car. As he was driving towards wherever she was taking him, Malcolm found some time to reflect. He could understand Nadejda's yearning for money, her urge for spending it. It must have had something to do with years of deprivation she had probably been subjected to in her childhood, in an unstable environment. Still, to go and buy trivial things that obviously she wouldn't use remained a mystery in his mind and he couldn't wait to get to the bottom of it. He drove automatically to wherever she told him to. Biting hard on the sandwich he got himself from the corner deli and washing it down with hasty gulps from a bottle of lemonade, he kept glancing at her, impatiently expecting her to give him further navigation. He drove along Burn's Bay road, passed over Tarban Creek Bridge and turned right into Victoria Road. "How far should I go now? Where are we going anyway?" He asked, trying not to sound too anxious.

Between sobs, Nadejda pointed to a side street and managed to say, "When you pass that street, go a bit more then make U turn, then I will tell you where to stop."

Malcolm passed Crown Street, drove further, slowed down and stopped in front of a huge building with a stone paved façade. He looked at the big sign hanging over the entrance, 'Gladesville Mental Hospital,' he read aloud, then he turned to Nadejda. "Why are we here?" he asked, feeling ill at ease with anticipation.

"Follow me Malcolm, you wanted to know, now look and you will know. This is my problem. I wished to keep secret but I was wrong."

They went in and walked through two long corridors. They passed lots of closed doors. Every now and then, they heard loud and eerie noises coming from behind those doors, noises that sent cold shivers down Malcolm's spine. Then Nadejda pushed him through one of those doors. Suddenly they were in a big hall full of people, or more appropriately, creatures that barely resembled human beings. Malcolm blinked a few times then looked closely. He had heard things about mad houses but never once had he tried to imagine how the inside of one of those places would look like. In a flash, he had a front seat view of a bizarre scene unfolding before his eyes. His stomach heaved by an unpleasant smell that hit his unprepared nostrils. It took him a while to get acquainted with the whole picture before he began studying the inmates, one by one.

There was a half naked woman sitting on the floor, rubbing some invisible cream on her outstretched arm. She was squinting at the faint light that came from the window above. Malcolm assumed that, in her mind, she was probably thinking she was sunbaking. Another one was cradling a rolled jacket in her arms. A maternal look in her eyes, she was pleading with the others to shut up because baby was asleep. One was combing another woman's long hair with her bare fingers, asking her, every few seconds, if she liked her hairdo. "Nice, nice," she kept saying, admiring her creation.

In the far corner, another woman caught Malcolm's attention. She was wrapped in multicolour lengths of fabric and looked like an Egyptian mummy in drag. A long moulting pink feathery scarf was trailing behind her, as she walked with the panache of a medieval queen. The woman turned around and, sweeping the floor with yards of material hanging from her waist, she clapped her hands ceremoniously. With a serious voice, "Silence," she ordered, to no one in particular, before bowing to an imaginary person and whispering, "Your Royal Highness." It was when she lifted her head that her eyes met with Nadejda's. Malcolm couldn't help noticing that his wife was staring at the wretched woman and seemed overwhelmed by mixed emotions. To his surprise, the woman grabbed Nadejda's arm and urged her to follow her, "Come, come, come and meet the Emperor," she insisted. Nadejda looked at the woman, then at her husband, "Malcolm, this is my mother Tatiana," she said, a sob in her voice and distress in her eyes.

Feeling nauseous, Malcolm's eyes went from the woman to his wife then, with a broken voice, 'Oh my God!' He whispered beneath his breath. "You poor, poor girl, what must you have been going through? I know now why you never wanted me to meet her. I am so sorry, so sorry, my dear."

Tatiana's gaze shifted from Nadejda to Malcolm. After briefly studying him, eyes blazing, she lifted her right arm in the air and moved her head from side to side, "No! This is not my Emperor," she said, frowning at Malcolm.

"No mamma, this is my Emperor, his name is Malcolm. Look, we brought you some more things from your palace," Nadejda said, feeling a bit embarrassed. Apprehensively, she opened the shopping bag and pulled out a few of those colourful marabous then, dipping in the bottom of the bag, she felt about and found the tiara. "And this is your crown mamma, wear it and you will feel like a real Empress." She added, placing the tiara on her mother's head

"An Empress," Tatiana screamed like a child. "Look Bronhilda, I am a real Empress. I told you I was."

Lost in their own special world, none of the inmates showed any interest in the matter.

"Which one is Bronhilda?" Malcolm asked, looking around to see whom Tatiana was talking to.

"She was mamma's friend, back home. Mamma not seen her for long time but she thinks she is here."

Tatiana became so engrossed in her crown that she forgot altogether about her daughter and the man who was there with her. Seeing no point in staying there any longer the two left the bedlam in silence. Nadejda held her head down all the way to the car but when he opened the door for her, still looking down she said with a trembling voice, "Now you know who I am, I am a crazy woman's daughter."

"How long has she been like this?" Malcolm asked.

"I don't know," she said pensively, then as she was settling in her seat, she continued, "On Shang-Sha, the boat that was taking us to Samar in Philippines, mamma started talking to herself and she did funny things. Not all the times, not really funny things but not normal things, you know? One day I heard two women talk about her, one said that her mother was crazy too. She said it is in the family. I am sorry Malcolm, I don't know what to say, my head is so....so..., maybe I am crazy like mamma."

"Nonsense, you are not crazy at all, you know Nadejda, you never told me anything about your life in China. I would like to know about the circumstances that brought you to Australia."

Turning her head towards Malcolm she stared at him for a while then, "OK when we are home I will tell you," she said, batting her eyes to let tears fall out.

At home, over a cup of coffee, using scattered, short and unsure sentences, Nadejda tried to give Malcolm a brief report of the events that led her and her mother to migrate to Australia. "I was young, I didn't exactly understand, I still don't know the real problem, I mean the war. I only know that, after the war, the red army took over Shanghai, that's when they put all the Russian people on boats and sent them to the Philippines. From there some got visa to go to America, some to Australia or Canada. Anyway in Manchuria, that's where we lived, I remember a bit. One day after school, I saw Mr and Mrs Petrov. They were waiting for me at the gate. They were my family friends. They took me to their house. They told me I had to stay with them because my mother had to go look for my father. My father was missing."

Nadejda stopped to catch her breath then she went on with her story, "Mamma was always fighting with my father about something she didn't want him to do. I think it was about writing things in the secret white Russian's paper. I heard her shout one day, "you will get all of us killed one day, but father didn't listen."

"What happened then?" Malcolm asked eagerly.

"One night he didn't come home and mamma was worried, she cried a lot. Her friends were worried that she will make herself sick, but she cried until the day she went away...."

"Did your mother ever find your father?" Malcolm interrupted.

"No, I stayed with the Petrov family for months, then she came back alone. She was so skinny, so sick. I don't know why we could never go back to our home," she went on.

Nadejda took a pause. She blew her nose and it made her face blotchy. It was obvious that she was going through a whole gamut of emotions. "Every time I asked mamma why, she just looked at me and she did this...." Nadejda sighed to make her husband understand what she meant.

"She sighed," Malcolm said, coming to her rescue.

"Yes, she sighed; those friends were very good to mamma, they took care of her. Mamma was very weak and sometimes she was saying things that didn't have meaning. Every time I asked her what is wrong, she said words I didn't understand. Mrs Petrov told me not to worry, she said she will be all right but I was sure she was hiding something important from me and I was scared. Father never came back. One day I was talking to Vladimir, the Petrov's son, about mamma, he said mamma was like that because when she was arrested they did bad things to her."

"Do you mean they tortured her?" Malcolm asked.

Nadejda lifted her head and looked at Malcolm, her eyes filled with tears.

"Yes, they hurt her to tell where my father was hiding. Vladimir thought I knew about that, it just came out of his mouth, he was sorry that I heard from him. I was very upset, I cried for long time."

Nadejda dropped her face in her opened palms and wept desperately. Malcolm had trouble finding soothing words that would give her comfort. He just put his arm around her shoulders and let her know he was there for her. A few minutes later Nadejda was a bit calmer, "That's why mamma never wanted me to see her with no clothes on. She didn't want me to see spots on her body, because they pressed her between pieces of wood with nails coming out of them," she added. Feeling exhausted but relieved for not having to worry about her secret any more, Nadejda went quiet for a while.

"Did you ever hear about your father?" Malcolm asked caringly.

"Yes. Mr Petrov heard from somebody that father was injured when he was running away from the pro-communists but they couldn't catch him. He escaped and he was hiding somewhere but with no medicine, he died from bad infection."

"Oh! I am so sorry to hear that, it must have been awful for you and your mother."

"Yes, we had very sad times," she said.

Feeling drained, Nadejda leaned back on the sofa and closed her eyes. Malcolm was deep in thought. He had just discovered that there was more to Nadejda than met the eyes. In a short time, he had seen her vulnerable side and it had saddened him to witness her sorrow. Affectionately, he persuaded her to go to bed, after drinking the warm milk he was going to bring her.

"Nadejda darling, you need your rest. Tomorrow we will talk some more about this. I am grateful that you shared your past with me. You know you can trust me, don't you? I can be your friend as well as your husband so you don't have to keep such painful secrets to yourself from now on, it's always better to open up and talk about things that bother you, all right?"

"All right Malcolm, I will remember in future."

"I have to be in the office early in the morning but I will try to be back in time, and don't worry about the house, I'll arrange a cleaner to come."

Unable to get a decent sleep, with the events of the previous day on his mind, Malcolm was up at dawn the next morning and was on his way to work. There he let himself in, stepped in the big hall crammed with desks and filing cabinets and headed towards his private office when he felt the urge for a strong cup of coffee. Having the impression that he was the first person present on the premises, he ventured out and walked towards the canteen to make his own coffee. Halfway there he heard muddled voices coming from behind a partition. His instinct told him to stop. Malcolm didn't mean to eavesdrop but he couldn't help hearing the voices of three women chatting away. They were going on about a subject he believed was about Lucas and his deceitful act.

Unaware that someone was within earshot, "Poor boss, fancy coming back to find that he has been cheated by someone he trusted most," one of the voices was saying. With an undisguised sarcasm, another voice that he recognised interrupted, "and he gave her everything, things I would give my right arm to have. I tell you, she doesn't deserve the easy life she has landed in. The nerve of that woman, the minute her husband's back is turned she goes and finds herself a beau, and a gorgeous one at that."

"Well, you just saw them hug, and Nadejda kissed him only on the cheek, maybe it is not what you think, maybe he is a relative of her's," Enid the new tea lady said, shrugging her shoulders.

"Don't think so, she always maintained she had nobody here."

"Maybe she felt lonely," the tea lady pleaded again.

"Of all the lame excuses, my mother and loads of other women slaved as Land Army members, while their husbands were out there defending their country but did they complain? Nope," the woman went on.

"Well, that was war time. Things are different now," Enid said, pouring tea in their cups.

Malcolm inched his way back to his desk feeling uneasy. His thoughts in turmoil, he was sure they were talking about his Nadejda. 'What? Is this idle gossip or a sick joke?' he asked himself.

Back in his office Malcolm couldn't stop his mind from racing. 'No, those innuendoes can't be anything else but nonsense. Nadejda wouldn't do that. Surely she must have met some man she knew in the past, from that boat she came on for instance. Giuseppe told me once about a bond of fellowship existing between people who came on the same transport. That gum flapping idiot must have seen them talking together. She was probably exaggerating the details, she is just one of those people who like to sensationalise what they see, people who have nothing better to do than spread nasty rumours. I have to put that bitch in her place,' he tried to rationalise.

Malcolm lit up a cigarette and filled his lungs with smoke. A few puffs further, unconsciously he began drumming his fingers on his desk. When he noticed what he was doing, he got more frustrated. Standing up impulsively, he took two steps towards the canteen, determined to go and confront the impudent woman and give her a piece of his mind. He was dead set to let her know where her insolence could take her but he stopped and reconsidered. He thought it was not like him to make a rash decision before having all his facts straight. The wise thing to do was to let Nadejda shed a light on the matter first. Nevertheless, the damage had been done. Exasperated, he found himself pacing the room. 'What is happening to me?' he mumbled, taking deep breaths to keep his calm.

Malcolm was known to be always in control of his nerves, always capable of rising above any situation but in this particular moment, this usually reserved and self-restrained man had reached a critical point. He actually doubted his ability to keep a straight face on a day he had so many things to sort out. For some reason, he felt as though he was caught in one of those unexpected storms that come every now and then and leave a lot of mess trailing behind. Both in his professional and private life, order had given way to confusion.

After an exceptionally cold winter they had that year, only a hint of summer's heat was being felt in the air, but Malcolm was seething inside. Grabbing a manila folder he fanned himself with it. 'Just when you think everything is all right, life turns around and kicks you in the teeth,' he muttered. Mercifully it didn't take long for the place to fill up with employees. Soon the daily routine and dealing with the Lucas affair got him so occupied that he hardly had time to think about anything else, at least not until way past lunch time. It was towards the end of the day that the subject of Nadejda being allegedly seen with another man began popping in his mind. Considering the trauma his wife had endured the previous night, he wondered what would be the proper way of tackling such a problem. Finally he came to the conclusion that a straight approach would be best.

After hours of punishing work, the last few days, tiredness catching up with him, Malcolm left the office and drove home automatically. He walked through the front door with a purposeful stride but stopped in his tracks when he noticed the sweet smell of roast and frying chips wafting in the air. He passed a spotlessly swept and carefully dusted living room and entered the kitchen. An aproned Nadejda was busy organising the fridge, "Oh! Hello Malcolm," she said with a smile.

"Hello, dear," he said, then seeing the inside of the fridge that was squeaking with cleanliness and stacked with all sorts of fresh food, he added, "Nadejda, I didn't expect to come to this, what a transformation, and you are cooking, I can't believe it."

"This not all my doing, cleaner woman helped me," she said with an honest voice, as she dried her fingers on her apron. "After we made living room and kitchen clean, we went shopping for food, and fabric shop person said kitchen curtains are ready, they will bring them tomorrow. Cleaner told me how cook roast, I am frying potatoes. Malcolm, I promise I will try to be more organised in future. I promise to be good wife for you," Nadejda declared, with the sincerity of a woman who had every intention of bettering herself and showing more devotion to her husband.

Overwhelmed by the change he saw in his wife and taking stock of the effort she had made to cook the evening meal, Malcolm didn't see any point in ruining things for both of them. With a tentative smile he looked at her and protested gently, "What do you mean? You have always been a good wife to me," then sampling a chip and pointing at the roast, "and if you do things like this once in a while, it will be all the better," he added, giving her a big smile this time.

"No Malcolm, after we eat I have something to tell you," Nadejda said with an air of sadness in the tone of her voice.

After dinner they went and sat on the opulent couch in their living room. Sipping freshly brewed tea, Malcolm was glad that he hadn't given his wife the third degree. He wasn't even sure if there really was anything to be concerned about. The phone rang and he went to answer it. When he came back, she was waiting for him. Malcolm couldn't help noticing the strange look she had on her face as she was nervously running her fingers on the piles of a velvet cushion. "Is something bothering you Nadejda dear?" he asked, his kindness giving her the courage to speak up.

"Remember last night, you said to me I shouldn't keep secret from you."

"Yes, and I meant every word of it," Malcolm said pensively, wondering if her speech had something to do with what he had overheard in the morning.

"Well, I saw Vladimir. Last week, when I went to see mamma, he was there. He was waiting for me. It was a shock for me."

"Vladimir? I have heard that name before. Is this the son of those friends you lived with, back in China?"

"Yes, I didn't know what happened to them, after we left. They said, maybe they will go to Canada, because Vladimir had uncle there. I thought I would never see him again, you know? With all the trouble there, I was not sure if they left alive." Nadejda went quiet, then turning her doleful face to her husband, "Malcolm, I am not a bad girl, I swear, I promise to myself I will be a good wife for you. Maybe it will be hard but I will try, I will do right thing," she said, sounding genuinely sincere.

"Did you and that Vladimir fellow have a history together?"

"Yes, we were young, very young, but we loved each other, just like children. We didn't do anything bad, you know?"

"Yes, I know what you mean," Malcolm said, encouraging her to continue.

"When mamma decided to come to Australia, I was sad, Vladimir was sad too. I told him we have to forget each other, but Vladimir made promise that he will find me wherever I go. I didn't believe it was possible. Not in million years I believe he can find me here. I told him I am married now and he must forget about me. If I knew he will show up...."

"You wouldn't have married me, is that what you are trying to say, Nadejda?"

Nadejda did not answer, she just held the cushion closer to her chest as though it could shield her from something she feared. Malcolm finished drinking his tea in an awkward silence that seemed to go on forever. Finally he put the empty cup down and broke the silence. "Nadejda, I want you to be frank with me. Remember I told you that I am your friend as well as your husband. I want you to listen to your heart and tell me something. If you were not married and you were free, would you have considered going away with Vladimir, no matter what sort of life he could offer you? What is he doing for a living anyway? Does he have a job?"

"He is a painter, he works with his uncle. He said to me he makes enough money for us to have good life. I can work too if we need more. I don't care about money. I am only worried about mamma, but sometimes when I visit her she doesn't know who I am."

"So?" Malcolm asked anxiously.

"Yes, I will say, maybe I will go with Vladimir. Malcolm I only say this because you asked me and I don't want to lie to you. You were so nice to me yesterday when you found out about mamma but you don't have to worry now. I will be a good wife, honest. I promise I will try to forget Vladimir but you have to help me, have patience... you know? Sorry I forgot to ask, do you want another cup of tea?"

"No, thanks," he said holding her shaking hand in his. "We will talk some more about this tomorrow. Let me sleep on it tonight, somehow we may find the best way to deal with this, don't worry for now," he added, looking in her frightened big blue eyes.

"You are not mad at me?" she asked.

Patting the back of her hand, "No! Not at all," he said, touched by her candour and integrity.

Chapter 6

It was a few years since World War II had ended. As their country was entering a period of economic reconstruction and development, Australian families were trying, as best as they could, to leave the past behind. Rich or poor, they worked hard towards putting their lives back on track and continue with their old ways. Most managed to even insert enjoyable moments in their everyday activities.

On that note, lately something out of the ordinary had been added to Australian's entertainment, something that had the potential to put their towns in a standstill mode for a solid fifteen minutes. Preoccupying a great number of people's minds, everyday, at the same time, their suburban routine was being disrupted. It provided them with a subject for casual conversation as well as some local gossip. In that short time, shopkeepers would be inclined to ignore their customers and housewives would forget all about their housework. And things wouldn't go back to normal until another episode of the lunchtime radio serial 'Blue Hills' was brought to air, attentively absorbed by everyone and ended. Listening to that program had become some sort of a ritual for the majority of Australians living in the country area as well as some city dwellers. They couldn't wait to find out more about the trials and tribulations of their favourite characters from the fictional Gordon family and their friends. Magnetically drawn and gathered around their wireless they used to religiously follow the heart warming storyline that transported the real life of country people to their homes, shops and meeting spots.

On a particularly windy autumn's day, while 'Blue Hills' enthusiasts were eagerly waiting for the program to start, 'Nelly', an American troop carrier converted to passenger ship, slid quietly into the Australian waters. The ship had been used for transporting a group of displaced people. Her voyage, that had begun in Naples, Italy, ended in Sydney with a long plaintive honk and a big huff of steam. On board were immigrants coming from all over Europe. After putting them through the tedious and tiresome formalities and the sickening routine of health inspection required by the Australian government, the passengers were allowed to disembark.

Amongst the passengers was a very attractive French woman who visibly stood out in the crowd. It was as if she had suddenly materialised on that spot by a strange phenomenon, if not by some bureaucratic bungle, because she didn't look one bit like she belonged with the rest of the group she had travelled with. Holding her head up solemnly, the woman stepped out of the ship. As she tossed aside an unruly strand of hair from her face, she displayed a hint of a widow's peak at the centre of her high forehead. The rest of her long, flame coloured hair that had lost its lustre during the horrendous voyage, was falling limply over her rounded shoulders. At first sight, one could easily believe she was an actress done up by a clever make up artist to play the part of a woman down on her luck. Despite her shabby attire and her gaunt face, she walked gracefully along the gangplank, one hand clasping her three year old daughter's tiny fingers. Her other hand was holding a dilapidated suitcase that looked like it had been kicked around a thousand times. Set in a pale oval shaped face, the woman had a pair of devilishly beautiful green eyes, a narrow slightly upturned nose and a perfectly contoured sensual full mouth. Her whole strikingly gorgeous head was complemented by her slender figure and long, smooth legs that could send any virile man's blood racing. Her name was Geneviève Melnic, at least that was her name on the ship's log.

As she stood on the firm Australian soil, Geneviève looked up towards the heavens, gazed at the bright blue sky, filled her lungs with the cool fresh air of the shore and exhaled with delight. She squeezed her daughter's little hand in her own and, with a motherly voice, "Ne t'en fait pas mon petit pinson, tout ira bien, tu vas voir," she told her over the commotion that was going on. Geneviève turned her head around and gave a last glance at the ship. Contradicting thoughts assailing her mind, she couldn't help doubting the reassuring words that she had just uttered to console her child. The coastal breeze began lashing at her, dispersing her hair from side to side. She stopped for a while, put her suitcase down and rearranged her triangular shawl on her back, throwing one corner of it over her shoulder to prevent it from slipping off. Her once tailor-made suit was soiled and crumpled. Aurore's dress wasn't in any better shape either. She was also wearing a dreary old hand-knitted jacket that looked a bit tight around her chest and the sleeves seemed to be getting short. Her bare feet hurting on the rough ground, she resented being dragged by her mother. Struggling to deal with her runny nose, she tried to comprehend what her mother meant when she told her not to worry and that everything will be all right because, at that very moment, shoes and a comfortable bed were the most urgently needed commodities weighing on her three year old mind.

On the advice of an Australian officer, Geneviève and Aurore joined a group of their co-voyagers and got on a train that was going to take them to Bathurst Centre. There, they were supposed to be sorted out and consequently sent to various job allocations. In other words, they were to start the first day of the rest of their lives in Australia, to eventually blend their old culture with one of the youngest in the world. Their arrival on this day was surely a far cry from the days British soldiers used to push convicts on shore, yelling, "Die you bastards," in their direction. Unloading them on this harsh sun scorched environment to fend for themselves, the soldiers expected them to survive the odds and make the best of a bad situation. Those same convicts and their descendents had come a long way in making this land an ideal place to live. Surely Australia hadn't earned the nickname 'The Lucky Country' for nothing. Indeed this enchanted land had become a sanctuary for people who had lost all they had. From their war torn homeland, they had come to the safe shores of this continent, hoping to find a new life.

On the train, throwing her arm around her daughter's frail body, Geneviève closed her eyes in a state of mental and physical exhaustion. As she began relaxing, scattered images of the last few years that she had lived back home came flooding into her head. Once again, those memories raised in her the same nagging question of whether she had done the right thing in uprooting herself to come this far in search of a better life. Anyway, like it or not, she was now in Australia and only time would tell what the future had in store for her. For the time being she had to wait and see. She was determined to try her darndest to pull herself out of that mediocrity she so despised. After all, she had an ambition the size of the Alps therefore she was prepared to go the distance and not rest until she had reached her goal.

Geneviève's mother owed her nickname 'Wilma La Rouge' to her lush long red hair that surrounded her face and cascaded around her shoulders. She was famous for her good looks in Bourg, the place of her birth, as well as the neighbouring villages that were all part of picturesque Ain. In addition to her fiery coloured hair, Geneviève had also inherited her mother's velvety complexion. Pierre, Wilma's half Swiss husband had lost his battle to tuberculosis only seven months before. He was a competent jeweller but, with his income gone, his wife and daughter were left to earn their own living. Luckily Wilma found a part-time job in the convent's refectory located behind the local Catholic school and was able to provide for the two of them.

In 1940 the Germans had already crossed the borders of France and they had reached and invaded Paris. Soon after, they had occupied the North of France and it was only a matter of time for them to come all the way down to sow terror in Wilma's peaceful neighbourhood. She could feel it in her bones that the war would eventually spread into the rest of the country. Wilma could almost hear the Nazi soldiers thumping their boots on the streets of her sleepy town. If it wasn't for Geneviève's sake, Wilma wished she had also died with her husband, and so wouldn't have to meet the Nazis when they would make themselves at home in her little corner of the world.

Wilma had a sleepless night, fearing for her daughter's safety. Restlessly she was rehashing in her mind the dangers Geneviève could be running into and what those bastards were capable of doing to a pretty girl like her. Towards morning she had reached a decision and knew she had to act fast. Wilma had no choice but to spread the rumour that she had managed to send her daughter to Switzerland to live with her paternal grandmother for a while. She thought she could always use the excuse of the war to justify why Geneviève had not been able to return home. To her daughter's horror, she stressed that, under no circumstances, was she allowed to show her face outside their home. After a long discussion that greatly displeased the twelve year old, Wilma gave Geneviève all the vital instructions about the where and how she was supposed to hide during the day.

For an added insurance, Wilma thought it was wise to get rid of their eye-catching locks and make themselves look as unattractive as possible. Now that Pierre was no longer with them, Wilma dreaded to be at loggerheads with her obstinate daughter. Still, with a bit of diplomacy she made her understand the gravity of the situation. Geneviève was growing up fast. At the threshold of puberty, she was a considerably good looking girl and that could very well work to her disadvantage. At dawn, in the anticipation of the grim days ahead, Wilma admired herself in the old mirror on the bathroom wall one last time and began with her mission. She snipped her own, then, her uncooperative whinging daughter's plaited hair. She rolled the precious red mass in a clean cloth then placed the bundle in a box and stored it in a closet. Turning to Geneviève she said, "Now listen carefully, in the mornings before I leave for work, you'll go to the basement taking all your clothes with you. Remember, you are supposed to be away, so don't leave anything lying around. I'll slide the trapdoor on top of the staircase and cover it with the rug. Do you understand, for no reason whatsoever are you to leave this basement or make any noise, understood?"

"Yes maman, I am not stupid." Geneviève said derisively.

"You are not allowed to light the lamp or a candle when I am not home."

"What if someone comes knocking at the door," the girl asked, a bored look in her eyes.

"Ignore it, remember you are not here, there is no one home. Even if they break the door and enter, you stay where you are and don't make any noise. Whoever they are, they will eventually leave. Nothing in this kitchen indicates that there is a basement under the rug. When I come home I will signal then you can come up. I will have to put something in front of that little window outside too, just in case the soldiers come to inspect."

"How would you signal?"

"I will sing the song 'Au clair de la lune'; in case you don't hear me sing but you hear me talk, just stay put, I may not be alone so be careful and very quiet, wait until the coast is clear before you come up."

"What if, for some reason, you don't come home one evening?" Geneviève asked, keeping her discontent in check.

"If that happens, you stay down there for a day or two, then wait until it's dark and come out carefully. Make sure there is no one here before you show your head through the opening. And watch out, because the kitchen table will be on the rug. You can never be too careful, you know?"

"So what will I do when I am up here?"

"Then you have to run towards the church and ask for help, but only if I am missing for two days and you have nothing to eat. I'll try to bring you as much leftover food as I can, that is if there is any and if I still work in the refectory."

"What will I do all day in the basement anyway?"

"You will keep yourself busy. Study, read, there are plenty of books down there and I will give you some fabric and whatever you need from my sewing basket. I'll help you study and I'll teach you how to sew, when I am back in the evenings."

"I wish papa was still alive," Geneviève moaned while reaching for the exquisitely crafted gold cross she was wearing around her neck. It was a piece her father had made for her a year before his death.

"I hope that cross protects you, my darling, as your father wished it would." Wilma said with a sigh.

"Yes maman, I wish the Germans never come here and the war ends soon."

A week later, Wilma saw for herself the way Nazi soldiers operated and realised her fears were not unfounded. On that cold day in November 1942, she was busy tidying up the mess boarding students had left in the refectory when several German army trucks lined up outside. To her horror she saw S.S. soldiers spilling out of them and swarming like killer bees towards the school and raiding the place. She observed them moving around swiftly, their stony faces generating terror and their savagery making them look like monsters. Without a scrap of humanity, without any consideration or a hint of compassion for the terrified school children, their long coats flapping around their boots, they barked orders to everyone in sight. As if they owned the world and everyone in it, they took over the premises to turn it into a makeshift hospital for their own wounded. Wilma was then forced to work longer hours. A local restaurant cook was assigned to cater for the wounded, the hospital staff and the officers on duty.

Besides washing stacks of dishes and scrubbing pots and pans, Wilma had to help the cook and wash the floors before leaving. For the first few weeks, pretending she had a bad toothache, Wilma decided to conceal part of her face behind an old scarf. Seething inside, she was hiding her beauty as well as her hatred for the intruders who were using her as a slave. Even the nuns were not exempt from doing their share of work. They each had to put a few hours a day, feeding, cleaning and helping the wounded get better, besides doing the back breaking laundry.

Every day that passed, Wilma found it harder to witness the cruelty her fellow countrymen were subjected to. How could one human being inflict upon another so much pain and misery, the answer was just out of her grasp. Nevertheless, as it had always been the case, Wilma and all the rest of her villagers got used to hardship sooner than they thought they would be able to. They realised that one is capable of adapting faster to hard times than to a sudden windfall or a newly acquired wealth.

After the initial shock of the Germans' arrival, things got a little easier since Wilma and the other members of her community saw less of those soldiers and more of the medical crew. Always busy bringing in and patching up their wounded, the Germans seemed to have less opportunity to exercise their power over the inhabitants of Bourg. Except for a few incidents that resulted in some locals being severely punished or in rare cases even executed, days went by, one at a time. Every now and then, Wilma could smuggle some food out of the kitchen in order to feed her emaciating daughter. At night, even though she used to be dead tired, she made sure to make the effort to pamper Geneviève and help her with her studies. As for her sewing skills, she taught the girl every stitch she had herself learned from the nuns. "Now this stitch is called 'Le Surjet', it is used to join two pieces of folded fabrics to each other, border to border."

"Is this important for me to learn maman?"

"Yes it is and you'd better believe it. Any kind of knowledge may come in handy if, God forbids, things get ugly all of a sudden. You never know, trouble can be at our front door at any time.

"I don't see how it can be helpful in these times of war."

"And I wish you never have to find out, but it is a fact, useful and skilled people have more of a chance to survive wars."

"You mean they can make them work instead of...."

"Yes, they wont kill them as long as they can use their expertise."

As far as Wilma knew, Geneviève had always been a difficult child, with a mind of her own. Self-centred, manipulative and insensitive to other people's feelings, she was particularly coarse with her mother. That was something Wilma had not understood why. She used to think, the fact that Geneviève was an only child and her father was spoiling her excessively had something to do with her impertinent behaviour. In her husband's eyes their daughter had always been a faultless princess. Sadly though, Wilma was aware that there was a nasty streak to Geneviève and often wondered where it had come from. She sincerely wished she could somehow keep her under control. She had often seen Geneviève make Pierre bend to her capricious ways with her uniquely characteristic impish smile and the roll of her eyes. "Your daughter is capable of charming a snake out of its nest, you are not doing her a favour by dancing to her every tune," she used to tell her husband.

"She is only a child, Wilma," he would plead with her, exaggerating his optimism.

"Yes, but it won't hurt her to learn some manners."

It was out of curiosity and also to get her mother off her back that finally Geneviève agreed to go down to the basement room and check her forthcoming hiding place. Normally she wouldn't hear a bar of it, but unfortunately the impending war had put an end to that sort of practice. Deep inside, her instincts were telling her she didn't have any other option but to accept her present situation. No matter what kind of friction there had been between her and her mother, she knew she had to listen to her.

Once Geneviève was down there, a glance around the uninviting place was sufficient to totally convince her she wouldn't be able to stay there more than an hour before getting bored to tears. Another look at the clutter that had invaded the place over the years and she believed there was no way she could come out of there with her sanity left intact. Nevertheless, with the war drawing near, she realised it was imperative for her to find something interesting to occupy herself with, when the time came. "I have to bring a few things down here, like something to sit on, for example, and enough bed linen," she thought aloud. And one day, sooner than they expected it, that time came.

After hearing her mother slam the front door to go to work, Geneviève started her first day of solitude. She was letting herself get used to the dim light when her eyes caught sight of a trunk filled with books, as her mother had said she would. She tiptoed towards the trunk and, from the top of it she took a hardback to flip through the pages, when dust rose up irritating her eyes and assaulting her lungs. A thick layer of dried up dirt spread across the cover prevented her from reading the title. As she opened the book, a nasty smell hit her nostrils and she cringed when she noticed a dead insect's remains stuck under the cover; "zut alors!" she heard herself almost scream as she creased her nose in disgust. She practically threw that book down.

Looking around, Geneviève saw an old and equally dusty feather duster hanging on the wall. She grabbed and passed it over the books a few times, reallocating the dust to other places, then took another book, a smaller one this time. She suddenly remembered the bucket holding some cleaning agents that her mother had brought down the night before. Searchingly looking in the bucket, she pulled out a clean rag and wiped a corner of the long sturdy table that used to be her father's workbench. Climbing on top, she tried a few sitting positions until she was comfortable enough to read. She had to hold the book up, in the direction of the little bit of light that was seeping through a small window. On that fairly bright day the place could have been brighter if her mother hadn't cautiously concealed the window with a hardy shrub growing in a clay pot. Geneviève placed a cushion under her elbow then flicked through a book and began reading a few lines here and there. Titled 'History of Bourg', it didn't seem to be an interesting book. She was about to put it down when her eyes rested on a caption that raised her curiosity, "Important people born in Bourg," it read. On top of the list, after a couple of names such as Quinet and Fabre, there was an intriguing name like Monsieur Joseph Jeremy De La Lande. It said that Monsieur De La Lande was an astronomer who had occupied his time researching the theory of the planets, his biggest concern being the planet Mercury. He lived between the years 1732 and 1807. 'Interesting,' Geneviève thought then, pressing the book to her chest, she tightly closed her eyes and, lifting her face up, she whispered in delight, "Geneviève De La Lande!!!" It sounded so posh, so respectful, so her. She wished that it was her real surname, as opposed to Caushon, the family name she was stuck with.

Geneviève couldn't help feeling anger and resentment, remembering how she had suffered at school because of her surname. She vividly recalled the cruel way her classmates used to torment her in the playground. Reduced to tears, she couldn't say a thing to counteract the irritating noises they were making to harass her. "Oink, oink," they used to squeal, imitating the cry of a pig. Even though they knew the real spelling of pig in French was cochon, to those contemptible girls it didn't matter, as long as they had some fun at someone else's expense. Oh! How she would like to scratch their eyes out and make them pay for heckling her like that. 'Yes, this is the surname I would want to see attached to my first name,' she decided, daydreaming about the possibility of it.

Geneviève stayed in her hiding place for as long as the war lasted. She cleaned and made it more acceptable, more comfortable but it still felt like a jail. It was a lucky coincidence that three years before his death, Pierre had decided to set a workshop in the basement of their house. He had a few jewellery designs of his own and had liked to make them in his spare time. Geneviève's cross was one of them.

After the first hour being down there, Pierre had realised that it would have been better if more fresh air circulated in the basement. He had racked his brain to find a cheap solution for it. It was Wilma who had come up with the idea to put another staircase going up to a second lavatory they had at the end of the corridor and right above the basement. The lavatory had a big enough window and just enough room to cut an opening on its floor. With both windows open, Pierre was happy to have a pleasant draught passing through his work area. So did Geneviève as she did most of her reading sitting on those wooden stairs and benefiting from the daylight and clean air. She was also lucky to have a toilet to use when nature called, except she was not allowed to pull the cord when her mother was away. For an added safeguard, with the help of her daughter, Wilma had to place a tall armoire in front of the lavatory door.

Mercifully nothing life threatening happened to Wilma and no one got wind that her daughter had never been out of the country and was down there in the basement for almost four years, surviving like an animal in hibernation. But unlike animals who pass their time in a torpid state, while she spent her days in the basement and her nights up in the house with her mother, Geneviève managed to read all the books in the trunk, plus a few that her mother smuggled out of the school. Any word she didn't know the meaning of, she asked her mother or looked it up in the big family's Larousse dictionary. As a result, her spelling, geography and history of France had improved to a degree much higher than it would have been, had she continued to go to school under normal circumstances, in peaceful times.

Geneviève read a lot of novels, they were her favourite because she was growing into a woman and those books were broadening her mind on the subject of romance and love. Geneviève couldn't wait for all the nonsense of the war to be over so she could get out, stretch her wings and go through the natural stages and the ups and downs of life. She wanted to fall in love and experience all that comes with it. She had enough of imagining and fantasising about the act of lovemaking. She wanted to truly feel the joys of being desired, sense the thrills of being chased by a man for real rather than read about the subject in a tattered old book. Nevertheless she kept on reading those romantic passages over and over. 'If only they were a bit more explicit so I could know exactly what lovemaking is all about,' she kept on whimpering impatiently, in the silence of her secluded space.

And then the day they all wished to see came about. The war ended and the people of Bourg got their birthplace back to themselves. No more enemy soldiers, with their unsightly helmets strapped tightly under their chins, were to lurk around. The dark shadow that had fallen across the entire country was removed for good. Even though their town was left half-destroyed, Wilma's fellow villagers were ecstatically happy to be there to reclaim it. Bit by bit, they were determined to rebuild and make it home again.

Unfortunately for Wilma, things were not going to be the same. For her, it wasn't so easy to go back to her old life and take up where she had left off, so to speak. The war had indeed taken its toll on her and, with all the efforts she had made to conceal her ordeal, mainly from Geneviève, the bitter reality was still there, tearing away at her inside. Just because she didn't admit it or confided to someone, it didn't make her any less of a victim and a casualty of the ugly war. She didn't have a wound or a mark to show for it but her scars were running deep in her soul.

Wilma's traumatic memories of what she had endured were there to stay for a long time. On many occasions, she had been taken advantage of, used as a sex object by any given German officer, whom she had the misfortune to serve something, in his office. For them, molesting her was too good an opportunity to pass up. It was their right as conquerors to help themselves and do as they pleased. One officer had raped her ferociously on the floor of the ex-school principal's office before she had time to clear the dishes off his table. The memory of his hard face and the sound of his heavy breathing were to remain in her nightmares for as long as she lived.

Another time, another half drunk officer had tried to invite himself to Wilma's house one evening, after her thankless task was done. A bottle of Bordeaux under his arm, a mocked courteous tone in his voice, eyes gleaming, he had asked her through his alcohol breath, "I hear you don't have a husband, what do you say if we go have a good time in your place, hem?" He had said, all the while, he was making this disgusting gesture with his closed fist and the index of his other hand, suggesting the act of copulation.

Terrified of what the officer might discover if he'd set foot in her house, Wilma had no choice but to fake willingness and impatience. Putting on an eager face she had gone to him to give in to his lecherous desires. Disguising her contempt, she had unbuttoned his uniform and helped him take off his boots that glistened in the dim light. Then, playing a made up seductive game she had let him do what he wanted to do, right there on the desk topped with military documents.

Every time such incidents occurred, Wilma went home feeling so miserable she couldn't face her daughter or look herself in the mirror. Pretending she was coming down with something and had a headache, which understandably she must have had, she had let her daughter eat alone and had gone straight to bed.

As usual Geneviève never once showed any interest in her mother's health and wellbeing. Too busy, feeling sorry for herself, she didn't have time to care about anyone else. Blinded by her own petty problems, she never bothered to go and check on her mother. If only she could guess the sacrifices Wilma was making to keep her safely tucked away from their oppressors, maybe it would ease a little of Wilma's pain. If it hadn't been for her daughter's safety, she wouldn't have to go on living with the shame of it all, after the first time she had been violated. In those long years of war, Wilma had changed so much, she couldn't recognise herself. Her once glowing skin had turned dull. She had a lot of wrinkles around her emerald eyes. Her glorious hair was left unkempt and hideously greying. She was aging at a staggering speed right under her daughter's eyes. The war was over, the nightmare was supposed to be over too, but not for Wilma.

Although the Germans were all gone and peace had come back to Bourg, Wilma had to act realistically so she kept Geneviève indoors for another month or so, "Just to be on the safe side," she told her daughter. Wilma was adamant to make her daughter's return look plausible. Knowing she couldn't do it on her own, she was forced to confess everything to father Perrault. The good priest was speechless at first but after getting over his shock he promised to help her with her problem. He told Wilma that in the following week, he and a couple of nuns were supposed to go to Chalamon. "We have to pick up some children from an orphanage and bring them here. I can smuggle Geneviève out of here and put her on a bus to come back to Bourg. You can go to the bus depot and bring her home. Pretend she just arrived from wherever she was and make sure a few people see you," he said.

Four days later Geneviève was officially back from Switzerland. Wilma was happy that she had taken precaution and had prevented later explanations, in case if what she had done was illegal in the eyes of the law. Even though she was still struggling with the mental anguish of her unyielding memories, her main concern was her daughter. Geneviève had also changed since the pre-war days. She had grown and her mother liked to believe that when she would mingle with the other teenagers, she would not be the odd one out. The fact that she was deprived of sunlight and sparingly fed would not seem unnatural since everybody else had gone through the same ordeal.

At last Geneviève had come out of her hideaway. She was free, free to be with others, free to tackle the world. She had dreams to fulfil, she had plans to put into action, but first, she had to live a little, have fun and make up for all the time she had lost. She was currently a tall and slender girl. She looked a bit boyish with her short hair, yet she was revealing a hint of the female curves. Nevertheless, time was on her side and even though life was still very tough, she was sure she would find a way to amuse herself. Her surname that had made her the butt of cruel jokes was still on her mind but that was something she had to leave alone for the time being.

Things had changed in Geneviève's neighbourhood. Ruined buildings were seen here and there. Geneviève decided to go to church one Sunday to see everyone, or whoever had survived. To her relief she didn't see any of the nasty girls who used to tease her years ago except for one, but it seemed that the war had changed her attitude for the better. Valentine had in fact turned into a sensible girl Geneviève thought when she heard her talk. With a genuinely concerned voice she had asked Geneviève if she too had felt the pressures of the war over there in Switzerland. "Was it really neutral, and tell me how does the Swiss chocolate taste like?" she had inquired in haste, as if that was the most important subject to know about. Geneviève couldn't help herself from smiling at the question.

"The chocolate was all right, as for my stay over there, well it wasn't easy. I was forced to live away until travelling was possible and grandma wasn't fun to be with, I mean she was not the best of company. I would rather have been here close to my mother, I was worried sick for her," she replied cunningly, hoping Valentine wouldn't ask too many questions about the country. With the little she knew about Switzerland, she could very well be caught lying.

"There is a gathering this evening in the church hall, would you like to go? Lots of people our age will be there," Valentine told her.

"I'll try, I will ask maman," she said, knowing her mother needed her help for spring-cleaning the house.

"See you there, then," her old classmate said, waving goodbye.

Geneviève went searching for her mother. She found her still praying at the last pew inside the church. Once again Wilma was thanking the good Lord for sparing her daughter's life. 'Please God I am begging you to help me erase the memories of war from my mind. If not for me then for Geneviève's sake, give me the strength to forget what went on between the walls of the schoolmaster's office. I have to be there for my daughter, I have to protect and guide her. She needs me now more than ever.'

Geneviève retained her pale complexion only for a while then, gradually, being out in the open air, lost colours came back to her high cheekbones. A few weeks later and her face was as radiant as it used to be. To everyone's delight she finally showed up at a social gathering, looking like a picture of perfection. Glowing with youth and feminine charm, she had what any woman would envy and any man would desire. Geneviève didn't realise how pretty she was until she saw the effect her looks had on the town's boys and that notion went straight to her head. She began acting like a goat confined to a small space for some time then let loose on a paddock. Hormones raging, frantically impatient, she was quivering with anticipation and couldn't wait to be part of the big scheme of life. She needed to savour and take advantage of her freedom to the fullest.

Wilma was working during the day and in her spare time she was taking part in helping father Perrault care for the increasing number of orphans that kept flooding in. With all her good intentions, Wilma was not able to keep a constant control over her daughter. It was no wonder that after a few months, Geneviève found herself pregnant and in deep trouble. Her biggest problem was the fact that she didn't have a clue as to who had put her in that unholy mess. 'Could it be François, the son of the local butcher or Amedée, the bread delivery boy who worked for the Boulangerie down the road,' she kept asking herself.

François was an arrogant, purse-proud, rotten brat with whom she had slept just to prove a point. It was her ambition to make him accept that she was more experienced in the field of lovemaking than he was boasting to be. She was not interested the least bit in him. In fact she despised him for putting his pigeons ahead of her. His main hobby was to feed his birds, clean their cages and watch them fly, from sunup to sundown. He was a chunky adolescent with bright coloured hair sticking out of his head like the bristles of a worn out brush. Nevertheless, he used to tease her relentlessly for the colour of her hair. "Poil de carotte," he used to call her, likening her hair to the strings hanging from a carrot.

The last time that Geneviève had met François, he was showing off his pigeons to a few friends. "Fire, fire, hair on fire," please somebody call the fire brigade," he had shouted, pointing at her. To save face in front of the boys, she had called him a frightened porcupine and had turned around to walk away from him. He had shrugged and told her, "Well cherie, you are not the only sweet pea in the pod and if you don't like my sense of humour you can leave, I assure you, you won't be missed."

Geneviève had ambled off afterwards without answering him back.

Amedée, on the other hand, was a very considerate boy. It was his innocent boyish face and his curly brown hair that had made her seek his company. He had the potential to be a caring husband to a lucky girl some day, but not to her. She had to forget about him because, despite his good looks and charming manners, Amedée was as poor as a church mouse, therefore dumping the responsibility on him was out of the question.

Geneviève could also blame her pregnancy on François and force him to marry her. Considering how financially privileged his father was, made this option more tempting in those post-war meagre times. Geneviève thought she could always turn François' life into such a living hell that he would want to divorce her. 'It's then that I would walk away with a lot of cash and get out of this godforsaken place for good, but do I want to marry that idiot? What am I thinking? Have I forgotten that if word came out that I have been sexually involved with someone, my mother would strangle me for sure? If only I knew where to go for an abortion, I could nip the problem in the bud without anyone having time to guess the truth.'

Geneviève's head was exploding with all these thoughts. Her mind kept going from François to Amedée, but the more she thought the more she became aware of the hot water she had put herself into.

The war had changed people's lives but in their tight knit community, curiosity was still rampant. One such faux pas was enough to ruin Geneviève's chance of a future she intended to build for herself.

Geneviève came to the conclusion that she couldn't let her secret be known to anyone in Bourg. In their circle there was no place for that kind of scandal. Tongues would be wagging incessantly for decades to come if she was to bring a bastard into the world. That night Geneviève flung some essentials in a small bag before going to bed. In the morning, she scribbled a few words for her mother telling her she needed to be on her own, to explore the world. She also advised Wilma not to make a fuss and not to go looking for her, because she felt it was time she was allowed to live her own life. After a last look around the house, grabbing a piece of bread, a bit of cheese and some money from her mother's insignificant savings, she fled to the city centre where she sold the heavy chain her cross was hanging from. Half an hour later she was on a fast train that took her to Paris, the place she had read so much about and was yearning to see.

For the first three days Geneviève walked and walked the streets, looking for a job. At night she slept under the bridge with the rest of the homeless people. The little money she had was not going to last for long. What if she didn't find a job soon, she began worrying. In the chill of early morning, feeling cold, hungry and disheartened, she was standing in a queue to buy a piece of bread when her eyes wandered across the street. She saw an old man scavenging for scraps in a big garbage bin. Two other younger men were fighting over something they had found in there. "I saw it first," one was saying.

"I don't care, it's mine," the other one screamed.

The thought that she could be doing the same if her luck didn't change nauseated her. Geneviève had heard the expression la chasse aux poubelles before, now she was seeing it with her own eyes and it terrified her. Winter was around the corner too. Stomach churning, sheepishly she tried to ask the man who served her if there was an opening in the boulangerie.

"No, sorry," he said, wrapping her bread in a piece of newspaper.

"Wait a minute, mademoiselle, I know someone who can help you," she heard a voice behind her say.

Geneviève's heart leapt as she turned to face the sinewy man who seemed to be serious about what he had blurted out.

"Do you mean there is a job somewhere? Where is it? Tell me please," she almost begged.

"If you care to wait, I'll take you there," the stranger said casually.

After paying for his loaf of bread, the man signalled her to follow him.

"By the way, I am Armand, my boss' name is Bertrand. He is running an agency, it's over there," he said, pointing at a shabby two story building.

"What sort of an agency is it?" she interrupted.

"You better talk to him, he can explain, here we are, go up the stairs and turn left, it's the first door, I have some more shopping to do."

Geneviève knocked at the door in question then pushed it open quietly when she heard a male voice say, "entrez, s'il vous plait".

At first glance the room looked like a regular office except for the skimpy garments hanging in the far end and the vulgarly made up female who was on her way out. Geneviève didn't have to be a genius to guess what sort of business Bertrand was running and what was going on behind the other doors in the building. The discovery numbed her senses but she also remembered the reality of her life. She had to survive. She knew she had the choice to leave but she stood there in front of the broad shouldered man who was staring at her beautiful features.

"What can I do for you," he finally asked.

"Armand sent me, he said you may have a job for me."

Geneviève took the job but didn't tell Bertrand anything about her pregnancy. 'It will be only for a short while, the minute I start showing I am out of here,' she thought.

Geneviève stayed in the brothel for two months, sleeping with every Paul, Pierre and Luc that her boss ordered her to but she didn't see any substantial money. Her income, after Bertrand took the lion's share went for food and lodgement that he was providing for her. She even owed him money for the winter clothes he bought her and was paying it off gradually. She could only borrow the outfits and accessories she had to wear on the job, charge free. Geneviève was not a prude, but what she had to do for the miserly money and that she couldn't save any of it, seemed unacceptable to her. She needed cash and she needed it fast so, with an eye to the future, she decided to come up with a plan that would free her from Bertrand's grip. She had to get out of there and try her luck elsewhere but without money her plans were of no use.

Suddenly Geneviève remembered something that had happened in the first days of working for Bertrand. After her client had left, she had gone to see her boss. As she had reached the door, another girl who was getting out of the office had held the door slightly open for her to enter. Through the sliver of light, Geneviève had seen Bertrand pull his desk drawer out and place a bundle in the space behind the drawer before pushing it back in. She had waited for a while before proceeding to enter and report to her boss.

Geneviève had wondered about the incident for a few days then she had forgotten all about it. 'Could it be money?' she wondered again and if so, she had to have it. The only question was how to get hold of Bertrand's keys and how to lure him out of the office. Then one day, the opportunity presented itself. Geneviève was lurking behind the clothes rack looking for a new outfit when one of the girls stormed in. She told Bertrand that Armand had been arrested after a fistfight he had with someone who had run into the back of his van. "He told me to ask you if you can take his papers with you when you go to the commissaire de police," she said, catching her breath between every word.

"I am on my way," he said, dismissing the girl.

When the girl was out, jumping off his chair, Bertrand walked towards a cabinet to get the papers.

It seemed that Bertrand had forgotten that Geneviève was still in the room. In his haste, he also forgot to lock the cabinet before leaving. 'So that's where he keeps our papers,' Geneviève thought, keeping as quiet as possible. Stashing the papers in his pocket, Bertrand left the room. When Geneviève heard the key turn in the door and after a few seconds, the downstairs door slammed, she went straight to the drawer and took out the bundle. It was money all right, but also there were four breathtaking chunky rings wrapped in a handkerchief with it. She rushed to the cabinet and looked for her own papers that the boss was holding on to. It was a precaution he was taking, in case one of his employees contemplated the idea of double-crossing him. Geneviève stashed the bundle in her brassiere and, squeezing herself out of the window, she climbed onto the fire escape ladder and fled. Without bothering to go around the block and get her belongings from the room she shared with another girl, she ran towards the metro. She jumped in a car not knowing where she would end up. It didn't really matter where the train was going, as long as it took her away, far away from Bertrand and his gang.

Aware of the sexually transmitted diseases she could easily catch, Geneviève had begun worrying for her health and the safety of her unborn baby. After seeing one of her colleagues being bashed by a client and discovering that there was no way out of that nightmare, she also feared for her life.

On the opposite side of Paris, far away from where Bertrand's brothel was located, Geneviève found herself an accommodation. It was in a partly bombed building, a reminder of the wartime air raids. Arlette, the lady who sublet her the small room was a good-natured person who turned out to be a fine friend to Geneviève in the following years. While knitting a multicoloured something, she gave Geneviève the grand tour of the house she jokingly called Notre palais, meaning our castle.

"This here is the bathroom," she said, referring to a filthy space with questionable plumbing facilities, "and this is Yanis' room."

"Yanis, is this your son?"

"No, Yanis is a Latvian young man. He is another tenant. The poor fellow has got a disability, he stutters. He had come to France only a few months before the war broke. He was here to learn all he could about the knitting machines. Anyway, he got stranded in Paris and since he had no one left back home he stayed here. He has a good job in a knitting factory now. Sometimes he brings me wool remnants and I just knit and knit," she went on, showing her masterpiece hanging from the needles.

"That's nice, what is it?"

"It's a shawl. It will come in handy in the freezing days. I have made a waistcoat for Yanis, you are going to meet him soon. Every now and then he stays the night at a workmate's place to save himself the travel but he always comes home for the weekend."

"I have to tell you something Madame, before moving in. I am expecting a baby, I hope you don't mind," Geneviève asked sheepishly.

"Oh! How nice, a baby! I don't mind at all. I adore babies," she said, looking at Geneviève's belly from the top of her glasses. "What about the father?" she asked casually.

"Don't ask me, the bastard was beating me for no reason. I got fed up with his temper, his constant abuse. I ran away before telling him I was pregnant. I couldn't risk my baby's life, staying with him. I had no guaranty that he wouldn't be bashing my child too, so I had to disappear."

Geneviève told Arlette lies after lies and when Arlette inquired about her surname, handing her some forged papers, supposedly signed by father Perrault, "De La Lande, I am Geneviève de la Lande, my real papers were destroyed during the air raids," she said.

Arlette half suspected that was not her real surname since she was on the run, but as long as the rent was paid in advance, it didn't matter.

One first look at Geneviève's beautiful face and Yanis was smitten. She sensed it and decided to use it to her advantage. It would be good to have a man around, even a stammering one, as long as he kept his distances from her. For someone who was so eager to be with a man, Geneviève had come to despise being touched by one, after working for Bertrand. She didn't intend to be pestered by any man, not even the sweet and harmless Yanis.

A week later Geneviève found herself a job, a seamstress job at a tailoring place called Maison de couture Mercier. The pay was modest but it was close to home. Her employer, René Mercier was married with three children, but that never stopped him from chasing anything that wore a skirt. His wife knew all about his weakness, a classic coureur de jupe, she used to call him. As days passed, Geneviève liked her job more and more. She learned a lot from René who restrained himself from making advances to her while she was with child. Nevertheless, the glow that her pregnancy brought to her skin was driving him nuts.

It was still dark when Geneviève felt the first contractions and yelled for help. Yanis pulled his jacket on and ran out to wake up Arlette then went after the midwife who lived a few houses away. Twenty minutes later he let her in and showed her the way to Geneviève's room. The first rays of the sun began shining through his window when he heard the cry of the baby. It was a girl and Geneviève called her Aurore, because she had come to this world at dawn. Geneviève also believed that the birth of her daughter was the start of a new life for both of them. After a much needed rest, holding the precious bundle in her arms, 'I will do anything to give you a good life. I assure you I will not rest until you have everything you deserve, ma petite poupée,' she promised her sleeping baby.

Arlette wouldn't have been more excited if that baby had been her own flesh and blood. She held her and pampered her whole-heartedly. A few months after the birth, as they had come to agree, Geneviève went back to work leaving Aurore in Arlette's capable hands. They had decided that Arlette would look after the baby during the day. In return Geneviève had to pay for the groceries and upon her return from work she would help Arlette cook the evening meals. It was a fair arrangement that suited Geneviève. The baby was doing fine and Geneviève continued to learn more about the art of dressmaking, extracting from René more and more techniques in that field. She asked a lot of questions and made notes of whatever she heard, but not without having to use a bit of coquetry to help her along the way. It was her brand of coquetry that landed her into his arms and later on, ignited the fires of an illicit affair between them.

Unable to keep his hands off her, René gave Geneviève more freedom in the workplace. She kept coming in late and left whenever it pleased her. Some evenings, she stayed late to make herself or her daughter an outfit. Without telling him, every time he was out on an errand, she carefully copied a pattern she thought would be useful to her later. In no time, she had a suitcase full of neatly folded patterns and a lot of confidence in her ability to, one day, run a business like René's, on her own. All was well, she was in charge of her life and fairly optimistic about the future, until that day when all hell broke lose. It was the day René's wife barged in to catch them in flagrant delit, as she kept repeating the expression to her close friends, in the following weeks. "I knew he was a flirt but those red hairs I kept finding on his clothes in the last few months confirmed my suspicion. I just couldn't wait to catch them in the act," she was telling them, over and over.

They used to creep behind the curtains of the fitting room and shamelessly give in to their forbidden desire. On that particular day, René had the fantasy to see her completely naked instead of rushing things along with only her skirt rolled up. Amazing each other by their sexual ardour, they were in an advanced stage of their lovemaking when they heard the swishing of the curtains being pulled over the railing. Instantly, they were exposed to the fury and the anger-filled eyes of a betrayed Sonia Mercier. For a while, Sonia just stared at them in disgust. Geneviève reached to grab her dress. René pulled his pants up and began fiddling with the buttons of his fly. All of a sudden, foaming at the mouth, hands on her hips and looking like a giant amphora, Sonia started screaming. "So that's what my beloved husband is doing when I am slaving at home, raising his three kids, washing his clothes, cleaning his house and preparing his dinner." Pointing her index finger in Geneviève's direction, she went on, "And you, you, I thought you were a putaine, the first time I cast eyes on you. I should have known, not to trust your saint-nitouche air of innocence."

Making a funny face, mockingly Sonia mimicked her husband's plea, when he had tried to justify the urgency for helping Geneviève. "She is a poor woman who is trying hard to raise her fatherless child, someone ought to give her a chance. Well, mon cheri, your good deed is done, now it's time to say goodbye to the slut, you hear me? And don't come to me for sex for a long, long time, not until I am sure you won't be transmitting venereal diseases to me."

Geneviève dressed herself in a big hurry, not knowing what she was supposed to do next. She grabbed her basket to get out.

"And don't bother to come back, you cocotte, you are fired, because I will do the hiring and firing from now on, since I am the owner of this establishment," Sonia blurted out.

Turning to René, "As for you, cheri, you can follow her now, but let me remind you, you don't have two sous to rub against each other, so make up your mind, choose between me, your kids, your home, your business or this miserable red headed harlot," she added.

Under the merciless glare of his wife, René stood there like a lifeless lump. Geneviève gave him a last glance and from the way he cowered and lowered his eyes, realising where she stood with him, she began walking to the door. Sonia followed her and, as Geneviève set foot on the doorstep, she lifted her heavy foot and kicked Geneviève in the backside then slammed the door shut. The kick was hard enough to make Geneviève fall in the puddle that last night's rain had left behind.

Geneviève walked home still feeling giddy from the shock of being discovered and disgraced. The next two days, pretending she was tired and unwell, she sat quietly in her room, deep in reflection. She didn't feel like going out and searching for another job. She couldn't help thinking about Yanis and his hints of the two of them joining forces and going to Australia together, hints that sounded like a marriage proposal to her. The very idea of moving to a new world was appealing to her and Yanis was a nice man, but he was also an ordinary man with very little to offer her. In other words, he was nothing like the prince charming she had dreamt about in the days she had been hiding in the basement of their house at Bourg.

Yanis had guessed that he didn't have any chance with Geneviève, so he had stopped badgering her about the better quality of life in Australia. He had restricted himself to just feast his eyes on her, every now and then, when she was playing with Aurore and didn't realise she was being watched. On the third day her mind was made up. Looking at the way Arlette was spoiling her daughter had often brought a question to the surface. She wondered how her own mother would have treated Aurore, should she have known about her existence. There was no better time than the present to find out. After all, her mother's house was her home too, and she had the right to live in it. She packed her bags and said farewell to Arlette and a disappointed Yanis. "Don't forget dear to drop me a line once in a while, and if you can, send some pictures of Aurore, I want to see how she is growing up," Arlette begged her.

"I will, I promise," Geneviève replied, and when Yanis shook her hand, he held it tightly for a while and, looking in her eyes, he whispered, "And if things don't work out the way you expected them to, come back but don't leave it too late, because I will be on my way to Australia next time there is a boat going that way."

Geneviève was standing in front of her home wondering if she was in the right place. The house was the same but it looked as if by magic it had been transformed into a dream home. The building was restored, the door and windows were painted tastefully, there were beautiful curtains hanging on the other side of those windows. The front yard was adorned with splendid pot plants. All sorts of flowers were growing in the tidy garden beds. 'Mother must have found a hidden treasure somewhere,' she thought. 'How could she have done this,' she asked herself as she walked closer to knock at the door. Exhausted by the trip and Aurore clutching at her skirt, Geneviève was surprised to see a stranger answer it. "I am Geneviève. Is my mother home?"

"Who is your mother?" asked the man, looking surprised.

"Wilma, Wilma Caushon, and who are you?"

"Oh!" The man said, "Your mother does not live here anymore. We bought this house from her almost three years ago."

"Oh! Where does she live now? Did she leave any forwarding address? Look, I came a long way and my daughter is tired, I would appreciate it if you tell me where I can find her," Geneviève said.

Turning his mouth down at the corners, the man spread his shoulder and shrugged. "I am sorry madame," he said, then as if he remembered something, "you'd better go to the convent, the nuns may be able to help you," he added.

Disappointed, Geneviève mumbled a merci beaucoup and walked away, dragging her daughter behind her. The wind was whistling past their ears and was messing up little Aurore's red hair. She couldn't see well, since she had lost the ribbon that was holding it away from her face, and that was aggravating her mood. They were half way there when Geneviève saw father Perrault on his bicycle. Recognising her, the priest jumped off his bike, almost running her over. "Mon père!" she exclaimed. The priest peered at her from tip to toe, then grudgingly said, "Hello, Geneviève, you are the last person I expected to see in this neighbourhood. What brings you back? Haven't you hurt your mother enough?"

"Hurt?" she asked, not believing her ears.

"Tell me, after all she did for you, how could you leave that poor woman the way you did?" Geneviève's eyes dropped down onto Aurore, who was bored and about to throw a tantrum.

"I had to leave," she managed to say, feeling she was standing in front of a firing squad.

"Oh, so you had to leave her without a decent explanation to hurry and join the big league of fallen women in Paris, hem?"

"Who told you that, mon père? Never mind, would you please tell me where my mother is because my daughter is tired, she needs her rest," she asked, feeling curious as well as discomposed.

"I am pressed for time, I have to give someone his last rites at the hospital down town. Go ask Mother Superior, she'll tell you," he said then; jumping back on his bicycle, he began pushing the pedals and off he flew.

"Bye," she said, not thrilled to be part of a conversation where she wasn't allowed to give her opinion.

At the convent, Mother Superior invited Geneviève to take a seat. For a split second, her gaze became fixed on Aurore as she wondered about the real age of the infant. Brushing her curiosity aside, she then decided to get straight to the point, keeping in mind not to allow her personal feelings about Geneviève to make her cross the line. In a rather neutral voice, she began speaking. "I assume you came here to inquire about your mother. Somehow I knew you would one day. Now, I am not trying to pass judgment on you, but let me first tell you a bit about the hell that your mother went through to keep you out of harm's way during the war. You might have thought you knew everything but you were wrong. There is something I feel I ought to tell you before I take you to her."

"Yes?"

"Throughout the war, more than once, your mother had been subjected to rape, by any one of the German officers. She had endured the degradation of being used by those animals and put her own life in danger, only to keep you fed and safe from them. She had kept you hidden all that time to prevent you from falling in their hands, and how did you repay her?"

Mother Superior's voice began shaking, as she continued, she tried to control herself but repressed anger got the better of her. "You came out of your cosy hideaway and couldn't wait to go looking for adventure. Tell me, did you enjoy sleeping with every drunk, every filthy sleaze who came to you with a few francs in his pocket? How could you do that to a woman who's only wish was to spare you from that sort of life?"

"I didn't know she was abused, she never told me, how could I have known, if no one told me. Now will you please tell me, where is my mother? Mother Superior, my daughter is getting very tired and she is hungry too. I am back now. What I can't understand is why am I getting grilled like this. After all it's between my mother and me, if she wants to forgive me or not." Geneviève went silent then, lowering her voice, she tried to ask again. "Where does my mother live now, will you please tell me?"

"Your mother waited and waited for a letter, a few lines from you, instead, she told me she had a visitor knocking at her door one night. A certain Bertrand, or was it Bernard. Does this name ring a bell? He was looking for you, and when Wilma told him you were not there, he became violent and roughed her up, leaving her bruised all over. Anyway, between punches and breaking furniture, he told her what kind of work you were doing for him. He also let her know that you had fled with a lot of his money and some things that were dear to him. Family heirlooms, I believe he had told her. Ah! He had also told her, before leaving her that he would get you even if he had to turn every stone you might have crawled under. Of course Wilma was too polite to repeat the obscenities that had come out of his mouth but I guess you are familiar with the colourful language he must have used."

"Get to the point, Mother Superior," Geneviève protested.

"The ugly truth had left Wilma devastated and horrified. Plunged in a state of total despair, she just couldn't cope with the way you had chosen to live your life. As for her life, a week later, she put her house for sale and let the first bidder have it for much less than it was worth."

Mother Superior stopped to take a deep breath before going on, "She had decided to donate the money to the orphanage and no matter how much father Perrault and I tried to dissuade her from doing so, we couldn't change her mind. She kept saying that the orphanage needed it more. Anyway she gave all she had to the kids who really appreciated the help and she came to live with us. She did nothing but pray while she devoted her entire time assisting the sick and the needy."

"Can I go see her now?" Geneviève asked with impatience. Rising to her feet, she began pacing the room.

"Sure you can but it's best you leave your daughter in here. I will tell one of the sisters to look after her while I show you the way."

Mother Superior stood up and walked towards the door, "Looks like we are in for a downpour, we better hurry," she added, adjusting her heavily starched headgear over her head.

They stepped out of the big entry door together. Geneviève followed the tall willowy nun almost automatically, her head aching by all that talk. Suddenly she came to her senses when she realised they were heading towards the cemetery. Anxiously, Geneviève clutched at the nun's habit and pulled at her ample skirt. The nun turned to face her and saw the burning question in Geneviève's big beautiful green eyes. Feeling a bit of remorse for not having her prepared enough for the bad news, she kept quiet for a while then nodded with sorrow. They walked past a few graves then stopped.

"There she is," the nun said, stretching her open palm to show Wilma's grave. "I will wait here, whenever you are ready, we will go inside and talk some more," Mother Superior said, as she turned around and took a few steps back, letting Geneviève alone to deal with her mother's death.

A wave of sadness washing over her, Geneviève approached her mother's grave and noticed a day old bunch of flowers held down by a rock, on top of it. Mixed emotions bringing a lump to her throat, to her own disbelief, she fell down to her knees and, holding the wilting posy to her chest, she burst into tears. "I am sorry maman, I am so sorry, please forgive me. I left you and this place to save you the dishonour. I made a bigger mess, didn't I? I should have known, you would have understood, you would have helped me. Now I know how selfishly I had acted towards you, you who has sacrificed yourself for me," she heard herself say with a broken voice.

Geneviève sobbed for a long time, oblivious of the gathering storm and the debris that the sudden violent wind scattered about her before the downpour. Within a few seconds she was soaking wet, her lower jaw shaking out of control. She was sprawled over the tomb, her limbs flung out, exposed to the elements, when she felt two hands grabbing her, lifting her with force.

"I think it's enough, crying will not bring her back dear, let's get inside, your daughter must be wondering where you are," the nun pleaded as she tried to get her to her feet.

It's only when Geneviève was standing up firmly that Mother Superior began fussing over her collapsing cornette that was drenched by the heavy rain. They walked towards the building in short steps.

"You need dry clothes and something warm in your stomach," the nun said, looking at the wretched woman and feeling badly about the harsh way she had spoken to her earlier when she had appeared unexpectedly.

"I need my mother, I came back because I thought we could be mother and daughter again. I came because of Aurore, she needs to grow up amongst her people."

"It's no use crying dear, I understand your situation, but you have to think about Aurore now. You need to think about her future as well as yours. It goes without saying that you can stay with us until you decide where you want to settle and what is it that you want to do for a living. I am sure you have a skill or two that would help you find a job, an acceptable job I mean."

Geneviève was listening without taking in a word of what she was hearing. Her mind was elsewhere and instead of a reply, she asked, "You never told me how she died, was she unwell?"

"She was not enjoying the best of health but that didn't kill her. A water heater blew up in her face, in the laundry. She was there, disinfecting children's clothing and bed linen. There was an epidemic and she was trying to get rid of germs and stop the illness from spreading further. Wilma was a bit absent minded at times, we couldn't really tell what had caused the over heating..."

At that time, there was a knock at the door and mother superior was called away to see to a pressing matter. While she was talking to the janitor, Geneviève was left alone in the office. Her survival instinct giving her a push, as swift as an arrow, she stood up and got herself to the desk. After checking the top of the desk, she opened a drawer and found the very thing she had always wished to put her hands on, 'these will do me fine,' she thought as she tore a few sheets off a pad with the logo of the convent printed on top. She rolled the papers and carefully stashed them in her bag before sitting down on her chair. When Mother Superior came back, she found her with the same desolate look on her face.

Geneviève and her daughter stayed with the nuns that night. Despite their tight schedule the nuns gave Geneviève enough of their time, they consoled her and listened to her sob stories. Licking her dry lips and occasionally blowing her nose, she managed to tell them a bit about her life in Paris, just to let them know she wasn't a prostitute all that time as they had come to think she had been. She told them that she was a seamstress and had a fairly well paid job waiting for her, "I also met a man, a very caring and reliable man who wishes to marry me, but I haven't given him an answer yet. For Aurore's sake I may accept his proposal, that is if he agrees to adopt her." She then inquired about François and Amedée.

"François joined the army, as for Amedée, he is engaged to Janine, one of our girls. She was amongst the first group of orphans who took refuge with us, after the war. While she was out on an errand, a bomb had flattened her home, wiping out her entire family. Janine was miraculously spared but it took her a long time to finally come to terms with her destiny," Sister Therese told her.

They were on the train going back to Paris. Aurore was peacefully sleeping, her head leaning against her mother's arm. Geneviève patted her soft hair, thinking about what Yanis had told her before they had parted a few days ago. She was hoping she wouldn't be too late to hold him to his words. As the train hurtled through the night, she kept mumbling to herself, 'I have to keep these last few days of my life out of my mind, blot them out of my memory, at least for now. I have to believe this thing with my mother never did happen. I will mourn her death and deal with my feelings of loss later. At present, my only concern should be the welfare of my child.

Aurore's future is the most important thing right now. If I get to Yanis in time, I will have to make sure his proposition still stands. He is my only way out of this rut. Australia may be the right place for us to be, and Yanis is my ticket to get there. I have to convince him that I came back because of him and not breathe a word about what went on in Bourg. I have to play my hand well or the ship may set sail without me.'

Arlette clapped her hands as she let the two travellers in, but good old dependable Yanis, grinning from ear to ear, seemed to be the happiest one in the house. It didn't take Geneviève too long to spill all the lies she had lined up for them. In a few sentences, like a well-rehearsed thespian, she led them to believe that her town had changed a lot since she was there last. That her mother was the same nitpicking nag she used to be. "I knew from the minute I got there that I would miss Paris and it would only be a matter of time before I would get bored and wished to leave. I just couldn't see myself living in that deadbeat excuse of a town, I tell you, the place did not look anything like the way I remembered it. Still, I owed it to myself to go and see that I have moved on and that Bourg should only stay in my past where it belongs. So here I am, happy to be back with you people, with you," she whispered, looking softly at Yanis, before lowering her eyes in her special seductive way.

Yanis couldn't believe his luck. Hope rising in his heart, his pulse racing, he brought himself to ask hesitantly, "You mean, you'll ma...ma.... marry me?"

Exaggerating her enthusiasm, "Yes, yes, yes," she said, planting her pouting lips on his blushing cheeks.

Overly excited with the latest developments in his life, after work, Yanis spent his free time running around and getting everything in order for their impending marriage. Ultimately he succeeded in securing a passage for himself, his wife to be and her child, on a ship that was due to depart in less than two weeks from Naples, Italy. Only a few passengers like Yanis had paid full fare for their voyage.

The ship had been transformed to mass transport a whole lot of immigrants to Australia. Under the auspices of the International Refugee Organization, it was all part of a scheme to assist displaced persons. The passengers were mainly from the Baltic regions, mostly Poles, Yugoslavs, Lithuanians, Latvians, Hungarians, and so on. They had been living in appalling conditions in refugee camps since the war had ended. Incidentally, Australia was a country with a crippling shortage of workers and in those postwar times, Europe was left with loads of such individuals in its ravaged countries. Later referred to as Balts, they were expected to slowly and smoothly fit in the Australian way of life, after their contract with the government was concluded. They were required to remain for two years in the employment allocated to them by the government and were promised to be paid exactly the same wages and receive the same conditions as their Australian counterparts.

Geneviève and Yanis had less than a week to pack up before leaving Paris for Naples. Yanis had a few loose ends to tie up at work in order to get his last pay. That morning they had gone to church and had been married. Arlette had thrown rice on them outside the church as well as on the doorstep of their house. She was making the newlyweds a nice wedding dinner, but they had to go to the shops first. They had to buy a proper suitcase, an overcoat of some sort for Geneviève and a jacket plus a pair of shoes for Aurore. Her old ones were getting small and were hurting her toes. Arlette had snipped the straps off the shoes so she could wear them till the shops without whinging.

Excited with the new look of her footwear, tapping her feet on the corridor tiles, Aurore opened the door, unable to wait any longer. She was about to venture outside when she saw a stranger standing near a van. The man was staring at her. Feeling uncomfortable by his presence, she took a step back and called her mother who showed up behind her. As the pair were about to cross the threshold, Geneviève turned her head around and cried out to Yanis, "We are outside, hurry up," when all of a sudden two strong hands grabbed her from behind. "So you thought you can do the dirty on me and get away with it, you miserable bitch," the stranger said, pulling her towards the van.

Recognising Bertrand's forceful voice, Geneviève began kicking and wriggling her body about and screaming. Between screams she managed to tell her daughter, "Get inside Aurore, call Yanis quickly," then, "Help! Help! Help me somebody," she went on shouting while she continued her struggle to free herself from her assailant.

In a flash, Yanis was outside. He jumped on the big man's back and, hanging from his neck he tried his best to fight him. Bertrand let go of Geneviève and instead began pounding Yanis in the stomach and upper body until Yanis fell to the ground. Arlette ran to the top of the street to call for help while Bertrand kept kicking his victim who was visibly not a match for the brute.

Geneviève was one second trying to help Yanis, the next second getting her petrified daughter out of the way. A policeman on a bicycle turned up finally. Seeing him, Bertrand left Yanis on the ground to twist and roll about in acute pain and, jumping in his van, he fled the scene before the agent de police had time to scribble his number plate in his little book.

Yanis' face was alarmingly distorted. Geneviève didn't know how to assist him. With the help of the policeman, they carried him inside. Later a doctor came and looked at his chest and abdominal injuries. He had two fractured ribs and heavy bruises with lacerated skin. For three whole days, the poor man was in agony but he kept reassuring his new bride that he would be all right and that nothing would stop them from getting on that ship. No one, not even the policeman thought of asking Geneviève if she knew the man who attacked her. Everyone assumed he was a sick bastard and that Geneviève was only trying to rescue her daughter from a child molester.

The night before they were due to leave Paris, Geneviève threw a few things in Yanis's old suitcase and promised Aurore she would have her new shoes whenever they reached that beautiful place they were going to. Arlette gave Geneviève the triangular shawl she was knitting the first day they had met each other. Finally they said goodbye to their tearful landlady and left for the train station. A hired car drove them there; the driver helped with the suitcase, since Yanis was in no condition to lift anything heavy. With great difficulty, after spending their last franc they got themselves to Naples. From there, the three of them went on board the huge ship but instead of breathing in relief, trouble was to follow them every inch of the way until they landed on the Australian soil.

On board the ship, Yanis couldn't have a moment of peaceful rest since the ship was fitted for mass transport. The beds were put up in stacks of three. There was no separate accommodation for the few married couples and families aboard, so he had to retire to the male section to sleep at night. On the fifth day, he just couldn't bring himself to get out of bed. He was very seasick from day one and vomiting made his side hurt atrociously. His bruises were still bothering him and, instead of healing, his lacerations flared up and gave him reason to be concerned. The ship had an Italian doctor on staff but there was only so much he could do for the unfortunate man who couldn't hold a meal in his already sick stomach.

The quarters being segregated by sex, Geneviève had difficulty getting to her husband's bedside to assist and comfort him. Finally they moved Yanis to the sick bay but his health went from bad to worse. His morale dropped to such a low that when he got hold of his wife, after apologising for letting her down, "If anything happens to me, you be brave cherie, take care of yourself and the little one," he said in a hopeless tone, like someone who was given a death sentence.

Geneviève turned her face away to blink back her tears, tears she wasn't sure were meant for Yanis or for her own disillusions. The men were ogling her and women were bitching about her. She couldn't stand the smell, the crowd, the lack of hygiene and her heaving stomach. It was no wonder that she was reduced to tears. If she had to eat another portion of what the cook was dishing out on her plate she wouldn't feel any better than Yanis. Oh, how she was missing the delicious meals she used to cook in Arlette's old but adequate kitchen. She wasn't expecting a cruise ship like the one she had seen in a film the previous year, but this gigantic tub was a symbol of misery and everything about it was revolting her and Aurore was crying incessantly for one thing or another. Furthermore she knew virtually nothing about the place she was to call home in another month or so.

Towards the end of the voyage Yanis was laying there semi-unconscious. The doctor had already washed his hands of him. Through an interpreter he had told Geneviève that if he hangs in there till they reach the shore, chances are, he may survive, providing he is transferred to a hospital straight away. When at last the ship landed in Sydney, the people in charge rushed him to the nearest hospital. They told Geneviève she would be informed of his condition once she is settled and they know where to contact her. The best news for Geneviève was that she was on dry land and breathing was easier. On the train that was taking them to Bathurst, the thought of facing her own arduous battle for survival came to add to her anguish.

Lifting her daughter up, Geneviève began following the soldier who had come to take her to his superior. She was almost sure it had something to do with her husband's state of health. When they got there, an old Australian army officer invited her to sit down. He patted Aurore's rosy cheek then, with the few French words he knew, he tried to tell her that her husband had died that morning. He also let her know that the Australian Government would take care of the funeral arrangement. Geneviève half expected that Yanis wouldn't make it, but to hear that it had actually happened left her numb for a while. Pour old, kind and faithful Yanis had died and she didn't know how to mourn his death. She sat there a little longer, looking sad and helpless. As she wiped a few tears off her eyes, she took her daughter's hand and left the officer. On her way out she thanked the officer for whatever she was supposed to thank him for and went back to work.

Geneviève had been assigned a job in the big kitchen where meals were prepared daily to feed the great crowd of new comers, the immigrants who were trying their best to adjust to their new life and surroundings. Aurore, being too young to attend classes, was always by her side. Strangely, she was the first one to pick up a few words of English. She made sure to relay them to her mother but Geneviève thought she would never learn the language, it all sounded so foreign to her.

Geneviève was telling the French-speaking lady at the immigration office that since her marriage to Yanis Melnic had never been consummated, she wished to have it annulled and return to her maiden name. "What was your maiden name?" the lady asked, looking at her from the top of her narrow framed glasses.

"De La Lande," Geneviève said then, and without waiting for the next question, she began giving the woman a highly inaccurate and fictional account of how their small town was bombarded during the war.

"So you don't have any papers to substantiate..."

"Well all our papers were lost in the fire. I only have the temporary note from the convent where we took refuge," Geneviève interrupted, handing her the forged note she had put together in Paris, in order to get a marriage licence.

"I think this will suffice, now I will ask you to fill this application, state what name you wish to be called by and sign here, here and here," the lady said, showing her the dotted lines she had to sign on.

"Don't forget to write your address here. You will be informed whenever your papers are ready to be picked up."

"Thank you."

Two weeks later Geneviève left the immigration office, feeling like a new person. With her new identity, she walked proudly on the streets of Sydney looking at everything with optimistic eyes. Finally, tired and hungry, she sat on a bench, pulled her feet out of her pumps and rubbed them against each other. She ate the little treat she had bought for herself from a milk bar then, her energy restored, relaxed and satisfied, she leaned back and began daydreaming. At the thought of the future she had ahead of her, she felt a powerful desire welling up within her. After months of hard labour in that camp kitchen, she had let herself to dream, even though she knew that dreams alone would not get her anywhere. Still, she had to remember that her dream would always be there and, should opportunity knock, she would be ready to grab it by the horns.

So far Geneviève had progressed only a wee bit. She had learned enough English to get by with and had a reasonably good income at a dressmaking factory in Surry Hills, but the giant Genie she had been waiting for hadn't come out of his bottle yet. Her wishes had not been granted but she was young and had all the time she needed to decide where she wanted to go and figure out how she was supposed to get there. As her green eyes wandered around, scanning the crowd of people who went past, the all so familiar question popped back in her mind. 'When will I be able to start my own business?' she lamented. Geneviève had the know-how to equal any other established fashion designer. She had enough patterns to start her off. She had learned a trick or two at the factory about speeding up the completion of a garment without the fuss of basting the pieces together. She had all the right ideas and knew how to implement them but without money her chances of getting her plans off the ground were next to nothing. She looked at her watch and rising to her feet she walked to the train station to get home in time to start the dinner. She passed a row of colonial style houses that developers hadn't yet put their hands on to demolish and build home units instead. 'One of these days, you too will have your day in the sun Geneviève De La Lande,' she murmured, as she saw an elderly lady sitting on a wicker chair, soaking up the sun on her little porch.

Geneviève was sitting comfortably in the first chair at the left of the steps, reading her Beginner's English book. Next to her a smartly dressed young girl was attentively filing her nails. As the train emerged from the Town Hall tunnel, Geneviève put her book in her bag and got up, ready to leave the train as soon as it stopped. "Excuse me," she said to the girl who gave her way, by moving her long legs to one side.

"Thank you," Geneviève added politely as she twisted her body and walked past the girl.

At that precise moment, two seats further down, a man who seemed to have fallen asleep woke up, visibly startled. Looking up from under his cap, his gaze met with Geneviève's. For a fraction of a second, his eyes twitched nervously. Maybe it was her voice that had pulled him out of his nap. Geneviève's heart lurched. 'Could that be Bertrand?' she wondered as she got sight of him.

In a flash, she turned around and ascended the few steps then rushed out and ran without looking back, just in case she was not imagining it and the man was indeed Bertrand. The thought of it put a knot in her stomach. The man let out an involuntary shriek while he stretched his hand towards her in a vain attempt to get a grip on her, even though she wasn't at arm's length. He stood up and began staggering along the aisle, making his way through children's school bags. He almost got to the doorway when the rounded handle of the umbrella protruding from his carry-bag got caught around the bar in front of the exit door. In a moment of haste, confusion, sleepiness and shock from finding himself face to face with Geneviève, his eyes never leaving her out of his sight, he lost his footing. Inevitably he slumped right into the narrow space between the train and the platform, his head hitting the sharp edge of the latter.

Meanwhile Geneviève was nearing the top of the long flight of stairs when she heard his roar mixed with the screams of a few passengers strung along the platform. No one did seem to have noticed Geneviève going up two steps at a time. They didn't see a connection between her and what had happened to the man. She stopped at the top of the stairs and watched the crowd gathering around the incident. Cautiously she came down again, curiously wanting to know if the man in the centre of the drama was the one she was running away from. She managed to get closer. He was lying on the cold concrete, his forehead bloodied, his lips trembling, his eyes suffused with rage. He appeared to be looking around, trying to find something or someone. When he saw her face he stared at it momentarily, tried to mumble a few words that no one understood then, letting out a deep breath, his head fell slightly to one side and his features went still.

The railway men who had rushed to assist him were telling the onlookers to clear the passage for the ambulance people. Giving a last glance at the odd expression of bitterness and hatred that had remained in Bertrand's frozen gaze, Geneviève left the scene, as pale as a ghost. She got out of the station and headed home. For a while it seemed that the traffic noise had died down and everyone on the street were keeping quiet for some reason. In total silence, she kept blinking then her eyes opened wide as she recalled the look on Bertrand's face before she fled. All of a sudden the silence in her mind, in her soul came to an abrupt end. The thunderous noise came back with a vengeance and, invading the air around her, it began closing in on her. Temples throbbing she ran the rest of the way like someone chased by a demon. She didn't feel safe until she locked herself inside her home. Later on, she knocked at her neighbour's door to pick up Aurore.

That night, the accident was briefly mentioned on the wireless. The next day, the newspapers had spared a tiny space to write about it. They had treated the matter as an unfortunate accident and had blamed it mainly on the man's sleepy state. Where Geneviève was concerned though, those few lines had pretty much closed the book on that chapter of her life. Like a leaf that falls off a tree, Bertrand's death didn't change anything on the face of the earth, but justice did get served. In a twist of fate, Bertrand had finally paid for hurting Wilma and killing Yanis. 'Was Bertrand in Australia in search of a better life or was he there hot on her trail?' That was a question that would remain unanswered for Geneviève for the rest of her life. There was a one in a million chance of their paths ever crossing in that part of the world but they did. Anyway, it was over and Geneviève didn't have to look over her shoulders any more.

Geneviève was very busy the rest of the week but on the weekend she decided to give herself a few well deserved relaxing hours. On Saturday morning she packed a picnic bag with some sandwiches, a bottle of Tarax lemonade plus two chunky pieces of Violet Crumble. After breakfast, together with her daughter, they hopped on a bus heading towards Balmoral beach.

They walked barefooted along the seaside, picking shells and listening to the shrill cries of the seagulls. Aurore particularly enjoyed the waves rushing and splashing up her legs before foaming back into the sea. Geneviève didn't have a proper bathing suit to go swimming in but she let Aurore play in the shallow waters. Towards noon they devoured their sandwiches. Aurore kept playing on the sand while her mother sat near her, eyes closed, deep in thought. As usual she was concocting another get rich fast scheme in her mind, ignoring the fact that none of her previous plans had ever had a chance to get off the ground. A group of teenagers walked past, snapping her out of her reverie. She looked around then her gaze became fixed on the horizon where the sky and the sea magically blended. For an odd reason her thoughts switched to Bertrand. She remembered her first meeting with him. He had looked like a nice person to her, until she got to know him better. A hint of a spark flickering in her eyes, a wicked grin lifted the corners of her lips as this less than human thought came crossing her calculating mind. 'Good old Bertrand,' she whispered, 'You came through for me once again didn't you? Your job saved me from starvation, your money helped me out of a life long prostitution and your punch up set me free from the shackles of a marriage of convenience. And now, with your death, you spared me the nightmare of one day having to answer to you.'

Geneviève closed her eyes again and sank further into the welcoming embrace of the sun's warmth, feeling strangely reposed. Instinctively she reached inside the front opening of her blouse and found the cheap chain she had bought back in Paris. Running her fingers on it, one by one, she felt the four rings she had stolen from Bertrand. Together with her crucifix, they were hanging from the chain, safely hidden close to her heart. 'Now I can wear these beauties and make my colleagues die of envy. Those Yugoslav and Greek women will be dazzled and will have to take me seriously when I tell them about my noble background. They will finally accept that I was not a poor peasant like them,' she whispered to herself.

A week later, proudly flashing two of her rings, Geneviève went to her work's Christmas party. With a pronounced accent and her limited English vocabulary, she tried to explain and convince her co-workers that her parents were from France's high society. "We were living in a big chateau, with lots of servants, until Germans came and took all our belongings away from us. These two rings and two other ones mother had buried in the garden, soldiers didn't find them," she was saying.

As months passed, Geneviève worked harder and harder. Her perseverance bordering on obsession, scraping and scrimping, as her neighbour would put it, she kept on pinching her penny until it screamed.

During the next six years, restlessly she jumped from one clothing factory to another and did three hours of cleaning every evening for pocket money. She made sure that Aurore was well fed, well dressed and shod. She spent very little on herself. She also changed boyfriends as fast as she found them, never getting seriously involved with any of them. She always picked the ones she could use and dispose of easily before they tried to get too cosy with her or her daughter. In her childish innocence, Aurore often asked her why she had so many uncles and not even one father, like the other kids did. Fortunately, as she grew older, to her mother's relief, she gave up asking that annoying question. Geneviève had told her on many occasions, that her father was a nice man who loved her very much but now he was in heaven because he was killed fighting for his country. How could she tell the poor girl who her father was when she didn't have a clue herself, since Aurore had inherited her own looks and her own hair colour. As for Aurore's character, that was another puzzle Geneviève had never been able to solve. Aurore reminded her of Amedée at times when she was calm and patient. Other times, when she behaved badly and acted frivolously, the arrogant mug of François used to pop in front of her mother's eyes. That's when she blamed her pregnancy on him.

Chapter 7

Smoke hugging the air above him, alone in his living room, Malcolm put out another cigarette in the heavy based and over-filled ashtray. He had once again retreated into his own mind. Once again he was going over the bizarre events that had happened throughout the last eighteen months, his marriage and the disillusion and disappointment that had come with it, for instance. Even though he was deeply happy for Nadejda to have been reunited with the man she loved, he couldn't say the same for himself.

More than ever, at that moment, Malcolm realised his life was lacking direction and purpose. Feeling crushed by a force he didn't have control over, as it had been the norm lately, he was guzzling coffee in between taking puffs of his favourite cigarettes, until it made him sick. Stifling a yawn, he pushed back the empty cup of coffee he had downed earlier, as if making more space in front of him would make him feel better. What he really needed was a generous dose of optimism injected back into his life. He needed a change in the atmosphere of his home. He needed something that would act like a catalyst to enliven his everyday existence.

Automatically, Malcolm turned the knob on the wireless but couldn't concentrate on the news. He took notice though, when he heard that the leader of the opposition, Mr Ben Chiefly, had died after a heart seizure, at the age of sixty-five. 'One of these days, it will be your turn, old boy,' he thought, focusing on his own mortality.

Seconds later, a new idea popping in his head, he rose to his feet and walked to his study. Sitting at his desk, without pondering the implication, he wrote a long letter to Adam, his nephew. In his letter, Malcolm asked Adam, who had been married for almost a year, if he would like to join him in Australia and be his right hand man. Since he himself didn't have the chance to see his own children run around his house, the idea that Adam and Freeda's children could, gave him a glimmer of hope. Suddenly Malcolm couldn't wait to hear the pattering of little feet on the tiles of his home.

Giuseppe Di Marco swallowed, rather noisily, the last drops of his Saint Agnes brandy left in his glass and looked speculatively at Malcolm. He put the glass on the table before addressing him, in a concerned voice, "Mal, we have known each other for a long time. You have always been a good friend to me. I know you must be feeling lonely at this moment, but do you think a boy fresh out of university is the answer to your problems? I mean, your nephew, is he mature enough to fill your shoes? Admit it, you don't even know him, well not lately, I mean the last time you saw him he was just a kid, now he is married and has a mind of his own. Will he really fit in with your life style and meet your expectations?"

Malcolm seemed a bit preoccupied by a thought. He appreciated Giuseppe's true friendship and had enough confidence in his fair judgment yet he paused a little before answering him.

"Amigo, I know you mean well but I have my reasons to want Adam here. Anyway, it looks like they have already started the preliminary procedures for their trip to this continent." After a pause, Malcolm continued, "There is something I have never told you or anyone else for that matter. It's a secret I intended to take with me to my grave but now that we are on the subject, I feel if I share it with you, you'll understand me better. I feel it's time I let you know, under this nondescript exterior, who is the real Malcolm and what was the incentive, the passion that drove him to become the person that he is now."

Malcolm lit up a cigarette and took his first puff then continued, "People think of me as a highly successful business man, maybe that's what I am, but why did I go to such length and work so damned hard at it is a different story. Mate, I didn't do it for the love of money, I never gave a damn for possessions. It was the love of a woman, a woman I could never have, that motivated me to be the daredevil I turned into. I had nothing to lose, so I went for the kill. It was a case of do or die. Every move I made was to prove something to myself, to the world and to her, especially to her. I felt compelled to show her that I was also capable of making something of myself. Leaving home and going on all those long trips in my young days, were only to stay away from them."

"Them, who is them?" asked Giuseppe.

"My brother Shimoon and his new wife Seraphima. See, she was the big love of my life. I was too young and too shy, I didn't have a shahi to my name at the time. One minute she was this lovely young schoolgirl that I adored, next minute she was the prettiest bride, smiling happily as she walked down the aisle on my brother's arm, and I was there, hand in pocket, playing with the tiny ring I had bought to give her."

"You bought her a ring?"

"Yes, I blew all my savings to buy it, I still have it in my safe, it's only a cheap ring. I was planing to meet her after the next Sunday mass and tell her about my feelings for her. I wanted to ask her if she would agree to marry me, wait for me, I mean wait with me until I was able to support her...us..." Malcolm took a deep breath, batted his eyelids and went silent. Automatically his hand went to his pocket for his cigarette box.

"Then what happened, did you ask her, did you see her?" Giuseppe inquired with interest.

"No, two days later my brother came home with a radiant look on his face and announced that she, I mean Seraphima, my Sera-phima had accepted his marriage proposal. Apparently my father knew about it, I was the only one in the dark. While I was busy fantasising about our life together, Shimoon, with his good looks and charm, his flair for literature and his use of poetic phrases had swept her off her feet. I thought that eventually I would get over her but as time passed she turned prettier and more desirable and I just couldn't take it any more."

His mood painfully nostalgic, Malcolm went on with his story as if he was alone and was reading loudly a passage from some romantic book he was holding. "When the reality of the situation smacked me in the face, I had no choice but to leave. I took a job in the south, learned a few tricks about export and import and, as they say, the rest is history. I came to Australia with a suitcase full of memories, a broken spirit and feelings of utter defeat and despair, in search of a magical potion to heal my bleeding heart. I hoped that time would cure my wound and help me forget the past. When I married Nadejda, I thought I could put an end to my obsession but it wasn't meant to be. I had all the good intentions to make my marriage work. I tried my best to make her happy."

"What went wrong between you and Nadejda, Malcolm? I never dared ask you the reason for your divorce, what happened really?"

"Vladimir happened, Vladimir Petrov came out of the shadows."

"You mean she was unfaithful to you?"

"No, they had feelings for each other when they were living in China. For reasons beyond their control they had to go their separate ways, she didn't know where he ended up. She even feared he might have been killed, but he reappeared, here."

"An old flame rides back into her life and you let her go, just like that?" Giuseppe asked, raising a querying eyebrow.

"Who am I to stand in the way of true love, my friend?" Malcolm uttered with a grin, opening his palms.

"Knowing you, you didn't let her go empty handed too, I bet you gave her away with a generous dowry."

"No and yes, she took all her clothes; I gave her a sable coat...Well it's cold in Canada, the girl would need a coat, wouldn't she?" he added humorously.

Giuseppe smiled, amused by the way Malcolm explained his motives for being kind-hearted.

"Go on, what else did you give her?"

"Some money to tide them over till they get settled, and I wrote a letter of recommendation to a relative I have there, he has a construction business. Vladimir was a painter, I was told."

"Don't you miss her?"

"Now that she has gone, I kind of miss her and her special traits."

"I say, she was extremely beautiful, gorgeous indeed, too good for an old stick like you. Just kidding, you have your distinguished qualities too."

"Yes, well, I agree she was something else but as for me, what can I say?" Malcolm added jokingly, as he ran his fingers through his salt and pepper hair that gave him the air of distinction Giuseppe was referring to.

"No, jokes aside," Malcolm went on with a serious tone, "Even though Nadejda was not the perfect match for me but in the short time we were together she managed to bring a breath of fresh air into my home. If it were not for Vladimir's resurfacing, maybe I would have ended up falling in love with her. I am glad that she is happy now. At least now I don't have the burden of guilt weighing me down, because in the days past, I used to blame myself for not trying hard enough to please her and welcome her into my life. I was still so wrapped up in my feelings for Seraphima, I couldn't stop hurting from not having her with me. In a way, I was the one who had sentenced Nadejda to the meaningless life she thought she had to live, a life without passion and warmth, without responsibility."

Realising he was blabbering far too much, Malcolm stopped suddenly. Lifting his head, he found his friend clumsily wiping a tear off the corner of his eye with the back of his hand. He rose to his feet and, walking swiftly to his bar, he grabbed an expensive imported bottle of spirit. He wiped it with a tissue. "Now, amigo, let's go sink our teeth into your good wife's pasta or is it lasagne today? I haven't had a decent meal since my maid went on her untimely holiday," he said with a forced neutral voice.

"Why, the one the agency sent, not good in the kitchen?"

"Oh, she is trying but she is a better cleaner than a cook. I think I need an Assyrian or an Italian cook."

They both laughed as they walked out of the door to go to Giuseppe's house for lunch.

After lunch, sunken in the chunky easy chairs in the living room, the two friends listened to the latest news coming from a wireless. In the kitchen, Mrs De Marco was placing slices of her scrumptious Tiramisu on serving plates. After the news, without realising it, the men had gone back to the previous conversation they had been having in Malcolm's place. "So you have decided to give your young nephew a chance?" Giuseppe asked, patting his overfilled belly.

"Yes, I believe I can teach him from an early age what business is all about and prepare him for the unavoidable day when I'll have to retire or just turn my toes, whichever comes first. See, Adam is the son I wished I had with Seraphima. He is part of her and I regard him as my own son. After all, one day, he will inherit everything I own, so why not let him come now. I can shape him into a good businessman while I still have the energy. I think, in a few years he'll make a fine young executive. In the meantime, his presence will save me from boredom. I am through searching for new ways to make money. I tell you, sometimes I envy those people who live a simple life with their family and are content with whatever they have. They just take life in their stride, they are less driven, less eager to go to the top and a whole lot happier I bet."

"Yes I suppose they are, or they seem to be," came the reply.

Sophie had trouble, making Marcus stand still for a while, so she could button up his shirt. At her age she was finding it hard to keep a three years old child under control. Jonathan and Liuba were in their room getting dressed too. They were all going to Shimoon's house to attend Adam and Freeda's first wedding anniversary party. Jonathan, having been Adam's best man, thought it was proper for them to be there before the other guests arrived. It turned out to be a very enjoyable celebration, with Adam and Freeda's family mingling as they savoured a great meal and some colourful desserts and fruits. Some time during the evening, Adam managed to pull Jonathan aside and, without preamble, told him about the letter he had received from Australia. "My uncle has asked me to go there and help him with his affairs."

"And, are you going?" Jonathan asked, creasing his eyebrows.

"Yes, I want to give it a go. Who knows, maybe this will be the best move I'll ever make in my life."

"I hope so," Jonathan said, tapping him on the shoulder, "see how it goes, maybe we will join you there some day."

"Now, wouldn't that be great? All of us together in a new world," Adam said, his chest heaving with the thought of it.

"But let's keep this between us for the moment, I don't want to rock the boat where aunt Sophie is concerned."

"I understand," Adam said, leaving Jonathan there with this new idea twirling in his head. An idea he had to chew over before discussing it with his wife.

Marcus was sleeping peacefully in his bed, recovering from a slight cold he'd had in the last couple of days. Liuba went to check on him. Despite his sickness, he had been very active during the day, which entailed a lot of running around the house. In his sleep though, he was nothing short of an innocent little angel, so lovely in fact that his mother felt like waking him up and covering him with lots of tender kisses. Carried away by that sweet sensation she smiled, but since she was also exuding practical good sense, she left him alone and walked away. She peered one more time through the half closed door before going back to her husband's side.

Jonathan and Liuba were cosily sitting on the floor, leaning on the sofa to get as close as possible to the heater and to each other.

Sophie was marking exam papers at the dining table when they heard a sharp knock at the window. Jonathan rushed to the front door to find his father's neighbour in a hysterical state. "You have to come with me, it's your dad," she began, her eyes twitching with nerves. "Last night, he must have left the kerosene heater on. This afternoon my husband went to see him about his car repairs, your father didn't open the door and..."

"Get on with it, what has happened? Is he all right?" Jonathan snapped, his eyes filled with panic. "Is he hurt or something, tell me," he went on asking as he brushed a strand of dark hair from his forehead.

"I am afraid your father is dead, overcome by fumes, he must have gone in his sleep, I suppose," she said wiping her eyes between sniffles.

After his father's sudden death, except for Liuba, his son and Aunt Sophie, Jonathan had no one else in Iran. His only sister was living in Germany with her Lebanese husband and their three children. Liuba had been very supportive of him during his mourning period, "I know how you feel darling," she told him one night, curling herself in his arms. "I hate to think that one day I may lose auntie, what will I do without her?"

"You will still have me and our son. We will always be with you, I promise."

"Oh! How I love you my sweetheart. I am sure of that. You and Marcus are everything to me," she said.

Watching his son having breakfast that day, Jonathan's mind drifted away, back to the day of his father's burial. He could see himself staring at the freshly covered tomb and for some strange reason, thinking about his conversation with Adam about moving to Australia. The thought of living in a new place, in his own place, had been nagging Jonathan ever since. Not that he had any complaint about living in Sophie's house, but it wasn't the same as being the king in his own castle. It was his pride that needed to be restored. A few weeks after Adam and Freeda's departure, he had come so close to telling Liuba about his secret dream but had not been able to open up to her and mention anything about it. He really wanted to move on, even though he had a good salary working in his new job at Point Four.

Point Four was an American enterprising project based in Iran. Being in constant contact with American workers, Jonathan had the opportunity to learn a bit of English, which he though would come in handy, should they have the chance to go to Australia.

Finally one day, in the intimacy of their bedroom, Jonathan dropped a hint about how he was missing Adam and their friendship then he casually asked Liuba. "Darling what would you say about us going to Australia?"

"Do you want to go to Australia?" she asked, leaning on every word and answering his question with another question.

Putting a confused expression on his face, "Yes...Well...I know we can't afford the fares or anything else right now but...I just needed to know your opinion. It's more for our son's sake, it's his future that I am more concerned about."

"You know, I'll go with you anywhere you want me too, as long as we are together. I will even go to the other side of the world, if that will make you happy."

"Actually dear, Australia is on the other side of the world," he said with a peculiar smile.

"I suppose it is," she giggled, "so what are we waiting for. Let's start saving money as much as we can and then, when we have enough, we will tell Aunt Sophie. She may be willing to go with us, after all she is due to retire soon."

Jonathan nodded but kept quiet about his deep desire of independence, he only sighed and changed the subject.

It was freezing outside on that last day of school before the Christmas Holidays. In the comfort of their well-heated kitchen,

Liuba was busy kneading dough for the nazook pastries she was planning to make for the festive season. It was her first attempt at baking those traditional Assyrian treats and Jonathan, who was free for the rest of the afternoon, was helping her in any way he could.

Jonathan was carefully brushing the egg yolks and yoghurt mixture onto the pastries when Liuba noticed a taxi stopping outside the house. To her surprise, she saw Sophie's schoolmaster pay the driver and head towards their door, a gloomy look on his face. Instantly she sensed something was wrong. Wiping the flour off her hands with her apron, she ran to greet the man. Jonathan followed her. "I have bad news. An hour ago, Sophie slipped on the frozen floor outside the school," the schoolmaster said without mincing his words."

"Is she hurt, how is she?" Liuba asked anxiously.

"I am afraid, she has broken her hip in the fall and her elbow is in a bad shape too. They took her to Sina Hospital, she is asking for you," he said, looking at Liuba.

Worried sick, Liuba looked at Jonathan, "what about Marcus?" she asked with a shaky voice.

"We can ask Mrs Hedayat next door to take care of him until we get back," Jonathan answered.

After weeks of agonising pain, Aunt Sophie's situation didn't improve. In fact, it seemed to be gradually deteriorating. Her broken hip had begun to knit but she had to be in plaster for a longer time. Her elbow that had been damaged rather badly was not about to be repaired without a snag. She had two unsuccessful operations and was still in pain. To make matters worse, she couldn't stand to be in plaster. It frightened her, especially when she was on her own. It made her feel like suffocating, as if she was trapped in a vice she couldn't escape from. Maybe it was some sort of a phobia that was making her irrationally restless. Someone had to be with her at all times or she would whine nonstop.

At one stage, Sophie was out of her plaster and returned home to rest, mostly at her incessant request. Liuba was always with her, catering to her every need. One night Jonathan and Liuba had to rush her back to hospital fearing an imminent heart attack. Between tests and consultations, Sophie managed to get hold of Liuba's arm and whispered a few incoherent words to her. "Go to Father Augustine, the papers are with him. He has my will and documents. My bankbook is in the bottom drawer of my wardrobe," she said, breathing hard with every word she uttered.

"You are going to be all right auntie, don't exert yourself now," Liuba almost begged her.

"I just want you to know, I am leaving you all my belongings. In case I don't make it, go to Father Augustine, the young priest, you know?"

"Yes I know, I know which one you mean."

Sophie didn't make it as she predicted she wouldn't. It seemed that she had a massive heart attack in the middle of the night. At school, they gave her a ceremonious funeral with all the school children singing a farewell song. In their eulogies, the schoolmaster and two of the members of the Assyrian association, as well as Jonathan, praised her for her hard work and her dedication in teaching Assyrian dancing to their members. Later, as the mourners were gathered in the church hall, Father Augustine approached Jonathan and Liuba and, after expressing his sympathy, asked them to meet him in his office the next day.

The Vardas already knew the reason why he wanted to see them. A wake was held in their home where lots of friends and acquaintances attended. With tears rolling down her cheeks, Liuba managed to say a few words to everyone. At the end when everyone had left, she noticed that her feelings were somehow different than those she had after her father or mother's funeral. Although bereaved, she felt less desolate. Losing her last blood relative didn't hit her as hard as she had imagined it would, mainly because this time she wasn't left alone. She had her dear husband to lean on and most of all she had her son to love and cherish. Her heart was afloat with the affection she was feeling for them and she thanked God for that blessing.

It didn't take Jonathan and Liuba too long to fill the necessary applications they needed to start their long journey. After selling the house, which Sophie had left to her, Liuba didn't have to skimp and scrape to raise money for their voyage. They could afford the fares and had a little left over for them to live on until they both found themselves suitable jobs in Sydney. It was just a little less than two years since their friends had landed on Australian soil and had lived with uncle Malcolm ever since.

At Sydney airport, Adam and Freeda went to welcome the Vardas and, at uncle Malcolm's request, took them straight to their house.

Jonathan and Liuba were too busy chatting with their old friends to glance out of the car's window and have a good look at the roads, the houses and the city that they were driving through. It was when the car slowed down at an intersection that they both noticed the cute little red brick houses on either side of the road. Each house had it's own front yard, consisting of a patch of tidy lawn surrounded by well planned flowerbeds. The red tiles on the roofs were also a novelty to them. "There are no walls around the houses," Liuba cried suddenly, thinking of the brick walls that surrounded the houses in Iran.

"No, no walls, just fences around the backyards," Freeda said in a slightly patronising tone.

"We will be there soon," Adam declared, making a left hand turn into a street aligned with bottlebrush trees. Minutes later, the Ford V8 turned into a driveway making the gravel creak under its tyres, then stopped.

The four adults took the luggage out of the car and carried them up the few cobble stone stairs. They dropped their loads on the porch. Adam opened the front door. They all went in through the inviting grand entry that was a transition from the stony porch to the warm and tastefully furnished living area, with its high ceiling. The illustrious crystal chandelier caught Liuba's eyes, then she noticed that the walls were papered in a soft sandy colour that went well with the antique green of the doors and windows. Through a huge archway, the newcomers could see the formal living and dining area filled with plush conservative furniture and decorative items.

Jonathan took a swift look around before his eyes became fixed on the opposite wall where the bar was located. 'Wow! This is what I call living,' he said to himself.

Jonathan was never much of a drinker. Back home, the most he drank was a glass of wine and only on special occasions, but the sight of such decadence left him breathless with envy. From the scintillating wine glasses lined up in the display cabinet to the multicoloured miniature drink bottles and the ornamental tools to open bottles, he admired them all from a distance. Liuba's heart had flipped a little too, but she kept her envy to herself and just observed the décor in silence. Malcolm's house wouldn't be the best house in the world, but it surely gave her a pretty approximation of what she believed a dream home would look like. When she got hold of Jonathan, she asked him with a whispering voice, "Are all those houses we passed so nicely decorated or is Malcolm just one of the filthy rich ones who can afford it."

"I don't know," Jonathan said hardly moving his lips.

While Jonathan and Liuba were unpacking in their appointed room, Marcus had found his way to the backyard and was chasing the household cat. Freeda was in the kitchen preparing a salad. She had already prepared the main course in the morning. When Malcolm arrived from work, after the handshakes and small talk, they all sat down to have dinner, then they moved to the lounge room for tea. On a few occasions, Liuba felt Malcolm's piercing eyes scanning her. He was sipping on his tea when he turned to her and asked. "You look kind of familiar, aren't you Sophie's niece?"

"Yes, did you know aunt Sophie?" she asked.

"I have known your aunt since we were kids, our forefathers were from the same village. Good old Sophie, always cheerful, despite... Tell me, did she ever get married after that unfortunate incident?"

Liuba looked at him puzzled. "No, she was never married," she said, confused by Malcolm's question.

"That's what I thought, the poor girl..."

"After what incident? I don't know what you mean uncle," Liuba said, her curiosity getting the better of her. She waited for an answer before continuing with her inquiry, sensing Malcolm may finally shed some light on something she had been wanting to know, a family secret she never got to bring out into the open.

"I knew there was a certain secret my mother was supposed to tell me when I became older but we never got around to having that conversation. Now I am old enough to hear it, please tell me uncle," she requested, eager and anxious at the same time.

"Well," Malcolm started. "It's a sad story but if you really want to hear it," he raised his hand and rubbed the back of his neck before continuing. "Yes! There was a reason behind Sophie's lonely life. Years ago, she was a pretty girl, very pretty indeed. She was engaged to this young man by the name of Alexander Hakim. My brother Shimoon had been asked to be his best man, they were schoolmates, you see? Anyway, the day before the wedding, Alexander and my brother went to pick up their suits from the tailor. On their way back, they hired a doroshkeh, you know the horse drawn carriages we used for transport in those pre-taxi days."

""Yes we still see them in parts of Tehran," said Liuba.

"As the doroshkeh slowed down preparing itself to turn comfortably from Shah Reza Road into Saadi Street, a lorry and a minibus were about to collide in the intersection. The flashing lights and the screeching of tyres and maybe the doroshkeh's driver pulling instinctively on the reins terrified the animal. Lifting its forelegs in the air, eyes rolled to the back of his head, the horse neighed frantically before bolting out of control, dragging along the carriage and the three men in it. Alexander threw his suit on Shimoon's lap and jumped to his feet to help the driver in placating the horse. At this moment, the wheel on his side broke loose and the lopsided carriage dropped to the floor. As he lost his balance in the fall, I believe Alexander's foot got caught between the jammed steps. His head must have hit the stone paved street a number of times before the horse was finally stopped and contained. My brother escaped with only a few bruises that he sustained by being knocked around, as he never let go of his grip on the handle. Unfortunately for Alexander, he did not survive the accident."

"Oh! Poor auntie," Liuba said, tears rising to her eyes.

After a pause, Malcolm continued, "Sophie was too devastated to face the world and go on with her life under the prying eyes of people around her. She took refuge in St. Vincent De Paul's convent. She stayed with the Catholic nuns for two years or so. We all assumed she would eventually join them and take the habit but she came back and went on with her teaching career. In a way, I believe she did live a nun's life, since, as you say, she never...."

"No, she was never involved with any man, as much as I recall," Liuba said, wiping her eyes.

"Now, that explains why she was so keen on bringing Liuba and me together," Jonathan said, a bit hoarse with emotion.

"Yes, your love story must have reminded her of her own. In helping you with your wish to be together, maybe she had tried to make up for her own situation. Your happiness had been the realisation of her own dream, a dream that had been so brutally interrupted all those years ago for Alexander and herself." Malcolm concluded as he put his empty cup on the coffee table. An eerie kind of silence descended the room, which Liuba then broke.

"Everything that happens in life happens for a purpose," they all heard her say in a trance like state, her fixed gaze giving her the semblance of someone talking under hypnosis. Wondering what had prompted that unexpected comment, everybody's eyes turned towards her.

"What do you mean dear," asked Jonathan, puzzled.

Without moving her eyelids, Liuba went on, "After my parents death, when aunt Sophie was taking me to Tehran, in that desolate state, I kept crying in the bus. I kept saying why, why, this had to happen to me. She told me just that, she told me, everything that happens in life happens for a purpose. The night of our wedding too, I was so happy I couldn't breathe, she told me that again. She also told me that my sad past had prepared me for that happiness, so I shouldn't take it for granted. Cherish every minute of it and try not to let anything spoil it for you, she told me. Still, I wonder what was the purpose of her tragic loss and her lonely life."

"It was you my dear, it was us, remember how she took us under her wings," Jonathan volunteered to answer. "If she had been living happily somewhere, with her husband and children, she probably wouldn't have been there for you when you needed her. Even with her death, she made it possible for us to come here, otherwise we wouldn't be having this conversation we are having now."

"I suppose so, I am sure we brought some joy to her life too," Liuba said pensively then, raising her head, she looked across the room, her eyes glistening with tears.

"You must have for sure," Malcolm added, "and now, let's talk about a matter of a different nature. What are your plans for tomorrow? Adam and Freeda are off work, they can take you sight seeing."

"That will be great and thank you again for your kind hospitality," Jonathan said, holding his wife's hand.

The following day, Adam and Freeda took their friends on a tour of the city. Malcolm had a surprise for them at home. When they came back they found a brand new Kelvinator washing machine in the laundry room. Marcus was not the only one intrigued by the all-electric washer with full-sized power wringer. The nice looking appliance had the adults equally thrilled to be so priviledged. "You know you should not touch any of these buttons," Liuba told Marcus.

"What will happen if I do?"

"You may ruin it or worse, you may electrocute yourself."

"What is electrocute?" asked the curious child.

The women and Marcus were having hot chocolate in the lounge room. Freeda was browsing in a fashion magazine, earmarking her favourite styles. Liuba had promised to make her a dress using one of the fabrics she helped her buy a few months ago when they went sightseeing. The young men were in the living room playing backgammon. Malcolm brought them an icy cold beer each, and the usual brandy for himself. "Tell me, I hear you talking about finding a place to rent. You haven't shaken the dust off your trip yet, what is the rush? Why do you want to leave us? He asked, turning to Jonathan.

"Well uncle, you were very kind to let us stay with you this long. We don't want to overstay our welcome. We are very grateful though for your hospitability. I have a job now and I think we can manage."

"Nonsense, this is a big house and we like having you here. The boy is happy, the women get along well."

"Thank you uncle, but it's not right for us to impose," Jonathan said apologetically.

"I insist, besides I have to thank you for the great job you did on my car and you don't want to deprive me of your wife's cooking," Malcolm said, then turning to Adam, he added with a grin, "No offence, Freeda is not the best of cooks, but don't tell her I said this."

Warming up his brandy in his palms, Malcolm returned his conversation to Jonathan, "Of course it is your decision but I suggest you stay with us a while longer, collect some money and when you are ready, buy a big enough house. Paying rent is not a wise thing to do, its money down the drain, and no, you will not be imposing on us." He lifted his glass to his mouth but stopped and continued. "Anyway, whatever you plan to do, may your difficult days be a few and your successful ones a lot, that's what I wish for you."

The Vardas did stay for a few more months, mainly because they didn't want to pull Marcus out of the school he was going to. Liuba found herself a dressmaking job at Princeton, a clothing factory in St. Leonards. They were able to put almost all their earnings in the bank, adding it to what they had brought from Iran. Life couldn't have been rosier. Liuba used to come home before everyone else did, therefore she could start cooking the dinner. She didn't mind working in that kitchen at all, since it was fitted with the latest models of labour saving electrical appliances. They all seemed happy with the arrangement, all except Jonathan, who was feeling the same way he used to feel in aunt Sophie's house. Lying in bed one night, he remembered years ago when he had tagged along with a friend to go and watch him practice boxing, in Atesh Stadium. Yourka, the trainer was a young Assyrian man who had migrated from Russia. A well known old boxing champion, he in fact was the first person who had initiated that particular sport in Iran. When Yourka had asked Jonathan if he wished to try boxing, "I don't have the time," Jonathan's excuse had been.

"All you have to do is to come here once a week then practice at home."

"At home? Our home is only a small room, more like a mouse house. I can't take one step without bumping into a wall or tripping over something. It's a useless place," Jonathan had answered, embarrassed by his poverty.

"Don't be ungrateful for having a home. Your home is your castle and no matter how small it is, it is still your home. You are the king within those four walls. You haven't been chased out of your house and home to know the importance of having a roof over your head," the trainer had told him with an unexpected chagrined tone.

In uncle Malcolm's house, despite the relaxing atmosphere and the kindness of the hosts, Jonathan was feeling out of place. He mulled the idea of moving out some more and in the morning he declared it was time they went house hunting. He couldn't wait any longer to be the number one in his own home and it didn't matter if it was a bit away from the metropolitan area. They might have to wait before they could afford their first car or even their own television set, it all depended on the price of the house they would be happy with.

In the first week of looking around, the Vardas realised that properties like Malcolm's were definitely out of their reach, the small old houses were not worth considering and a flat was not Liuba's idea of a home. She had always dreamt of having a big garden where she could grow all the herbs she needed for her cooking. In the few months they had stayed in Malcolm's house she had converted a corner of the backyard into a veggie patch. She had turned every empty pot or container into minuscule herb gardens, herbs that were much needed in Assyrian and Iranian cooking. Anyway the following weekend, Adam drove them to see a real estate agent at Raine and Horne Realtors, where he had seen a pair of newly built houses advertised in their window.

Chapter 8

Peter was really and truly at the end of his tether, right on the verge of losing his power of tolerance. He kept moaning desperately, unable to bear the stabbing pain in his shoulder any longer. Exasperated, he was about to scream when the door of the big hospital room swung open, letting in a full figured nurse, wearing the biggest smile. Like a breath of fresh air, her presence alone brought a feeling of relief into the dreary atmosphere of the place. Nevertheless, it was fair to say that the injured men had no ground to complain because where they were, was far more comfortable than those temporary medical tents they had been in. Even the boat that brought them back home didn't have anything better to offer.

The good nurse chatted gaily with every patient, telling them exactly what they'd needed to hear. She did her very best to lift their spirit with her contagious optimism, until she reached Peter's bedside. Bending her head to one side, she regarded him with the similar attention an art connoisseur would give to an object d'art. "A new face hem? Let's see how we can cheer up this young, and not so bad looking man," she said, raising her eyebrows and nodding approvingly.

Peter stared at her for a second then, hope bringing a shine in his misty eyes, "Thank you," he said, a wee bit embarrassed by the compliment, then he added, "nurse, I will be grateful to you if you could give me something for my pain."

"When did you get your last medication?" she asked, changing her tone to a more professional one.

"Four hours ago, but my shoulder is killing me, can you do something to stop this pain, please," he almost begged the new nurse. Holding up his chart, Martha read about his condition attentively then looking at him, she said, "Mr Peter Goddard, it looks like your injury has been contaminated and it needs to be taken care of as soon as possible. Unfortunately we have a short supply of the stuff you need to combat the infection but I'll try to get you something. By the way, my name is Martha, Martha Leigh."

After disinfecting the wound, Martha applied a yellowish cream on it and changed the dressing then handed him two Aspros.

"Take these for your pain and try to stay calm and get some sleep," she advised, before leaving him to go and tend to other injured men. Trying to boost their morale, she gave a few words of encouragement to each soldier. She talked to them about anything except the war, as if the horrible thing was not happening out there.

Martha had a kind heart, and looking after the sick and the injured was the part she played in that war. It was a war that saw so many of her fellow men march to the front line, high on patriotism, only to end up physically as well as emotionally incapacitated. She saw them carried in on stretchers to be patched up, somehow. They were then left on one of those hard and uncomfortable beds, hopelessly alone, struggling with their pain and trying to make sense of their situation.

Peter and Martha became the best of buddies during his stay in that military hospital. Although he was still in a lot of pain, he was about to be discharged to make room for more pressing cases. Besides, they could only do so much for his shoulder. The infection had cleared, the wound was healing over gradually but the annoying pain returned every now and then and made him absolutely fed up with everything.

Peter wondered what would happen to his friendship with Martha once he was out of the hospital. On his last day, when she went to visit, he clung to her arm and asked if he could see her sometimes for a coffee or a walk in the park. In Peter's eyes, Martha had been a godsend, a saviour. That is after the soldier who had carried him to safety when he was shot outside Tobruk on that cold day of January. That compassionate infantryman's face would never fade from his memory even if he tried.

Peter met with Martha the next days after his discharge. They had a nice picnic lunch together in the nearby park. She provided a few cheese sandwiches and he brought the grog. Martha didn't drink, as she had to go back to work, but she couldn't help noticing Peter taking a gulp out of the bottle at regular intervals. "Looks like you've come up with a cure of a different nature, a self-prescribed medicine, now that's naughty," Martha said, half joking, half serious.

"It's calming my pain to a certain degree Martha, since I can't have any morphine, this is the next best thing. Even ordinary pain killers are hard to find these days anyway," he replied, tossing his sandy blond hair to the side.

Peter had grown dangerously dependent on Martha, his Florence Nightingale, as he used to call her sometimes in the hospital. At the end of their third get-together, they exchanged an amicable kiss and agreed on another date, during which, "How about us getting married?" He blurted out, in the simplest of manners.

"Why not, let's go for it," she answered, just like that, without giving it a second thought.

'How can I say no to a man with such a gorgeous face,' Martha was thinking, not believing her luck as her own looks were on the plain side.

They both felt it was fate that had put them on the same path and that they were destined to be together. Martha had another year of training to be a full-fledged nurse. For the time being, she was a volunteer nurse and her help was greatly appreciated. An orphan, she lived in Redfern, sharing a room with two of her friends. As for Peter, a farmer's son, he was born in Albury and had lived there until he was drafted. His only aspiration was to study and become a journalist, against his father's wishes, who wanted his first born to stay on the farm and help with the daily chores.

When Peter's high school days were over, he began working as a freshman in the local newspaper. Starting at the bottom of the corporate ladder, he hoped he could scratch his way to the top by studying hard in the evening classes.

Under the scornful eyes of his father and his younger brother, Peter worked by day and studied till late at night, in a candle-lit corner of the house. Unfortunately for Peter, things didn't pan out the way he wished them to. The war took care of his wishful thoughts of success and his desire of being a big shot in the world of journalism. Whatever plans he had for his future came to a sudden halt the day he got drafted and sent to fight for his country.

On the battlefield, when the war was going on in all its fury, Peter couldn't help imagining himself being sent there as a reporter. Looking at the events unfold before his eyes, he was wondering how he would describe them. In a way those thoughts helped him keep his sanity and temporarily put a lid on his hatred for the untimely war that had robbed him of his dreams. When he got shot, he though it was the end for him. It could have been, had the bullet hit him a little bit more towards the centre of his torso, then he opened his eyes and found himself in a dimly lit place. Gazing around, he saw other soldiers who were in more or less the same shape as he was and the world began caving in on him. Lost in despair, he felt like he was being sucked into a bottomless pit. And every time one of those excruciating pains came shooting through his entire body, he really wished he had died, he and his dreams together, dead and gone for good, but he didn't die.

After weeks of struggling with pain, Peter felt that he had just turned into half the man he used to be and a fraction of the man he had wished to become. Now that he had met Martha, at least he was not alone, he was so attached to her, he couldn't envisage going through a day without seeing her. He loved her in his particular way.

He was sure he had some romantic feelings for her but needing her was another contributing factor, if not the biggest on the list. He wished to marry her and make her a permanent part of his future life because she had touched it in ways he never could have imagined.

Peter needed Martha in his day-to-day living, as a guide, a decision maker and someone to watch over him, with the warmth and kindness that only she knew how to give. There was a big snag in their marriage plans though. They didn't have a place to live after their marriage. Between the two of them, they didn't have a dime to spare on rent and on any kind of furniture. Peter was staying with a war mate of his, sleeping on the floor of his sunroom, a space not big enough for him to stretch his long legs. Tossing and turning on his borrowed sagging mattress, he kept wondering in the middle of the night, where on earth would he take his bride, should they get married. "The good Lord will help us," Martha kept telling him, and they continued seeing each other every afternoon.

One afternoon when Peter went to pick Martha up from the hospital, Martha came out of the door twirling her cardigan about. Peter noticed that she was beaming with exuberance. "I have good news for you, for us," she said, before saying Hello.

"What kind of news?" he asked, his mouth gaping with curiosity.

"A solution to our housing problem. If you agree to it, we can get married as soon as possible," she said excitedly.

"All right, shoot," he said, not able to wait another minute.

"Well, it's my Aunt Rachel. I went to see her yesterday. I hadn't seen her for a long time. Anyway we had a good heart-to-heart and when she asked me about my personal life..."

"Go on."

"I told her about us. When she heard about you she said, and wait until you hear this, she said we could have one of the two bedrooms in the place where she lives. It is in Paddington."

"I didn't know you had a relative who lived so close."

"I do, she is a widow and lives on her husband's war pension. He served in the First War. Anyway, after he died my aunt continued living in the same house. It's a semi, a dual occupancy, you know? Now most of her money goes for rent and other things. She has little left to pay for food so she told me if we take her other room, which is fully furnished, she will still pay the rent and all we have to do is to provide food and pay for the winter heating fuel. I think she is feeling lonely and needs our company too."

Out of breath, Martha stopped talking.

"That's the best news I have heard in a long time, this is an answer to my prayers, what are we waiting for, as you said Martha dear, let go for it."

The moon had a superb silvery glow that night when the newly-weds entered their very own bedroom. It was after the small reception party that Martha's two roommates had put together in the church assembly room. Aunt Rachel, who used to work in a millinery workshop in her younger days, wore her best hat and her everlasting Sunday dress, jazzed up by her favourite diamante brooch that was pinned a bit clumsily on the collar.

Martha went on working in the hospital while Peter was running around looking for a casual job, a job too hard to find in those difficult times. The pair lived on bread, cheese, a bit of mince and Weet-Bix, but only if they could find a pint of milk, and an occasional Marmite jar. Rarely were they able to buy a few pieces of fruit or vegetables. They tried to make do with whatever they could afford until on one glorious day, the end of the war was announced on the wireless.

On Wednesday 9th of May 1945, the three of them, together with the rest of the Australian people, celebrated V.E.Day, Victory in Europe and the surrender of the Germans. Acting Prime Minister, Mr Chifley, declared that day a public holiday, but the best news came on Thursday the 16th of August when sirens were sounded and crowds cheered, after the Prime Minister announced the end of the war with Japan. Martha and Peter went to the Domain to join in with an estimated one million people who were gathered there and in Kings Cross, to celebrate the fall of Japan.

At home, aunt Rachel kept wiping her eyes listening to the wireless when she heard. "On board H.M.A.S. Moresby today, Colonel Kaida Tatsuichi, the Japanese commander, signed the surrender document." Lifting her eyes to look at the heavens, "Praise the Lord," she whispered, before dozing off on her personal chair.

That night Peter and Martha returned home exhausted but happy that the demons of war had been finally chased away from their country. They were also happy to share a secret with aunt Rachel. It was a very special and private matter, one they were sure would make her jump for joy. Martha's physician had told her, only a few weeks ago, that she was in the family way. The three of them were hardly making ends meet but they couldn't think of anything that could stop them from looking at life in an optimistic way. Now that the spectre of the war was no longer hanging over their heads, they had hopes that things would eventually change for the better.

Grateful to aunt Rachel for putting a roof over his head and treating him like she would if he were her own son, Peter regarded her like a mother. Very seldom did he receive a letter from his real mother, but when he did, there was always some petty complaint mentioned. If it wasn't the draught, it was another thing to whinge about. Peter had his own problems to worry about, but he never imparted a word of them to his parents. He just wrote back that he and his wife were doing all right and wished them luck.

On Martha's suggestion, Peter had been getting trained to be an English teacher and his efforts payed off when he found a job in a boy's high school. The Australians were beginning to breathe easier as they were leaving their memories of war behind, although things were still a bit rough, regarding the state of the country's economy. Unemployment, shortage of food and rationing still on their minds, they were determined to soldier on, hoping they would eventually get back on their feet.

When Martha gave birth to a baby boy, Peter was over the moon. "A son, a son of my own," he cried, holding him lovingly. They called him Samuel, a few minutes after his arrival.

Rearranging things in their small bedroom, they tried, without any success, to squeeze a second hand cot in. At the end, Martha and Peter had to move an old chest of drawers to the living room and put the cot in its place. It wasn't an ideal solution but they were happy to have Samuel sleep close to them. At least, unlike in many other families, one of them had a job, which meant food on the table and clothes on their backs. Martha had three more months to start work, as she had been promised.

During the next four years, aunt Rachel proved to be a tremendous help in babysitting little Sam. Lately though, she was feeling a bit under the weather, with her old age aches and pains and blood pressure. Martha was preparing the evening meal one day when Samuel ran to her, urging her to follow him. "Aunty is on the floor, she is not talking," he cried, eyes dilated with shock. Martha ran to investigate, fearing the worst.

"Go call David," she told Samuel who rushed outside, on the balcony and yelled, "David! David! Come quickly, mummy needs you." When David, the neighbour's teenage son showed up in their window, Martha asked him to run and call the doctor.

"She has suffered a minor heart attack, but hopefully she will be over it, there is no need for hospitalisation. All she needs is plenty of rest and a healthy diet. Being a nurse, you sure know the drill Martha, and I will come to see her every day," the good doctor said, handing her a prescription.

"Give her these drops three times a day but if there is a problem, call me immediately," he added, before leaving.

While the friendly doctor was examining aunt Rachel, Martha noticed a key hanging from her neck but didn't give it much thought. Maybe she has some memorabilia, pictures or even letters that are valuable to her, Martha supposed. She couldn't imagine her aunt having anything else worth keeping under lock. One day, during her recuperation, aunt Rachel told Martha that she was leaving all her belongings to her. She also casually mentioned the fact that the neighbours had witnessed her will.

"When the time comes, you can keep whatever you want and give the rest to the Salvation Army."

"All right auntie, don't worry about it now, you should rest, you are not in any danger at the moment so there is no need for this sort of talk," she tried to reassure her aunt.

Martha couldn't help thinking about the few custom jewellery items her aunt wore so proudly on special occasions. Then her old-fashioned dresses and crocheted knick-knacks came to her mind and she cringed at the idea of having to go through them. She would feel a little embarrassed, sending them to the Salvos, but if that were what her aunt wanted, she would have to do it for her sake. "Who knows, aunt Rachel's trash may be someone else's treasure," she assumed.

Peter was too busy cherishing the moments he could spend with his son and was counting his blessings for having Martha by his side. She was taking such a good care of him and their little boy that his unrealised career dreams had become a thing of the past. In those difficult times he was even grateful for having a job to go to. As for his shoulder pain, there were a few prescribed painkillers available to him. He could also take the good old Aspro tablets or Bex powders whenever he would exert his arm and the affected nerves bothered him. Unconsciously he had gone easy on the booze and only drank a small amount on special occasions.

The thing about war and its effect on people is that when your country is in turmoil and you live under the threat of an invasion and the loss of your freedom, all you can think of is how to deal with that common foe. The problem is of such magnitude that all throughout that period and long after, people forget who they were and what were their aspirations, before their very existence was jeopardised. This rule applied to Peter and even though the war had been a considerable hindrance to his career prospects, for a few years he was content with his life. How could he not be anyway? Just looking at his son's baby face, topped with a mop of golden hair was enough to fill his heart with glee. Samuel's smile had brought such an unequalled joy in his life that he didn't have time to speculate how things would have been if the war hadn't happened. He never had the opportunity to consider himself a victim of circumstances, let alone a failure.

The sky had been covered with thick black clouds all day. Martha put her jacket on and left work an hour earlier and hurried out. On her way home she stopped at the milk bar near their house and bought a few things she needed to make a cake. Once home, she took the eggs, a block of Western Star butter, a packet of sugar, the pint of milk and the fresh cream out of her shopping basket and placed them carefully on the kitchen bench. She also brought the bag of flour, the tin of cocoa and the baking powder out from the cupboard. She was going to follow a recipe printed in the latest issue of the Woman's Weekly magazine. Martha intended to make the yummiest and the most skilfully decorated cake for Samuel's fifth birthday. Things were looking up for them, as the economy seemed to be picking up in the country, even though the recession was not quiet over yet.

That night, after they finished with dinner, Martha and Peter placed the candles on the cake and lit them up. Together, they sang Happy Birthday to a very excited Samuel and afterwards Martha cut the cake. When she took a thin slice of it to her aunt, she noticed that auntie's eyes were shut. She also remembered that, after having her light dinner, aunt Rachel had left the table. She had gone to sit on her cushioned cane chair and had pulled the patchwork blanket on her legs. Since then she had been silent throughout the whole birthday ritual. Outside a storm was brewing, "Auntie, auntie," Martha called, pushing aside the hand knitted shawl hanging on the back of the chair, but auntie didn't answer. Martha examined her pulse worriedly then asked Peter to take Samuel to their bedroom. Sensing something was wrong, "What is it?" he asked, without actually sounding the words.

"I think she had another attack, I am afraid she is not with us any more," Martha whispered to her husband.

Peter took his son to the bedroom and let him play with the tricycle they had given him for his special day and returned to the living room.

"I am sorry, Martha dear," he said, putting his arms around her.

They buried aunt Rachel in the local cemetery located only a few blocks away from their house. The few mourners were soaking wet, standing there under that torrential rain that had been giving the city a lashing for the past couple of days. Martha had taken the key off her aunt's neck before the undertakers had arrived. Aunt Rachel had told her that she had saved for her own funeral. Peter had already paid for everything, using whatever they had in their saving account in the New South Wales Bank and Martha didn't mind if they ended up paying for the funeral. Nevertheless, she couldn't help wondering how much her aunt had been able to save on her scarcely sufficient pension. At the end of that day, after Samuel went to bed, not quite understanding what all the fuss was about at that strange place, and why aunt Rachel wasn't there with them, Peter and Martha tiptoed to auntie's room.

The rain was throwing itself against the window, giving an eerie feel to the room. After a quick look around, Martha tried the key on the top drawer of the antiquated dressing table, which was the only place that seemed to be locked. Beside a stale and unpleasant smell that hit their nostrils, they found a few old rusty containers that had been holding cough lollies, tobacco and other things, in their days. There was also a tall canister covered by a faded paper with the Bushell's Tea logo barely visible on it. Martha opened one of the small cans. It contained a pink cameo sitting on a bit of crumpled paper and topped with some cotton wool. In the next can, she found a string of pearls, some of them peeling and feeling sticky at the touch. There was also a partly discoloured golden chain with a broken clasp. From under the little cans, she pulled out a flat and bigger cigar box that housed a collection of brooches, some with missing stones here and there.

"Fakes, all fakes," Martha said, shaking her head. "This will make for an embarrassing donation," she added, moving to the next tobacco box. She struggled a bit to open it but once she did she saw two bundles of bank notes, neatly tied with string, "Now we are talking, here it is," she told Peter who was trying to open the tea leaves canister.

"How much would that be?" he asked, starting to show signs of sleepiness and a bit of boredom.

"I don't know, not much I guess."

They unrolled the musty bundles, flattened the bills, one by one, then they counted them. At the end Martha declared, "Twenty-two pounds, not bad, it's even more than what the funeral cost, now what's in that can?" Using the key for the drawer, Peter flipped the lid open and saw a piece of paper folded in four with something written on it. It looked fresh, as if it had been put there only recently. Holding it up, he began reading it loudly.

"To Peter and Martha

This money is for you. I had been saving it for a rainy day, since the day I was left alone, but you came along and took care of me. I can't thank you enough for that and for bringing Samuel into my life, filling it with so much joy. Put it towards a home in a quiet suburb and be happy, you deserve it."

They looked at each other with misty eyes before emptying the content of the can on aunt Rachel's bed. They sat down, gazing in awe at a multitude of bundles, tied the same way as the first two. They untied and counted them too. "Eighteen hundred and twenty pounds! Wow! This is great, this is absolutely great, this is just what we need to get a new start," Peter said at the end.

Turning her head towards the heavens, "Yes, thank you Auntie," Martha said, closing her eyes to let tears of gratitude roll down her cheeks.

"Now, considering the circumstances, an extra bedroom would give us enough space to live for a while longer, but imagine moving into our own house. Even if we have to borrow some money from the bank, it wouldn't matter. We would be paying mortgage instead of rent. We would be moving in with the knowledge that one day that house will be ours, all ours," Peter said, looking all emotional.

"I'll call on a few real estate agents tomorrow. Raine and Horne, here I come," Martha chanted, overcome by happiness and excited by the idea of going house hunting, even though she felt a bit uneasy to rejoice so soon after her aunt's death.

"Yes, let's do it. Bless her soul, if that's what auntie wished us to do, then that's exactly what we will have to do."

On the weekend, beaming with happiness, the Goddards went to find their dream home.

The real estate agent met with Adam and the Varda's in Crow's Nest, right in front of the two houses. Built in a mirrored image of each other and nearing completion, both places were open for inspection. One first glance and Liuba was already convinced she would love to live in any one of those two houses, just by looking at their fresh facades. Remembering the few places they had seen the previous week, 'Who wants a dirty old house near the city anyway,' she thought. 'And who feels like cleaning scum from other people's bathtub, kitchen floors and oven, not to mention dirty carpets.'

The agent opened the door of one of the two houses in time to wipe the unpleasant memory from Liuba's mind. They went in to investigate the interior of the house. Then they stepped out to the empty land behind it. Once fenced, that space was to be the back-yard. While they were busy checking that place, another couple were inspecting the house next door. They smiled at each other, said hello and exchanged a few words on the weather. They even talked a bit about the big tree the two houses seemed to be sharing. Finally they ambled inside to discuss the financial side of it all, with their respective agents. As they were signing the papers, the agent was telling them something about the reason why the houses were built that way but Jonathan didn't care why. All he wanted to know was when they would be able to move in.

Two months later, Jonathan, Liuba and little Marcus were settling in house number twelve while Peter, Martha and Samuel were making number fourteen their home. Soon, both families began landscaping their front and back yards. The Goddards were more inclined towards Azaleas, firs and palms, whereas the Vardas took a more practical and rustic approach to their choice of plants. They planted a selection of citrus trees at the far back of the yard and a few other fruit trees at the sides. They had a big pergola erected along the left side fence, past the carport and planted two vine trees, entwining them around the supporting poles. They were to grow and cover the top of the pergola, in years to come. Jonathan could almost see bunches of red and green grapes hanging from the branches. Most importantly, they reserved a few square pieces of land for their favourite herbs.

In the front yard, Jonathan transplanted a row of fourteen rose shoots alongside the right fence. Hot pink Begonias were chosen to grow and climb over the opposite fence too. Adam, of course, was a big help in taking Jonathan to the right places for buying plants as well as digging and planting them. He even gave them a few big clay pots with colourful flowers thriving in them, as part of his housewarming present.

In the months to come, at Liuba's request they secured Geranium filled little boxes outside the living room windows and several hanging baskets made the carport more interesting.

The Goddard's garden beds were looking equally nice, especially when the Azaleas were in full bloom. The two neighbours were as usual courteous to each other. They had talked a couple of times about the big tree that had its roots in the Varda's yard but, growing at an angle, it was leaning towards the Goddard's side. They had both agreed that it would be a shame to cut it down so they let it be. Peter had decided to place something under it to prevent it from falling on the fence and damaging it. A sturdy ladder he had thought would do the job acceptably.

Jonathan never minded giving a bit of advice to Peter who didn't know much about horticulture. As for Liuba, she kept on sharing her herbs with Martha. Every now and then, she also gave her a plate of whatever she had cooked, after noticing that Martha was getting thicker around the middle. Suspecting that she could be pregnant, it was only human to let her neighbour have a taste of her food, in case its definite aroma gave her cravings. Peter used to comment about the mouth-watering flavour of the authentic dish she took over to them. Once, jokingly he mentioned that Liuba shouldn't bother giving the recipe to Martha because she would always find a way to muck it up. He liked to tease his wife for her lack of interest in trying her hand at cooking exotic foods. Admitting that he was telling the truth, Martha didn't get offended by the remark. "But she makes the nicest cakes, puddings and scones," Peter added to make his wife feel better.

Life went on for the two friendly neighbours. Liuba's English began improving just by talking to Martha, who taught her the right way of pronouncing words. As for Peter, he had his car regularly checked and tuned. Both appreciated the fact that their so-called over the fence friendship was developing into something more tangible. The first time they met on a social level was the day Peter came home with a concrete birdbath in the boot of his car. As he got out of the vehicle to untie the rope holding the birdbath, Jonathan, who was busy pruning his roses, heard him groan like he was in agony. He looked in Peter's direction and saw him struggling to lift the heavy mould, let alone carrying it somewhere. He put the secateurs in the back pocket of his overalls and rushed over. Without saying a word, he held the other side of the birdbath and together, they took it to the place designated for it. Peter thanked and shook Jonathan's hand then, automatically his own hand went up to his shoulder and, grimacing with pain, "It's this stupid joint that goes out of whack in the wrong time. There was no one in the shop to deliver the jolly thing and I wanted to surprise Martha with it," he said.

Jonathan asked if he had hurt his shoulder recently.

"Oh! No," Peter replied promptly, "It's an old war wound, I fought in Tobruk, I got shot just before the Italian forces were about to get defeated by the allied troops," he elaborated.

"Oh!" said Jonathan, embarrassed by his lack of knowledge about the details of the wars Australia had been involved in.

Peter invited Jonathan over for a drink and Jonathan, accepting the invitation, followed him inside and on their patio. Over a glass of cold beer, they talked a bit about the war times. After that day, any excuse was good enough for them to get together and have a chat, sharing a glass or two of their favourite grog and nibbling on some little savouries. When the gathering was at the Varda's house, Liuba used to serve them some of her tasty snacks that Peter liked so much.

Fixing cars was Jonathan's job but carpentry was his second fiddle. He liked to make little wooden things in his spare time. He decided one day to use his capable hands at making a scooter for Marcus. Painstakingly he accomplished his task and gave the toy a finishing shine. Marcus was so impressed with it that he asked his father to take him next door so he could show his treasure to Samuel. Samuel looked at it so enviously that it made Jonathan promise him on the spot that he would make him one too. "Only if you two play together on the driveways and put them away in the garage when you finish playing. We don't want to see them lying around, do we?" he said looking at Peter who nodded approvingly.

When the second scooter was done, Jonathan got the idea of doing something about the temporary postbox the builders had left at the side of the driveway and which was still being used. He though he would make one himself, one that would look like a little house, but large enough to hold big envelopes. On that note he began sawing away the left over wood from his previous jobs. He was halfway through it when he saw Adam's car stop in front of the house.

Adam came down holding the prettiest wrought iron green postbox, another housewarming present, no doubt. Jonathan covered and put away the one he was making and rushed to greet his friend. "I thought I'd better bring this before you go and buy one," Adam said with his usual jovial smile.

"Actually, that was on top of my list for next week's shopping day," Jonathan said, bending the truth a tad. He also thanked Adam for his kind gesture before letting him drive off to go to a meeting.

On a windy day in November 1955, Martha gave birth to another baby boy. The over exalted parents named him Jeremy. Liuba went to visit Martha in hospital. She took her a box of Cadbury's Chocolate and a little jar of the jam she had made herself. Martha was busy browsing through a very old issue of the Woman's Weekly opened on her lap. After the preliminary talks, she pointed at a picture in the magazine. It featured Anderson and Sally tying the knot in the Blue Hills program. "Rod Taylor is a very good looking actor," she commented casually. Liuba leaned over to have a look.

"Yes, nice eyes he has," she agreed and before sitting down again, she kind of whispered in Martha's ear that she too would have a baby in another seven months. Soon after, Liuba realised that she had shared her good news with Martha before letting Freeda know about her pregnancy.

It was five o'clock in the morning when a panic-stricken Jonathan ran to the Goddard's house. Martha was awake and had just finished breastfeeding Jeremy when she heard the knock. Throwing a robe on her back, she answered the door and found Jonathan babbling nervously. "What is the matter?" she asked, fearing that something might be wrong with Marcus.

"She is bleeding, I don't know what to do, I am sorry to have bothered you at this hour," he was trying to say.

Seeing the poor man in that state, Martha bundled her baby and, holding him tight to her chest, she followed Jonathan next door to assist her friend. At Martha's suggestion, hands shaking from worry,

Jonathan began to dial for an ambulance. As soon as he hung up the phone, "Do you think she is miscarrying?" he asked Martha, fearing her answer would be affirmative.

"I am not sure," she said and went on holding Liuba's hand and comforting her while they waited for the ambulance to arrive.

Jonathan lifted his head from the edge of his wife's hospital bed. The dim light on the wall was barely illuminating the soft contours of her pale face. He looked at it lovingly and sighed. The morning stubble and the black circles under his eyes were the telltale signs of the kind of night he had just been through. He could feel himself trembling at the thought of being so close to losing her. Liuba had lost the baby but the doctor had assured him that she was out of danger. He sat there listening to her quietly breathing and thanked God for giving her back to him. The Goddards were taking care of Marcus so Jonathan could stay with his wife. He looked at her some more, dreading the time he would have to tell her what had happened. How she would cope with her loss was something he didn't have an answer for. "Poor darling," he whispered as he covered her hand with tender kisses.

The two families lived next to each other in perfect harmony. Since Marcus had started to go to school, Liuba was able to go back to her old job in the clothing factory in St Leonard's. They had agreed that in the mornings, on her way to work, Liuba would take Marcus and Samuel to school. In the afternoons, pushing Jeremy's pram Martha had the job to pick the two boys up and take them to her house. Marcus would then stay with her until his mother was back from work. The two women ended up being the best of friends, sharing each other's happy and sad moments.

Jeremy was two years old when, after trying very hard, Liuba became pregnant again but later had another miscarriage. This time it was even scarier than the one before but she came through it alive. Unfortunately after that, she was told she wouldn't be able to conceive again. The news distressed her immensely but gradually she resigned herself to be content with having just the one child. She went on with life, giving all her motherly love and attention to Marcus who was growing tall and handsome like his father. When Jeremy started school, Martha applied for employment in North Shore Hospital and got the job but she had to attend a refresher course in nursing before she could start working.

The friendship between the two neighbours kept growing stronger. They visited each other every now and then. On the cold weekends, they used to get together in one's sunroom to soak up the sunshine and in warmer days they gathered on the veranda. The women used to chat over a cup of tea or coffee and occasionally a piece of cake while the men told anecdotes about their youth, enjoying whatever they liked to drink. Jonathan who had never really been keen on beer, used to have a nip or two of his Seppelt's wine but Peter stuck to his favourite ale, Foster's Lager. Lately though, Jonathan had noticed that Peter was showing a tendency to overdo it at times. One evening after dinner, while they were watching the news on their brand new Ecko Television set, he relayed his worries to his wife. Licking her upper lip, a pensive look on her face, Liuba began recounting a conversation she'd had with Martha just a few weeks earlier. "Martha was telling me again the story of how she had met Peter during the war."

"Aha?" Jonathan said, interested

"She said, because of shortage of medicine, he used to drink, to dull his pain I suppose. Anyway, she said he got over his habit and after they got married, he seldom drank. She also told me that now she doesn't know what is his excuse for boozing and that she sure doesn't wish to see him end up like one of those winos she trips over on her way to work." That conversation was interrupted when Jonathan became engrossed in the news about Australia winning 38 gold, 36 silver and 31 bronze medals in the Commonwealth games, in Perth.

Chapter 9

On the other side of the world, in Chicago, members of another Assyrian family from Iran were trying to learn the ropes of living in a foreign land. From the day they got married, sometime in the year 1936, Daniel and Jenny Sarkis were dreaming of migrating to America. They wished to go to that land of opportunity, to where the streets were paved with gold, as people used to say, exaggerating the possibilities offered to newcomers. Many of their acquaintances had already moved there and, blinded by their first impression of the new place, they had sent letters, praising the quality of life in their adoptive country.

Daniel's grandfather Ivan had initially crossed the Iranian border and entered the Russian soil to find work. On the other side of the boundary line, because of some road construction plans, there had been a big demand for capable workers. Ivan worked hard and stayed in Russia for a couple of years. When he had saved enough money, he dashed back to his homeland to get married. Straight after, bride in tow, he returned to his job. The two lived in Russia for a long time. They had a happy life together, especially after their son Joseph and their beautiful daughter Maya came along.

As soon as Maya reached a mature age, she got married and followed her husband to Kiev, where her husband's parents lived. Joseph grew up to be a decent looking young man who, after a few years of schooling, found himself a position in an inn as the cook's helper. He was in the process of marrying Daisy, his good old childhood sweetheart when, in the dawn of the First World War, his mother died from the complications of a simple chest cold left untreated. Being a diabetic, Ivan didn't live much longer after his wife.

The country was going through rough times, heavy defeats had sapped Russian morale. In utter distress, Joseph and Daisy found out that the Tsar had abdicated and the Bolshevik revolution was being followed by armistice negotiations. Still worried about the outcome of all those changes, Daisy found out that she was pregnant. Daniel was born a few months after the humiliating treaty of Brest-Litovsky had been signed and Russia had gone out of the First World War.

Soon after, when the communist party became established, all the foreigners residing in Russian territory were given a choice. They could either put everything down and return to their country or stay and adhere to the new regime. Unable to tear themselves away from their cosy old life and their precious belongings, some Iranians had kept on procrastinating. Consequently, they were given the ultimatum to stay or leave within the next forty-eight hours.

The Sarkis family, being in that category, had reluctantly left their home and grabbing whatever they could carry with themself they had fled to Iran, scared for their lives. All the people who were thrown to the Iranian side of the frontiers were labelled the White Russians. In the coming years, the American government, opening the doors to all the White Russians and their dependents, had invited them to take advantage of the opportunity and apply for a permit that would allow them to set sail to their shores. Therefore, a great deal of eligible people did just that. They went and put their names on those application forms to migrate to America. The only snag was that the waiting list was miles long and some had to wait years before they could pack their bags.

Life could have been a lot more difficult for Joseph and his family if they had come to Iran with what they seemed to be bringing with themselves. A brand new and heavily hand carved table, two kerosene lamps, a few blankets and feather down pillows and a trunkful of warm clothes were all they had arrived with, at the inspection point.

Understandably, the table didn't get the approval to pass. Its legs, that looked suspiciously thick, had attracted the attention of the guards who thought they were filled with gold coins and jewellery. Therefore, the Sarkis family, putting on a very convincingly unhappy face, had taken the rest of their things and had crossed the border without it. Joseph had heard about people who had been caught trying to smuggle their valuables in their carriages and the legs of their tables, had the clever idea to play dumb in order to fool the guards. His eye-catching new table had made it easy for the rest of their belongings to go unchecked.

In Iran, as soon as they got settled, Joseph and Daisy got their treasures out of their hiding places and took them to the Bazaar, exchanging them for cash. They had chunky gold chains hanging inside the many pleats of Daisy's old skirt and a few gold coins were in the soles of their old shoes. With that money, Joseph opened a small café in Lalehzar Street.

Lalehzar was a busy, narrow street in the heart of Tehran. Aligned with shops and business offices, it was the ideal place for all sorts of wheeling and dealing. During the day, it was a trade centre and naturally people working in those cooped up places had to go somewhere to buy their lunch. The majority of them used to walk to the nearest café. In the evenings, they used to go back there for a shot of Vodka or Arag, their common alcoholic beverage and for some mazeh, which consisted of small hors d'oeuvres or a skewer of kebab. After a hard day of work, they believed they needed to relax their nerves before going home to their families and their late supper.

In its little alleys, Lalehzar had also a hidden nightlife. All sorts of clubs, unseen during the day but ever so lively after the sunset, were open to the public, with music, singers and belly dancers. Again, people leaving those establishments, half drunk, used to feel the urge to drop into a café before heading home. Joseph couldn't be happier to see his culinary skills pay off in that tiny little place.

It was in those days that, following a friend's insistence, Joseph had applied to go to America, but he was so caught up with his open-all-hours café that he had forgotten all about those papers he had filled in. To Joseph's delight, Daniel was doing very well at school. After a few years, Joseph rented the shop next door to his café and turned the whole space into a Bistro, a foreign name recently in vogue given to that kind of restaurant. Business began booming. Joseph was doing well, so well that he bought a nice house in a good neighbourhood. Daniel was fourteen years old when his mother got pregnant. As months passed, Daisy became so big she could hardly walk. Her midwife, Madam Shishlo, told her that she was carrying twins and advised her to go to hospital when her babies were due. This was also because she was busy looking after her own daughter who had been diagnosed with cancer and needed her mother.

One night, Daisy felt pain and discomfort. She started having contractions before her due time. In panic, Joseph ran to Madame Shishlo's residence but she wasn't home. Her neighbour told him that poor madam's daughter had died and she had gone to church for the funeral. With great difficulty, Joseph managed to get Daisy to the hospital, where, after hours of agony, she gave birth to a pair of underdeveloped babies. Doctors did everything they could to save the mother but, with all their efforts, they couldn't stop her from bleeding to death.

In all the chaos and with no one to care for them, within the next three days after their birth, the babies died too. Devastated, Joseph was in such a deplorable state that if it wasn't for Daniel's sake he couldn't tell what he would have done. He pulled through eventually and went on with taking care of his son and his business.

The shock however left its mark as he also developed diabetes. In the days when his father was told that he had sugar, as they called it, people were a bit ignorant about this debilitating disease but Joseph was aware of the gravity of it. He tried his best to keep his condition under control for a long time. Daniel used to go and help him in the bistro.

In the years that followed, Daniel met a nice girl called Jenny. They fell in love with each other and got married. A year later, their son Matthew was born. In the year 1947, when they least expected it, the Sarkis family received a letter from the American Embassy informing them that their application for emigration had been accepted. It was good news but there was something they had to consider before making any plans. Joseph was not fit to travel and Daniel was left with a big dilemma. He could take his wife and child and go without his father or stay and forget about America. After mulling it over, staying appeared to be the best choice. He even decided not to tell his father or anybody else about it. It was fate or coincidence that all of a sudden Joseph decided to go visit his cousins in Urmia, his birthplace in Azerbaijan. He was away for five weeks and it seemed that he had gone off his diet during that time. When he came back, his condition took a turn for the worse and eventually he slipped into a coma. Three weeks later he died without regaining consciousness.

Matthew was at the right age to go to school so, after Joseph's funeral, Daniel and Jenny thought it was best to hurry things along and leave as soon as possible and not let their son miss any school time. They went through all the formalities and got their papers in order. They sold the bistro, their family home and house contents and finally headed for Tehran's train station with two big suitcases, a carry bag and their little boy. They had a long journey ahead of them before going on board a liner to cross the Atlantic Ocean and sail all the way to America. The voyage was tiresome but the thought of at last being in their version of the Promised Land made it bearable.

Once in Chicago, the Sarkis family banked all their money and looked for temporary jobs. They needed some time to think and study the various possibilities of putting their nest egg to use. Daniel found a job as a waiter in an Italian restaurant and Jenny, who had never worked anywhere before, was employed in the meat section of a big grocery shop, packaging and labelling different cuts of meat.

During the first school holidays, Daniel and Jenny went to visit one of Jenny's relatives. It was at their place that they were told about a diner being on sale in their neighbourhood. The couple went to check it out but were of two minds; once they had a good look at the place, they contemplated the idea of starting their own business. They took the chance and went for it. The good news, even though untimely, was that Jenny was pregnant with her second child. Jenny was faced with a dilemma. On the one hand she had to keep on working until the diner showed profit, on the other hand she would have to quit her job anyway. Those boxes of meat were too heavy for her to lift in her condition. She was worried, but she didn't suspect that the diner would still do reasonably well as it used to and that money would keep coming in, despite the change in the management. Only for the first few days did Daniel feel like he had two left hands but soon he was on top of the situation. Her confidence restored, Jenny left her job for good and went to help her husband in the diner. She thought it was time they made some changes to the place as well as the menu.

After replacing the name Stavros' Diner to Danny's Diner, Jenny made her plans for some serious remodelling. She stripped the floor from the drab, sad looking, greasy vinyl covering and had it paved with light grey tiles. In the parts alongside the two adjoining walls opposite the counter, she laid a length of two metres wide burgundy carpet. She then placed round tables on the carpeted sections. Each table was then covered with a round burgundy tablecloth, topped with a dusky pink smaller square cloth, allowing the burgundy one to show from underneath. Small glossy burgundy vases were placed in the centre of every table. Each vase was holding a beautiful posy

made of silky lily of the valley flowers and a few dainty pink buds
in view amongst them. She hung half a dozen posters of peaceful
sceneries on the walls and placed healthy pot plants in the corners.
Beside the colourful doormat, two giant umbrella threes, at either
side of the door, made the entrance look all the more inviting. They
also hired waitresses, two of them working only in busy hours. They
were wearing white uniforms, with pink piping around the collar
and lapel. Each girl had a lacquered burgundy nametag pinned on
her chest.

Word went around and customers began pouring in, either for
eating or taking food away. A far cry from the dingy place it used
to be, the restaurant appealed to a better class of clientele. People
who knew about it didn't mind paying car park fees at the top of
the street and walk the rest of the way, to sit down and enjoy a meal
cooked in Danny's kitchen. Gradually, Jenny became bigger and
bigger as her pregnancy progressed but she never stopped doing her
part in the diner. She single-handedly cooked most of the Assyrian
dishes she had added to the previous menu. They still ordered a lot
of the more affordable pies and other pastries from bulk producers.
The cook continued to prepare roasted and grilled chicken as well
as fry chips and eggs, and make hamburgers. Jenny's specialities
were those scrumptious cabbage rolls served in pockets of flat bread
baked on the premises. She also served shish kebabs on a bed of rice,
cooked the Persian way.

On a glorious day in March 1952, Jenny gave birth to a beautiful
little baby girl. They called her Clara. She was a delightfully quiet
baby and posed no problem whatsoever to her mother. After a few
weeks of absence, Jenny returned to her duties in the diner but not
without baby Clara who was calmly sleeping in her pram. She used
to leave her in the little room behind the office. The room had been
cleaned from its clutter that consisted mainly of Matthew's toys
and books. An easy chair was left for Jenny to sit on at feeding time.
There was enough room to move around and the sun was shining
through an adequate sized window.

All the while Jenny was home nursing her baby, her cousin's son, eighteen years old George was hired to help in the kitchen. George was a placid teenager, slightly timid and not highly educated, but whatever he lacked in the academic department, he made up for it in ethics, dedication and hard work. He had an older brother Robert who had been even less keen in furthering his studies but who was big and strong. Sometimes Daniel used to ask him to do odd jobs, like lifting heavy boxes and cleaning the windows.

Daniel liked to keep Robert around the diner mostly for his strong build, as an insurance against thugs and undesirables. He knew that his presence in the background could make hoodlums think twice before trying to put any malevolent plan into action. Robert was free to come and go, eat whatever he wished to eat, as long as he was seen from outside. He had a part-time job with a furniture removalist company. With his pay and the amount of money Daniel used to stash in his pocket every now and then, he was happy and didn't mind to be hanging around. The two brothers adored Clara who was growing into a cute little girl. With her big hazel coloured eyes, a delicate face that was topped with curly chestnut hair, they likened her to a brunette version of Shirley Temple, the child actress.

When Clara was old enough to go to school, she was as always a cute and sweet little girl that everyone admired. She loved her brother Matthew a lot; even when he nagged her for bothering him, she used to listen to him and respect his wishes. Over the years, Matthew had turned into a chubby and spoiled brat, a teenager hard to get along with. He had the responsibility of taking his little sister to school in the mornings but Jenny used to go and collect her in the afternoons, as her son had always something to do after school, mostly football or any other activity he liked to participate in. After picking her up, Jenny used to bring Clara into the diner and resume her work in the kitchen. In the back room, after having her customary glass of milk and a few of her favourite cookies, Clara used to do some drawing or her homework if she had any. Sometimes she used to go and watch or even help her mother with little tasks until closing time.

Clara learned a lot from her mother just by observing her doing her daily chores. After the age of twelve, she knew exactly how to make Baklava, how to thread little pieces of lamb, onion and capsicum bits on skewers for the kebabs and how to prepare the stuffing for cabbage rolls. In a way, she became her mother's right hand. Jenny felt very lucky to have her by her side, as long as her help didn't interfere with her studies.

After the first two years of running the diner, Daniel and Jenny had been able to buy their home, the proverbial suburban nice house with picket fences and a swing on the veranda. They even had enough room in the backyard to put a swimming pool later on. Gradually they had filled the house with the best of furniture and electrical appliances. They had also added a rumpus room for games and activities and had built a barbeque area for parties. Life couldn't have been kinder to them. Everything around them seemed right and so good, almost too good to be true, until that night when a dark cloud came hanging over their heads and refused to be blown away.

It was Christmas Eve and Jenny was home preparing for the big reception she was giving. All their friends and relatives were invited. The whole house had been decorated and fitted with lights that flickered gaily and added to the Christmas atmosphere. The kitchen was abuzz with people scurrying around and pulling their weight with party preparations. The waitresses, working overtime, were arranging hors d'oeuvres on big silver trays. George had just arrived with the chickens that were baked in the diner because they didn't have enough oven space to do them at home. Robert was sent by Daniel to pick up the continental torte that Jenny had ordered for the occasion from the Italian cake shop.

Jenny was checking the last details of the many dishes she was going to serve to her guests. No expense had been spared. Everything had to be perfect, since this wasn't only a Christmas Party; it was more like a celebration of their life, of their dream that had come true. There were flowers on every table. Dozens of presents wrapped in dazzling colourful paper and topped with superb bows were placed under the huge natural Christmas tree. The tree itself had been adorned with lots of sparkling ornaments and the lights that went on and off were adding joy and an air of mystery to the ambiance of the huge lounge room.

Earlier Jenny had phoned Daniel asking him to bring some more soft drinks, just in case, and he had told her that he was about to close and be on his way home. He was just waiting for the last two clients to leave. It so happened that those two did not intend to leave, or not until they robbed Daniel of all his day's takings and maybe have a bit of fun on the side.

Julio and Phil had made a big effort to dress decently that night so they wouldn't look suspicious when they entered the diner. They almost looked like two businessmen working out the last details of a deal over a friendly meal. Under their clean attire though, unfortunately for Daniel, they were the same scum of the earth, the same low life thugs who used to terrorise the elderly and prey on the innocent residents of the area.

Followed by Phil, Julio walked towards the counter with a steady gait, looking calm and collected. He stood in front of Daniel brandishing a twenty dollar note between two fingers of his left hand. Happy to see them finally ready to leave, Daniel looked down at the list of the food the two had consumed then began punching numbers on the cash register. At the end, pressing on another button, the drawer of the machine opened noisily. He stretched his hand to take the money from Julio, but Julio retracted his hand and, "No pop," he casually said. "I'll keep this, you don't have to worry about giving me change, instead you will take a bag and fill it with all there is there and hand it to me without a word," he added.

Surprised, Daniel looked up and only then did he notice the barrel of a gun shining in Julio's right hand.

"Now slowly do what I told you to do and don't even think of making a stupid move or I'll blow your head off," Julio added with the same cool voice.

"All right, all right," Daniel mumbled swallowing hard. All this time, Phil was standing a step back watching the scene, thinking how easy it was to get money if you just pointed a gun at someone. "Cool man!" he said under his garlic smelling breath. Julio could have taken all the cash Daniel handed him without argument and leave, but that wouldn't be fun. Bloated with pride, he was too keen to show off, too eager to let his newest recruit know what a daredevil he was. Julio always enjoyed teasing his victims, he loved watching them squirm and beg for mercy. Daniel's fixed gaze though had him feeling uneasy for a moment. He turned and gave a quick look at Phil then, smugly gathering his filthy lips together, he sent a kiss to Daniel, and, "Adios amigo," he uttered then he pulled the trigger. Not expecting to see a killing, Phil got confused and, acting like the idiot that he was, he yelled, "Merry Christmas!!!" from the top of his voice.

For a fraction of a second, Daniel kept staring at Julio with wide open eyes, the question, 'why,' etched on his face, then he slumped to the ground. He shuddered for a painful moment but before giving up the fight he managed to put his hand on a button under the counter. That was to alert Mario the fruiterer who called the police, knowing his friend next door was in trouble. Unfortunately their secret wiring didn't stop Daniel from getting killed.

When Robert got the cake, he carefully placed the box in the back of the van and made sure to secure it so it wouldn't move. He was supposed to go straight to the house but, as he put the key in the ignition, his instincts told him to go back to the diner. He thought he might be needed in closing time, even though Daniel had told him that he would be all right on his own. It wouldn't make so much difference if the cake arrived a few minutes later anyway, he thought. He made a U-turn in front of the cake shop and drove back. He had to drive past the diner to go and park the van in the car park behind. As he approached his destination, Robert noticed people gathered in front of the diner. Sensing something was wrong, he stopped at once and, leaving the van unattended, he jumped down and ran towards the crowd. He pushed his way through when, to his horror, he saw two policemen wheeling a stretcher out of the door. Instantly he recognised Daniel's familiar face, as one of the policemen began pulling the zipper over his bloodied body.

Suddenly, out of the throat of that gentle giant, an unhuman sound, a roar, like the cry of a wounded beast escaped, paralising the onlookers to their spot. The horrified cry travelled far, every decibel cutting through the frozen air of December. For a split second it was as if everything had stood still. Even the scantily falling flakes of snow seemed hanging in midair, turning the atmosphere all the more gruesome. Robert slid down onto the hard concrete of the footpath, reduced to a mass of despair. "It's my fault! It's my fault!" he cried over and over, as his warm tears descended down his distorted face. "I shouldn't have left you alone Danny. It's my fault. What am I going to do Danny? How could anyone do this to you? Oh Danny, what am I going to say to Jenny?" he kept on crying.

Clara was checking the presents under the Christmas tree to make sure none of the children of the guests had been overlooked. The headlight of a car turning the corner grabbed her attention. Through the laced curtains she saw a police car pulling into their driveway. As she went to find out what they wanted, a cold winter breeze rushed in through the front door, a cold winter chill that was to remain within the walls of that house for many, many years to come.

While undoing her apron strings, Jenny came to see who was at the door. At the sight of the two uniformed police officers, an uneasy feeling came over her. Interrogatively she just stared at them, finding it hard to swallow the lump she felt growing in her throat.

One of the officers asked if they could go inside. They both entered and asked Jenny to sit down. "Mrs Sarkis, there has been an accident," one of the officers began saying, trying hard to keep his voice from giving away the disquiet in his mind. This had always been the hardest part of his job.

"What accident?" Jenny murmured.

"I am afraid Mrs Sarkis, an hour ago, there was a shooting in your diner. We are sorry to inform you that your husband Daniel Sarkis was shot during an armed holdup."

Petrified, Jenny's eyes scanned the policeman's eyes, wishing to see a sign, hoping that he would tell her that Daniel was still alive but the officer continued, "I am sorry, Mr Sarkis didn't make it, he died on the way to the hospital."

Jenny's face turned to ash before she began screaming. "No! No! Not my Danny. It is not true. It can't be true."

Guests started to arrive but instead of the joyous party they were expecting to participate in, they stepped into a nightmare. Screams and wailings were all that filled the house in place of Christmas cheers. Even the children, seeing their parents in such an unhinged state, couldn't keep themselves from crying. Someone turned off the lights on the Christmas tree as if to say that the happy days were over. Jenny's cries could melt the hardest of hearts. Light had gone out of her life too. Devastated and feeling like her insides were mauled, Clara kept on holding her mother in her arms. Setting aside her own bereavement, her own heartache, she tried to comfort her mother to her best ability.

In all the pandemonium, nobody could tell exactly how Matthew took the bad news. It also seemed that no one knew his whereabouts, until one of the guests said that he saw him running towards the park.

Everybody who knew Daniel attended the mass that was followed by the burial ceremony. All the shopkeepers in the street where the diner was came too to extend their respect to the family. Mario the fruiterer next door, sobbing openly, kept wiping his eyes with a big crumpled handkerchief and saying, "He was like a brother to me." His wife Angela helped Jenny get off the floor when she collapsed in the church at the sight of the coffin sitting on the bier. Covered with an impressive flower arrangement, it was placed between the altar and the first rows of chairs.

When Jenny came to, she could hear the distant voice of the priest. Feeling lost in a whirlwind, she couldn't tell how much time had passed. At some stage, she became aware of someone delivering a eulogy. She tried to comprehend and grasp the meaning of what she was hearing. "This poor excuse of a human being needlessly ended the life of a decent, hard working and kind man who never hurt anyone. He was a man loved by his wife, his children and respected by all his friends and people who devotedly worked for him. Yes, they worked devotedly because they knew how understanding and just he was with them. He treated them as equals and was there for them whenever they needed a helping hand. His good deeds will surely not be forgotten."

Feeling ashamed of her weakness, Jenny felt that she had to get a grip on herself. She straightened her posture and listened to the other eulogies in silence. Discretely she wiped the tears that still rolled down her cheeks. At the cemetery, when the men, including Matthew, lowered the coffin in the dug up ground, she stood up tall, a dignified look on her pale face. Without uttering a word, in her heart she said goodbye to her beloved husband and there and then she promised him that she would be brave. She also promised that she would do her very best in taking care of their children, their home and the business and that she wouldn't let his hard work go to waste.

Two days later, from the description Robert had given of the last customers he had seen enter the diner, the police found Phil. Detecting a weakness in his character, they interrogated him rather harshly hoping he would crack under pressure. After giving him a graphic description of life inside, with no one to protect him, Phil who was indeed a born coward didn't hesitate to squeal on his small time hero. Julio got wind of his accomplice spilling the beans. He had been hiding in a girlfriend's house. Fearing that she might also be implicated, the girl friend let him stay one last night and kicked him out in the morning.

The next afternoon, the police spotted Julio's car. At the end of an elaborate car chase that left a number of parked cars damaged, Julio got out of his car and ran. The police cornered him in a back alley and after a brief struggle they handcuffed and pushed him into one of their cars, wiping the neighbourhood of one of its vermin.

After Daniel's funeral, Jenny's existence changed dramatically. It felt as if something inside of her had died. She had lost interest in life but for the sake of her children and because she had promised Danny, she was determined to be strong and brave. Throughout the sad ordeal, especially at the cemetery, somehow Matthew's attitude had not made sense to anyone. He, who had always been projecting the image of an insensitive, self-serving brat, had looked peculiarly numb, like he had been in a trance. He hadn't cried, he hadn't said a thing. It was as if an arctic blizzard had blown about him and had turned him into an icicle, an icicle with a haggard look in the eyes. In particular, Jenny's cousins were having trouble knowing what to make of his attitude. They had wondered if he was really hit hard by his father's death or he was just putting on a clever act. Robert and George, who had always loved and respected Clara, had watched her silently cry and had tried to comfort her. At one time, she had hid her face in the hollow of Robert's chest and had sobbed. As for Matthew, they had never been too keen on him. Their dislike of him had been growing at the same rate as he had grown older. It was mainly because of the nasty way he had been treating them and the rest of the staff. They had never dared to complain to his parents but they had joked a lot about his odd behaviour behind his back. "What do you think is going through his mind?" Robert had asked his brother at the wake.

"Don't rack your brain figuring him out, the amount of food he is likely to stack on his plate will tell us plenty about what's going on in his mind," George had answered.

The two had been baffled even more, realising that Matthew hadn't even gone close to the banquet table. "It's only a matter of time, I am sure he will soon go back to his old habits," George had said.

"Yes, once a brat, always a brat," Robert had agreed.

During the following weeks, although Clara loved her father dearly and was missing him an awful lot, she managed to bear it out. Miraculously she found in herself the strength to deal with her sorrow and help her mother cope with the tragedy that had plagued their lives. Eventually Jenny went back to work, but since she needed two extra hands in the diner, she gave more responsibility to George. Robert too was employed on a full-time basis to help with anything he could. He was mainly assigned to act as a bodyguard to the children and to herself, also to keep an eagle eye on the customers and anyone who could possibly pose a threat to them. Matthew had also been asked to put a few hours everyday after work and at least half a day on the weekends.

Matthew hadn't been able to go too far with his studies, so Daniel had advised him to find a job elsewhere, rather than hang around the diner. Aware of his son's self-centred nature, he had thought it wiser to have him work under someone who would have more authority over him, someone who would teach him discipline and expect respect from him. Not exactly thrilled with the idea, Matthew had found a storekeeping job in a large Toy Manufacturing Factory. He had been working there for only six weeks the day Daniel got killed.

After his father's death, when everything settled down and work resumed at the diner, a bizarre idea burgeoned in Matthew's head. In his immature mind, he believed that he was now the man of the house. He decided that it was about time that he started exercising his power. With that false assumption of superiority, he gave himself the carte blanche to boss everyone and throw his weight around. The waitresses were his first victims. He picked on them unnecessarily until they had enough of him.

Criticising their every move, the two cousins were equally fed up with Matthew. They were at a loss, not knowing how much longer they could tiptoe around him. Although they continued respecting him, for his mother's sake, they secretly hated his guts. A few times, detecting tension in the air, Jenny had set her son straight. Matthew had sulked for a day or two then had gone on being the same attention seeking, pain in the neck that he was before. Once, Clara heard him talk rudely to Robert. She pulled her brother to a corner and, regardless of her younger age, she chided him with a semi-serious tone. "Grow up and stop being so obnoxious. They are doing their best to make things go smoothly and what do you do?"

"What?"

"You piss them off, that's what. Don't you see you are hurting mum? She has enough problems to worry about and you are here to help not to make yourself sandwiches after sandwiches."

"What is it to you? You say I shouldn't eat when I am hungry?"

"You can, but not all day long, in case you hadn't noticed, you are getting fat and ugly."

It seemed that Clara's words had hit a sensitive chord because after that, she noticed a radical change in Matthew's attitude. At times, she found him in an unusually pensive mood that made him look almost well meaning and decent and she couldn't help feeling sorry for him. She even came to believe that inside that arrogant exterior, there could be a nicer person screaming to be let out.

Chapter 10

Geneviève's first break came when she overheard a conversation between two ladies at the hairdressing salon where she used to visit once in a while for a trim. "My friend said it's a posh fashion house in Rose Bay. She told me that the boss is a nice French lady by the name of Josephine Joubert. She makes clothes for the most important ladies of Sydney, and my friend heard that Madame Joubert can do with another pair of hands in the workroom," one of them was saying.

"And do you want to apply?" the other one asked.

"I can't go this week but I'll try to be there first thing on Monday morning."

Geneviève kept repeating the name until she was able to scribble it on a piece of paper. The minute she was out of the salon, she rushed home and, after a few phone calls, address in hand and dressed appropriately, she was on her way to see Madame Joubert. The next day she started working in the fashion house, but only on a trial basis. It was decided that she would be fully employed should the boss be happy with her work. A few months later, Madame Joubert could, in all honesty, consider Geneviève to be one of her valued employees, as far as her sewing skills were concerned.

Madame Joubert never had any problems with Geneviève's performance in the workplace, but from day one she couldn't help having suspicious feelings about her. There was this little voice inside of her that was telling her not to fully trust the green-eyed woman who's behaviour seemed too good to be true. Josephine kept reminding herself that she should watch Geneviève closely just in case she had mischief on her mind. Fearing industrial espionage, she tried to keep Geneviève away from the patterns and leave her in the dark about her newest designs and the financial aspects of her business. Nevertheless, Geneviève proved to be more resourceful and cunning than her boss could ever have imagined her to be. She was not interested in patterns, not even the latest dress designs. All she was after was to know a few names and the details of some of the clients who came for made-to-measure garments. In fact, in no time, she had managed to put together a list of names, addresses and phone numbers of most of Josephine's less demanding customers. She had also found out the whereabouts of some suppliers who, every now and then, delivered those first class fabrics and haberdashery.

Often assigned to help in the fitting room, Geneviève could listen attentively to the conversations the socialites were having with their friends or with Madame Joubert. She had the opportunity to hear the correct way of speaking the English language. In the meantime she came to learn a lot about the way people from the Australian high society were living, including: where they were staying, when they were on their holidays, and what were their favourite subjects of discussion, their good and bad habits and the subtle way they criticised and gossiped about others. In her free time at home, she kept reading and reading. She borrowed books from the library and even bought the daily papers, in the bid to keep abreast with the latest events in the world. She acquired the necessary knowledge on cars, fine furniture, gourmet food, wine, sports, arts, horses, music and even politics and the stock market.

After paying her rent and putting some cash aside for the electricity and other regular bills, Geneviève only kept a minimal amount from her pay as housekeeping money. She was adamant to leave the rest of her earnings in her ever growing account in a branch of New South Wales Bank. Talking to neighbours and anyone she met on her errands, she was able to slowly gather a small clientele. Her customers appreciated the fact that they were getting their clothes made for a fraction of what they would have to pay elsewhere for the same standard of work. Her clients were mostly migrants and, at her request, they came to her in the utmost secrecy and only told their relatives about her.

Growing into a beautiful young girl, Aurore never posed any problem to Geneviève who made sure to provide her with everything a girl her age would need. Always meticulously dressed, Aurore could easily be mistaken for a rich, spoiled girl. Her classmates, intimidated by her appearance, didn't feel confident enough to approach and welcome her into their group. Often on her own, Aurore pretty much learned to keep to herself and she didn't mind it. She had always been content and used to being in her mother's company.

Geneviève's love life had also come to a quieter phase. In the last eighteen months, she only had been seeing a young doctor with whom she met at the hospital where Aurore had been admitted for an urgent appendectomy. That affair had died on its own soon after it had started. With her tight schedule, Geneviève had hardly any spare time for socialising and having fun.

Aurore was fourteen when, sheepishly, she went to her mother and expressed her desire to become a model. "I will ask around and find out if there is a school where they train models," her mother replied, worried that her daughter may not be planning to go further with her education.

"Oh, don't worry maman. I know of such an agency and I don't have any intention of neglecting my studies. I will keep going to school and, after high school, I will attend a business college for one day you will be a well known fashion designer."

"Wouldn't that be wonderful? And I think, by then, I'll be ready and honoured to put you on my payroll," Geneviève said with a smile.

There were rumours that Madame Joubert had decided to retire and go back to France, but no one knew exactly if there was any truth in that. No one knew when this was supposed to happen and who would be the one to fill her shoes, should the rumours be true. With artful planning, Geneviève had shrewdly managed to lure some of Josephine's clients to her house. They went to her for the less important outfits that they needed. Quite by accident, the boss had found out about it but she had restrained herself from admitting it. She was waiting for a series of orders to get out of the way without a snag before bringing the subject up with Geneviève. Ranging from a bridal gown, six bridesmaid's dresses, the mother of the bride and the flower girl's outfits, all had to be completed in less than three months.

Josephine had decided to let Geneviève go, using the excuse of being old and fatigued and that she wished to reduce her workload as well as her staff. Towards the end though, when one of her clients reported that Geneviève had dropped hints in the fitting room about making her clothes for less, Madame Joubert's patience ran out. She confronted her and, throwing her last pay in her face, she sacked Geneviève on the spot. Caught off-guard, Geneviève's face turned to a greyish white with resentment. Anger making her voice hoarse, she didn't leave the premises before spilling her venom first.

"You think I stabbed you in the back? Think again. Ever since they heard about your retirement plans, the girls can't wait to see your back so they can take over your business."

"Oh, yes? What retirement plans and how many girls are we talking about?"

"Everyone of them, from Eva, the snake in the grass, to the goody two-shoes Egyptian woman, and the good for nothing, harebrained Dina. And let's not forget Adrienne, the girdled cow, who has a closet full of copies of your patterns, not to mention a trunkful of your haberdashery that mysteriously go on missing every now and then."

"Apart from being a dishonest person and a compulsive liar, you are nothing but a big mouth and a lot of hot air. Now get out of here before I lose my temper," Josephine said, her tone changing from resentful to angry.

Livid, Geneviève stood there wanting to answer her back with a sharper, more biting comment, when, "allez vous en tout de suite," Josephine screamed, pointing her finger at the door.

Outside, Geneviève couldn't help remembering the way Madame Mercier had thrown her out of the door in Paris.

Since Geneviève had not received any reference letter from the House of Joubert, she was well aware that it would be useless for her to look for a job elsewhere. Her misconduct was bound to come up and ruin her chances of being hired in another fashion house. Her bruised ego was urging her to take the affront she had been subjected to and use it as an incentive to forge ahead. Her pride dictated her to throw caution to the wind and risk her life savings to prove her point.

Geneviève wanted so much to show everyone that she could easily equal and even outshine any other fashion designer out there. 'Madame Joubert and her gang will know the show is far from over when they hear about it. Josephine will just have to wait and see how her clients will desert her, one by one. Mark my word, I will have them all or I'll die trying to do that.' Those were the thoughts on Geneviève's mind the rest of the day until she went to bed, all hyped up with her plans of success. In the morning, she was calmer but not any less driven. "Let's put the show on the road," she told Aurore, after telling her daughter about her wish to be her own boss.

"Good luck maman," Aurore said, as she grabbed her books and left to go to school.

Recklessly, Geneviève went to see everyone on her list. She was more than ever determined to strive, to seek, to find. So she searched and found every place and everybody who could help her in her new undertaking. From bankers to solicitors and real estate agents, she shook hands with them all.

Two months later she was busy deciding the décor of her small but well positioned boutique, somewhere on Ocean Road in Double Bay. The workroom behind it had enough space to squeeze four industrial sewing machines. She had already placed an ad in the local papers hoping to find reliable machinists and a capable cutter. Everything was going as smoothly as possible. Her old clients were informed of her new place of business, so were some of Madam Joubert's regular customers who each received a note in their post box. Pamphlets were dropped at all the neighbouring houses too. It didn't take Geneviève too long, to say with confidence, that she was getting close to being known in the area. She believed she was on her way up, as for getting there, she just wished she could accelerate the process a little.

In that pre-holiday period, Geneviève worked as hard as it was physically possible to meet her clients' satisfaction. They all wanted to see their made-to-measure outfits ready for Christmas, and they did.

Christmas and New Year's Eve came and went, the boutique reopened with great expectations for the year to come but, after the yuletide rush, things didn't look so rosy. There were a few passers-by who came in once in a while to inquire about the off the rack garments as well as made to measure dressmaking but they usually left, hardly adding any outstanding amount of cash to the coffer. Geneviève had some irons in the fire and even though for the moment work prospects didn't seem too bright, she didn't allow her optimism to diminish. She ordered a lot of fabric and had some eye-catching numbers made to keep her workers busy and also to fill the boutique. Thinking that in all probability business would pick up again, she decided to stock up in preparation. She was ready to do anything to keep her dream from crumbling down but at the end of every week, when she looked at the books, she couldn't help feeling anxious.

Geneviève managed to sell a few unsubstantial items here and there but the expenses continued to be a lot higher than the earnings. Thinking about her present situation in a positive way was getting harder. Only a few days ago, crushing her hopes, her accountant had told her, "I understand you being jarred by what I am saying but the fact remains, you cannot keep on losing money. Unless you pull a new moneymaking scheme out of your hat, in the near future, I am afraid you have to close the shop."

Sensing Geneviève's distress, Charles, her cutter who had previously worked in a couple of rag trade factories, found the courage to make a suggestion. He advised her to take work from big manufacturers, "I mean, just to keep the workroom going until something better comes up," he said. Geneviève agreed and made a few phone calls that proved fruitful. Money started coming in, like a trickle unfortunately but it was enough to stay afloat. To Geneviève, it felt like doing forced labour.

One day, Aurore came home beaming from joy and all excited about getting her first modelling job.

"It's not much but it's a start," she said enthusiastically.

"I am glad for you, ma cherie," her mother told her as she kissed her smooth forehead. Aurore was offered more jobs, modelling dresses in shopping malls for big retail clothing shops. The money she earned from that couldn't have come at a better time. It helped pay for the things she needed for school and her mother couldn't always afford them when times were difficult. Geneviève was getting restless. Making up garments for other manufacturers was not exactly the thing she had dreamt of doing for a living. Her self-esteem badly bruised, she didn't know which way to turn. On many occasions, the thought occurred to her to phone her clients and find out where she was standing with them and every time her pride got in the way of actually doing it. She just hated the idea of crawling to them, because that's how they would interpret it. She would rather die than allow one of Josephine's girls to learn that her glamorous business had hit rock bottom.

The only customer Geneviève was sure to have a valid excuse for not showing up was Mrs Davenport. The poor woman was supposed to have a mastectomy straight after Christmas. 'She must have recovered by now,' Geneviève thought. Never exactly knowing what a woman undergoing such a rueful and dispiriting operation goes through, Geneviève shuddered at the thought of someone losing one of her breasts. Looking down at her perfect chest, "I am glad it's her and not me," she whispered when the phone rang, making her jump off her chair for some unexplained reason.

"Haute Couture Studio," she uttered, after a pause.

"Hello, this is Elaine Davenport," a very weak voice came from the other end of the line.

'Speaking of the devil,' Geneviève thought before answering.

"Hello Mrs Davenport, it's nice to hear from you, how are you feeling now?" she asked, still startled by the strange coincidence of the call.

"Thank you. I am not so bad, still a bit crook but I am recuperating. It was hard after the operation but thank God, I am getting better. The main thing is that it's over for the moment. Listen, the reason I phoned is that I have a favour to ask you and I hope you can help me with my problem. I have lost a fair bit of weight and have nothing to wear, nothing that doesn't fall off me, that is."

"No worries Mrs Davenport. I am sure we can take in the side seams of anything you wish to wear for the time being or maybe you are thinking of a new wardrobe," Geneviève asked hesitantly trying not to sound pushy.

"There is this charity function I am supposed to go to. Considering my health I am not really looking forward to it but it is imperative that I make an appearance, at least for the first few hours."

"Yes I understand your dilemma."

"I wonder if you could make me something in this short time if it is possible."

"Of course, everything is possible, when can you come."

"The fact is that I am not up to driving yet. Would it be possible for you to come to my house so we can discuss the details of the dress I would need? I would appreciate this immensely, you are not too busy I hope."

"I am never too busy for you, Mrs Davenport. I will bring my fabric swatches and my tape measure with me, now let me check and see when is the first available time," Geneviève said.

After a few seconds, pretending she was looking in her appointment book, "Actually I have a cancellation, I may be able to come this evening, but oh, no, my car is in the garage for repairs, excuse me a minute," she added, then called, "Charles, can you give me a lift to Wahroonga."

"Yes," a voice said from the room in the back.

"It's all right, Mrs Davenport, I'll be there at five o'clock."

"Oh! Thank you Geneviève, I'll be waiting for you, do you have my address?"

"Yes, are you still in Wahroonga Avenue?"

"Yes."

Clad in a cool, crisp dress, Geneviève walked through the big gate and went knocking on the door after Charles dropped her in front of the newly built Davenport mansion. A uniformed housemaid let her in and showed her to Elaine's bedroom on the upper floor. Looking around with curiosity and awe, Geneviève couldn't get over the beautiful things her eyes saw gathered under one roof and that was only a small part of the house that she happened to see. It took her and Elaine an hour and a half to decide on the fabric, the colour and the style of the dress while they sipped on their tea that the maid brought over to them. Exhausted, Geneviève was packing her things to leave when she heard the muffled sound of a car door closing gently. Minutes later she heard a masculine voice talking to the maid then the sound of footsteps coming up. "Can I get you something, Mister Davenport?" The maid said, from the bottom of the stairs.

"Not at the moment, thank you," the man answered. Geneviève was halfway through the doorway, ready to say goodbye to Mrs Davenport when her eyes met with those of the man of the house. Caught unprepared, she glanced at the well dressed and literally tall, dark and handsome man and, "Good afternoon," she blurted out.

"Good afternoon," he said then, turning to Elaine but his eyes still glued to Geneviève's face, "I didn't realise you had company, dear," he added apologetically.

"This is Geneviève De La Lande, the dressmaker I told you about yesterday. She was kind enough to come all this way to show me some sketches and fabric swatches."

"Nice to meet you Geneviève," he said shaking her hand, "sit down, please," he added, showing her a chair.

"And this is my husband Harold," Elaine went on without noticing that the tired face of her other half had lit up all of a sudden and that he had held Geneviève's hand a bit longer than etiquette would allow. Out of politeness, Geneviève put her bag and things next to the chair and sat down. Harold began asking her a whole lot of questions about her background and how did she like living in Australia. Eventually the subject of business came about.

"Business is not bad, there is always work for someone who is willing to make the effort. Nevertheless, unless you are sitting on a gold mine, no matter how hard you work, by the time you pay your rent, electricity, wages and all sorts of overheads, there is not much left," she said with a degree of sadness in her voice.

"Yes, that's the same with almost every business. There is also the matter of competition. It can be very tough in some lines of work."

"It is, but see, all the other boutique owners are usually ladies who are running it for their enjoyment. They consider it as a hobby, a pastime, a way to meet people and chat. They are having fun while they make a little pocket money on the side. Most have a husband capable of providing them a good living so, when business is slow, they can afford to sit and wait till it picks up again."

"I gather this is not your case," he asked, then after a pause, "is there a Mr De La Lande in the picture?" he went on with his query.

"My husband died two days after my ship landed in Australia."

"Oh! How awful," Elaine said, cutting into the conversation.

"I am sorry to hear this," Harold added compassionately, "it must have been rough starting your life in a foreign country, on your own."

"I managed. My daughter and I have been lucky so far."

Geneviève was enjoying talking to Harold but it was getting late. Rising to her feet, she gave her hosts the hint that it was time for her to leave. "I have to hurry if I want to catch the last bus that goes my way," she said politely.

"Didn't you drive here dear," Harold asked, looking out of the window as if to see whether a car was parked nearby.

"Not today, one of my employees gave me a lift but I have to find my own way back."

"No worries, I have to take some papers to show to a client. I can take you wherever you are going, if you don't mind waiting a bit. I just have to pick up the papers and we are out." Turning to his wife, "I may be late dear, don't wait up for me. I may have to grab something to eat at the office if the meeting goes on forever."

'In her early sixties, Elaine looks more like Harold's mother than his wife,' Geneviève couldn't help thinking on her way out of the Davenport mansion.

As the black Mercedes purred down the driveway and out onto the street, Harold turned to Geneviève and, contemplating her exquisite profile, he asked her for directions. Shyly she told him where she lived and urged him to drop her across the road and opposite of her street, "to save you time," she explained. Ever the gentleman, Harold wouldn't hear a word of it. He drove further, turned around, entered her street and insisted to stop right in front of her door.

Putting all the charm in her voice Geneviève began thanking him for his kindness when she felt his warm hand on her knee. "The pleasure was all mine Geneviève," he said, his hand persuasively still resting on her knee. She turned to look at him questioningly. The late rays of the sun shining though the windscreen were trapping the emerald green of her eyes beneath the lids. Her vision was blurred but that didn't prevent her from seeing the intensity of his gaze, as he was catching sight of her face, mesmerised by the classic beauty of her features. Suddenly aware of his unconscious act, Harold retracted his hand and apologised sincerely, looking like a child caught with his hand in the cookie jar. His embarrassment brought a smile to her face. Her sensuous lips half opened to say something but decided to keep silent.

"You have such a beautiful smile," he commented.

"Thank you," she said hurriedly while reaching for the handle to open the car door.

"I really don't have to go anywhere, no one to meet," he ventured to say; bringing her attention to the folder he had taken from home. "Is it all right if I asked you not to leave just yet? Don't get me wrong. I am only craving for company. I have a lot on my mind, a lot of decisions to make and Elaine, being sick and all; I have no one to talk to. It can be so stressful at times. I try to drown myself in my work but there must be more to life. A human being is not just what he or she is doing for a living," he concluded, a hint of discontentment in his tone.

"I'll vouch for that," she said in accordance.

"You said it with such conviction, is something lacking in your life too?"

"I don't have time for a private life. Except for my daughter, it's a big zero in other areas."

"You shouldn't work so hard, a beautiful, young woman like you deserves to have some fun and recreation once in a while."

"I can't see how."

Through her narrowed eyes Geneviève surveyed Harold for a bit wondering why they were having that conversation altogether.

Putting a philosophical air on his face, "You have to start by throwing away the negative thought pattern," he said, sitting back in his seat a little.

"Look who is talking, I was just going to advise you to do the very same thing. Stop, think, sort out your priorities and then act upon them. And throw away, as you said, all the irritating parts of your daily routine. See, I have a goal and I am working hard to achieve it, that's where I get my energy. Every now and then I get disheartened but I don't let it get to me. I never give up," Geneviève uttered with conviction.

"That's good, that's very good and I am sure you will get your wish some day if you persevere to keep your spirit up this way. With me, it's a horse of a different colour, but enough said, I don't want to burden you with my problems."

"As I was saying, I am trying to take my first step on the long path of success. You, on the other hand, can fill a book with your achievements, I have no doubt, judging by the way you live."

"I did achieve a few things, I can't deny that but, am I keeping you from something? Is your daughter waiting for you inside?" he asked worriedly.

"No, my daughter goes to evening classes, she won't be back until eight-thirty. Would you like a cup of coffee or something?" she asked, an idea brewing in her head.

"Are you inviting me in?" he asked in surprise, "I would love a cup of coffee," he added, unable to keep the eagerness out of his voice.

They entered the house in silence, him wrestling with his own thoughts and desires, her, wondering if it was wise to get so friendly with a good client's husband. 'Oh! What the heck,' she thought. In these times when her love life had taken a nosedive, she could do with the company of a man and Harold seemed to be a willing candidate. Anyway, he might have turned to her just seeking a sympathetic ear at the end of a frustrating day. For the time being he was there and that was enough. She was a vivacious, sexy woman and he was showing the all so familiar signs of being the kind of man who would go for a woman of her calibre.

Sipping coffee, Harold and Geneviève talked about everything and nothing but Geneviève managed to find out that he was an architect and that he had built the house he and Elaine were living in. She knew for sure that Elaine was enormously rich and had two children from a previous marriage. She had also learned that his marriage with Elaine must have put a couple of noses out of joint because his stepson had nicknamed him the gold digger. To Geneviève, Harold looked like a man in his early forties, except for his silvery side burns, the only indication that he could actually be older. Nevertheless, he must have been a lot younger than his wife and penniless perhaps to earn that nickname. "Now enough about me, let's hear your story," he had said, after his little heart to heart talk.

Geneviève didn't feel it was proper to whinge about her being on the brink of bankruptcy, since she was doing business with his wife, so she told him a little bit about Aurore. "You know how it is, a mother can't stop worrying about the safety and the future of her daughter. I am always busy, I wish I could spend more time with her instead of working so hard for money that comes and goes without letting you see the colour of it."

"Do you have enough clientele? It must be very difficult to be able to cut it, in this competitive world, especially when you are on your own with no one to assist you and give you moral support."

"Tell me about it," she said with a sigh, no longer able to play the dignified role of keeping face when you are financially embarrassed. Sensing a note of despair in her voice, Harold said then, "If I can be of any help, just let me know, would you? Better still, I will do some inquiries, talk to a few people in the trade. I have heard a lot of good things about the quality of your work. Obviously you are a woman of taste and refinement and I know you wouldn't dream of doing something that was less than perfect. All you need is a kick-start in a new direction. As you mentioned, one person cannot single-handedly run a successful business." Rising to his feet, he added in a reassuring manner, "I'll call you in a few days and tell you what I've learned," as he grabbed his car keys off her outdated, second-hand coffee table.

Her eyes glowing above her chiselled cheekbones, she said, "Thank you, I'll be waiting for your call," while she scribbled her phone number on a piece of paper. He kissed her high, rounded forehead and walked out to his car.

From the next morning onwards, whether she was at work or at home, Geneviève kept glaring impatiently at the telephone, willing it to ring. She waited five long days and was about to give up on him when he finally called. Going straight to the point, jovially, "I have some interesting news," Harold declared, then, "are you free this evening?" he asked eagerly.

"Yes, I'll be home after seven," she said.

"See you then," he said and hung up.

He rang the bell a bit after seven. As she let him in, his blue eyes met with hers in a direct frank gaze, putting an end to her suspicions that he was only there for reasons of a different nature. Dressed in her casual best, she didn't look like a woman waiting to greet a lover either. She was still of two minds about getting involved with him. "Is your daughter home?" he asked looking around.

"No, she is attending her evening class, she will be back at nine or so. Geneviève offered him a cup of tea with a slice of Aurore's left over birthday cake. He sat down and talked about trivial things that were irrelevant to the inquiries he was supposed to have done. She waited to hear the good news he had mentioned on the phone. At last he began tackling the subject. "My partner and I have been looking for a suitable place to build a small shopping complex. We are still looking without success but three days ago, in our search, we came across this old factory in Surry Hills. The place is not big enough for our project but it will be ideal for a clothing factory. It needs a bit of doing up of course, a lot actually, but I can say that it has possibility. Now, I have inherited some money from my aunt, bless her heart. If you are interested, we can join forces and together we can make this work."

"But I don't have any money for partnership."

"We won't be needing your money. As I said, I have the dough and you have the know-how, meaning you will only manage the place. We will hire the personnel needed to start with. Of course everything will be legal. We will start it small then and, God willing, we will let it grow. Our solicitors will draw up the papers and agree on the details, like deciding how much your contribution in the work is worth. They can calculate the percentage of the profit you are entitled to. Once we are both happy, we will get the ball rolling. I have already put a deposit on the place so it won't be shown to others. Oh! And before I forget, I would appreciate it if you didn't tell a word of this to my wife or anyone else, please. It is important to me," he said, searching her eyes to see if she understood.

"What about my boutique?" she asked, a little curious about his request.

"You can keep it for the time being, until we know what is going on. You can employ someone to help manage it. It will not hurt to sell the best pieces from the factory production in the shop anyway. The garments I have in mind to produce will have to be simple and easy to make, costing as low as possible, things that will appeal to a younger generation. More and more women are joining in the workforce. All these girls who will be working in the offices of the future will need to be dressed in chic but more affordable suits. I know you specialise in high-class work but that's not where the money is. What do you think? Will you at least consider it?" he asked, his voice vibrating with urgency.

"I'll think about it; right now I feel a little dazed by the whole idea, let me sleep on it a day or two," she said.

For a nervous moment, Geneviève thought he was a con artist trying to cheat her out of whatever he thought she had, or he was talking about something that could never happen. As tempting as it sounded, the idea couldn't be anything else but an absurd dream. Harold must have invented it to earn her trust and consequently get her in the sack, yet, one look at his open face and those childlike eyes told her otherwise. After all, what did she have to lose? Her business had hit rock bottom and the only way to go from there was up. She was definitely sick of worshiping money from a distance. So far, her dreams of prosperity had come hard up against reality.

The more Geneviève thought about Harold's proposal, the more she became convinced that it was not such a bad idea, but could they make it work, was a different matter.

Harold had given Geneviève his work number and had asked her again not to let anyone know about his plans. "Let's keep it between us, I will tell you why some day, if we end up working together. I am at a crossroad of my life at the moment. I need to be independent, that is why my wife and I no longer live in her house in Mosman. I hated the place anyway. It looked more like a mausoleum than a house. Her son is living in it now – the relentless sycophant – and he had the gall to call me a gold digger, while all the time, he was and still is sponging off his poor mother instead of earning his keep," he had told her.

The rest of the day and part of the night, Harold's words echoed in Geneviève's ears. In the morning, she phoned, "When can we go and see the site?" she asked.

"Whenever you are ready," Harold said calmly, kind of suspecting she wouldn't let an opportunity like that slip out of her fingers before looking into it closely.

The next time Geneviève set foot in the Davenport's residence it was for Elaine's first fitting. Once she entered the impressive heavy oak front door with its superb tinted glass sections, she noticed the pricey Persian carpet covering the floor of the large foyer. "Mrs Davenport will be with you shortly," the maid said, letting her in the living room.

While waiting for her client to appear, Geneviève had ample time to have a good look around and admire the décor. Besides the superb handpicked pieces of furniture, she spotted a few genuine paintings adorning the walls before letting her eyes travel and linger on the antique vases and figurines sitting on the coffee tables. Everything she saw was definitely worth a second glance and she couldn't help but to feel envious towards the lady of the house, just for the fact that she was able to live in that house. 'What is the problem between the odd married couple?' she wondered. 'And what did Harold mean when he mentioned his need to be independent? Was he preparing himself for a certain day when he could break himself away from his marriage? These questions kept floating in Geneviève's mind, as she was pinning the long and delicate sleeves on the armholes of Elaine's dress.

Geneviève was due to see her solicitor the next day and was confident he would advise her to go ahead with the deal. In her mind, she could already see doors opening in front of her. She had realised the lifestyle of the rich and was dead set to do her darnedest and go for it. It was impossible not to see Harold's proposal as a turning point in her fortune. In the little free moments she could find, she had filled a book with several new sketches of the outfits she would like to try for her first show.

That evening, when Harold examined the designs, he was pleased, really pleased with her work. He always had an eye for recognising that touch of genius in people and he was glad to be right about Geneviève's ability to deliver. He was glad he had not been wrong to trust his instincts. Closing the book, he nodded and admitted his delight with a big smile.

Soon after establishing their partnership, Harold couldn't wait to remodel and give a fresh look to the dilapidated old place. Geneviève used her time to interview and hire a group of machinists, both for indoor and outdoor work. An Italian lady by the name of Regina Martinelli who had come to Australia only recently had caught Geneviève's attention. Having a big family, Regina badly needed a job but she was over qualified to just sit behind a machine and run seams. She was a former student of Nada, a famous dress designing school in Rome run by a certain Concetta Boscolo.

Regina had also worked at the prestigious Shoubert Fashion House. Shoubert and his brother were well known designers to famous movie stars such as Gina Lolobrigida and Sophia Loren and the first ladies of many Eastern countries. The bad thing about Regina was that she had only five words in her English vocabulary and a few more in French. Regardless of the language barrier, Geneviève hired Regina to take care of the clients at the boutique and went on looking for a suitable person to manage the shop and be able to communicate with Regina.

With all the customers that Elaine and her friends were sending her way after the charity function, Geneviève needed a lot of help in the workroom. Elaine had been informed about Geneviève's endeavour to start a clothing factory and was meaning to congratulate and wish her luck; she had no idea that the silent partner who was financing Geneviève's new pursuit was none other than her own husband whom she hardly saw at home because of his demanding career.

Regina and the new Italian and English speaking lady, whom Geneviève had hired to manage the boutique, had just left. It had been a full day of teaching the two the way she expected them to run the place on their own. She needed to make sure she could count on them.

Everything was happening so fast in Geneviève's life that she didn't know where her head was at times. Finally she had a few minutes to herself. She sat down to have a cup of coffee in peace. Her eyes following the faint steam that escaped from the dark liquid and curled up before vanishing in the air, she began thinking about the new challenge life was presenting her with. No matter how worried she was, a voice inside her was telling her, 'this is only the beginning, the start of a journey to something big.' The phone rang in time to pull her out of her daydreaming and her illusions of grandeur. "The sewing machines will be delivered in an hour," Harold told her through interfering noises on the line.

"Do I have to be there?" she asked loudly, as if that would help clarify the bad connection.

"Only if you want to, but don't forget to tell Charles that he has to take whatever he needs for sleeping over there tonight. We can't risk being burglarised before we are properly insured."

"Yes, he knows what to do," she said before the line went dead.

Geneviève placed the receiver back on its cradle and returned to her coffee, her mind suddenly occupied by a feeling of dread and anticipation, of what ifs, like what if something goes wrong. She took a few more sips of her brew and felt slightly relaxed.

Harold was sitting on the edge of the desk in the office of Très Chic, the factory he had created with the help and output of Geneviève. He was attentively checking the figures on a sheaf of invoices. Once in a while, turning his attention away from them, he glanced at Geneviève's beautiful face surrounded by her glorious russet hair. She was resting in one of the two comfortable easy chairs in the room. A number of the latest fashion magazines were scattered around her feet. She had been peeking through them for inspiration. In the last few months, her sales representative had come with huge orders from the big department stores. To meet their urgent demands, she had to call in enough outdoor workers in order to ensure the completion of those garments in due time. And now, relaxing in the glow of her achievement, she was thinking of all the things she could do.

They had accumulated enough money to expand or invest. A dreamy smile on her face, she looked as if she was about to drift into sleep but she was awake. Eyes shut she could almost see the path of success blazing in front of her. In her mind, she was reliving the day she and Harold found themselves unable to hold back their desire to go that one step beyond being just two business partners. Until then, they had each followed their conviction that people who work together should never be involved with each other. 'It's bad for business,' she had kept telling herself. 'Maybe one day,' he had hoped. But it had happened.

It was the day, she recalled, that the rep came with the big orders. Geneviève phoned Harold and told him the good news. Knocking off work a little sooner, Harold rushed out to buy a bottle of wine and some savouries. He showed up at the factory looking like someone who had been informed he had won the first prize in the Opera House Lottery. On his way out, Charles put the lights off in the workroom. Apart from her and Harold, the place looked suddenly deserted. They were the only ones left on the premises. Grinning from ear to ear and brandishing the bottle, "We did it," Harold cried out.

"We did it," she murmured, closing her eyes in glee. They clinked their glasses and took a sip of their drinks. They both put their glasses on the desk and hugged. A simple hug it was, just to show their happiness, to acknowledge that they were on a winning streak. But that simple hug was enough to weaken their resolve in staying just friends. Holding her tightly, "I wanted to do this for so long," he said longingly, pressing her a bit harder against his chest. A smile crossing her full lips, "Really, what took you so long then?" she replied with an alluring voice.

"I was scared to spoil things between us," he answered before his lips went to lock with hers.

It started with a soft kiss, the first of many that followed, longer and more sensual kisses. Dropping to their knees on the newly carpeted floor, they began tearing their clothes off their restless bodies. He was kissing her one more time when, letting go of her face and her hair, his feverish hands began travelling down. Lingeringly, they reached and cupped each of her firm rounded breasts, the velvety texture of her skin taking him to the heights of ecstasy. All throughout those intense moments of intimacy, Harold was feeling like a wet behind the ears adolescent making love to an unattainable mythical goddess. Finally, out of breath, they laid there in silence. She turned onto her side and closed her eyes. His heart still thumping, he let his eyes sweep over her naked back. He lifted his hand and lightly caressed the supple line of her thighs. "I suppose we have to get dressed and go home," she said, breaking the silence.

"Unfortunately yes," he agreed, searching for the softness of her neck one more time. He gave her a few furtive kisses all over her face before he finally scrambled to his feet. They got dressed in a hurry and were ready to go. "See you tomorrow," she was about to say when Harold grabbed her in his arms and kissed her with so much more passion that it took her breath away. "Let's stay together, Gen."

"How do you mean?" she asked, unsure of his intentions.

"We will find a way, I can't live without you, Gen. I love you. You must have known that all along."

"I can't say I didn't," she whispered through half opened lips.

"Will you marry me if or when I get a..."

"Let's not be hasty, all right, this is not a good time to rock the boat," she added, holding her hand in front of him.

"I will do anything for you, you know that, don't you?"

"We will talk about this some other time, for the moment it's best that we concentrate on getting the new orders on the road."

The next six weeks happened to be so hectic, both at the factory and at Harold's workplace that every time Harold showed up, they could only talk about business and nothing else. Aurore had also started to come home at unpredictable times so Harold and Geneviève couldn't meet in her house. They were only able to steal a few minutes here and there for a kiss and a cuddle. They were rarely able to stay back in the office to take their eagerness a little further. Occasionally when they didn't have company, Harold had tried to reopen the awkward subject but every time she had found a way to leave his question unanswered by diverting his attention elsewhere. Her attitude not adding up, Harold had begun wondering if she ever had any romantic feelings for him.

Geneviève's shilly-shallying was mainly due to the fact that she remembered Harold mentioning, a long time ago, something about a certain prenuptial agreement he had signed prior to his marriage. It said that he wouldn't get anything from his wife should there be a divorce. That was mostly to prove to Eton, Elaine's son, then in his teens, that he wasn't marrying his mother for her money. Geneviève had kept Harold in suspense thus far because she wasn't sure if tying the knot with him was a sensible thing to do. In her calculating mind, getting hitched to a man who, after an unpleasant divorce, would walk out of his marriage with only a suitcase and some diplomas was not the best of moves. She couldn't help remembering her union to Yanis and how she felt relieved when it dissolved by itself with his death. She loved her freedom far too much to give it up without getting something out of it.

No longer struggling against impossible odds, Geneviève wouldn't worry her pretty head for anything that didn't have a dollar sign attached to it. She had enough money in the bank to make her feel less intimidated. The seed she had planted by going into business with Harold had truly flourished yet her ambition and appetite for success were far from being fully satisfied. Geneviève's biggest wish was to, one day, buy Harold's share and be the sole owner of Très Chic. She was living for the day she could at last see herself placed firmly in the driver's seat. Of course nothing was wrong with the two of them having an affair, as long as his wife was left in the dark about it.

Once again Harold and Geneviève were left alone in the office. They had just started to talk business when the phone rang, making her jump off her seat. 'Who could it be?' she asked herself, stretching her arm to get the receiver. It was Benson, Harold's associate, the only person who knew about Harold's part in Très Chic. After exchanging a few words with the caller, Harold grabbed his jacket from the back of his seat and said, "There seems to be some kind of emergency at home, can you please close shop," and then rushed out without waiting for her reply.

Geneviève began putting the desk in order when she heard a knock at the door. She went to answer it thinking Harold had forgotten something when a stranger pushed his foot through the front entrance and, inviting himself in, walked into the office and threw his cigarette in the ashtray sitting on a stand next to the door. An involuntary shudder going through her, Geneviève asked , "Who are you and what do you want?" as she grabbed an umbrella from the corner with the intent to use it if she had to defend herself from the intruder.

"So you are the French trollop Harold baby is shacking up with," he said, leering at her from tip to toe.

"Shut your mouth and get out before..."

"Before what? Don't you want to know who I am before giving me my marching orders? I am Eton."

"And I am the Queen of Sheeba, now out," she yelled.

"Eton, Elaine Davenport's son," he stressed, waiting to see her reaction.

"Oh! That Eton. You mean the freeloader who sponges off his ailing mother instead of earning his living."

Trying to say something to squash her biting comment, "I see you had a little bit of informative pillow talk with good old Harold. So the old boy couldn't wait to share all the juicy gossips with his whore."

"How dare you, no bastard will call me names, get out of here right now," she yelled again, her blood boiling.

"Oh, no? What are you then, just a plain garden variety husband snatcher, hem?"

Putting all the disdain she could muster into her voice, she uttered, "What I am is my business. What is it, are you jealous or something?"

"Don't flatter yourself," the man said, ogling her again. "And it is my business when it concerns my mother," he added.

"I have a great deal of respect for your mother and I feel sorry for her to be lumbered by a parasite like you. Actually, sycophant was the word Harold used to describe you. A son who is not ashamed to let his sick mother cough up for all his debauchery."

"We are not talking about me, we are talking about you and you're a kind of shameless opportunist who will use any sort of trick to entrap gullible married men. I don't blame you, what he is worth can bring all sorts out from under their rocks. And you my dear, you are no exception, no sirree. No one can say no to ye old lucre, as they say."

"What lucre, didn't you make him sign a pre-nuptial agreement before he married your mother?"

Looking at her through half closed eyes, and as if talking to himself, "Yes but that was sixteen years ago. Now he doesn't need her money, since lady luck had been on his side. The rascal, his mother dies and he is left with their family home full of antiques, not to mention those bounteous shares in big companies which he sold to build the house they are living in," Eton blabbered, unaware that those revelations were news to Geneviève's ears. "And as if that wasn't enough, the lucky devil inherits acres and acres of land in Galstone and a chunky sum of money from his old aunt. Now, let's be frank, is it him that you have your eyes on or his windfalls, because if you say you are not after his money I won't believe you. I happen to know your brand of woman," he continued to let slip out of his mouth.

"I don't have my eyes on anything, but since we are on the subject, let's be frank. Tell me why are you so interested in Harold's affairs all of a sudden? Don't tell me that you have his best interest at heart and that you are not shaking in your boots at the possibility of a divorce between him and your mother. Now wouldn't that be a shame if she returned home? No more freedom, no more wild parties for you. I bet that would feel like a kick in the teeth if you had to share the mansion with a sick old woman left in your care. Where will you entertain all your promiscuous friends, you poor thing?"

Eton's face turned ashen with contempt, he came to answer her back but Geneviève attacked him with some more home truths.

"What is it now, you can dish it out but you can't take it, who is the opportunist then, you or me? Answer me."

"I love my mother, I'll have you know," he could only manage to say at the end.

"Sure you do and pigs can fly too, and for your information, Harold and I are not shacking up, we are here running a legitimate business. Your private eye should have been more thorough with his findings. Next time get your facts straight before shooting your mouth and making accusations. Now that you have said what you came here to say, get out, out," she ordered him haughtily, pointing the end of the umbrella in the door's direction. Feeling outmatched, Eton resorted to a bit of jocularity to cover up his defeat.

"How about a kiss for the road then?"

"Get out I said, out before I knock the light out of your miserable life," she said, threatening him with the umbrella again.

"I am going, I am going," he said, putting a phoney scared look on his face, then added, "They say you should look for snakes before you pee in the bush. I know now what this saying means."

"You are full of it, aren't you?"

Eton's ploy to get Harold out of the factory so he could pay Geneviève a surprise visit didn't get him anywhere but she benefited from it. She ended up with the knowledge that Harold owned the big house and probably most of the contents. She had also learned that he had inherited a lot more from his aunt and was in fact substantially wealthier than he had led her to believe. That notion distinctively put a different complexion on things. It had her mind in a spin all the while she was driving home and in the evening as she was nursing Aurore who had come home with a bad cold. And to think that she was giving Harold the run around because she thought he had nothing much to offer her except his monthly pay and maybe some other benefits from his architectural job.

Geneviève had come a long way since her ship had landed in Sydney but all her efforts and smart-aleck moves had not yet given her the ticket to shoot to the level she was aiming at. She wondered if Eton had any idea that he had given her vital information about Harold's personal wealth and if he did, would he go to him and make an issue of it. In case Harold was still willing to be with her, she had to secure her place by letting him presume that she had said yes to his request without knowing how much he was worth. She thought of several ways she could bring him to reopen the old subject of their staying together. She also came up with a few damage control ideas, just in case anything happened to go contrary to her plans.

First Geneviève had to determine if the problem that had Harold rush home had anything to do with her. There was a possibility that Elaine had been informed about her involvement with Harold and was declaring war to him. She had to find out where she was standing with Harold, then, using her charm, make him want to be with her badly enough to leave his wife and marry her.

Harold used to show up once a day at the factory or at least he used to give her a call, just to touch base. Two days had passed and Geneviève had not seen or heard from him. She was worried sick and the machinists, particularly the sample maker, had to bear the brunt of her bad mood. Geneviève's edginess nearly cost her a valuable employee if it wasn't for Charles' capabilities of handling and sorting out awkward situations.

It was almost closing time when the phone rang. It was Harold telling her that he had to stay home to ward off a full-fledged attack of the flu. He sounded terrible. Between coughs and sniffles, he managed to put her mind at ease, "See you in a few days or whenever I am over this cold," he said.

"I wish I could be there to nurse you back to health."

"I do too. I am missing you an awful lot, Gen. I can't wait to see your pretty face again."

"I am missing you too," she said then asked if he was alone at home.

"Yes, Elaine had an appointment with her therapist and I sent the maid out on an errand, so I could call you."

"What was the emergency that made you run home the other day?" she asked casually.

"There was no emergency, the message must have been for someone else. When I arrived home everything was all right."

"Take good care of yourself darling and call me as soon as you can," she said with a kind tone.

"I think someone is back, I'd better say goodbye," he said and hung up.

Harold was on his feet again and every time he went to see Geneviève, he was surprised to find her so responsive to his desires. His heart melting by her amorous glances, everything about her was telling him that she was as much in love with him as he was with her. Giving another look at every one of the six little trinkets hanging from the heavy gold chain he had brought to give her, he entered the office at the end of the day. After a furtive kiss, he sat her down and, once again, he told her that he couldn't live without her. He then asked her if she would share her life with him. Wasting no time, her green eyes blazing with delight, Geneviève said yes, happy that Eton hadn't spoiled things for her.

Harold's car was far enough from the house and the coast was clear for Eton to knock at the Davenport's door. As soon as he entered, without preparing his mother for the shock, he told her about his discovery. He felt compelled to let her know of her husband having an extramarital relationship with her dressmaker. Unfortunately, his good intention backfired and left him aghast when Elaine told him calmly that she already knew about it.

"And what have you decided to do to get the slut out of his life? Surely you can persuade her to take her hands off him."

"I don't see why I have to do such a thing," she said flatly.

"I don't understand you mother, whatever happened to hell hath no fury like a woman scorned?"

"You remind me so much of your father."

"In what way?"

"He couldn't say anything without using a saying."

"I mean, mother, will you sit down and let the opportunist seduce and steal your husband?

"If that is his wish...."

"Don't you care about him?"

"I do, but if he is ready to be seduced he will be, by Geneviève or someone else. Don't tell me you care about him now, you used to call him the gold digger, remember?"

"So I was wrong about him but that doesn't excuse her, she is still not a saint and you have to put her in her place."

"Leave that to me son. Harold has been good to me and I don't intend to do anything that will bring him pain. I love him far too much to wish him anything other than contentment."

Harold arrived home all tensed up. He went up the stairs slowly. He was gasping for air with every step he climbed. He remembered the day of his wedding with Elaine, the strong-willed, glamourous socialite who had fascinated him with her charm and witty conversations. She had told him, just before the ceremony, "If things don't work out between us, there is no reason for any of us to grin and bear it. All we have to do is to speak up then, without any hard feelings, we can solve problems or decide to go our separate ways. There is no need to make each other miserable by staying married if the spark has gone out of our union." Nevertheless, Harold was finding it hard to go to his wife and remind her of the pact they had made sixteen years ago. He was at the top of the stairs, composing himself when, "Is that you Harold?" he heard his wife call from the bedroom.

"Yes, it's me," he said, entering cautiously.

"Get something to eat then come back here Harold, we have to talk," she said in her usual sedate voice.

"It's all right dear, I am not so hungry," he uttered wondering what was on her mind and would that stop him speaking his mind.

Trying to hide his sombre mood, Harold nervously wiped the sweat off his brow and sat on the edge of the bed, waiting for Elaine to tell him what was bothering her. Somehow he had a feeling that Eton or someone else had found out about his connection with Geneviève and had alerted Elaine. He felt a great deal of guilt for wanting to leave her at that crucial time when she needed him most, but his love for Geneviève was stronger. Going straight to the point, Elaine began with, "Harold my love, I can't thank you enough for all the kindness you showed me during my sickness and all the love and support you gave me throughout the years we were married. I got sixteen absolutely glorious years with you and that was more than I expected to get from life, considering the age difference between us. I feel that the time has come for me to set you free. That is if you so desire."

"What do you mean?" Harold asked, not believing his ears.

"I mean you are free to go live your life the way you want it. I'll call the lawyers and start the divorce proceedings and I'll move back to my house as soon as the papers are signed. You have my blessing so go and be happy. I am sure the young woman you have chosen has the power to give you all the love and happiness that you deserve."

Flabbergasted, Harold rose to his feet, unable to stop the batting of his eyelids.

"I don't know what to say Elaine," he said then, bending down, he kissed her forehead, "thank you, you are an angel, a true angel," he added, holding her hand firmly.

"Don't be a stranger though, you know you can come to me if you need to talk, I will always be your friend."

"I know," he said before letting go of her hand.

Taken aback by Elaine's graceful act, Harold couldn't help feeling sorry and indebted to her, especially that she never even mentioned Geneviève's name. With just a few words, she had spared him the agony of opening up to her and to ask her to give him his freedom.

Chapter 11

Alice Yousif was an Assyrian girl who lived in Sydney Australia with her parents and her twin brothers. Her father was from Iraq but her mother was born in Iran. The family could barely get by with Mr Yousif's salary and what the mother was earning in her part-time job. They lived in a home unit close to Fairfield's shopping centre. Mrs Yousif had an elder sister called Cecilia who had moved to America with her husband a few years after they were married. The pair had never been blessed with children and, after the husband's sudden death, which had happened in a work related accident, Cecilia was left with a fairly big house and a lot of money. To people who knew her, Cecilia had the reputation of being a bit careful with her money.

Alice was seventeen years old when, before Christmas, she decided to send her aunt a greeting card in which she cheekily wrote that if ever her lottery ticket happened to win something big, she would love to go to America and visit her. Alice had never bought any lottery ticket to have the chance of winning but that card made luck magically shift to her side. Three weeks later, she received a letter from her aunt. In it there was a return airline ticket to Los Angeles with Alice's name on it. Alice was over the moon; nothing like that had ever happened to her. Good old aunt Cecilia wasn't so mean after all, she thought. This was the first time that she had something she didn't have to hand over or share with her twin brothers, as it had been the norm in their household.

To Alice's father, girls held second place in the house. In his eyes, the twins were God's gift to the family and everything good had to be theirs first and Alice had no say whatsoever in that matter. Anyway, aunt Cecilia had also mentioned in her letter that it would be better if Alice used her ticket in summer time, because they could go to Chicago and visit the other relatives they had there. She had explained that her arthritic pains would probably give her trouble in a city that would probably be covered with snow all throughout the winter months.

Alice did exactly that. She got her passport and visa ready and, on a warm and sunny day her plane landed in Los Angeles. After staying a week or so at her aunt's place, the two left for Chicago. A few days later, one of Cecilia's cousins took them to a party organised by Chicago's Assyrian Association. Chaperoned by her aunt, Alice went from group to group of people and was introduced to the rest of their relatives and other fellow Assyrians. Alice had always been a skinny girl by nature, one of those rare individuals that people believed could eat all they want but never put on weight. Maybe it was a case of opposites attract or it was Matthew Sarkis'lot that their eyes met across the crowd and, as they say in fairy tales, their gazes locked and their lives entwined together. It seemed the two had fallen in love instantaneously.

Matthew had not planned to be at that party in the first place and he surely didn't intend to dance that night. It had only been a few months since they had buried his father and, thinking it wasn't the proper thing to do, he had declined his friend's suggestion to go with them.

Somehow Jenny found out about the whole thing and, not only did she not object to her son having a bit of a good time, she even encouraged him to feel free to consider going. "It's all right my son, you are not expected to mourn forever. Nothing will bring your father back, we all know that, so go and enjoy yourself. Life is short and you will be young only once," she had told him. So there he was shaking hands with Alice.

Matthew was surprised to find himself, not only smiling at Alice but small talking with her, only minutes after his arrival. The newly assembled band began playing Assyrian music and at least one third of the people present rushed to participate in the dance. Seizing the opportunity, tightly clenching his hand in hers, Alice practically dragged Matthew onto the dance floor. Matthew felt awkward since he didn't know how to dance but she didn't let go of him. Finally the music stopped and the two retreated to a corner where they chatted for a good part of the evening with aunt Cecilia watching them from afar. No one noticed the change but it seemed that, away from her father's objectionable influence, the restricted and somehow victim-ised Alice had grown wings right under everyone's eyes. Amongst people who had met her for the first time, she had managed to assume a new personality. In fact, she was transformed into this outgoing and sweet-talking girl who, in no time, had Matthew smitten and wrapped around her little finger.

The two lovebirds met each other a few more times after that night. Matthew, the boy who had always been a bit gauche around women, had come to believe he had found the girl of his dreams. The last time they were together, he casually told Alice that some day he might fly over to visit her and also to see Australia, because he had heard so much about it.

Her visa expiring, Alice had to return home. After she left, Matthew began missing her. He decided to tell his mother about his desire to travel to Sydney but he didn't know how to bring up the subject without having to mention Alice. He feared his mother would take it as a desertion and lack of responsibility towards her and his sister. Finally one day he gathered enough courage and, beating about the bush for a while, he told her how people were praising life in Australia. Jenny was not foreign to his little romance with Alice, gossipmongers had seen to that and she had asked the necessary questions to have a better idea about it. She decided to spare him the humility of asking by giving him the opportunity to express his wish. "Matthew, I was thinking, wouldn't it be wise if you took some time off work, we can manage without you in the diner, I am sure," she started casually.

"What for, mum?" he asked nervously.

"I though it would be a good idea if you went to Australia and saw the place for yourself. Check the Down Under, I believe that's what people call that country nowadays."

"Do you mean it mum?"

"Yes, it's worth a try and if you like it, I can't see why we can't all go, I mean move there for good. If it is as good a place as everyone keeps saying, we can sell everything and just go. I don't think we will have any problems doing that."

"I didn't think you would consider taking such a big step," Matthew interrupted, not believing his ears.

"We left Iran, didn't we? And son, it is not a secret that my heart is not in America any longer. Since your father was taken from us in such a cruel way, I'd rather be somewhere where the horrible memories of his death won't be haunting me as much as they do here."

Never recovering from the shock of her husband's senseless killing, Jenny had indeed been constantly looking over her shoulders in Chicago. She hadn't been able to stop worrying for her children's safety, so she made it easy for her son to make that trip. She even talked to him about Alice and reassured him that she would love nothing more than to see him happily settled with the girl of his choice.

Matthew left for Australia with a considerable amount of money. In fact it was most of the cash his mother could spare from her savings. "This is part of your inheritance, be extra careful with it. In case if you decide to stay there, use this money to put a deposit on a good house. On the other hand, if things don't work out the way you wanted them to or you don't find life in Australia interesting, transfer the money back and return home," she had told him before his departure. To her disbelief, Matthew had listened to her attentively and had promised that he would not disappoint her. He had even thanked her for her thoughtful advice.

Four months after his trip to Australia, Matthew married Alice in a small and private ceremony. His mother and sister were not able to fly over for the wedding. Clara had exams and Jenny couldn't leave her home alone. There was also a matter of organising the anniversary of Danny's death and the crisis of the cook being away from work because he had to sort out a certain family problem.

As his mother had suggested, Matthew put most of his money towards a three bedroom house in Fairfield. He was working as a store manager in the straight to the public sale's section of a factory that was manufacturing light fittings. He had a good salary but that job wasn't what Matthew had in mind to do for the rest of his life. He always dreamt of being his own boss. Like his father, he liked to be self-employed and not to have to answer to anybody else. He kept inquiring about various small business possibilities and decided that if and when he had enough money, he would open a gift shop. He was also waiting to find out what were his mother's plans about moving to Australia. Being married to an Australian citizen, Matthew had a better chance to apply for permanent residency. Eventually he was accepted to stay as a migrant and was able to begin the process of bringing his family over. He couldn't wait to see them settled in Australia, especially after knowing about his wife's pregnancy.

Matthew had given Jenny the thumbs up about his adopted new country and ever since, leaving America had been on Jenny's mind. Nevertheless, for some unknown reason she had kept procrastinating in taking the first step. As if she wasn't the same motivated person, lately she just couldn't find enough energy in herself to do her normal everyday chores. She had started to feel discomfort over her abdomen and experienced ill-defined digestive disturbances. For the last eight months, she had been taking drugs for a peptic ulcer that she had developed but recently things were getting a little more complicated. Clara and everyone else at the diner, seeing her drink antacid liquids straight from the bottle, had kept nagging her and urging her to consult a doctor and seek proper medication. "You can't continue ignoring it, you are not well," they had kept telling her.

"I'll be alright, I am just a bit over worked that's all. Soon business will get quieter then I'll take a few days off," had always been her answer. And so Jenny kept dilly-dallying and hiding her more doubtful symptoms as much as she could. One of those was a bad backache for which she kept rubbing various ointments on the tender area and slept with a hot water bottle stuck to her back, but the pain persisted. Apart from her strength, Jenny was also losing weight. She had no appetite for certain foods, particularly meat, and had a feeling of fullness after eating the smallest amount of food. When Clara inquired about that, she told Clara, "Well I am not complaining, I always wanted to be slim but couldn't stick to any diet," pretending she was happy about her emaciating figure.

Jenny and Clara were informed a few months earlier that Alice was pregnant. Finally, on one of the first days of December, Jenny received a telegram from Matthew. He was telling her the good news that she was the grandmother of a pair of baby boys and that Alice and their sons, James and Jason, were all doing well. Jenny and Clara celebrated the birth of the twins in the privacy of their own home. The next day, they sent lots of nice presents for the babies and their parents. However, the good news didn't get to lessen Jenny's persistent pain. Her symptoms became more pronounced and worrisome, especially when she began experiencing nausea and vomiting.

In a state of panic, Jenny had no choice but to consult a physician who sent her straight away to a specialist. After putting her through a lot of sophisticated yet unpleasant tests, the specialist found disturbing signs shown in the X-rays, indicating the possibility of cancer developing around the existing ulcer. He suggested exploratory surgery to assess the extent of the illness and decide on ways to tackle the problem. Jenny tried to put Clara's mind at ease.

"It will only be a simple operation, I assure you. The doctors just want to see if they can get rid of the ulcer once and for all. I'll be all right darling, you'll see," Jenny told her and insisted that there was no reason for her to worry.

After the operation, the doctor went to visit Jenny in the intensive care unit. "I am afraid Mrs Sarkis, the cancer has spread to your pancreas as well as your small intestines. This may explain the backaches you are having, unfortunately the situation is not an easy one to be dealt with. I have discussed your case with a couple of my colleagues and we unanimously believe that it is inoperable," he told her in no uncertain terms.

Jenny was pretty much expecting to receive some unsettling news but to hear that the doctors had washed their hands of her had bowled her over. Her biggest concern was how her children would react to the fact that her days were numbered. The plug had been taken off her hopes of recovery so her sickness was no longer something she could cover up.

"Isn't there anything anyone can do for it, any last resort?" she began asking the doctor.

"There are a few good drugs on the market that I can prescribe for you, they will alleviate your pain temporarily but, by all means, if it's your wish to get a second opinion, feel free..."

"I get the picture, I am dying and if that's the case, I don't see any point in being poked and prodded unnecessarily. I'd rather have my illness take its usual course."

"I understand Mrs Sarkis. In the meantime, please try to rest and see your general practitioner whenever you need anything."

"Now tell me doctor, how long do I really have? I must know. I have to sort out a lot of things before I kiss this world goodbye. I have to prepare my daughter and prevent her from being affected by my death; her safety and her state of mind are my biggest concern, so can you tell me doctor," she asked again, trying to hold herself together.

The, I am not really sure look on the doctor's face, more than answered her question.

In the following weeks, Jenny went through all the stages that people with terminal diseases go through. From denial to anger and hope for some sort of a miracle cure then, search for an alternative medicine and eventually feeling extremely depressed, she experienced them all. Only behind drawn curtains could she sob openly when she was on her own. Then came the last phase when she came to accept her fate. She accepted that death was also a part of a natural life. The inevitable was drawing near. Even though telling Clara and Matthew about the hopelessness of her illness was something that Jenny had been dreading all along, it had to be done. With the help of her strong pain killers, she waited a few more days until Clara's fifteenth birthday passed then, one afternoon, she told Clara, "I need to go to church, I want to light some candles for your dad, you know."

"I'll go with you," Clara said, sensing something unusual and pressing in her mother's voice.

"Thank you dear. I was just going to ask you that."

Inside the church, mother and daughter knelt and prayed together. Afterwards, they walked out to the garden behind the church building. It was a fine day and the sun that was shining through the foliage of the trees could have made it a relaxing one, in better circumstances. Mother and daughter sat on a bench placed under a gigantic oak tree and kept silent for a while. Strongly aware that her mother hadn't taken her there for nothing, Clara turned and looked Jenny straight in the eyes. "Mum, what is it, why are we here?" she asked her in a firm tone.

Jenny didn't waste any time; another second and she probably wouldn't have the courage to utter a word so she abruptly went to the point.

"Clara, there is no easy way to tell you this, I am dying, I have cancer," she said, without looking at her daughter.

For a split second, Clara stared at the void, feeling as though her heart had been ripped out of her ribcage then took a deep breath. Digging her nails in the fleshy part of her arms, she pressed hard, hoping that the pain would prevent her from screaming. Swallowing with great difficulty, her body numbed, she pushed her head back and lowered her lashes, unable to say a thing. Desperately she tried to close her mind and keep the words she had just heard out, but she couldn't dismiss the fact that her mother wouldn't say such things if they were not the absolute truth.

After a draining silence that seemed like an eternity, Jenny noticed a single tear shining in the corner of Clara's eye. She held her daughter's hand in hers and softly caressed it. "I need you to be brave, Clara darling, I lived a good life. I had the best family. Truly, I was given more than any woman would desire and if this is God's will that I should join your father I should look forward to it. Together we may be able to keep an eye on you and on your brother. By the way I want you to talk to Matthew and tell him I want to see him before..."

"Before what mum? You are not going to die, there must be a cure," Clara said while, 'Isn't there any hope?' her eyes were asking.

Jenny understood and, shaking her head, she lovingly looked in her daughter's eyes.

"It's all right, it's you that I am worried about. I don't want you to be alone. I am sure that you are capable of taking care of yourself. You are more mature and level headed than any other girl your age, nevertheless, I would be happier if you lived with people I know and trust."

"I would still feel lonely without you," Clara said as she wiped her eyes.

"You'll be all right."

"Why us mum? After what happened to dad, I thought I was lucky to have you at least. I thought you were indestructible, always there for me, like a tower of strength."

"You were my tower of strength too, my darling girl. I wish I could live long enough to see you get married and have your own life. My only regret is that I will not be able to see your children. Clara, I have thought a lot about your future and I don't think that Chicago is a good place for you to live," Jenny said with a sigh and then went on. "Given the circumstances, I believe it's best if you went to Australia and stayed close to your brother, even if it's for a trial period. I am sure he is missing you too, and being around children may also be beneficial for you. As for Alice, although you have never met her, she may turn out to be a good friend after all, like the sister you never had. I wish you'd give the matter some thought."

Clara listened to her mother then nodded approvingly.

"Mum, I will do whatever you say but now, allow me to help you. Please, don't hold anything back from me, whatever you need, just ask me. Whenever you need me, don't hesitate to let me know. I don't want you to suffer on your own, trying to spare my feelings. We are in this together and together we will try to face it. We will deal with it one day at the time," she said in a trembling voice, visibly distraught.

As the days ticked away, Clara stayed at her mother's side, leaving her only to go on important errands. The bond already existing between them until then became even stronger as though they were sharing one single soul in their two separate bodies. Together, they took care of all the necessary changes around the house and the diner. Clara stood behind Jenny like a rock. Feeling like she was dying inside, she carried her pain within. Pain so unbearable that, at times, she feared she couldn't take it any longer but she found the force to keep her anguish to herself.

In a short time Jenny and Clara managed to sell their most valuable furniture and object d'art they had accumulated over the years. For a bargain price, Danny had purchased a large piece of land years ago. They sold that too and made an unexpected profit.

Thinking of Matthew and considering the tension there was between him and her cousins, Jenny decided to leave her son another big sum as the rest of his share of inheritance. The house and the diner were therefore bequeathed to her daughter. "I want you to have a place to come back to, when or if things don't work out with you and your brother. Also times are not favourable for selling properties right now," she had explained to Clara who couldn't care less about what she would be left with after her mother was dead and buried.

"Anyway, I had a talk with my cousins, they are more than willing to stay on. Together, they will run the diner." Jenny said.

"Do they know about the nature of your sickness?" Clara asked.

"Yes, I told everyone the day after I told you."

In fact, Jenny had gathered all the staff around after work and had told them all they had to know. Robert and George, overcome with sorrow, were left speechless for a while. Finally, when the reality had started to sink in, realising the gravity of the situation, they had given their solemn promise that they would do whatever she wanted them to. They were given more responsibilities and a big pay rise. The two had to report regularly to Mr Brighton, who in turn, had to take care of the financial side of things. He was supposed to send Clara regular cheques from the diner's takings, and the rent the house would bring.

"As I was saying, I have already discussed the matter with our lawyer. He has agreed to help and supervise you, should you need any further assistance in making decisions. Mr Brighton will be here tomorrow and we will talk some more about the small details. Anyway, he has to keep you up to date whenever something unusual is happening. Meanwhile, should the market improve, he has to inform you and sell the business or the house as soon as you give him the go ahead," she continued uttering in a trembling voice.

While the cancer was aggressively invading her body, Jenny said goodbye to her daughter almost every day, as if that day was her last. With all the energy left in her, she gave Clara a few last motherly advices on any subject she could think of, until the day they had to rush her to hospital. Her tired body attached to all sorts of tubes, for three whole days, Jenny kept waiting, her eyes asking for her son but

Matthew never arrived. Eventually, she slipped into coma without seeing him. Her heart heavy, her eyes dry, Clara kept a constant vigil at her mother's bedside. A lot of people came to see Jenny. They waited outside the door, not knowing if there was anything that they could do to help.

After Clara's phone call and the telegram that George had to send, everybody believed that Matthew would show up any minute. "I will do my best to get away and come," he had said, genuinely saddened by the news he had heard about his mother's condition. Forty-eight long hours passed and Jenny's time ran out. Nestled in her daughter's arms, quietly life seeped out of her tired and debilitated body.

During the heart wrenching times of her mother's illness, Clara tried hard to keep herself collected and in control. As her mother took her last breath, she felt free to exhibit her grief. She cried like she had never cried before. She cried all the tears she had held back for so long.

Still unable to really make sense of her loss, Clara accepted the fate that had befallen on her. She dialled her brother's number one more time, thinking he might not be there, but he answered the phone. When she told him what had happened, she could only hear him sob on the other end of the line. "I will call and tell you why I couldn't come," he just managed to say before he hung up.

Clara was torn to pieces with sorrow and loneliness, yet she still managed to thank all the mourners who came to present their last respects to Jenny. They did nothing but praise that courageous woman. They told a lot about her good nature and her unselfish behaviour towards everyone with whom she had come in contact. After the funeral, Clara and Matthew had a long phone conversation during which she told him about her decision to go to Australia. Matthew assured her that she was welcome in his house and that he was looking forward to seeing her.

Within the next few months, Clara had to ready herself for her long journey. It was her mother's wish that she went and lived with

Matthew and she was determined to give it a go. Still, now that she was so close to meet with Alice, she began wondering about her sister-in-law's character. Clara wasn't sure what kind of reception she would get from her. All she knew about Alice was whatever she had seen in the few wedding photos and a couple more that were sent to them after the birth of the twins. From those snapshots, she had gathered that Alice was a very skinny woman with light brown hair, a palish complexion and a face with no particular beauty to brag about.

With the help of her cousins, Clara sold the last items left in the house and changed the family car to George's name. In the meantime, Mr Brighton sent Matthew a cheque and a note telling him to accept that as the rest of his inheritance. "The first amount your mother had given you when you left America and this cheque are equal to today's price of what Clara could get from the sale of the house, and the diner that were left for her," he had explained.

When Matthew read the note and saw the sum on the cheque, he couldn't be more content with his share. His first thought was to start the business he always wished to own. Luckily, in a quiet street in his suburb, a shop was on the market. Matthew went for it and, as soon as the deal was closed, he was able to begin putting up the appropriate fittings for a gift shop. He worked hard to get it started and succeeded to a point, with a few tricks of the trade that he had acquired back in America. Like a child, he was all excited about it and, being busy helped him cope with the loss of his mother.

Matthew couldn't wait for his sister to arrive. He needed her approval at selecting the right merchandise for his shop and he wanted her to see how clever he was at decorating the window. Thankfully his wife never showed any enthusiasm in that regard because he dreaded to see her poke her nose in his business plans. That part of his life, he would rather keep off-limits from her. His shop was his baby, his project, his world and his sanctuary. It was the only place he hoped to find a bit of peace, away from Alice's nitpicking and neurotic needlings.

Chapter 12

A listair, Elaine's brother, couldn't have found a more opportune time to up and die. He was the eldest of her three siblings and the only one still living. Alistair had never been married and had no next of kin to inherit his assets. It was quite normal therefore that he would leave his manor and the adjoining lands to Elaine, with just his life savings to go to charity. Prior to his death, Alistair had instructed his nurse to phone Elaine and inform her of his ill health. The nurse had tried to contact Elaine but had never been able to get hold of her. When she finally located Elaine, Alistair had already died. Beside the bad tidings, the nurse had also divulged the contents of his will. Soon after the nurse's phone call, Elaine received a letter from a certain British lawyer, telling her that her presence was required for the reading of her brother's will and the transfer of his property to her name.

Elaine spent a whole afternoon moping about her departed brother. Her old family album on her knees, she kept looking at some tarnished black and white family photographs. There was one of Alistair and Timothy. Timothy was the brother who had lost his life in the war. After a long sigh, Elaine blew her nose then switched her mind to the will, wondering what she should do about it. She had the choice of giving her son power of attorney and to send him in her place or go there in person. In this case she could have a better idea on what would be the best thing to do with the property. She believed that the manor and the grounds must be in great need for some serious renovation. So too, she could guess that it had surely kept all the charm of the old world and it would be a shame to sell it and let others make it their home.

Elaine couldn't help remembering living there for a few months, almost thirty years ago, before travelling to Australia with her first husband their daughter and their little boy. A wave of bittersweet regrets swept over her at the thought of leaving Australia and her memories of the good times she had with Harold. She glanced at an elegantly framed picture of both of them, still taking pride of place on her bedside table. All of a sudden, she came to acknowledge that maybe it was wiser to go and avoid being the subject of idle gossip, when Harold marries Geneviève.

That night Elaine kept tossing about like a boat that had skipped its anchor. By morning she found herself still wondering about the whole thing. Feeling the need to talk to someone, she phoned her trusted friend Lady Foley who used to live near Harold's house. A few words later, her mind was made. She was as good as packed and ready to jump on an aeroplane. "But don't burn your bridges behind you. You may want to return home," Lady Foley had advised her, sensing that Elaine was toying with the desire of cutting her ties with her Aussie life. As a matter of fact, that wasn't far from the truth because Elaine had begun contemplating the idea of leaving the past behind and starting afresh back in her motherland. Taking her state of health into consideration, Elaine asked her son if he wouldn't mind accompanying her on her trip. "Pack enough clothes, we may have to stay longer than we dare to anticipate if we decide to keep the estate. There would be a lot of running around to organise the repairs the place would probably need," she told him with a soft but resolute tone.

"I will," he echoed politely while rebellious thoughts passed through his mind. 'If we decide! As if I have a say in the matter,' Eton groaned inwardly. Nevertheless, he went on asking, "Is there anything you want me to do for you before we leave? I mean do you need any medicine? Is your passport in order?"

"No, I am all right, but thank you for asking."

Geneviève heard from Harold that Elaine and her son were about to go on a long trip. The news of their departure was the best present Harold could have given her. She felt as free as a bird to have them, especially Eton, out of her hair at that critical time. She had carte blanche to go to every length in organising and getting herself ready for her big day.

With the enthusiasm of a seventeen years old girl, Geneviève searched, studied, deliberated and decided every detail of her wedding day. The dress she chose to wear was of a pale shade of pink but it had all the trimmings of an elaborate wedding gown. It was a gown every girl half her age would have dreamt of having on while walking down the aisle. As she had wished, on the actual day, besides her dress, the church decorations, the limousines, the flower arrangements, everything was spot on. The whole marriage ceremony also had all the pomp that Geneviève had intended to put into it, to make it as memorable a day as it could be. It was an event that her few friends and Harold's acquaintances were not to forget even if they tried.

Geneviève wasn't off base to have believed that Harold was a good catch. Not only was he financially sound, he was in every way the man she needed, a true husband material, one that she had come to love in her particular way. "Honey, what is there not to love?" she had told him, the day before the wedding when he had asked her if she really loved him. She was adored and pampered by him beyond her expectations. Harold would grab the silliest of excuses to shower her with gifts. It didn't take too long for the fancy jewellery box he had given her for Christmas to be filled with some exquisite pieces. Living in the impressive and tastefully furnished house was her dream come true. It was unmistakably ideal for her as well as her daughter.

From the first day they moved in, Aurore took to the place like a duck to water, fitting in her new lifestyle so snugly, one could think she was born into it. Gone were the memories of the meagre days when she had to make do with the basic meals and skimpy wardrobe her mother could provide for her. In the subsequent four years, lady luck happened to smile on the happily married couple. With what Très Chic, the boutique at double Bay, and Harold's partnership in the building company were bringing in, they managed to buy the big property next door to the factory. They had the old building knocked down and had a three level brand new factory and office space built instead. Six months later, basking in the after glow of their success, they closed the deal on a chain of clothing shops. On the verge of bankruptcy, resulting from expanding too much, too soon, the owners had no choice but to sell and cut their losses before sinking deeper in debt.

In the pursuit of excellence, Geneviève did her best to tart up the shops. Using a brilliant shade of light grey and a hint of silver and navy, she turned them into first class boutiques. Stocked with her latest creations and smart imported accessories, the boutiques attracted a lot more customers than they could wish for. Meanwhile, huge orders kept pouring in at the factory. Without jeopardising the workmanship, Geneviève and her hard working employees managed to get all of them completed and dispatched in due time.

It was unfortunate though that in those blissful first years of their marriage, their hectic schedule didn't leave Harold and Geneviève enough time to enjoy their togetherness. During the day, if Harold ever had the opportunity to escape, he'd give her a visit at her office but they could only talk shop. Then, in the evenings, after talking some more about their respective responsibilities, over a wholesome dinner, they used to retreat to their bedroom. By then, they were so tired that they could hardly enjoy their time together before drifting into a well deserved sleep. Often, after a few kisses and a cuddle, Geneviève had fallen asleep in her husband's arms.

On the weekends, if they didn't have to go anywhere, Geneviève made sure to spend a bit of time with Harold and pamper him. Forcing him to forget about work, she tried her best to make those short hours pleasant as well as restful. Caring about his wellbeing, she made sure that the maid cooked healthy meals. Aurore ate very lightly. Still busy with her studies, her exercise routine and her slowly increasing modelling jobs, she was dead set on keeping her slender figure. As for Geneviève, she never had time to eat during the day. She survived mainly on coffee and maybe a piece of fruit. It was only for Harold's benefit that the evening meal was supposed to be lean. The trouble was that Geneviève had no control on what her husband was packing in his stomach when he was eating out at lunchtime and his frequent coffee breaks. On a few occasions, she had given him hints that he should be careful with his diet. "You are putting on weight darling and I am worried about you," she had muttered with a frown.

"Maman, leave the poor man alone. Actually, I think that Harold is tall enough and those few kilos look good on him," Aurore had intervened.

"Yes, but too much fatty food is bad for the heart, that's what the doctors say," Geneviève had argued, sending a reproaching glance her daughter's way.

"Blame it on the restaurant that has opened near work. Their tasty dishes are responsible for this," Harold had said with a smile, proudly patting his rounded stomach.

"And the Italian cake shop, but you don't have to eat there every day dear. I can have Sonia pack a lunch box with healthy sandwiches and some fruit to take with you."

"Boring!" he had replied under his breath, then kissing his wife on the cheek, "I'll be alright, don't worry. I am as healthy as an ox and if it will make you happy, I will join the gym, I promise. I have to run now, bye you two," he had added, grabbing his briefcase.

"I will be happy if you saw a doctor to have your blood pressure and cholesterol level checked," Geneviève had continued nagging, while Harold was half way through the door. Turning to her daughter who was busy contemplating her own picture in the fashion section of a store's catalogue, "Il a gagné de l'embonpoint, haven't you noticed the spare tyre around his waist," she had scolded her, anxiously.

"Yes," Aurore had nodded.

"So he doesn't need you to encourage him to eat everything in sight. With all the stress he is under at work, his health is at risk, dear. His father had a heart attack when he was almost Harold's age, you know?"

"Okay maman. Nevertheless, I am sure he knows what he is doing and he said he'll join the gym. Maybe you can use your charm to persuade him to keep his promise but don't go on nagging him about every morsel he puts in his mouth. Men don't like that."

"Since when do you know what men like or dislike, hem?" Geneviève had asked, putting a pretend shocked look on her face.

"Maman, I am not a four year old, I can read."

Geneviève finished ordering next season's fabrics and was getting rid of the rep; "See you next time Monsieur De Plechet, and merci beaucoup."

"See you Madame Davenport," and the little French salesman was out of the door when the phone rang. "What now?" she grunted, taking off her chunky earring to answer.

"Hello," she said with a tired voice.

"Hello, Geneviève. It's Benson here. You have to come. I am afraid I have bad news," she heard Harold's partner say, as though he was calling from the bottom of a pit.

"What is wrong Benson?" she asked worriedly.

"It's Harold, he is on his way to hospital," Benson's voice trailed off abruptly. After clearing his throat, he continued, "He...he collapsed behind his desk. When I entered the office, I saw him through the glass door, he was standing there, I put my briefcase down and I was about to hang my raincoat when I heard a crashing noise inside. I looked and he was on the floor. I called for an ambulance. They just left. I thought I'd better call you before following them there.

"I am on my way," Geneviève cried out.

Hanging up noisily, she grabbed her handbag and dashed out, almost running to her car. Geneviève was in the dark about the reason behind Harold's collapse but the closer she got to the hospital, the more she became worried that it might be something serious. At the emergency room, the grim look on the doctor's face confirmed her fears. At once, any hope of seeing Harold back on his feet and back in her life dissolved on the spot. She learned later that Harold had died seconds after his arrival into the emergency room. "We tried our best to revive him but unfortunately he didn't respond, we just couldn't bring him back," said the doctor.

"He was all right this morning. What could have brought this on?" Geneviève asked, sounding hoarse with grief.

"We won't know until we have the coroner's report," the doctor replied before he was called away on another emergency.

Geneviève was devastated. After years of struggle she had finally felt the security she had wished for and had acquired a certain sense of belonging. She had enjoyed the warmth of a family life, and that was thanks to Harold. His unconditional love for her had transformed her into a completely new woman. A woman so cherished, so fulfilled, she couldn't comprehend why things had to alter so drastically in a matter of seconds.

A dependable man, Harold was unbelievably kind and so patient with Geneviève and her daughter. But 'was', was the operative word. He wasn't with them anymore. No longer could Geneviève consult him when she had a decision to make. That chapter of her life had been closed suddenly and she was beginning to feel the sting of it, yet there were no tears appearing in her eyes. Only later, after Aurore and a few friends were informed of the tragedy and had rushed to her side, had Geneviève been able to shed her tears.

Finding solace in her daughter's embrace, she came to wonder if there was something she could have done to prevent such a disaster from happening. She had been concerned about the long hours Harold and his business partner had been putting in to make their company grow and prosper. She blamed his work related stress, his lack of physical activity and even his unsupervised diet for having joined hands in cutting his life short. He had so much to live for, so much more happiness to spread around.

Geneviève and Aurore had another crying session when Benson and his wife helped them enter their home and when Charles and a few of her top employees arrived to console and commiserate with them. Utterly shattered by the loss of a good friend and a valuable associate, Benson was finding it hard to control the flow of his own tears. He sobbed for a long time before he could apologise to Geneviève, "I am here to comfort you Geneviève, but look at me. I can't even stop myself from falling apart."

"I understand how you must be feeling. It will be hard for all of us to go on without him. He will be missed enormously," Geneviève said, pulling a few tissues out from the tissue box.

On the day of the funeral, despite her bereavement, Geneviève couldn't help feeling the need to look her best. That's how Harold would have liked her to look anyway, she thought. Without flaunting it, she made herself appear elegant when she entered the church, flanked by her daughter. The church was packed with her late husband's and her own friends, acquaintances and employees. As she walked to her seat, a lot of heads turned to sneak a peek of the recently widowed woman. They all admired her for looking simply stunning on such a sombre occasion. They found her even more captivating in that body hugging black crepe dress, accessorised only by a strand of pearls that added sparkle to her teeth and depth to her eyes. Softly pulled back in a French bun, her hair was partly covered by a wide brimmed hat with a white satin ribbon around the bottom of the crown.

Barely listening to the priest conducting the service, Geneviève was crumpling a delicate handkerchief between her gloved fingers when her engagement ring caught her eyes. With a genuine sigh, she recalled the day Harold had presented it to her. The lustrous diamond looked so grand, so magnificent, it had blown her away even though she knew he could afford it. Tears in his eyes, he had officially proposed to her and after hearing her affirmative answer, "Do you like it?" he had anxiously asked.

"I love it," she had answered, adding that she would marry him even if he gave her a plastic ring.

"There is more," he had said, brandishing a blue box with a big golden bow on top.

"What is it?" she had asked excitedly as he was taking the lid off the box. Folded between sheets of fine white tissue, she had seen the sexiest and most exquisitely embroidered satin teddy and matching negligee.

"This one is more for me," he had said and they had both laughed.

The sound of the organ bringing her out of her reverie, she murmured, 'Oh! Harold, why did you have to leave me?' She cried, as she pressed her handkerchief to her tear stained eyes. She had come to depend on him and his pleasant company and now he was out of her life, a life that seemed to be so full of promises. Following the burial ceremony, one by one, the attendants passed before her to shake her hand and express their condolences. To her surprise, Geneviève realised that Elaine was there too. Earlier, standing amongst the mourners, she had spotted a man with an uncanny resemblance to Eton. The man was wiping his eyes so it couldn't have been him, besides, Eton was in England, she had thought. But if Elaine was there, there was a possibility that her son was there too. Giving Geneviève a hug, "Life can be so cruel," Elaine began to say.

"Very cruel." Geneviève said between sobs.

"He was a special man, our Harold. No amount of tears will wash away the memories we have of him. Dear Harold will be greatly missed, but what can we do. I know it will be hard for you to live without him but life goes on...."

"Thank you for coming," Geneviève could only say.

Catching her on her own, Eton was the last person she had to shake hands with. Wearing his usual scornful grin, he ogled at her and managed to whisper a few nasties in her ear.

"You killed him, didn't you? Tell me, how does it feel to be sitting tall in the saddle? I bet you can't wait to find out how much you stand to inherit from the poor man," she heard him utter.

In a different time or place, Geneviève would have a witty response to throw at him but she was not in the mood. She left his distasteful remarks to hang in the air like a bad smell and only stared at him with a blank expression.

"I'd better excuse myself, we ought to be careful, that's how rumours get started," he muttered before leaving her.

From between her clenched teeth, only the words, "In your dreams," came to escape but they were muffled in the general humming sound that was surrounding her. She was too depressed to give importance to anything that the miserable being could say. Eton had successfully made her sad day even sadder, yet the memory of seeing him cry still baffled her.

Staring down at the scattering crowd, Geneviève recalled the day that Harold had told her that he would love her and take care of her, for as long as he lived. Yet at that very moment, as long as he lived, seemed to be such a shorter time than it was meant to be. Tears misting her eyes again, she turned to Aurore. She was still fiercely devoted to her only daughter. "It's you and I, again, my darling but we will be alright. We will miss him for sure but we will have each other," she articulated with sorrow.

Aurore was also chagrined by the death of her stepfather. She had come to love and admire him for the tolerant and kind person that he was. In him, she had finally found the father she had never known. Harold had treated her with both respect and affection and she was sure that his loss would leave a big void in her future life.

Geneviève had always been a popular woman on the social circuit. After her husband's funeral, besides her closest friends, most of the men who knew her found it their humane duty to call her. They persisted in offering their hand in helping her get over her grief. They kept ringing and asking her to accompany them to various functions. If it wasn't the theatre, it was to go to dinner, to see a musical or anywhere they could think of. They used to advise her that she needed to go out more instead of being cooped up at home. A good friend of Harold had gone as far as suggesting that it would help if she could keep away from the places that would remind her of her late husband. Even if the invitations sounded sincere, Geneviève wasn't ready to believe that the callers didn't have any ulterior motive behind their calls. Every time, after politely declining their proposition, she presumed, 'The rascal, he only wants to get into my pants or put his hands on my money,' as she slammed the phone down.

Geneviève had a small number of good friends who were genuinely concerned about her dispiritedness but they had reasons to believe that she would bounce back eventually. In fact, after the initial three weeks of mourning, Geneviève began feeling her own self again. She made a few phone calls to see how things were going at work. She answered a phone call from Benson too and agreed to go to the meeting he had arranged with the company's accountant and solicitor.

Geneviève came truly back to life the moment the accountant gave her the details of how much Harold's part in the building business was worth. One look at that figure and the thought of adding it to their personal wealth, like the shops, the factory, the house and the shares would amount to, made her head spin. Pepped up by her finding, she couldn't help thinking about the next step up the ladder of success she had yet to climb. She wondered whether her dreams of riches, her outrageous fantasies were all met or were there some other achievements she still had to go after.

Sitting at the breakfast table, Geneviève finished writing a few nice words on each thank you card meant for anyone who had come to Harold's funeral. When she put the last card in its envelope, she got up to tell the maid to post them all. On her way, she saw her reflection in the glass panel of a door in the hall and felt it was time she let go of her sad looking attire. It was time to get on with the rest of her life and make plans for the future. 'I have to recharge my creative juices and let them flow,' she thought, remembering the French fabrics that were probably delivered by now and were sitting in her office. It was time she took matters in her hands and forged ahead but before putting another rung up the ladder in the fashion world, she had to pay a visit to Elaine.

During those weeks of mourning, something had kept nagging at her. It had started with something Benson had said in the hospital, the day of Harold's heart attack. He had mentioned that Harold had a visitor in the early hours and whoever it was, the visitor had left before Benson had arrived at the office.

"What makes you think he had a visitor?" she had inquired.

"A cigarette butt was in the ash tray on the coffee table near his desk. We know that Harold is not a smoker and the cleaners had left the place spotless the night before," he had replied. Later, when Geneviève had gone to collect her husband's personal effects, she had noticed the cigarette butt and had realised it was the kind Eton used to puff. It was a brand not many people smoked. Was it a coincidence or had the so and so dropped in on Harold. If that was the case, then there was a possibility of him being the catalyst that had precipitated Harold's death. Geneviève had to find out about this and Elaine was the only one who could tell her of her son's whereabouts at that particular time. "A Dieu ne plaise, God forbid, if Eton was the mysterious caller, mark my word, the degenerate will have to answer to me," she had cried aloud.

The thought of Eton and Harold being in the same room gave her a sickly feeling in the stomach. For four years, she had let Harold think she didn't know about his wealth before accepting his marriage proposal. Geneviève wasn't even sure that Eton had the presence of mind to realise he had some vital information worth using against her, but with him around, her secret was like a ticking bomb, ready to go off at any given time. Her chances of happiness were under constant threat of Eton opening his mouth and ruining everything for her. She was glad to have him out of her hair, if only he had stayed wherever he had been.

Geneviève's visit with Elaine was pleasant and fruitful. On the one hand she had a good tête-à-tête with her old customer. They cried a bit, they talked a lot about Harold and they both parted feeling peaceful. On the other hand, Elaine told her that they were on their way back to England because her son was getting married. Apparently Eton had met the nurse who used to take care of his uncle and they had fallen in love with each other. "It was kismet. After all, true love was what he needed to come out of his shell. You never got to really know Eton. For so long, he had been at war with himself. He was always in a sarcastic mood and that pained me. Anyway, now I am very happy for him," Elaine had added.

"When did you come back exactly?" Geneviève had asked casually.

"I came about three weeks before dear Harold's funeral but Eton's plane landed a couple hours prior to the service. He just put his bags down and we rushed to the church, that day."

"Yes, I saw him. He looked very sad and, to tell you the truth, I was a little surprised to see him at the cemetery."

"Eton was very fond of Harold, even though he was adamant not to show it. He was counting on my marriage to last forever, hoping he could get closer to Harold. He regarded Harold more like a big brother than a stepfather. I had a feeling that, deep down Eton admired him and wanted nothing but to have him on his side. That's why he resented you for taking him away from us. I knew

I couldn't hang on to Harold for too long, therefore I didn't mind seeing him with you. Another woman might not have been able to understand him and make him happy like you did. Alas, we all lost him at the end."

The next day, meticulously dressed and coiffed, Geneviève ascended the long sweeping steps to the foyer of her house. She grabbed her car keys and went out of the door. A few seconds later, her Mercedes glided along the gently curved street and headed towards Surry Hills. She was ready to get out and start marking her territory, ready to tackle the world. Reassured that Eton hadn't told Harold of her deceit, she was delighted to know that he had died a happy man. Harold had gone to his grave believing that she loved him for who he was and nothing else.

Geneviève had always a voracious appetite for success and the money that came with it. She had acquired a fortune, with Harold by her side, but since he was no longer with her, she couldn't see any reason for her to sit idle. It was far too soon for her to rest on her laurels. She was young and energetic and there were other achievements she could come to grips with. She had no doubt that, at times, she would have to face major problems but etched in her memory were Harold's wise words. "Problems are here to teach us valuable lessons. They can help us grow and be strong, therefore they should not be considered as hurdles and deterrents," he had told her on a few occasions.

Reorganising her desk and feeling confident enough, Geneviève stood up, sleeked her black skirt against her body and walked out to have a chat with her staff. They had to see that things were back to normal and that she was in control. She began by telling them about her wish to be called by her maiden name De La Lande from then on. While she was letting them know of her future plans, in her mind Geneviève was psyching herself up to aim for the stars. 'I have to do my best in turning all my little undertakings into well oiled machines, make them work and bring me fame as well as fortune.'

Money came to Geneviève as she had wished and planned and with it came her ever increasing power. A power she had no qualms to exercise to get things done her way, no matter how unreasonable her expectations could be at times. It was only natural therefore for a variety of nauseating incidents to occur between her and anyone who dared express his or her views or even oppose her. They would surely be chewed up and shown the door mercilessly. As time passed, Geneviève put her hands on a few more failing businesses and, after some remodelling she turned the lack lustre outfits into moneymakers. Her clever and innovative ideas were paying off. With her carefully put together garments, it didn't take her long to attract sufficient attention and to get the media exposure she was craving for. Her designs began appearing in the top magazines.

An upsurge in the country's economy had started to be felt, as more and more immigrants were making Australia their home. Every day new businesses were popping up, making unemployment a thing of the past. Life was easier for those holding high positions. Having more money to spend, people were becoming a lot more fashion conscious. It was an ideal time for anyone to get ahead. By now, Geneviève knew a great deal about stock and shares to invest her earnings wisely. With her financial future sewn up, she was on her way to become a household name, a celebrity. Convinced that she was a force to be reckoned with, it mattered very little to her that some people actually resented her for one thing or another.

Aurore's modelling career was also coming up shining. Since the day she had been able to put her makeup on properly and had learned to walk straight on her high heeled shoes, she had not been without job offers. In the late sixties, looking refreshingly pretty, she had been frequently in demand by top agencies. She was seen parading alongside famous models like Maggie Eckhardt but these days, she was photographed exclusively in her mother's best designs. Once her studies were completed, Aurore went on Très Chic's payroll. To get the necessary training, she worked alongside the big wigs who were helping in the smooth running of 'mummy dear's' empire.

Before long, Aurore became actively involved in every aspect of her mother's business. Being in constant contact with Geneviève, in no time, Aurore realised that her mother was a different person at work. At times, she found it hard to cope with her nitpicking attitude and her highly unreasonable demands regarding the workmanship on her cheaper garments. It's fair to say that she was even concerned by her mother's unsound hiring and firing of staff. One day, when she finally tried to voice her opinion, her mother quickly cut the argument short by saying, "Ma chèrie, business is business and fortune favours the bold, as they say. You can't get anywhere if you stop and think about every individual who may get hurt in the process of you doing your job well. If I didn't take my goal seriously I would be left in the dust and we would still be knee deep in mediocrity. Now, tell me what is more important, our future or the future of a bunch of no-hopers who can't keep their jobs? Remember ma petite, in this world only the strong survive."

"But maman! Are you so blinded by your self-righteousness or do you enjoy watching people squirm under your thumb? Sometimes I can't recognise you. What has happened to you? You were such a better person when you were with Harold."

"Well, that was then," Geneviève said, slightly moved by that remark, then, pretending she hadn't heard it, "I have a question for you, are you trying to take the zest out of my achievements or are you missing the sour taste of poverty? I could swear that you had actually acquired a taste for the best things in life and didn't mind sharing the spoils of my winning success."

"Yes, but!" Aurore began to argue but stopped right there, preferring to let go of the subject if she desired to continue the lifestyle in which she had become accustomed to.

"No buts!" Geneviève interrupted, throwing her arms in the air to show her exasperation.

Aurore wished in her heart that her mother could find another man like Harold. Someone who could keep her temperate and end the frustration she must have been feeling.

"By the way, what do you think I should wear for that television interview?" Geneviève asked, changing the subject.

"Oh, yes. You have to appear on the Midday Show. What about your new blue suit? You look nice in it."

"Oh, no. I need something more elegant. Don't worry. I'll find a suitable outfit. I am after that particular look. That sophistique personifiée, if you know what I mean," she added, half closing her eyes and giving her face a mystified look.

Chapter 13

From the day he was born, Jeremy was a difficult baby. As a toddler, he put his mother through the wringer with his never-ending tantrums. Martha dreaded the day she had to take him to pre-school and, a week after she did, she was told that her little boy was one of those hard to control kids. At the primary school, he was branded a restless and troublesome child. His round-the-clock disruptive pranks often made his teachers wish they had chosen a different line of work. At her wit's end, Martha organised a lot of pastimes to keep Jeremy's mind occupied. She even let him invite his schoolmates over to her house to play, hoping some of their good manners might rub off on him. Unfortunately, nothing like that seemed to happen. For one reason or another, his friends refrained from showing up again. Patiently Martha tried to reason with him. Occasionally, his father had to threaten him with severe punishment, but Jeremy refused to be intimidated by mere words. He believed his mother would not allow his father to raise a hand on her baby. And Jeremy remained as unrestrained as ever. His bad behaviour at home and elsewhere began generating disputes between Peter and Martha. Every time Samuel heard his parents quarrel, he snuck to his room and hid himself behind his study books.

Marcus and Samuel lived in separate houses yet they almost grew up together. They played together. They went to school together. They were involved in sports and extracurricular activities together. They participated in each other's respective birthday parties as if they were brothers. The two shared a lot of happy moments in each other's company. However, even though the bond between them was strong, when it came to choosing the subjects they wished to study, they had nothing in common. So when they started high school, following their relative career paths, they slowly ended up running in different circles. Certainly, this didn't mean that they had stopped being friends and that in times of crisis one wouldn't rush to assist the other. And crisis was what they kept having on their hands every time Jeremy took the wrong step and gave them reasons to worry.

Unwittingly, Peter grew tired of Jeremy's misconduct. He began to disassociate himself from the problem, leaving Martha to deal with it as she saw fit. After every clash with his son, it became a habit for Peter to go on drowning his anger and disappointment in his drink. As days went by, Peter became more oblivious of his fatherly responsibilities. While Jeremy was missing out on the guidance and the discipline he badly needed, Martha was having a taste of a sorely empty life because she stood to lose and to be neglected the most.

Unlike his big brother, Jeremy was not the studious type. In fact, as he grew older, he didn't display any ambition, any inclination whatsoever in anything worthwhile. All he wanted to do was watch action movies on the television and imitate the actor's movements. The storybooks, the games and the crafts that were given to him for his birthdays or at Christmas time were mostly dismantled and ultimately scattered around or thrown away. His favourite belonging was a toy gun that he used to twirl around his index finger like cowboys did in those western movies he liked so much. Growing a bit too tall for his age, he had a peculiarly gaunt face that made him look noticeably hard on the eyes compared to his father and his elder brother. It seemed that he had inherited his mother's features in an exaggerated way, a bit like a caricature drawing.

It was a rude awakening, a bitter revelation to Jeremy when, at the age of nine, it came to his attention that his teenage brother was turning into a very handsome young man. Disenchanted to be the ugly duckling of the family as well as the recalcitrant, Jeremy began drinking secretly from his father's supply of alcohol. One day, Marcus saw him on the veranda, busy downing a big bottle of beer when no one was home. He went in and told his parents about it. "Are you sure it was a beer and not a lemonade?" asked Jonathan.

"Dad, I know what a bottle of beer looks like," Marcus replied.

"The boy is not even ten, do you know how fast he can become an alcoholic if he indulges so early in life?" Jonathan said, turning to Liuba.

"I wonder if his mother knows about it," she said worriedly.

Marcus took it upon himself to tell Samuel about his little brother's binge drinking. They both had a talk with Jeremy and gave him a lecture that didn't seem to impress him. "What is it to you?" he asked them with a nasty frown. Two days later, Jonathan saw Jeremy outside the shopping centre with two of his colourful mates. They were trying to fit a box of beer in the basket behind a bike. He pulled him aside and, with a concerned fatherly voice, gave him a few words of advice, urging him to act according to his age.

"Son, do you know what your behaviour is doing to your parents, think about your poor mother and your future for a change."

Trying to look blasé, "Stuff you," Jeremy spat out scornfully before walking away to join his friends.

"What did that bloody wog want?" asked Scott, one of the boys.

"He wants to be taught a lesson for sticking his nose where it doesn't belong," Jeremy said with a gloating smugness.

"Did you tell the old fart to go jump?"

"I did better, I told the moron where to shove his opinion, or else," Jeremy added with a devious smile.

The following weekend, Jonathan went outside to mow the lawn but found his new mower wrecked beyond repair. After further inspection he noticed his toolbox and some small gardening implements were missing too. He didn't report the theft, as he knew who was behind it. Jeremy had left his calling card. It was a piece of cardboard hanging from the mower with the words, "Tough, isn't it?" written on it, and this could only be Jeremy's modus operandi.

Jonathan decided not to tell the Goddards about the incident, he only mentioned it to Liuba because she would find out about it anyway. It upset her a great deal more than he thought it would.

Unable to resist the temptation, ever so tactfully, over a cup of tea, Liuba told the story to Martha. She even showed her the piece of cardboard with the writing. Recognising her son's style of curling the bottom of the letter G, Martha kept on whimpering in shock, "I will have to tell Peter and I promise you, we will replace everything that they have taken or damaged. That is after we have a good talk with our naughty boy," she attempted to reassure Liuba.

Refusing to believe that her son could do such a callous thing on his own initiative, "The little imp needs a good spanking for befriending those hoodlums. It's their doing, Jeremy is not exactly a model child but he wouldn't do something like that," Martha added, trying to shift the blame onto the other boys.

Martha sounded sincere and strong willed in her neighbour's house but once she stepped into her own place, her determination to inform Peter of Jeremy's wrong doing weakened. Her past experiences made her rethink her decision. Eventually she went back to the Varda's home and pleaded with Liuba to keep the whole ugly matter under wraps. "I will gradually reimburse you myself. I will also try to knock some sense into my son's head but I really think there is no need to aggravate the already tense situation between father and son," she said before leaving.

'What good would it do to tell Peter, anyway? It would only make Jeremy all the more motivated to mischievous behaviour and Peter more driven to the blasted bottle,' Martha thought bitterly while walking back to her house. She remembered the time when the schoolmaster had asked to see them in regard to their son. He had complained about Jeremy's poor marks and bad manners in class. "Young man, you are becoming a great source of disappointment to us, you know that?" she had heard her husband yell at Jeremy.

"Oh, yeah! And what else is new? Go on say it. Can't you be more like Samuel?" Jeremy's derisive reply had been. Jeremy had then slammed the door on his way out and Peter had gone to his beer guzzling, a lot sooner than usual. That incident had generated yet another row between her and her husband, in which he had repeatedly blamed her for their younger son's improper conduct.

"The rascal doesn't have a snippet of respect for me. Sometimes, I wonder if it is not you who is putting him up against me," she remembered Peter telling her at the end.

"Oh, yes! And I suppose it was my lifelong ambition, my secret desire to end up with a rebellious offspring and a cockeyed drunk of a husband. Some caring mate you turned out to be for me, a true companion for my old age. Thank you very much," she had answered after giving him a cold, hard stare. They had made up the next day after; apologetically retracting his unwarranted accusations, Peter had made a promise not to repeat them. A promise she knew he wasn't going to keep.

A few months later the mower affair was almost out of the way. Still not satisfied by the trouble he had caused Jonathan, Jeremy decided it was time to move to the second stage of his retaliation. He and his two stooges followed Jonathan to the market and saw the spot he parked his new Ford Falcon. In his rear window, Jonathan had seen the three imps pass him on their bikes but hadn't made much of it. He was busy shopping when Jeremy got off his bike and walked closer to the car. His friends kept watch as he took a sharp object out of his pocket and scraped a couple of lines along the shiny body of the vehicle. A glint of satisfaction in his eyes, Jeremy jumped on his bike and fled the scene followed by his accomplices.

Jonathan came out of the shopping centre pushing a trolley full of goodies that Liuba had asked him to buy for the party they were having at the weekend. He had fetta cheese from Bulgaria, vine leaves from Greece to make dolma, seeds and nuts from Iran and Iraq, halva from Israel and curry powder from India, not to mention a few bags of Lebanese bread and baklava made locally by an Iranian lady. Grateful that the continental shop carried all those items in recent times, he was happy to have found everything Liuba needed. His happiness was short lived though, as his heart skipped a beat when he saw his beloved car in that appalling state.

On the weekend, after his guests, including Peter and Martha, arrived, Jonathan managed to take Adam to a corner and fill him in on the feud that was going on between him and the neighbour's son.

"I was about to ask you how did that happen," Adam said, pensively scratching his head.

Jonathan and his guests were all having a good time when Adam carefully sneaked out of the house and went knocking at the Goddard's door. Adam had seen Jeremy ambling in his parent's backyard. He knew the boy was on his own. When Jeremy answered the door, Adam grabbed him by the front of his shirt, making it hard for him to budge.

"Listen boy, I know what you are up to. You and your friends think that you can do whatever you want and get away with it, don't you? Well think again, because I too have friends and they will be watching your every move from now on, so listen and listen carefully. If anything happens to your neighbour Jonathan, his family or his house, car and anything else that belongs to him, I'll hold you responsible. So pray hard that no harm comes to my friend. Because if I hear that a hair is missing from his head, if there is a scratch at the sole of his shoe or his fart sounds a bit out of tune, I'll come on to you like a ton of bricks. Is that understood, boy?"

"Who are you?" Jeremy asked with a trembling voice.

"I can be your worst nightmare, so start praying. You can never tell what's around the corner, understood? One wrong move and...."

At that point Adam let go of his grip and made the gesture of cutting his own throat with his index finger. Faking a smile, he then looked straight into Jeremy's eyes to make sure he did grasp his meaning. Wide eyed and intimidated, Jeremy was left in the doorway while Adam tried to sneak back into the Varda's house before anyone noticed his absence. He slid inside as his two daughters, Violet and Juliet, were helping Liuba serve the desserts.

Jeremy got the message and left Jonathan alone but his reprehensible nature combined with the bad influence his friends had on him, made him commit numerous misdemeanours. Martha's blood boiled every time she had to clean up his mess without letting Peter or Samuel hear about them.

More and more engrossed in his studies, Samuel decided to move out of his parents place to live somewhere closer to his university. Even though he dropped in every now and then for short visits, he never got wind of what was really going on in his parental home. He was aware of his father's penchant for drinking but branded it as a normal Australian way of life and recreation. He seldom met with his friend Marcus who, after finishing his year ten, had put himself into Technical College to learn all about the real estate business.

Samuel was studying to become a journalist, a profession his father was still secretly yearning to have had, if only situations had been different. Now, in the dawn of his midlife crisis, it seemed that Peter's wound had reopened. His hopeless desire of doing the job he liked was reignited to give him more of a reason to feel cheated by life. He didn't know when he had started to resent being a teacher but the hatred was present and eating at him. Since he had found out about Samuel's choice of career, he had given him all the support he could, especially in those rare moments one could say he was still sober. As the night progressed though, and alcohol began clouding his judgement, he couldn't help himself from feeling envious of his son. That's when he used to mumble under his beer breath, "Some people have all the luck. If only I didn't have to go to that blasted war. If only I had a father who had been willing to support me, I would have shown the world what kind of a reporter I was cut out to be." He used to drink some more then, after a period of eerie silence, he used to break in tears, ashamed of having those sorts of feelings towards his own flesh and blood.

Martha used to feel drained every time she found Peter in that pathetic condition. She had no choice but to help him to bed and talk to him until he drifted into sleep. To some extent, she could understand him and at times she sympathised with him but his exasperation and his belief that he was a failure had made him a man hard to live with. Tired and sick of watching him fight with his demons, she had come to realise how empty and dull her own life had become. Constantly fretting Peter's next temper tantrums had turned her into a nervous wreck.

On many occasions, Liuba had seen Martha wandering in her backyard or sometimes she had spotted her on the veranda, sunken in her wicker armchair and lost in her thoughts. Liuba had wished she could somehow help her neighbour but didn't know if it was her place to mention, let alone discuss Peter's flare-ups, with Martha. In the bid to lessen the chances of Peter going overboard with his drinking, the Vardas had tried to space their social meetings. They just didn't want to risk being indirectly responsible for the occurrence of any domestic quarrel between the couple.

Jeremy was twelve when he was arrested for stealing a tape recorder and a few tapes from a music shop. When the police informed his mother of his detention, she went and bailed him out. She tried, once again, to shut up about it, hoping Peter would never get wind of her secret action. At home she chided Jeremy but one look at his unrepenting face and she wondered if it wouldn't have been better to let him go to prison or wherever they would send such a young lawbreaker. She thought maybe, just maybe somewhere, somehow Jeremy would reach a turning point and would rethink his life, because she believed he could do with some serious adjustment. On the hearing day, the magistrate had indeed ordered Jeremy to get his act together or bring a toothbrush to his next court appearance. "Next time young man, I may not be so lenient toward someone who is determined to be chronically insubordinate," he had said.

That afternoon Peter came home in a very foul mood. It seemed that he had found out about Jeremy's latest stunt. After thumping his clenched fist on the table, he faced his son and, eyes bulging, he began pouring his anger at him. He screamed and cursed and, addressing Martha, he even threatened that he would kick the rapscallion out of his house if from then on Jeremy didn't obey the household rules. For quite a long time, he went on and on about how he had been busting his behind to put a roof over Jeremy's head and food in his belly, "and how does the ungrateful wretch repay me? By hanging out with a bunch of no-hopers, by drinking, by smoking and by stealing. To make matters worse, I had to hear it from my own students," he added, then turning to his son and regarding him with disgust, "I tell you, you are an embarrassment to us, a big, big disappointment. Why couldn't you take a guideline from Samuel and, like him, aim for a concrete future instead of throwing your life away?" he said.

Jeremy didn't flinch under the verbal onslaught but when he heard his father harp on about his elder son's good deeds, he found it hard to stay silent. In a visible rage, he stood up, made a funny face and, as he moved his head from side to side, he blurted out, "Samuel this, Samuel that, Samuel is the son every parent would wish to have, Samuel can even walk on water. Why doesn't anyone inform the Vatican, so they rush in and canonise him, and I suppose you think you are a saint too. Well I have news for you Mister Perfect. You are no better than me. Always off your face, stinking like a flaming beer brewery. Did you really think I liked the smell of your breath all those years when I was an impressionable little boy? Do you have any idea how much you have embarrassed me in front of my friends? They stopped coming in to play with me because they got annoyed with you asking them silly questions and interfering with our games. What right do you have to criticise the friends I have now. They are the only friends I can get these days after you scared away the others. As for your very precious Samuel, I have had a bellyful of you singing his praises. And one more thing, I'd rather die than become a bloody bore like him. Let him bust his ass for that concrete future, because I don't need it."

Gobsmacked by the realisation that whatever Jeremy had just spewed out was based on a nugget of truth, Peter went quiet suddenly. Seconds later, head down he walked to the kitchen, grabbed a bottle of spirit from a cabinet and, retreating in a crab-like motion, he pushed his way into the sunroom and closed the door as he mumbled, "If that's the case, have it your way, you're on your own buster." Without further discussing the matter with his wife, it appeared that Peter had completely washed his hands of Jeremy. From that moment on, he let Martha shoulder the responsibility of dealing with their thieving son.

Maybe it was the confrontation with his father or it was just something waiting to happen that sped up the process of Jeremy going from bad to worse. As if it had been in the cards, Jeremy switched from alcohol and cigarettes to drugs and joined the ever growing number of people dependent on cannabis. In the beginning it was only once in a while that they could get the stuff but later on, thanks to a newly found friend who had connections, the boys were able to have a regular supply of dope. Jeremy kept wagging school, came home later and later and acted strangely around the house. His eating habits had also noticeably changed. Martha was worried sick seeing the blank look he had on his face sometimes. He seldom gave her precise answers to her questions. Many times she found him slumped in a corner of his room asleep at odd hours. Often he looked unconcerned of whatever was going on around him. His clothes had this singular smell that Martha couldn't or didn't wish to recognise. He incessantly asked her for money, inventing unlikely excuses for why he needed it. Martha couldn't say no to his demands. He would persist and wouldn't leave home until she gave him whatever sum he presumably needed. Then came the stage when a few little but pricey items started missing from the house. When she asked him about them, he answered with a shrug, "How do I know, I am not the only one who is living in this house. Why don't you ask Mr Wonderful what he did with them?"

Martha didn't know where to turn. She didn't want to admit it but after consulting a doctor and browsing in a few medical journals that contained references about drug addiction, she was convinced that her son had gone down that track. She was also sure that it was only a matter of time before Jeremy used violence or any form of crime to get the cash he required for a fix.

Distress scrunching her face, Martha finally decided to reach out and confide in Liuba. Talking to Liuba had always calmed her nerves and eased some of her stress in the past. Even though they came from two different backgrounds, the trust and the devoted friendship that had developed between them remained intact. Liuba listened attentively as Martha talked about Jeremy's unconventional behaviour and shook her head in awe. It wasn't that long ago when she had heard of a similar story from a colleague of hers who went on a holiday to America. There she happened to hear of her nephew's friend who was known to be smoking marijuana. "My friend told me that the boy was acting the same way when they first found out about his addiction. She told me that he made his mother's life a living hell before...."

"Before what?" Martha asked, fear in her voice.

"Before he became.... I don't know, I think something got mixed up in his brain, he became mental," Liuba answered unwillingly.

"How did that happen?" Martha stressed again.

"I shouldn't have told you this. I am sorry Martha. I only know that the poor woman blamed herself for not doing enough to protect her son but there is only so much one can do when children are not prepared to listen. Today's children have a mind of their own."

"You didn't tell me how did he become brain damaged."

"Apparently the police had discovered a crop of Indian hemp and had it sprayed with some sort of poison to kill it. The plants were gathered in the night and taken to the streets before the police moved in to arrest the people who had planted them. He must have smoked the sprayed herbs," Liuba whispered, regretting having let the conversation stretch that far.

Her mouth dry, her temples throbbing, Martha went back to her home, more distressed than before.

A few days later, carrying a big bunch of fresh parsley from her garden, Liuba called to see how her neighbour was doing. Martha put the kettle on. Avoiding the subject of dope, the two friends were immersed in idle conversation when Jeremy came home and, seeing Liuba, he went straight to his room. Liuba left the parsley on the table and, rising to her feet, she excused herself. The minute she was out, Jeremy showed up, "What are you doing home at this hour?" Martha inquired.

"I need some money, twenty dollars exactly," he said.

"I don't have any money left, I had to pay two big bills this week. What is it for anyway?" she asked, trying to sound casual.

"Whatever, I just need it."

Martha thought it was about time she stood up to him and ignored his outrageous demands.

"If it's for school. I'll give you a note and explain...."

"I don't need your fucking note," he said, raising his voice.

Bringing his face closer to hers, he looked her straight in the eyes then, dangling a long chain from his index, "Do you understand? I need twenty dollars now," he shouted, stressing on every word with a rather authoritative tone.

Unprepared for such outburst, Martha saw her son twirl the chain around his finger and send Liuba's parsley flying all over the place. Eager to make a bigger impact on his mother Jeremy began throwing her shopping on the floor. "You have money for these, don't you?" he said, clearing the table with one movement of his arm. A small tin of Ardmona peaches brushed against his mother's ankle and made her groan from pain. Martha was terrified of what he might be capable of doing next if she continued resisting him. Since she didn't want him to know the whereabouts of her secret stash, "I can borrow some money from Liuba, if it's so important," she said, running to the door.

After Jeremy left with the cash, Martha rushed back to Liuba and, trying hard not to cry in front of her, she reimbursed her the money.

"You can't continue doing this, you know Martha? I don't want to tell you what to do but you are not helping him by giving him money every time he asks for it."

"Do you think I don't know that but what am I supposed to do? How can I stop him? His father would never be able to get through to him. As for Samuel, he is studying so hard to get his degree. I don't think it's fair to distract him before his exams. Besides, the way Jeremy thinks about him, I seriously doubt if Sam's words would have any bearing on his younger brother. God only knows how much I have been praying for a solution but I cannot see any miracles happening soon."

Martha went through a lot of long hard days from then on. Putting up with her son's condition became a way of life for her. She didn't know where else she could turn for an answer. A few times she dared to tell Jeremy that he had a problem and needed to seek professional help. "What are you talking about? I am perfectly capable of taking care of myself, thank you very much. Your husband is the one who needs help," was all he would say to get her off his back.

Two months later, Jeremy and his friends broke into a car and took it for a joy ride. They were all high on something they had put their hands on. Jeremy was at the wheel. They were cheering and savouring the thrills of being in charge. After a short time of so-called ecstatic fun that the raucous bunch were having with a series of reckless zigzagging and stupid stunts, Jeremy found himself driving against the traffic. "Nothing to it," he said with self-assurance, before attempting to right his wrong.

The lights must have changed because a few cars rolled towards Jeremy, making it hard to do a U-turn in time. He swerved to the left and, jumping onto the median strip, he tried to get to the other side of the road. From the corner of his eyes he noticed a van getting dangerously close to him. It was too late to get in front of it so, to dodge it, he had to cut in front of it and go to the other lane. That's when he saw another car advancing on that lane. Unable to turn to the right and merge with the traffic he was forced to dodge that passing car too. Arms stretched, holding firmly on to the wheel he pushed harder on the accelerator. It felt like he was flying as the car sped towards a concrete retaining wall erected on the curving edge of the road. The passenger's corner hit the wall first. The speeding car kept moving, scraping on the side of the wall then overturned and landed heavily on its right side. There was an earsplitting noise of shattered glass and metal. Jeremy heard cars screech and stop around him before he passed out. When the police arrived, the two tyres on the left side of the vehicle were still spinning above the wreckage.

After carefully freeing the four occupants trapped in the mangled scraps of metal, the ambulancemen that were called to the scene took them to the hospital. The three friends of Jeremy had a good chance of surviving the accident but unfortunately things didn't look that promising for Jeremy.

Martha was on duty when she was called to her son's bedside after the police found out about his identity. Within half an hour, Peter was there too. Jeremy was coming in and out of consciousness. He had lost a lot of blood. Two doctors were doing everything they could do to stabilise him, under the circumstances. Muddled by the shock, Martha kept repeating that she didn't know when and how her son had learned to drive. Pulling her away, a nurse practically forced her to take some sedative tablets, while another was busy adjusting the drips and regularly checking Jeremy's blood pressure.

Later, Martha began praying silently as tears were rolling down her cheeks. From a distance, her eyes were begging God and the doctors to give her son back to her.

Anticipating the hopelessness of the case, the doctor let Peter come closer to Jeremy's bedside. Peter bent down and wiped his son's brow with his handkerchief. All choked up, he tried to say something but just couldn't utter a word. As if he sensed his father's presence, Jeremy came to. In a brief lucid moment, his eyes became locked with those of his father. With a tremendous effort he managed to let a few words escape from his parched lips, "I aimed for a concrete something after all dad," he said in a slurred speech as a semblance of a smile crossed his blood stained face.

"Shush," Peter whispered.

"I guess I stuffed it up for good, didn't I?" Jeremy added before he closed his eyes.

There was a tiny moment of total stillness, then his head dropped to one side.

"No! No! Jeremy, No! Please doctors hurry, do something," Peter heard his wife screaming behind him. He turned his head and saw her distorted face. Bewildered he looked around. From the expression on the doctor's face he realised that Jeremy was no longer with them. Martha was frantically caressing Jeremy's face and kissing his hands, "My poor baby, why did this have to happen to you?" she began lamenting.

Letting out a bitter sigh, Peter tried to lift his woebegone wife off Jeremy's lifeless body. He put his arms around her and awkwardly attempted to console her and let her know that her pain was his pain too and that he was there for her, sharing her grief, her loss.

Everything happened so fast that neither of Jeremy's parents had the opportunity to call Samuel or the Vardas. Samuel had to get back from an assignment and hear the dreadful news, two days later. Jeremy might not have been a well-adjusted young man but his death, at the tender age of fourteen, was undoubtedly a tragedy for his family. Considering his tendency for reckless behaviour, Martha and Peter kind of expected something unpleasant to happen to him, sooner or later, but never in their minds did they think that Jeremy's mistakes would cost him his life. In Martha's case, she wished that he would be caught, be set on the straight and narrow, and let out with a clean slate. She was harbouring the hope that the penitentiary treatment would open his eyes and make him see the errors of his ways as well as restore his self-respect.

Scott became a paraplegic and the other two boys escaped with a couple of broken bones and some cuts and bruises.

During the funeral and long after she had toned down her vociferous cries, Martha remained feeling bitter and inconsolable. Despite her best efforts not to lay blame on Peter, deep in her heart she couldn't help doing just that. Predominant in her mind was the belief that it was her husband's lack of character and his drinking habits that had prompted Jeremy to make some bad choices in his life. She found it hard to let go of the thought that Peter's neglectful behaviour had played a part in Jeremy's subsequent death, and that concept played havoc with her mind.

Every time Martha had her eyes closed, scenes of the past rushed to her head, haunting her and preventing her from being reasonable. She couldn't stop remembering the way Jeremy used to react whenever Peter mentioned one of Samuel's accomplishments as he often boasted to friends and neighbours. With an arrogant air on his face, Jeremy used to put his hand in front of his mouth and pretend he was about to throw up. While a feeling of guilt was tormenting her for allowing that to go on, Martha couldn't help resenting her husband for constantly criticising Jeremy for his shortcomings. She often found herself muttering gloomily, 'Being a teacher and educating teenagers, Peter should have known a thing or two about bruised egos and the negative effect they can have on young children. He should have known that Jeremy would be running the danger of developing an inferiority complex every time he was compared to

Samuel for one thing or another. Who knows, maybe they were those same little blows that caused Jeremy to stumble.'

Sometimes, tired of pointing the finger at Peter, Martha used to lay off him and pass judgment on herself. It wasn't like she had never come in contact with young patients who had tried to end their lives because they were passed over and misunderstood. And not forgetting those who were hospitalised for their drug related problems. Considering Peter and herself took care of other people's kids with a degree of success, then how come they failed in the upbringing of one of their own? Why was it that they hadn't seen Jeremy's tragic end coming? Martha ended up accepting that she was as much to blame as Peter was and having nothing to say in her own defence became the core of her private hell.

Feeling sorry for their neighbours, the Vardas tried to be there for Peter and Martha, even though Jonathan seriously believed that Jeremy was nothing but a bad seed. "He might not have been the apple of his father's eye and for good reasons, but surely the boy hadn't exactly been an uncared for kid. Jeremy had the love and attention of his mother to fall back on. A lot of youngsters didn't see eye to eye with their fathers but they didn't rush to mess up their lives. Even abused children have been known to have dealt with their ordeal and gotten over it. Why couldn't Jeremy rise above it all and lead a normal life?" he used to tell Liuba every time she attempted to make an excuse for Jeremy's faults. In any case, Martha wouldn't be able to cope with her loss if she didn't have Liuba to listen to her, every time she felt the need to pour her heart out to another human being.

For the first few weeks after Jeremy's funeral, no one knew how to act around Peter. Peter himself didn't know how to mourn the death of a son who caused him so much heartache. To his best ability, Jonathan tried to come to his rescue. To lend Jonathan a hand, his friend Adam planned to take him and Peter on a few fishing trips on his boat. Jonathan volunteered to teach Peter backgammon and everyday played a game or two with him just to keep his mind occupied after work. He figured that's when Peter would be most inclined to remember Jeremy and be tempted to hit the bottle.

Jonathan and Liuba had all the good intentions but, as neighbours, there was only so much they could do without overstepping their boundaries. Inevitably their frequent meetings dwindled down and each couple went about their own affairs. Peter retreated in his particular world and Martha clammed up in her own sad cocoon. They both went on dealing with their grief in their own way. While he acted as a normal person during the day, Peter was a different man in the evenings, mainly after he had a few drinks too many. None of his co-workers and friends detected how inebriated he had been the previous night.

As for Martha, she was gradually coming to terms with the fact that Jeremy was dead and that she couldn't do anything to bring him back. Sure she was missing him but the person she missed and needed more was the Peter that she had fallen in love with and married all those years ago. Left with her memories of the good old days, she was reduced to clinging onto the hope of seeing Samuel more often, ignoring the fact that soon after his short visits, she would be back in the same old rut. A few times, fed up with Peter's never ending nitpicking and his unjustified arguments and when their house smelt like a pub's lavatory, she took her pillow and went to take refuge in Jeremy's room. Those occurrences became increasingly frequent as years went by. Eventually, keeping it a secret from Samuel and their neighbours, Peter and Martha did the most plausible thing there was. They went on sleeping in separate bedrooms. They used to discuss their domestic issues together, cook their meals and eat it together, shop and visit friends together but they were strangers for the rest of the time.

Very rarely, when Peter was in the early stages of being dead drunk, he used to call his wife by her full name as he used to do in their happier days and during their intimate moments. "I miss you Martha Leigh, my precious Florence Nightingale," he used to say before creeping in between the sheets with her and holding her tightly in his arms as if nothing was wrong with that. Martha couldn't say no to Peter. She had learned, by experience, that if she tried to stop him, it would only be the start of a clamorous disagreement. Doors would then be slammed with thundering echoes and some very harsh words would definitely be heard, words he would not even remember saying, in the morning. It was therefore obvious that Martha's love life was almost nonexistent. Deep in her soul, she had often wished for a solution, an escape of a kind but, not even once, the thought of leaving Peter had crossed her mind. To Martha, the sacrament of marriage was a serious business, an institution. It had always been for better and worse, as she had said in her wedding vows. No matter how dreadful her existence, Martha stayed tied to her husband and, with time rushing her by, she felt all the more trapped in a situation with no way out. It seemed like she was marooned on Peter's island and was doomed to live his life.

Peter picked up the local papers off the floor then, taking his keys out of his pocket, he opened the front door, slamming it shut once he was in. In his haste he dropped the rolled up papers. Cursing under his breath, he kicked them out of his way and staggered towards the kitchen. Grabbing a can of beer from the refrigerator, he made his way to his personalised easy chair and slumped heavily into it after pushing the button on the television set. It was a bit after twelve. "Hey Charger," a couple of female voices filled the room.

"Sluts," Peter heard himself grunt.

He took a big gulp out of the can, watching with contempt the advertisement for the newest Chrysler car on the market. Inevitably, his thoughts switched to a much more pressing matter that was obviously bothering him intensely enough to have put him in such an ill humour. "The bitch, who does she think she is, telling me what to do or not to do in my own spare time? She thinks she owns me for the bloody pittance she's paying me. I think you'd better go home now and come back to teach tomorrow, when and if you are sober, she has the gall to tell me, as if I give a damn what she thinks," he went on grumbling like some broken record.

That morning was the third time since Christmas, that the new school principal had called Peter to her office. It was only to give him yet another earful about the way he looked and behaved in class during the last few weeks. "I don't have anything against social drinking but when you show up with bloodshot eyes and bring your mood with you, it's a different story. My point is your irresponsible conduct is bound to reflect on your work and on the school's repu-tation. It's not helping your case and it's certainly not in the best interest of your students. Besides, by not setting a good example you are likely to make yourself expendable," the headmistress had concluded prior to sending him home to recover from the previous night's over indulgence in alcohol.

It was the way she had said it that gave Peter a fair idea that he had worked her last nerve. This time her words were more like threats of dismissal rather than friendly advice. They were, "Shape up or ship out," kind of threats.

Peter took another gulp of his beer then, "She wouldn't dare sack me. I'll tell her where to stick her stinking job first," he mouthed, trying to convince himself he wasn't about to be intimidated by the woman. That was Peter's anger talking because he knew that she was the one holding the trump card and she could easily ruin things for him.

The advertisement for the Chrysler car had ended. After another ad, the TV presenter was about to interview a certain fashion designer by the name of Geneviève De La Lande.

Glammed up for the occasion, Geneviève was sitting regally in an art deco style chair. Her neatly done up hair and the latest designer's outfit that she had chosen to wear looked spot on. Even the keyhole opening in the neckline of her black silk top, that allowed the crew at the network to feast their eyes on her magnificent cleavage, was a testimony of her self-confidence and extreme sophistication. It even caught Peter's attention. After the introductions, the preliminary talks were mainly about fashion and Geneviève's background in the field. A few kind words were also exchanged about Coco Chanel who had died a month or so earlier. The host began asking Geneviève about the motivation and drive that had raised her to that level of success and had sprung her to fame. "Sheer determination and hard work," she declared categorically. "You have to want something so badly that you would be prepared to do anything to get it," she added, batting her eyes to accentuate her words.

"Anything?" the presenter asked with a toothful smile.

"Anything," she replied with the professional cool of a person in control. "I can say that I scratched my way to get where I am now."

"I believe you recently opened a few more boutiques such as, Pour Toi, Indulgence, Paris Paris, F For Fashion, to name a few, and let's not forget Jeune Toujours, in that modern shopping complex in North Sydney."

"They are just an added bonus," she replied calmly.

Taking advantage of the opportunity, the presenter fired the question that was burning on his mind since the beginning, "Can you tell the viewers what is your response to the rumours that you have got where you are by using some slippery and unorthodox ways," he queried expecting a vague answer that wouldn't reveal much. Instead Geneviève answered his question with another, more to the point, question. "You mean the rumour that I have slept my way to the top or something along that line?"

"I didn't say that but people in the industry are using the words back stabbing and..."

"Well people can say whatever they want dear, and if that's what they think of me, I won't disappoint them. I admit with a certain pride that I did some back stabbing, used a lot of clever tactics and also exercised a great deal of my seduction skills. And yes, I slept my way up when I absolutely needed to, and I am not about to apologise for it. Desperate times call for desperate measures, as you say. I did what I had to do in the circumstances and that was a lifetime ago, soon after my ship arrived in Australia. It was dog eat dog then. Come on, we all know this is a man's world. I had to survive, didn't I?"

More aggravated, Peter pressed a button on the remote control of the television set and changed the channel in a great hurry. His head was still pounding with the residual anger that the headmistress had sparked. He didn't really need this, "The trollop, she has the bloody hide to sit there and declare on National TV that she made her millions lying on her back. I, on the other hand, have to bust my arse to make ends meet and still Madame the headmistress is not happy," he uttered as he struggled to get up from his chair.

"Hire a woman in my place, see if I care, the world is ruled by strumpets like you two, anyways. Gone are the days men were in charge and women stayed at home where they belonged, and they obeyed their husbands. Those were the days," he kept mumbling, his incoherent words mixing with the lyrics of the song My Sweet Lord, coming from the TV set.

Unconsciously Peter began walking back and forth in the space between the television and his chair, as if he was hoping to outpace the disturbing thoughts that were racing in his head.

Martha arrived home that afternoon to find her other half in one of his worst moods, a mood that lingered until he went to bed. She tried hard to stay out of his way, solely because she too wasn't in the mood for another repeat performance of his infamous temper flare-ups.

Chapter 14

I t was raining heavily when Clara's plane landed at Mascot Airport. Throughout her flight, she looked forward to seeing her brother but as she was getting closer to meeting him, she could feel her heart pounding uncontrollably. The fact that her new life was about to start robbed her of ease. She was unable to visualise the kind of situation she would land into at her brother's place. Being always treated like a princess at home, she had no idea what to expect, living in someone else's house. Sure she was prepared to make some adjustments but it was the unknown that had her frazzled, as she was getting off the plane. Once she was out of the customs area, after a brief kissing and hugging with Matthew and Alice, they grabbed the bags and the three practically ran towards Matthew's car that was parked a bit too far from the entrance door. Matthew struggled with the two big suitcases while Clara pulled another one on its swivelled wheels, her shoulders bent under the weight of a heavy carry bag and her uncomfortably big vanity case.

Alice was holding a colourful umbrella over her own head, probably to protect her bizarre hairdo. Clara couldn't help noticing that her sister-in-law was bulging in the middle. Another thing that didn't escape Clara's attention was the hem of Alice's shortish skirt. It was unattractively rising at the front to accommodate her at least five months pregnancy. Alice had dyed her hair blonde and had it highlighted with streaks of a bright shade of orange.

The whole wispy mass was worn high over her head. She had tiny ringlets hanging over her forehead, giving her a rather ridiculous look.

Clara also realised that Matthew had lost a few pounds. With narrower shoulders, a sunken chest and a premature middle age kind of spread, altogether he looked a lot different from the chubby young man he used to be. In other words, nothing resembling the Matthew she used to know.

Matthew drove in silence, listening to the latest news about the war in Vietnam that was broadcasted on the car radio. Once in a while he asked questions like, "How was your trip Clara?" and "are you comfortable back there?" Alice said nothing to Clara but issued a few orders to Matthew and criticised his way of driving. Chewing gum, she unsuccessfully kept pulling her skirt down to cover her bony knees. Beginning to feel irritated, Clara couldn't wait to get to the house and have a bit of rest.

When they finally arrived, Matthew took his sister's luggage to the room designated for her and Clara followed him. The two dropped their load down then, hugging each other, and they burst into tears. They both knew in their hearts that the crying was just a delayed grieving for their mother whom they both missed so much. Alice went to her room to change into something warmer. She came out wearing a pair of pants with the legs exaggeratedly flared at the bottom. She declared that she was on her way to pick up the twins from her parents' house. Matthew made tea and he kept on asking random questions. They had a lot to talk about but they didn't know where to start. When the two finally had every subject covered, in a very embarrassed way, Matthew tried to explain and justify the reason why he hadn't flown to America for their mother's funeral. "My heart was torn to pieces, imagining you going through all that heartache on your own. I just couldn't leave her alone. She wouldn't have been able to cope with the boys and the morning sickness she was having," he said, referring to Alice.

"We didn't know she was pregnant."

"Clara, I will never be able to forgive myself. I should have been there. I let mother and you down. Can you forgive me, at least?" he asked, wiping the new tears that were flooding his eyes.

"Shush, it's all right, mother understood, we all did."

"Mother was an angel," he said, putting a platter of assorted biscuits on the table.

In those few minutes together, Clara realised that her brother's appearance wasn't the only thing that had changed. There was a distinct difference in his demeanour as well. It seemed that he had gone from one extreme to another. The way he was talking to her, he sounded so caring, so affectionate, so unlike the Matthew of yesteryears.

In the days and months that followed, Clara had the chance to find out why. The transformation couldn't have been anything but the result of being mercilessly needled and vehemently told off by his wife. Oh! How her mother was wrong thinking that Alice could turn into a friend for her and that it would be good for Clara to be close to her relatives. A harmless entity, Clara had believed her sister-in-law would be, but that was only for the few first seconds of her arrival. Her mother couldn't have been further from the truth because Alice did not have the ability nor the desire to be anyone's friend, especially not those who had the misfortune of living under the same roof with her. "A thorn in my side," Matthew had called her when he had it up to his neck with her inconsiderate deeds and the way she could cunningly twist every situation to her own advantage. Many times, Clara had to witness Alice's hysterical moods that made her so unbearably unique, so much like a giant fingernail on the blackboard of one's soul. To top it off, even though she didn't look like much, it seemed that Alice had an overly inflated opinion of herself.

In the beginning, Alice was almost civil with Clara for a couple of days but soon her true face had begun to show. Alice never missed an opportunity to make fun of Clara's American accent.

Not a day passed that, in a derisive way, she didn't give her tips on how to dress and how to lose weight. Matthew became exasperated, when once, he heard his wife mention how many calories were in the single toast and jam that his sister was having for breakfast. "Give the girl a break, I can cut myself on your bones, for heaven's sake," he protested, then, looking at Clara, "come to think of it, I believe Clara's feminine figure goes well with her cute face and, just because she is one notch over size eight, doesn't exactly make her one of nature's abnormalities."

"So I am not feminine, hem? Sorry for breathing," Alice muttered, feigning indignation. She then ran her long fingernails in her hair and added, "That's the thanks I get for being helpful and sharing my knowledge. You are both welcome to stay in the dark ages. I'd rather go with the times. Mankind is made to progress not to go backwards," she uttered.

Clara kept eating in silence even though she found it hard to swallow. She was fuming inside but she was mostly feeling sorry for her brother who, for her sake, had taken a stand against his wife and had his head chewed off. To see that Matthew had to endure living with such an insignificant and grossly irrational woman distressed Clara immensely. Alice was decidedly unburdened by intelligence yet Mathew, who was a terror in the diner back home, was putty in her hands. Clara often wondered if Matthew enjoyed being a victim. Looking at the way he was tolerating the cross he had to carry, she came to the conclusion that in those few years of living with Alice, her brother had been re-educated. He was trained to a degree that he was acting more like a puppet under his wife's control. Alice's nerve wrecking silent treatments were her way of proving her point and her disparaging remarks had indeed helped Matthew lose his self-esteem, his identity.

In the early days after her arrival, Clara had tried to play the role of a peacemaker between her brother and his wife a few times but then, seeing the futility of it, she had given it up altogether. As the days stretched to months and years, she got accustomed to staying in her room and keeping out of their noisome bickering, in which Alice was always the one ending up with the upper hand. Trying to keep herself busy and far away from that insufferable woman, Clara went from one art class to another and mastered all the skills possible. Rather than being constantly under intense scrutiny, she learned pottery, leatherwork, flower and jewellery making. Sculpturing small figurines with breathtaking accuracy was her forte.

During the day, Clara used to go and help her brother in the gift shop where, for reasons of her own, Alice never set foot in, except for once or twice when she needed money. After dinner and, of course, after washing the dishes, Clara used to retreat to her room. There, using all her know how, she used to create two to three dainty little articles that she took to Matthew's shop to be sold. Clara insisted that her brother took his percentage from the sale just like he would with any other merchandise he acquired from other suppliers. People who met Clara believed she was a happy young girl, mainly because she was smiling a lot, but they had no idea what was going on in her heart. They couldn't see that, deep inside, she was nothing but a hopelessly lonely and depressed person.

Clara was convinced that nothing would ever happen to change her life for the better. More than once, the thought had occurred to her to pack her bags and go back to where she belonged, to the place where her good memories were laid to rest but, thinking of her brother had made her stay.

Clara used to feel guilty, every time she came close to giving up and leaving. Nevertheless, the pressure was mounting, making her wonder how much longer she could take it. Like all the girls her age, she couldn't help dreaming of that knight in shining armour, who would appear out of nowhere and take her away from all that unhappiness. Since Alice had given birth to her daughter Caroline, Clara didn't have a moment of peace. She loved the boys and the baby and was willing to pull her weight when it came to housework but the way Alice was bossing her around like a hired hand was a bit over the top and not exactly what Clara had expected her trip to Australia would turn into.

According to Alice, Matthew was having it too easy at the shop. He was supposedly twiddling his thumbs most of the day so Alice had decided that he should get up at night, bottle-feed and change the baby while she was having a well deserved sleep. As for Clara, she had been given the privilege of feeding, cleaning up and dressing the twins in the mornings until their grandmother came to take them to her house for the rest of the day. Alice always had time to take long bubble baths, try new hair styles, paint her toenails, read the latest women's magazines, put all sorts of face masks on and yet, she never stopped complaining that she was run off her feet with three kids to take care of.

In the mornings after the twins were gone, Alice used to put her baby in her pram and walk to the shops to browse and buy clothing items and toys for her daughter. While the boys had to make do with their outgrown outfits, Caroline had twenty times the amount of clothes she could possibly wear. After shopping, Alice used to have her lunch in a posh café before returning home to have her beauty sleep while baby was having her nap then, dragging her feet she used to start preparing dinner. If it were not for Matthew's love and Clara's little gifts every now and then, the boys would not have anything to wear or any new toys to play with.

Having no life of her own, no friends and no one to share her thoughts with, Clara had no choice but to do everything to please Alice. She couldn't even say a word of it to Matthew from fear of creating squabbles. Tiptoeing around Alice to prevent recurring arguments in the house became another one of Clara's occupations until one day, in the gift shop, Matthew initiated that long awaited conversation and apologised for his wife's unwarranted behaviour. "Never mind me, it's you I am concerned about. She is using every trick in the book to keep you on a short leash. I cannot begin to understand why you are putting up with this sort of treatment," Clara said, looking him in the eyes.

"Clara, if it wasn't for the children I would have left her long ago but knowing about mother's sickness, I couldn't add to her worries," he said.

Matthew then confessed that Alice had thrown a tantrum and had discouraged him from flying to Chicago when their mother was on her deathbed. Letting out a sigh, he quoted the exact words of his wife, "You want to leave us here to go and sit there for who knows how many months, until she dies, and what if she doesn't? Yes, what if she doesn't die within a certain time? Do you know you may not have a job to come back to if you don't return soon enough, she kept yelling. In reality, I am sure she feared that, once I'd left, I might not have wanted to come back to her. That fear was also the reason she planned her second pregnancy. Purposely, she didn't take the pill. She just wanted to tighten her grip on me, to suck me more into her web." Matthew took a long breath before continuing, "and what's so damn unfair is that she thinks that I am always the bad guy and she is convinced of it too."

"You have to be strong Matthew. You have to put your best foot forward and do something about it before it's too late. It's one thing to make a sacrifice and another to be a martyr. Imagine what our father would have done if he was in your shoes," Clara spoke out, creasing her forehead.

"It's easier said than done. You see, I can't afford to divorce her and she knows it. I will lose half of everything I have and my children. Then there is child maintenance to think about. Where will I get the money? I don't see how I can get out of this mess, can you? I mean you can always go back to America. I wouldn't blame you if you did, even though I don't wish to be left alone without you here, but it would be selfish of me to dissuade you from leaving."

Clara consoled her brother as well as she could and reassured him that she was not about to throw in the towel and desert him.

"Can I ask you something?" she said, then, straight away she fired her question before changing her mind, "what was it that attracted you to her in the first place?"

"Let's face it Clara, girls were not exactly losing sleep over me, you know? So, when I saw her interested in me, it was a big boost to my ego. I lost my head, I daresay. Besides, how was I supposed to know, in such a short time, that she came with a built-in attitude?"

"That's true," Clara said, nodding pensively.

"I tell you Clara, if I could take my children and run, I would do it so fast, I would leave skid marks behind."

Matthew had a lot on his mind. He just couldn't stop spilling his guts to his sympathetic sister. It wasn't everyday that he was able to have a heart to heart with her even though she was more than a decade younger than him, he needed her as a replacement for his mother.

"I wish it was only her bad temper I had to put up with. To tell you the truth, I am scared, I think she is sick," he whispered, anxiety altering his voice.

"What do you mean by sick? Do you think she is mentally sick?"

"Yes and I told her once that she should see a psychiatrist."

"What did she say?" Clara asked, curiously amused.

"She said I was the one who needed to have my head examined."

"What do you think is the matter with her?"

"The fact that her parents favoured her twin brothers over her and openly ignored her needs must have had something to do with it. For all I know, they could have scarred her for life. She wasn't this bad at first. I mean she craved for attention all the time but after the birth of the twins she became unbearable. No matter what I did for her, it was never enough. She kept nagging me that I was acting like a typical man. She still does. She probably thinks that because I am a man, automatically I am crushing her, dictating her and she has to lash out and retaliate. She feels the need to punish everybody for her past sufferings, or for having been born a girl."

"So you believe that she has a problem worth looking into?"

"Yes. I know for a fact that, as the boys were growing, she felt more threatened. Many times, when one or both of them were crying, I heard her say things like, no, you are not going to have your way, just because you are boys or over my dead body, if I let you be the centre of attention. One day she was saying, wait until you have a sister and you'll see who is the boss."

"OH!"

"You know, Clara, one day I met one of her relatives. I asked her a few things about Alice's life at her parent's house. She told me that Alice was always wearing her brothers' hand-me-downs. She had never seen Alice in a dress or a skirt. Her father used to shave her head whenever he shaved the boys'. And listen to this. He used to call her Savanta, as a term of endearment. Can you imagine that? I remember our father calling you Princess."

"Oh! That's cruel. I wouldn't have liked to be referred to as the ugly girl, especially in front of people, no wonder she is the way she is."

"Yes, in a way I cannot blame her for being so spiteful."

"I wish you could convince her to go and get some help," Clara said, feeling sorry for Alice.

"I talked to a doctor once. He told me that she has to offer herself for treatment. He said, you can't drag someone to a shrink and hope for a quick cure. The patient has to admit that he or she has a problem and ask for a psychiatrist's help."

"I suppose it's true."

"In the meantime she will keep maltreating my boys. Caroline is my daughter too and I love her dearly but the way Alice is pampering her is outright sickening. I wish I had the power to miraculously eradicate the misconceptions that have been implanted deep in her subconscious. Don't laugh Clara. I am only repeating what I heard the doctor say."

"I knew those were not your words but nevertheless, this is a job for professionals. At least the boys have you. I think you have to stand up for them as well as for yourself. Maybe you have to appeal to her motherly love. She must have some feelings for her sons, hidden somewhere inside of her. Maybe if you use a scare tactic just to snap things into focus for her. After all, what can she do without you and the children, go back to her parents who are the cause of her problems or work for her living?"

"She was never interested in work. Work is for men, she reckons. In any case, if things come to a crunch, I may be forced to suggest a trial separation period but for now I have to wait and see," Matthew said, then went to lose himself in his paperwork.

Christmas being around the corner, Clara had to work a bit harder. It so happened that the little trinkets she was making were ideal gifts to give or hang as decorations on Christmas trees. She was also asked to teach her techniques in the same art classes that she used to attend.

Matthew took his sister's advice and tried to reason with Alice, hoping against hope that she might at least be kinder to their sons. Since Clara learned about Alice's childhood calamities, she felt a certain degree of compassion towards her but the fact remained that they were not cut from the same cloth. Alice didn't have the background that inspired trust, therefore Clara stayed on her guard. She kept her distance from her sister-in-law and never ever asked her for a favour or confided in her. Clara knew that the chances of Alice turning into an angel in the near future were very slim.

Money kept trickling in, adding to Clara's bank balance. Considering her earnings in the gift shop and her teaching salary plus whatever her mother's solicitor had been regularly sending her, one could say that she was doing well. Once or twice she came very close to talking to her brother about joining their resources and going into a partnership. She figured that they could both benefit from a revamping or an expansion to the shop, for instance. After kicking the idea around for a while, with Alice in the picture, she let go of her futuristic plans. Instead she went on spoiling her nephews and trying to mother them a little, to make up for the affection they were missing. As a result, the boys were getting quieter and better behaved and more attached to her.

Chapter 15

I t was an ordinary day that should have just flown along like any other day. Geneviève rubbed her eyes. She was tired. Tired of going through so many résumés of all those applicants she had interviewed in the last two days. A few had good qualifications and would probably have been capable of replacing her previous accountant who had to move to Brisbane. His wife badly needed the kind of treatment that a hospital over there was providing for the rheumatic arthritis sufferers, he had explained. Nevertheless, for some undetermined reason, none of the men and definitely not the boastful female applicant appeared to be the person she would have liked to work with closely and on a regular basis. They all lacked that something special she couldn't put her finger on.

Sitting back in her chair, Geneviève let her mind wander for a while. Lately she had been feeling stressed. Her work responsibilities eating up most of her time, she hardly had a moment to spare for fun and recreation. Her social life had a lot to be desired. For weeks she had not been in close contact with anyone interesting. She was craving for a bit of excitement. In other words, she was bored to tears and badly needed a man, a real man, in her life. What Geneviève could never have suspected though, was that her life was about to take a significant turn, in a matter of minutes.

Geneviève was immersed in her thoughts when she heard a knock at her office door. It was her secretary informing her that

Mr Foroohar was there for his three-thirty interview. "Let him in," Geneviève implied with a movement of her hand.

"Mrs De La Lande is ready to see you," Geneviève heard the girl say outside of her door. Lifting her head to see what the man with the strange name looked like, Geneviève felt something flip inside of her chest. The sensation was so acute it took her by surprise even though her eyes gave nothing of it away. Alarmed by the sudden quickening of her pulse, she watched the impeccably attired and well-built figure enter and walk towards her desk. At first glance, one could bet that the man was coming from a Latin background but Geneviève soon realised that besides his name, there was something else that was unusual about him. "Mr Foroohar, am I right?" she asked, slightly uneasy.

"Good afternoon Mrs De La Lande, and that's right. My name is Farhad Foroohar."

"Good afternoon Sir...." she said extending a long fingered hand to shake his, "have a seat please;" she managed to finish her sentence in a lower voice.

While the newcomer was making himself comfortable in the visitor's chair, Geneviève couldn't help contemplating his high, smooth forehead and those big black eyes that seemed to be kohl rimmed. She even had time to notice his slick hair that he had brushed away from his open face and the bluey shadow that a recent close shave can bring to a man's jaw line. Another twinkling glance at Farhad's splendid fair complexion and Geneviève was undisputedly sure she had found the man who had filled her dreams since her early teens.

Farhad seemed to be from a totally different world, at least as far as appearance goes. "So, you are here for the Chief Accountant's position?" she began, and before he answered, flipping through his neatly typed résumé, "what makes you think this job is suited for you? Of course, you come highly recommended by the agency but I'd like to know your point of view," she continued, lifting her head to look him straight in the eyes.

"With all due respect Mrs De La Lande and in all humility, I believe I am qualified for this job and, if necessary, I am prepared to work hard and long hours to prove it. Also we live close by and my wife works two streets away from here. We are new in Australia and this is my first interview," Farhad replied with a firm tone and a slight American accent.

Going over the papers one more time, "I can't see any mention of your place of birth here but it says that you lived in America."

"Yes Ma'am, my mother and I left Iran some twenty five years ago. I was born there but I grew up in America."

"Interesting! I have inherited a pair of Persian carpets from my late husband and I am enjoying having them in my house now."

Geneviève searched for another question to ask him but deep in her heart she had no doubts she had found the right man, both professionally and personally. 'He is too good looking. I'd be a fool to let him slip out of my fingers,' she was thinking, mesmerised by the poise and mystical air of the man sitting at a short distance from her.

"How soon can you start?" she queried, a bit stirred by her unethical and not so business orientated thoughts.

"I can start on Monday, if it's all right with you."

"Then Monday it is. Be here at nine and I'll introduce you to the rest of the staff, while giving you a tour around the place."

"Does that mean I have got the job?" he asked candidly.

A gleam entering her eyes, "You've got the job," she answered with a cheeky smile. Then, noticing the perplexed look on his face, in a more serious tone, "Of course you will be hired on a trial basis and with the salary proposed in the ad then, after three months, if we are both happy, your pay will be reviewed and adjusted and your position will be permanent. Is that all right with you?" she asked.

"Yes, I am happy with that."

"And I have every confidence that you are the right person for the job and we will get along nicely," she added and put the résumé down.

Farhad stood up, "Thank you Mrs De La Lande. I am looking forward to working in your establishment," he said, sounding cheerful.

"See you on Monday and it's Geneviève from now on. By the way, Mr Bennet, your predecessor, had to leave suddenly. He might have left his desk in a chaotic state but I bet it will not be a monumental task for you to put things back on track and bring the accounts up to date."

"No worries, I'll try my best," he said as he shook her hand and left, leaving her dazed for a short while.

Grinning mischievously, "A bientôt, see you soon, gorgeous creature," she whispered under her breath.

Out of the blue, Geneviève suddenly remembered something Harold had advised her once, in the first year of their marriage, "You have to think you're an eagle. Circle overhead long enough, until the time is right, then pounce and grab your prey." Of course Harold had been talking about a business acquisition not a man but that's exactly what was passing through Geneviève's mind at that moment. She sighed at the thought of her late husband, "Poor darling," she muttered but straight away, pushing Harold's memory to the back of her mind, she began anticipating the good times ahead.

On Monday, flanked by the dashing Mr Foroohar, Geneviève went from desk to desk, proudly introducing her new Chief Accountant to everyone who was somebody in Très Chic's main office. On her rounds, she couldn't help noticing that every female employee was taken aback by the gentleman's imposing figure and perfect looks. They were on their way back to his office that was conveniently located opposite of hers, when suddenly Farhad bumped into Eddy, a little man holding a big bundle of colourful belts. While apologising, Farhad bent down to retrieve the few belts that Eddy had dropped to the ground. "No harm done, it was my fault," Eddy said shyly.

Geneviève began introducing them to each other when, to her surprise, recognising Farhad, Eddy screamed, "Shahzadeh, is that you?" he asked, dropping all the belts to the floor.

"Yes, it's me, Eddy. What are you doing here?" Farhad asked in Iranian, as they grabbed each other's hands, blatantly excited.

Perplexed, Geneviève looked at the two men talking a foreign language she assumed was Iranian, since she recalled that Eddy had also come from Iran. She decided to leave them alone to chat some more. "I'll talk to you later," she told Farhad and disappeared into her office.

The day passed with Geneviève and Farhad meeting a few more times as he kept coming across issues that needed to be clarified. Towards the end, when he went to her office to drop some documents she had requested, Geneviève remembered the incident with her belt supplier. "By the way, how do you know Eddy?" she asked curiously.

"Oh! I knew him back home when we were kids. It was a long time ago. His mother was a dressmaker and my mum used to go to her for her dresses. During the fittings, Eddy and I used to play together."

"He called you Shah ... something. Is that your middle name?"

"No, Shahzadeh is some sort of a title."

"What sort of a title?"

"It means ... don't worry about it, it's not important," he said, visibly disconcerted by the question.

"I am sorry, I didn't mean to pry," she said.

"No, I am sorry. It's just that I don't particularly like to go through the rest of my life, carrying that title."

"Fair enough!" she uttered. Dropping the subject, she diverted the conversation to business again, yet she remained intrigued by his refusal to comment about the matter. She could always ask Eddy, she thought.

Things were hectic for a few weeks. Geneviève and the rest of her staff were up to their necks in paperwork. Christmas was fast approaching and the workers had to complete, check, pack and dispatch a lot of orders before the machinists left for their four weeks' leave. For the last few months and even amidst the chaos, Farhad had ample time to get acquainted with all the ins and outs and requirements of his job. Having the opportunity to observe his performance, Geneviève had come to realise what a dedicated and precious asset he was turning out to be for her fashion house. She mostly appreciated his overdeveloped sense of responsibility and decency. He was also very courteous towards her and everybody he had to work with.

They were supposed to have a late lunch party on the last day before the holiday break. The fact that Farhad had never shown any sign suggesting he was one bit interested in her personally, had made Geneviève want him even more. She was consumed with desire and itching for his touch. Presuming that she had waited long enough to make her first move on him, she thought, 'No more fantasising, it is high time for me to cosy up with Farhad, and what a better time than the eve of the festive season,' relishing in advance the delightful moments she would have with him.

While all the machinists and the office employees were packing their stuff and fixing their faces, Geneviève ambled into Farhad's office and invited him for a drink after the party. "Just the two of us," she stressed.

"I am afraid I can't do it today," he said earnestly. "Actually, I may have to leave way before the party ends," he added apologetically.

"Nonsense! She blurted out with confidence. Then, placing both hands on his desk and ogling him seductively through her devilish eyes, she began, "Let's not beat about the bush," then, feeling the titillating rise of excitement in her entire body, in the nonchalant way of a woman used to getting what she wants, she dropped the unscrupulous question. "We both have our needs, urges. Isn't it time we gave in to those sexual longings, together, after we send everyone home, hem?"

Put out by her directness, Farhad's wonderful dark eyes widened in disbelief. He tried to pretend he didn't hear the distasteful suggestion by nervously shuffling some papers, mainly to hide the disquiet in his mind. The bewildered look on his face must have answered Geneviève's question but, blinded by her self-assurance, she didn't see it. She paused waiting.

"So! What's the verdict?" she queried as she lifted her hands off his desk, letting her gold bracelet fall away from her wrist. The multitude of shiny little charms attached to every link of the chunky chain produced an annoying jangle. When the din dyed down, without looking at her, he uttered dryly, "Begging your pardon, Mrs De La Lande, I have to remind you that I am a married man. To be precise, a very happily married man."

A brief and uncomfortable silence fell in the room. Seconds later, Farhad continued, "Did I just break some sort of an unwritten law here? I am under the impression that I did. If that's the case, please accept my apology and if you wish, I can leave my resignation on your desk before I go."

Farhad's harsh words producing a vague disturbance in her mind, her heart thumping, Geneviève realised she had bet on the wrong horse, so to speak. Recognising a brush off, with her hopes of a passionate get together utterly destroyed, she had no choice but to say or do something to save her face. She searched for a clever and witty reply, anything that would have the potential to make him believe she had talked that way for a purpose. At last, stretching her first words, "I startled you, didn't I? And it worked," she let out with a chuckle. "Don't be alarmed, there is no need for your resignation and if I embarrassed you, I am sorry. I just needed to make sure you were genuinely trustworthy. This was my way of giving you the ethic test," she tried to explain.

"The ethic test?" he asked, feeling both bothered and curious.

"Yes! I needed to know if you were capable of resisting any kind of temptation, or if you could be corrupted in any way. See, I always admire a man with principles, with moral values. Only a solid, dependable family man can be trusted in business. One who cheats on his wife can cheat almost anybody. I know by now that I can rely on your work but it's your honesty I had to make sure of."

Geneviève stopped for a while then, tossing her newly dyed hair to one side, she went on, "As you see I am not the crazed sex predator I led you to believe I was," trying to sound as sincere as possible and hoping that her half-baked story had been convincing.

"I thought you already knew about my honesty before we signed the employment contract, five months ago."

"That was a bit too soon for me to know. Now, chin up. Friends?" she queried, trying to make eye contact with him.

"Friends," he replied in a low, muffled tone, his eyes still fixed on the papers he was shuffling earlier and finding it hard to compose himself.

A quiet moment that seemed too long and unsettling to Geneviève passed.

The question of, 'Did he buy my explanations,' still burning in her head, she broke the silence by saying, "Now, are you prepared to put this behind you and continue being the competent accountant that I hired in the first place?"

Farhad didn't really buy Geneviève's explanation. With his over attractive looks, he was more than aware of the kind of effect he had on women. Back in America, he had his fair share of being chased by them. There was no reason to expect anything different from the Australian girls. He just didn't think Geneviève would fall into the man hungry category of women. Finally, lifting his head to face her, "I suppose I can but, for heaven's sake, give me notice next time you intend to drop a bombshell like this on me," he said, making her feel the chill of his stare.

"Rest assured, it will not happen again. I was only acting in the best interest of the company. Speaking of which, you are going to have a raise in salary, commencing in the new year," she said half smiling, trying her best to minimise the effects her undue bomb-shell, as he had called it, could have had on him.

"Thanks! That's the kind of talk I don't mind to hear," he said, with a happier disposition.

Unable to utter another word, with tightness in her throat, Geneviève felt the urge to get away from there. Towering above Farhad, "Try to stay a while at the party," she whispered and turned around to leave.

'I always manage to slither away from tricky situations but boy that was not an easy one,' she thought, as she stepped out of the room. On her way, she glanced at her reflection in the glass panel of Farhad's office door and realised that her face had paled to a greenish grey. 'Am I losing my touch?' she asked herself, while she dashed to her own office where she slumped in her chair, nerves on edge. Diverse thoughts assailed her fogged up mind. One minute, she was thinking, 'I can't let him go. For the moment, apart from money, I have little else to offer him if I want to keep him here.' The next minute, 'If only he was aware of what he will be missing by rejecting my advances. Does he know to what he said no to? I bet he doesn't have the slightest idea how exciting I can be if I want to. Well, that'll be his loss. He had his chance and he blew it for sure,' she kept muttering.

Wondering if the air conditioners were working efficiently, Geneviève fanned her face with her hand, as she felt the heat of that midsummer's day together with the anger gnawing away at her. Gradually, a strange sensation began washing over her. She couldn't sort out her feelings. She couldn't say why she wanted him to stay and why she was finding herself so at a loss. Not only was she feeling insulted and hurt, she was feeling nauseous. She was feeling suffocated. She thought she had to do something to clear her mind before showing up at the party and facing her employees. 'Come on Geneviève, pull yourself together, you are not desperate for this man and furthermore, no man is man enough to rattle you,' she pleaded with herself, yet something remained amiss in her mind. Nervously snatching the receiver off the phone, with a sweaty hand, she took her earring off and dialled a number. She called the nearby gym she used to visit once in a while when she needed a workout or just to unwind in the sauna.

Occasionally Geneviève used to ask a masseur to help her relax after a hard day at work. Aldo had the prestige to call at her home sometimes when she urgently needed to get rid of the tension in her tightened muscles. Lately he was promoted to double as a lover. This became a regular practice after the day that her maid left a bit earlier than usual. Besides his fee, Geneviève slipped a few bigger bills in Aldo's pocket and asked him if he would like to stay for a while longer. Aldo got the hint and stayed. They never talked about their secret arrangement, never before and definitively not after the fact. Recognising Aldo's voice on the other side of the line, she murmured in the phone, "Hello! It's me. I need you at seven o'clock this evening."

"I'll be there," she heard him say and she hung up.

The distant clamour of the machinists did not help her mood. Plunged in her chair, Geneviève found herself staring at the dust particles swirling in the strip of sunshine coming from the window. She tried to recall what had transpired in Farhad's office when the crushing sense of reality overcame her. The notion that he was less than keen and had the audacity to tell it to her face had her in a tizzy, once again. She really trusted her powers, where men were concerned. In the past, there was no stopping to her wicked ways, when she had her eyes set on a good looking man. All she had to do was to drop a hint and they were at her mercy. She was the one who called the shots. The way her resolve had weakened by Farhad's abrupt unwillingness to play her game had both muddled and infuriated her. She was mostly angry with herself for being in that quandary. 'There's always a first time for everything, isn't there?' she thought. How could she not have thought of the possibility that Farhad could let her fall flat on her face the way he did. She was so confident that by the end of the day they would embark on a voyage of discovery. She could see their sizzling affair get off the ground. It felt so real she could taste it. 'And of all the pathetic, flimsy excuses, I am a married man, he said. Big deal! As if that stopped my previous conquests from blotting their precious wives right out of their minds, at a snap of my fingers,' she was thinking.

Consumed with rage, Geneviève didn't realise she was talking to herself. She was too upset, too indignant to recognise her true feeling at that time. She was too preoccupied nursing her bruised pride to sense that twinge of jealousy igniting inside of her. Geneviève was in for a surprise. She had yet to discover that, what Farhad had come to mean to her, was on a higher plane. That she had indeed fallen in love with the man and needed him in her life more than the air she was breathing.

That evening, Geneviève put herself in the capable hands of Aldo and let him do whatever he was there to do. Unfortunately for her, neither the massage nor the lovemaking that followed came close to alleviating her disappointment. Throughout the evening, she kept closing her eyes and wishing it were Farhad who was holding her, touching her. Instead of Aldo, she thought she saw Farhad's beautiful dark eyes staring at her accusingly and her whole body stiffened. Calling Aldo was an attempt to drown the heady desires that Farhad had awakened in her but it seemed that she hadn't gone for the best of plans. What she needed was something more than just a sexual release. She realised she was hopelessly craving for a merging of body and soul. Something she never had with any man she had been with, not even with her dear Harold. Again Farhad's fabulous features haunted her mind and she found herself aching to caress his face. He was the one she wanted. He was the one she needed.

Once Geneviève paid Aldo, she all but told him to get lost. He was long gone when she got up and walked across her bedroom, her slender legs taking turns to emerge through the opening of her soft satin negligee. She stood in front of the large bay window and, staring at the darkness beyond, she called, "Farhad," but no sound came out of her dried throat. She felt a shiver take hold of her body. She embraced herself and finally, with a wail in her voice, "Farhad! My adorable Farhad, what am I going to do without you?" she cried aloud, every letter in his name twirling around her with a thundering sound. Breathlessly astounded and alarmed by the state she was left in, Geneviève had a first taste of how it feels to be a loser, when she felt the crushing pain of her heart breaking into pieces.

Chapter 16

His apprenticeship days behind him, Marcus was presently working in a very reputable company. On top of buying and selling houses, his firm was building lots of new houses in every corner of Sydney and major cities of Australia. Marcus was a young man, ready to make his way in the world of the Real Estate business.

The weather was at its best on that particular day of May 1971. It was the Saturday before Mothers' Day and flower vendors were seen on the footpath of almost every main road. Marcus and Patrick, a colleague of his, together with two of the senior staff, were sent to the Fairfield area to conduct an investigation on a big piece of land. Newly released by the Government, it was a space large enough to build eighty to a hundred houses on. While doing his job, Marcus kept reminding himself that he had something to do before going home.

Buying a present for his mother was becoming a difficult thing for Marcus lately because there wasn't anything he could think of that she didn't already have. Liuba had all the electrical appliances she could fit in her little kitchen. The cabinets were bursting with glassware and crockery items. As for personal articles, 'How many dressing gowns, slippers, handbags, nighties, dresses and suits, can a woman in her forties have?' he thought. Very seldom did his mother have the opportunity to wear her real jewellery and she had never shown any inclination to wearing costume jewellery or fancy accessories. Marcus was therefore left with not so many options. Still, he had to make time, go and look for that special item that he hoped was out there, waiting to be discovered by him.

After they finished their mission and wrapped up whatever was expected of them, the two real estate recruits were free to leave. The other two remained on the site to go over their notes and clarify a few more things. Patrick had been invited to a barbeque party for lunch, "Do you feel like going with me?" he asked Marcus.

"No, but thank you, just the same. I have some shopping to do. I'll see you on Monday," Marcus said, excusing himself.

They said goodbye and each walked to their respective cars. Marcus drove towards Fairfield's shopping centre. He parked his car in the first vacant space he could see and began walking on the road that was festooned with all sorts of shops. He thought maybe it was best to try the chemist and check the toiletry section when, unexpectedly, he found himself standing in front of a gift shop with a very appealing window dressing. A few clay figurines placed on glass shelves at the sides grabbed his attention. They were made with utmost skill and taste. Different shapes of snowflakes, cut out from a white velvety paper, were stuck on the glass at the back of the window case. The floor was covered with artificial snow. An attractive golden tree was standing in the middle of that supposed snowfield and had knitwear items hanging from every branch. A reddish coloured cardigan caught his eyes. It had sequins and small clear beads artistically scattered around its neckline. Marcus pushed the door open and stepped in. As he went through the door, a light beam activated an alarm to inform the shopkeeper that someone had entered the place. At first Marcus didn't see anyone there, then he heard a soft female voice asking him, "Yes, how may I help you?" He looked in the direction where the voice was coming from and, emerging from behind the counter, he saw a pair of big beautiful eyes set in a rosy face and his heart throbbed a bit faster.

Marcus could not help noticing that the young girl's clear fore-head was surrounded by a mass of long curly chestnut hair that she had tied at the back of her head. Nor did her sensuously full lips escape his attention. They were opened slightly to reveal the sweetest smile, a smile that melted Marcus's heart. When she stood up, Marcus's eyes swept down to her bodice, allowing him to feast on a perfectly formed bust and narrowing waistline. Altogether, in that short moment, it became his firm belief that the owner of that face and bust exuded all the charm and femininity that he would wish to see in a woman. She was one heck of a girl, the kind of girl that his dreams were made of. Still holding his gaze on her, Marcus waited till his thudding heartbeat slowed a bit then hesitantly uttered, "I am interested in that cardigan." For the first time in his life, Marcus was lost for words and this didn't bother him one bit. He actually enjoyed the fuzzy feeling he sensed inside of his chest cavity.

Absorbed in her thoughts, Clara was sitting behind the counter and was hand knitting a tiny pink jacket for a doll when she became aware that someone was entering the shop. Without lifting her head, with her usual calm voice, "Yes, how may I help you?" she asked. No one answered but Clara got the sensation that the caller was staring at her. She looked up and saw a charming young man on the other side of the counter. She put her knitting down, stood up and smiled. Slightly embarrassed, the customer paused then, pointing to the golden tree in the window, he let her know that he was interested in the red cardigan. "I wonder if it comes in any other colour?" he asked.

"What colour did you have in mind?" she asked, her eyes going from his dark brown hair to his becoming long side burns.

"A colour more suitable for a lady. It's for my mother actually," he added with a smile. Clara looked around for a while, unable to focus on anything then turned to the curtains behind her and called her brother's name. She was still sensing the warmth of the man's gaze.

It was a gaze that kept sending soothing waves all over her body and wrapped her in an unexpected joy. Matthew came out from the room in the back of the shop. Clara asked him in Assyrian if they had the red cardigan in a subtle colour when, "Are you Assyrians?" the stranger asked with an inquisitorial tone.

"Yes we are," said Matthew, puzzled by the question.

"I am Assyrian too," then switching to his maternal language, "I am from Crow's Nest. I am not so familiar with this area. I have been told that there are a lot of Assyrian families living in Fairfield. By the way, my name is Marcus, Marcus Varda," he elaborated in a more relaxed tone, extending his hand to shake Matthew then Clara's hands. Clara's heart was pounding. Her palms were clammy. She was feeling heat rising to her cheeks. After the full introduction, Matthew placed a big box on the counter. While she was helping Marcus make up his mind on the cardigan's colour, Clara was almost sure that she too had made an impression on the young man. If love at first sight was a possibility and not just a myth, then that was for sure the beginning of one such love story. A romance that Clara couldn't have imagined in her most daring dreams.

After Marcus left, Matthew didn't mention a word about him yet Clara had a feeling that her brother had liked him. Matthew's hunches were also telling him that this wasn't going to be the end of the story and that Marcus would call again.

A few days later, Marcus showed up telling them how happy he was that a pottery item he had admired last time was still there in the window. The piece depicted a family of rabbits sitting at a table and having a meal of carrots and lettuce. It was indeed a very intricate piece made with a great deal of patience and a keen eye for detail. Clara had made it only recently. As he carefully placed the masterpiece on the counter, Matthew made sure to point out that Clara had actually created it. His face lighting up, Marcus congratulated Clara on her exquisite skills. "This belongs in a museum, it does, honestly," he said then, taking his wallet out, he got the full price ready. Feeling mildly abashed by the compliments, Clara began carefully wrapping her handiwork in tissue paper. Marcus helped her put it in a padded box.

"I think I'll keep it for myself. It's too good a thing to give to someone else as a present," he whispered. He then casually asked Clara if she would like to go to the party organised by the Australian-Assyrian Association held in Fairfield's Civic Centre.

Clara didn't smile but Marcus sensed a slight softening of her mouth and a glint of excitement in her eyes and that gave him a bit of confidence to pursue his request, "It's a yes, I hope," he asked timidly. Clara then smiled openly. She had known about the party for some time and had wished she could go but she thought it was proper if she'd ask her brother's permission to go with Marcus.

"Why don't we all go? Alice may be able to leave the children in her mother's care for a few hours," Matthew said, trying to be helpful.

The next day, Matthew insisted that Clara go and buy herself a pretty evening dress. Without looking like he was pushing her, in a fatherly way, he encouraged his sister to go for it. It was apparent from the way he talked about Marcus that Matthew had every intention of letting any little spark there was between him and Clara, to kindle.

When Alice got wind of the incident, she acted as if she was Clara's best friend. Putting a sudden concern in her voice she began devising plans to attract Marcus. She volunteered to arrange other get-togethers and outings to "ensnare" him. It was the word ensnare and the sick idea behind it that terrified Clara. Aware of the meddlesome nature of Alice, she realised she had to stop her. Stop her and her desire to take over and consequently spoil things before they had the chance to start. Patiently she allowed her sister-in-law to finish with her prattle then, with a good choice of words and a great deal of tact she made Alice understand that she didn't wish to push things along so quickly. In other words, keep your plans to yourself, was the message she gave her.

Nervously, Alice lit up a cigarette and drew deeply on the acrid smoke then, staring at nothing in particular, she stubbed it in the ashtray. Blowing the smoke in the air, she rose to leave the room, her face crimson by Clara's categorical rejection of her brilliant plans, "Have it your way, see if I care," she mumbled as she passed through the archway. Continuing with her insolent discourse, she walked towards the kitchen to start her version of lasagne.

"Opportunities like this may never present themselves again for all I know. Who do you think you are anyway, Elizabeth Taylor or Miss Universe? Dilly-dally all you want. You are the one who will be left on the shelf if you don't play your hand wisely," she was saying through clenched teeth but loud enough for Clara and her brother to hear every word.

Clara felt the need to scream but she forced herself to maintain a dignified silence. She was determined not to let Alice taint her newfound joy. Frozen to his chair, Matthew displayed an unwillingness to react too. Knowing that one word out of him and Alice would embark on yet another of her never-ending arguments, hurling more hurtful phrases his and Clara's way. He just rolled his eyes in a meaningful way and let his wife stew in her own juices. Later on he advised his sister not to let his chatterbox wife bother her. "She is more bark than bite, you know?"

"Don't worry Matthew, I don't take these mere words seriously any more. I only want this relationship to take its natural course without outside interference. Alice may mean well but it's her condescending talk that makes me see red."

"Yes, Alice seems to draw sustenance from criticising people but we have to ignore her."

The next day dawned with the promise of sunshine. Clara woke up feeling good about life even though nothing had happened yet to give her that sort of confidence. Still, she sensed a boundless supply of optimism within herself. It gave her the energy to get up and face Alice and the rest of the world. Something was telling her that her destiny was about to manifest itself, that things were on a roll. She hugged herself and twirled in front of her dresser as she hummed one of the Beatle's songs. Marcus dropped in at the shop pretending he was still working on that land business. He asked Matthew and Clara if they knew of a good place he could have a decent lunch. Matthew directed him to a well known take away food place for which Marcus thanked him before asking if they would like to go and have a bite with him. Clara tucked wisps of hair behind her ear and faced her brother, an interrogative look in her eyes.

"You can go Clara. Unfortunately I have to stay. I am waiting for some leather goods that are supposed to be delivered any time now. I'll be all right," Matthew said casually, as if there was nothing odd about the invitation.

Pretending her daughter was not feeling well, Alice decided not to go to the party but she met Marcus when he came to pick up Matthew and Clara. Secretly impressed by Marcus's looks, "I'll be all right, you go and have a lot of fun," she said, feigning a regret when they left without her. As soon as they were out of the door, her physiognomy changed. Jealousy brewing inside of her, 'Some people have all the luck,' she muttered bitterly as she walked to her bedroom. There, looking at her reflection in the mirror of her dressing table, 'What has she got to deserve a hunk like him?' she added.

Marcus couldn't get away from work every day and drive all that way to see Clara but he phoned the shop regularly and almost at the same time. Every time he called, Matthew let Clara pick up the phone and if he picked it up, he usually talked to Marcus briefly then, "It's for you," he used to say before handing her the receiver and making himself scarce.

They were invited to the Vardas for lunch. Jonathan and Liuba couldn't wait to see this artistic girl their only son had lost his heart to. Clara was eager to meet them too. Her only worry was whether the children would behave and whether Alice would embarrass her in front of Marcus's parents. Her fears disappeared as soon as she shook hands with them, a feeling of warmth swept over her and she knew she was amongst nice, sincere and trustworthy people. Adam and his family were there too and from the way they greeted her she believed they were decent people who would not judge or criticise anyone unnecessarily.

After exchanging the customary banalities, Matthew couldn't shake this feeling of déjà vu. Puzzled, he stared at Jonathan, racking his brain, searching in his memory to find an answer to a pressing question, 'Where have I seen this man before?' Suddenly rising to his feet and pointing his finger at Jonathan, "It was you! You were the man, you were the one who danced in the street," he exclaimed with a gleeful voice.

"You danced in the street?" Liuba asked Jonathan dumb-founded.

Everyone looked at Matthew, waiting to hear more about the subject, as he went on.

"I said you looked familiar. You are the young man who danced in the street to the music of that what's his name, the scruffy violinist.

"Paganini," Jonathan declared, "but how do you know this?" he inquired, surprised that someone had knowledge of what had transpired that afternoon when he had left Aunt Sophie's house.

"I was there," Matthew replied, "I was this tall," he added, holding his hand down to show how tall he was. "We used to live two houses away from where it happened. I saw you and that Paganini fellow."

"Small world," Marcus uttered.

"You never told me that," Adam complained jokingly.

"So you two know each other already," Alice joined in then, pressing her lips together, she tilted her head sideways and let the universal gesture that means I don't get it to appear on her face as she asked, "but why were you dancing in the street?"

"It's a long story, I'll tell it in a while. Now what do you wish to drink Matthew, my new old friend?" he asked, turning to his guest.

That incident, in all its simplicity, started the meeting on a cheerful footing and, as the day progressed the three families bonded over a very appetising meal. Subsequently it made it easy for the young lovebirds to get to know each other better in the following similar gatherings. Marcus and Clara therefore did not have to find plausible reasons to spend time together. Clara was blissfully happy to know that her biggest wish could one day become a reality. Every day that passed made her more appreciative that fate had snatched her from the jaws of despair by bringing Marcus into her life.

The day was shaping up to be another beautiful day for Clara. Away from the annoying presence of Alice, she was serving customers with her habitual good nature. Joy in her heart, she couldn't wait for Marcus to come and pick her up at five o'clock, as he had said he would, "I have something of utmost importance to discuss with you," he had stressed in the morning when he had called.

Clara was waiting for Marcus outside the shop. Her hazel eyes lit up when he showed up, grinning broadly. She matched his smile and when he saw her smile, he felt hope rise in him. "Hi beautiful!" he said with a cheerful voice. In their candour, Clara found those two words so strangely intoxicating that her body stirred. It was as if she had discovered the secret door to paradise.

"Hi," she replied, slightly embarrassed, her heart wobbling with anticipation, wondering what important thing he had to tell her. Marcus's brown eyes twinkled at her embarrassment.

"Let's go for a walk. I had to park the car a bit too far. I hope you don't mind."

"Not at all."

Hand in hand, they walked along that familiar street of Fairfield, indulging in small talk till they reached the local park. Watched by two adults, a group of children were using the playground's equipment. Marcus led Clara towards a bench but before she sat on it, he stood in front of her and, grasping both her hands and without preamble, "Will you marry me, Clara dear?" he asked, searchingly looking in her eyes. Her heart leapt as she gazed in the passionate darkness of his eyes.

"Yes," she blurted out, tears misting her own and her answer went straight to his heart. He put his arms around her and pressed her head against his chest then, caressing her full head of Shirley Temple curls, "Oh, darling, I won't let you regret your decision. You know how much I love you, don't you?" he asked, giving a spontaneous expression to his emotions.

"I kind of guessed you did but I also feared that it could have been my wishful thinking," she replied, blinking her eyes to let the tears roll freely down her cheeks.

Smiling, Marcus bent down and kissed her lips, softly at first then, with a growing passion that left her breathless. They sat on the bench and talked some more. On the way to the car she linked her arm through his, practically clinging on to him as they ambled along in silence. It seemed like they didn't have a care in the world.

Later, when they got to her home, Marcus gently kissed her goodbye outside the door. She entered the house still feeling the warmth of his breath that sent a ripple of desire through her body. She braced her shoulders and quietly retreated to her room. Joy clutching at her heart, Clara couldn't help reflecting on the days when she used to feel so depressed, so lonely between those same walls. Her sadness was now an insignificant term, a memorandum of events that were devastating to her in distant times. Clara was now living a wonderful, incredible dream. She could say, for sure that Marcus and his love for her had taken care of the big void she was so anxious to fill.

In the following weeks, the romantic episode of Marcus and Clara's relationship continued. It went on till the Vardas, together with Adam and Freeda, appeared at Matthew's house and officially asked for Clara's hand in marriage to their son. In the traditional way, they presented her with various little gifts, as well as a superb engagement ring. The next day, Clara began running around, buying bridal magazines and collecting swatches of fabric and trimmings. When she wasn't with Marcus, she was thinking about and searching for the perfect dress that she would like to wear on her Wedding Day.

Chapter 17

Geneviève was on the phone giving all the necessary instructions to her trusted florist, "I want the roses to be delivered at exactly ten minutes after nine o'clock. Make sure that my secretary receives and signs for them and not a word about the sender's name, OK? Don't forget what I told you to write on the card."

"Everything will be as you specified, don't worry Mrs De La Lande. I will deliver the flowers myself."

"Thank you, I would appreciate that," Geneviève said as she put the receiver down and lifted it again to dial her Travel Agency. She booked a flight to Queensland as well as a room for two nights at the most prestigious hotel on the coast. She made a last phone call to her secretary informing her of her trip, purposely dropping hints to let her deduce that she wouldn't be alone there but with a certain man she had been dating for quite a while. Geneviève was absolutely sure that, in no time, Brenda would manage to make her discovery public knowledge.

On the first day after the public holidays, coffee in hand, all the office people, including Farhad, were gathered around, talking about whatever each one of them did during Christmas. Pretty soon the conversation turned into gossip about the boss's secret lover, all because a bunch of red roses had been delivered earlier with a card prominently on display, saying, "Dear Geneviève, thank you for the unforgettable few days we had together. Hope to see you again soon." There was a semblance of a signature. It started with a letter looking like an M or maybe an H. The rest of the letters were also not any clearer for the signature to be deciphered.

Geneviève arrived at the office later than usual that day. Her made-up face kind of concealing her state of mind. She had tried hard to make herself look like she had had a few good days of rest and recreation. "Did you enjoy your holidays?" her secretary queried.

"Yes, we had a tremendous time! It rained a bit but we didn't care," Geneviève answered rather loudly, trying to sound convincingly pleased. The truth was that Geneviève stayed cooped up in her hotel room reading a book for the whole two days and ordered her meals in – meals she hardly touched as she practically lived on coffee and juice – only because she needed Farhad to believe that she was happily vacationing with another man and was not moping around without him. Little did she know that Farhad didn't give a damn about the where and with whom his boss had passed her time? He had his own life, his own worries and his own problems to deal with.

It was imperative for Geneviève to keep a straight face whenever she was in Farhad's proximity. In the meantime, she had to make sure that he was comfortable enough to willingly stay in his current employment. The very thought of him leaving the company terrified her.

A couple of months passed during which Geneviève tactfully tried to gain back his confidence. At times she resorted to confide in him by talking about her problems, her fears. Sometimes she even had to pretend that she had hit a snag and needed someone else's advice, a two heads are better than one kind of advice. She hoped he would detect that, despite her bossy exterior, there was a vulnerable and softer side to her.

Scared to give her true feelings away, Geneviève tried not to make eye contact with Farhad as much as possible. The two managed to work together in total concord. At times it seemed that the faux pas she had made before the holidays had never happened. She became a completely different woman whenever she happened to be in his company. Nevertheless, she remained her old distinctive self with all the other employees, often venting her inner anger and frustration on the meekest, regardless of age and gender.

Feeling a bit more relaxed with her, once Farhad found the audacity to criticise the way Geneviève had handled an elderly cleaner who hadn't done his job to her satisfaction. Since she was the big cheese, she wanted and insisted that everything was done her way. "Is a bit of dust, left here and there, so important? Goodness, the way you yelled at the poor man, I thought he had committed an unforgivable crime," Farhad scolded her in a friendly way. She was impressed and quite elated by his faint show of intimacy. "Untidiness is a crime in my eyes," she said.

"Yes but..."

"I don't really like to act like a tyrant but I have to keep the workers on their toes. If I let them get away with a small mistake, the problem will escalate and it will be harder to keep them under control after that. Also, I have a low tolerance level when it comes to incompetence," she added with a smile.

"It's your business but if I was you I wouldn't create enemies. I am afraid all your moves are not necessarily in your best interest. One day, one of them may be less forgiving. Safety comes first, these situations can be a bit hairy if you are not careful."

"Don't be melodramatic. So I am a demanding boss, what else is new? I have heard a few things they say, behind my back. Why not give them an excuse to make up more jokes about me, if it amuses them.

"They say things like what?" Farhad asked with a cheeky boyish tone.

"Let see, things like, what do you get if you cross a sac of bones with a rattle snake?"

"Heard that, what else?"

"Oh! What ever, I can't remember," she answered, putting an end to that line of questioning with a movement of her hand but Farhad could see that she was not so cool and comfortable with what the staff thought of her.

"It bothers you, doesn't it?"

"What? She asked nervously."

"What they say. I personally believe that everyone respects you for the remarkable lady that you are and those jokes are only a pastime. You shouldn't take them seriously."

"Do I look like I give a damn what they say?"

"I think you do."

"Bah!" She said, throwing her shoulders in the air, a little hope budding in the depth of her heart. 'Remarkable lady he called me. Is that what he thinks of me? Is it possible that he is not so indifferent towards me? That he has not slipped away from my grasp, after all? Is there any chance that all is not lost for me?' The thought of it overwhelmed her. She gave him one last furtive glance and began discussing work matters with him, glad that she had him as an ally of a kind. One thing Geneviève had no doubt about was that Farhad was the only person who truly spoke his mind. Nothing about what he said or did was dictated by his fear of her or the need to keep his job secured. Geneviève had not yet found even one shred of hypocrisy in him and that concept made him all the more desirable to her, all the more dear to her heart.

A big proportion of the employees from the office and just about all the machinists had gathered in Très Chic's canteen to say farewell to Angela who was leaving her job for an indefinite time, if not forever. Angela was only two months away from having her first baby. Geneviève made her way to the platform, grabbed the microphone to say a few words, before presenting the mother to be with the gift from the management. With their collected money the staff had also purchased a present and were eagerly waiting to give it to their good friend.

Clearing her voice, Geneviève blew in the mouthpiece and began with, "Can I have your attention please," but faced with technical difficulties she decided to speak loudly instead. The place was not so big anyway to need that sort of equipment. She repeated her opening sentence then added, "Once again, because of the stork, we are about to lose a valuable employee and while we are very happy for Angela, myself and everyone present are sad to see her go. Nevertheless, we all hope that our best wishes will follow her during the last months of her pregnancy, throughout the delivery and afterwards when she brings the precious little bambino home.

At this precise moment, as if drawn by a strange force, Geneviève's eyes went from Angela to Farhad who was standing a few feet away. To her surprise, she noticed a distinctive sadness in those gorgeous eyes of his that she had come to adore so hopelessly. Her heart sank as she stared at the expression his face had taken. Automatically, her mind went back to a few hours earlier when the pram she had ordered for Angela was delivered at her office. Coincidently, Farhad was with her, they were busy discussing a business transaction. She remembered the way his eyes had travelled from his folder to the big white bow on top of the gift. He had let out a big sigh then walked a few steps towards the pram and actually had run his fingers around the edge of the canopy with the same distressed look in his eyes. 'What am I missing here?' She asked herself, while continuing with her speech.

Geneviève couldn't wait for the formalities to end so she could have a moment with her accountant. She hoped she could somehow convince him to open his heart and tell her what was bothering him. By the time she was able to be alone with him, in her mind, she had put two and two together and had come to the conclusion that Farhad and his wife were childless. 'Could that be the proximate cause that had him sad eyed?' she had wondered. As Farhad entered her office, his very posture revealed that something had pained him. Geneviève casually glanced at him. "Angela looked pleased with her gifts and the way this whole farewell affair was conducted," she said simply.

"Yes! She seemed happy enough," came his neutral reply.

"Say, you and your wife have been married for some time now, if you don't mind me asking, have you ever considered starting a family?" she asked with nonchalance."

"We did." he answered, a bit hesitantly.

"So, what is preventing that from happening?"

"It's not happening," he said with a broken voice, after trying to clear the tension from his chest.

"You mean you are all for it but...."

"That's right. We have been unsuccessful so far."

"Oh!" she only said, then after a brief silence, she queried caringly, "it's never too late, have you been to see specialists?"

"Yes, a few, but nothing has changed."

"Well, a close friend of mine who works in a family planing clinic in the city, was telling me once of a particular obstetrician who is using this amazing new way of dealing with infertility. She told me it has been eighty per cent proven to be successful with couples that had tried everything and failed," she said, wishing she could hold his face between her hands and wipe sadness away from it. "Wait a second," she added, as she reached for a notebook in her drawer. Looking into it, she grabbed the phone and dialled a number. A few seconds later, after a short conversation with her friend in question, she went straight to the point and began scribbling the doctor's name and address on a pad. "Dr G Abernethy, Macquarie Street, yes, I got it. Thank you, I'll call you one of these days to arrange a date for lunch, bye for now," she said and hung up.

Geneviève handed Farhad the paper, urging him to give it a try. "Ask your general practitioner for a referral, as soon as you possibly can. Who knows, this doctor may have the answer to your problem, you have nothing to lose anyway," she pleaded with him.

"Thank you, we truly have nothing to lose as you say and maybe he is the one with the cure," he said.

Taking the paper from her, Farhad left, leaving Geneviève wondering what sort of an idiot she was volunteering to help the couple. What if the fertility program worked? It would only mean that she had put the last nail in her own coffin where her hopes and desires towards him were concerned. 'Geneviève, tu es une imbecile,' she reproached herself, her spirit sagging at the thought of Farhad getting closer to his wife in the event they became parents. Gradually a spiteful idea began flourishing in her selfish mind. 'Then again, his wife may never get pregnant. Their marriage, probably an arranged one, may not stand the strain. Their relationship may suffer to a critical point. I will then see to it that he comes to me for comfort and, when the bottom falls out of their marriage, I will be there to reap the rewards.'

Chapter 18

I t was a toss up between Samuel and another young journalist to go and cover a certain fashion parade. At the end the boss decided to give the honour to Samuel. "Boring!" Samuel mumbled to himself but, accepting that every job must have its tedious moments, he got ready to go and make the best of it. "Andiamo, let's go," Enzo said, tapping Samuel on the shoulder.

Enzo was an Italian born photographer and father of two who was assigned to execute the task of taking the necessary photos. They arrived there just in time to grab their places amongst other members of the media who had come to report on Très Chic's annual show. Samuel stood patiently through the preliminary speeches, the first one being made by none other than Mrs De La Lande, the fashion designer herself.

Occasionally, Samuel scribbled some notes on his pad till the pencil thin models began prancing on the catwalk under the bright light that was following them every step of their way. Enzo was able to take a lot of pictures, as the girls were giving their flexible bodies the characteristic movements in order to reveal every detail of the garments they were modelling. There were also the constant flashing of blinding lights from the cameras of professional photographers that the Très Chic fashion house had hired. Nevertheless, the girls were used to the glare and did their bit without batting an eye.

When all the different categories of ladies' clothing were put on show by various models, the speaker announced that it was time for the pièce de resistance outfit. "And now, the last but not least, a wedding gown worn by our own Miss Aurore De La Lande," Samuel heard him say.

All eyes became glued on the doorway from which the top mannequin was going to emerge. Enzo lifted his big camera, ready to capture the model at her best poses. The lights dimmed momentarily then intensified as the gorgeous creature stepped out and walked gracefully towards the centre of the catwalk, eclipsing the male model walking with her and playing the role of the groom.

For a while the world seemed to stand still for Samuel. The attendees gasped and cheered at the sight of the girl's slender, eyecatching figure that made the moment come alive. "Mamma mia!" Enzo exclaimed while he turned to Samuel to check his reaction. Samuel's eyes were stuck to the cloud of ruby red coloured wavy hair, falling so luxuriantly around the statuesque shoulders of that astonishing goddess. Never in his life had he been so captivated by a woman's looks. In his eyes, the girl was nothing but the personification of his dreams.

Unable to write anything, Samuel gave Enzo a nudge, urging him to take all the shots he could, as she was nearing their spot. The floor was vibrating by lively music. Mesmerised, Samuel continued contemplating those stunning features set on that glowing oval face. In a split second his eyes met with hers or he thought they did and he felt a rush of pleasure invading his entire body. The dress she was wearing consisted of an off white silk taffeta skirt, tightly fitted around the hips but flaring at the bottom. Ankle length at the front, it was very long and amply trailed at the back and was finished by a slightly undulating frill all around the hem. The superb skirt was complemented by a body hugging, heavily beaded bodice. Loads of silky cords, threaded with a few gold beads at their ends, were loosely tied around her tiny waist then let to hang all the way down to the floor, at her left side. "Aurore," Samuel whispered, "What a befitting name, and to think that I almost missed being here tonight."

In a dramatic move, Aurore turned around, her long trailed skirt sweeping the floor in a luxurious rustle. As she came closer to Samuel, she turned her head to his direction and smiled encouragingly. Awestruck, Samuel smiled back as she continued her retreat towards the doorway. It all appeared so natural, so as may be expected. It was as if they already knew each other. Applauding frantically, the crowd cheered some more and asked the couple back as they disappeared through the curtains. The memory of her chiselled cheeks and provocative lips still on Samuel's mind, his every instinct urged him to do something before she vanished like Cinderella did at the stroke of midnight. Clutching his pad to his chest, 'I have to see her. I have to find a way to talk to her,' he was thinking.

Aurore came back on her own at first then all the other models joined her. People threw flowers at their feet. Several big bunches of flowers were brought and given to them from the management. Samuel could hear a few spectators whistle but he just stared at Aurore in utter disbelief that such a beautiful being could actually exist.

Five minutes later, Samuel found himself peeping through the changing room's door, hoping to catch another glimpse of Aurore and possibly exchange a few words with her. A guard asked him if he was waiting for one of the models. Holding his journalist card in the man's face, "I am from the Sydney Morning Herald, I wonder if I could ask a few questions..."

"The press will be received a bit later when Mrs De La Lande has the place to herself. The models shouldn't be disturbed, they need time to relax and change."

"But I have to see..."

It must have been fate that Aurore saw him and came to rescue him from embarrassing himself any further, "It's all right Alec," she said casually, dismissing the over protective guard then, staring at Samuel's open and honest face, "who is it that you have to see sir?" she asked politely.

"You, Miss Aurore. I wonder Miss if I could ask you a few questions. My name is Samuel, Samuel Goddard." Like some schoolkid caught doing something he wasn't supposed to be doing, clumsily he pretended he was looking for something in his pockets. "Oh well!" he said, giving up on his search, "first of all, allow me to tell you that you are by far the prettiest girl, I mean model that I have ever had the pleasure to see. How long have you been modelling?"

"Thank you. I have been modelling for almost eight years now. How many fashion parades have you been to?"

"Not many," he said timidly, "and another question," he added.

"Yes?" she asked, tilting her head to one side with curiosity.

"May I ask you if you are free this Friday afternoon?" he blurted out, surprised by his own boldness. It was a shot in the dark but it was worth the risk. A smile creeping across her mouth, Aurore creased her nose and, making a face as though she was thinking, "Let me see, no, I don't believe that I have something special on Friday," she whispered through her beautiful lips.

"How about if I picked you at, let's say five o'clock, at ..."

"Outside Très Chic. You know where Très Chic's offices are, don't you?" she asked, confident that her mother would not be there at that time.

"As a matter of fact, I do, then it's settled, bye for now," he replied gleefully before leaving.

A few steps away from them, still giddy from all the applause and compliments, Geneviève was engaged in an animated conversation with some prospective buyers. Nevertheless, the look on Samuel's face as he was chatting away with Aurore didn't go unnoticed by her prying eyes. The minute she could tear herself away from the would be clients, she rushed to her daughter's side, "What was with Pépe Le Pew? Was he bothering you?" she inquired reproachfully.

"Oh, no. He was just a reporter trying to do his job. Pépe Le Pew," Aurore repeated, trying to control a fit of the giggles.

"Still, he looked a bit too pushy to me, too unpleasantly persistent," Geneviève said with the assertiveness of a controlling mother.

So far, things had come together for Geneviève with a pattern of perfection. She didn't wish to have her day of glory obscured by some undesirable individuals hanging around her daughter.

Samuel went out and looked around to find Enzo. 'Why should I be so lucky,' he wondered, thinking about Aurore consenting to see him. When he took the chance and tried to talk to her, in his mind, he was ninety per cent certain he would be subjected to some of that arrogance that comes so naturally to the perfectly beautiful people. Instead, he found himself having a cosy chat with one of the sweetest persons he had met in his life. He couldn't wait for Friday to arrive.

Samuel and Aurore kept seeing each other. Their tight schedules taken into consideration, their meetings were usually brief and far in-between. As time passed, Samuel's genuine admiration towards Aurore turned into a deeper feeling. He ended up being passionately in love with her.

In Aurore's case too, Samuel was becoming a lot more than the Adonis she had the chance to see the day of the parade. It so happened that, on the day of the parade, every time a girl went through the curtains to go onto the catwalk, someone standing close by was able to have a glance at the audience. Aurore was the one waiting there for her turn to get out, therefore through the beaded curtain's gaps, she was able to peep many times at Samuel's stunning face glowing in the lights. Aurore could say that she had been interested in him first and she knew that she was getting inevitably close to falling in love with him.

Samuel and Aurore were two young people caught in a hormonal haze and alarmingly unable to keep away from each other. Their tender feelings for one another had a big chance to launch them into a heated romance. Normally, there would be nothing wrong with the picture, except there was a fly in the ointment, as they say, a fly by the name of Geneviève.

With her grandiose expectations of the most perfect son-in-law, Geneviève would hit the roof if she ever found out her precious daughter was involved with a common guy. Having no other choice, Aurore had to keep her relationship with Samuel under wraps and was adamant to continue doing it for as long as she was able to. She could not possibly know every detail about her mother's escape from the abject life, back in France in the post-war times, but she remembered enough about their humble beginnings in Australia. Nevertheless, having observed Geneviève's attitude over the years, Aurore had a clear notion that her mother would make an issue of the wide social gap between them and Samuel. With Geneviève's visions of grandeur and highly inflated ego, Aurore was sure her mother would urge her not to take her fling with Samuel any further.

Over the years, Aurore had heard her mother repeatedly say, "Go out with boys, have fun, you are only young, but make sure you don't give any of them a sense of progress." Lately, it was, "String them along and when the time comes for you to get married, don't short change yourself, you deserve nothing less than a prince."

Samuel was also keen at keeping his affairs of the heart from people around him but he couldn't fool Enzo, who kept questioning him so much until Samuel couldn't conceal the feelings he had for Aurore any longer. His enormous smile and his blue eyes lighting up every time Aurore called him on the phone, were distinctly positive indications that she had seriously captivated him. In fact, there were not enough adjectives to describe the excitement he felt whenever he got the chance to steal a few moments with her. Samuel was convinced that fate had something to do with the way the two had come together and that belief brought him a blessed sense of happiness. Every time he was with Aurore, his heart would be thumping with the longing to see her again.

Samuel's job was often keeping him away from home. His mother was missing him an awful lot, since he was the only man in the house with whom she could have a pleasant conversation every now and then. Peter's attitude towards her had changed so much lately. Gone were the days she found his minor faults endearing. Most of the time, when he was at home, there was nothing but harsh words and cold silences left between them. These days, she often found herself on a ledge trying to find a reason to continue living with him and his unrealised dreams that he was grappling with.

Lost in his own hell, Peter failed to realise the loneliness his wife was feeling. Night after night, as the effects of alcohol came to surface, he kept travelling into his own imaginary world. It was a place where he could see himself interviewing politicians, asking them all the trickiest of questions, making them cringe before answering him. There, he could have the opportunity to dig for dirt and corruption in high places, he could be the first one on the spot gathering information wherever he sensed a scandal was brewing. In his mind, the dust of a certain war had finally settled. He was in foreign countries meeting with the who's who of the movie industry, discussing intriguing subjects with the celebrities of every continent. In the eyes of his mind, Peter could see his name at the top of every daring article printed in the Australian Newspapers.

There was a ray of hope left for Martha, and that was to see Samuel married and settled at last. She yearned for the company that a son and a daughter-in-law would bring, and she couldn't wait to be a grandmother. The anticipation of this future happiness was the only thing that gave her the strength to go on, and to slowly let go of the painful memories of Jeremy.

The times that Samuel passed at home were getting shorter and shorter but even so, recently, Martha's intuition had told her that her son might be in love. She had noticed that, lately he was putting a lot more care into his appearance. He was buying expensive clothes and was wearing even more expensive aftershave. That wasn't all. Martha had also detected some sort of overall transformation in him. Her curiosity getting the better of her, she cornered him one weekend and urged him to tell her whom the lucky girl was. "Won't you tell your mother who has put that permanent grin on your face?" she had asked.

"All in good time mum, all in good time. You'll know when you have to know," he had only said, smiling openly as he had caressed her cheek with the back of his hand.

Chapter 19

A dam was back from Iran, a trip he had to take because of his father's unexpected heart problems. Luckily, by the time he got there Shimoon was out of danger and was recovering steadily. Adam spent a few days with his parents before taking the plane back home. He came back to his wife and two daughters, his job and most importantly to get a head start with the preparations for Marcus and Clara's wedding. He was the best man and he intended to do his part to perfection. Malcolm was also away from home. He had to fly to Japan to finalise a business deal but he had prompted Adam to get to his father's bedside and not to think about the company. "Don't worry Adam, the company will still be here when either one of us returns first," he had said.

As soon as Adam put his suitcase down, there was some disturbing news thrown at him when he asked about the girls. "Juliet is all right but Violet, I am afraid, her relationship with her husband seems to be on the rocks. I will tell you all about it after you shower and get some rest."

"Is it serious?" Adam asked worriedly.

"It may be. They have been having problems for some time. I thought it would pass and I wouldn't have to worry you with it but apparently it didn't."

"The twerp! I knew he was a no-hoper the day I set eyes on him. I can kick myself for allowing her to go out with him in the first place. She was far too young for that sort of thing anyway."

"What could you have done? It's not like she would listen to you. She was in love and we both know how persistent our daughter can be when her mind is set on something. She wanted him and nobody could dissuade her from that. Thank goodness she had the good sense not to fall pregnant. That would have been something to worry about," Freeda said, visibly upset about her daughter's marital problems.

"He is rude, unreliable, and has never held a steady job. He is just wrong for our daughter. She could have done so much better if she hadn't rushed to get married."

"If only we knew about his gambling problem," Freeda blurted out.

"Gambling problem? What else do I have to hear about the little parasite? I tell you Freeda, we'd better have a serious talk with the two of them and resolve this situation as soon as possible. If it were up to me, I would say that the best solution for them is to go their separate ways before they mess up things any further. I knew it wouldn't work. I had this sickening feeling inside of me the day they got married and believe me, it wasn't because he was not from our background. No matter how hard I tried, I just couldn't bring myself to accept him as someone you can bring into your family."

"It's two years of her life and a lot of our money but you are right, it's best to let Ari know that he has us to answer to if he does the wrong thing by our daughter."

"Yes! He'd better clean up his act or else. By the way, any news from uncle Malcolm?"

"Actually, he phoned yesterday. He told me that he had considered changing his plans and fly to Tehran but, feeling under the weather, he had decided to come straight home."

"Oh, what is wrong with him?" Adam asked with curiosity as well as concern.

"I don't know exactly. He said something like a chest cold, difficulty breathing. He was evasive."

"Nothing serious I hope," Adam said, staring at her anxiously.

"I am not sure. I think he should consider giving up smoking. He didn't sound well."

"Yes, that makes things worse probably. By the way, Freeda, remind me to phone Jonathan after my shower. I have some news for him."

Adam stepped into the shower unaware that his uncle had chosen not to tell Freeda anything about a small matter of his sputum being streaked with blood.

It was the day before the wedding. Jonathan was not home. Adam was delivering the extravagant gift that uncle Malcolm had prepared for the bride and groom. He also handed Marcus a card in which his uncle had expressed his sorrow for not being able to attend the wedding because of health problems. "Oh! What is he suffering from?" Liuba asked, inviting Adam to sit and have a cup of tea with them.

"Uncle is fighting a nasty kind of flu he must have contracted while he was overseas," Adam explained.

"Pity he can't come, I wish he gets well soon. Give him my regards please and tell him thank you from Clara and me," Marcus said.

"I will. Sorry I can't stay. I have to meet the florist at the church," Adam said, turning to Liuba. Thanking her for her offer, he left.

Aside from Freeda, Adam had only told Jonathan of the real nature of dear Malcolm's illness. "Let everybody enjoy the wedding for now," Adam had suggested.

Malcolm had arrived five days earlier in a dreadful shape. He was coughing incessantly. After a restless night, Adam had rushed him to see his doctor who had ordered a series of tests. Days later, when they went back for the test results, they were given the alarming news that Malcolm's symptoms of what seemed to be a chest cold were actually the first telltale signs of a more serious illness. He was told that he indeed had cancer of the lungs. Deeply concerned for his uncle, Adam couldn't help remembering what his wife had said about uncle having to lay off cigarettes. He wasn't surprised to hear the doctor give him the very same advice or more like order him to stop smoking there and then.

Almost aware of the fact that his days were numbered, Malcolm tried his best to keep his cool and treat the matter as if it was not a big deal. His wish was to prevent the family from worrying or making a fuss around him. Adam had learned all about the business he was going to inherit eventually, yet the thought of not having his uncle by his side and benefit from his expertise and guidance had begun giving him a panic attack. Running a company of that size on his own was suddenly appearing scarier than he could have imagined.

When Adam went to the church to check on the decorations, he made a halt in front of the altar. Even though he always claimed that he wasn't particularly inclined towards religion, he found himself having a chat with the figure on the crucifix. In a clumsy way he went on his knees and began begging Jesus to have mercy on his uncle, "Make his remaining days not too unbearable please! You know what a nice person he has always been, let him die with dignity," he prayed.

The wedding preparations were going according to plan. Every detail was checked and rechecked. Clara was happy with the choices she had made regarding her own gown as well as her bridesmaids' outfits. Adam had given Jonathan the good news that their old dancing friend Saul and his son Israel would be flying to Sydney. "They will arrive just in time to attend the wedding," he had said.

There was a jubilant feeling floating in the air at the Varda's and at Matthew's home. Matthew had been bending backwards to do his share in making sure everything went smoothly on the big day. Even Alice had tried her best to participate.

The schoolmistress had called in sick. Apparently she had contracted the latest flu virus and Peter couldn't ask for a better opportunity to sneak in and teach his class in peace. His first hour after lunch was free. Peter could have taken a long break and drop in the nearest pub, as he would have done in the past. Instead, he decided to stay in the classroom and eat his cheese sandwich quietly. He felt the need to reflect on what the boss had told him the other day. After a disturbed night, he had come to realise that it was time he did something about his drinking habit. He was aware that his dependence on alcohol was progressively destroying his life. His career seemed to be in danger of extinction too.

Peter recalled the days after Jeremy's funeral when he had resorted to booze in the bid to forget the fact that maybe he could have done something to prevent the tragedy. Yet the old ingrained feeling of failure had kept poisoning his life. He had been convinced that if he had been the man he had aspired to be, none of this would have happened. He would have been a hero in his son's eyes. Jeremy would probably have walked in his footsteps and made him proud. Still, in the rare moments of sobriety, especially when he was teaching in class, the thought had occurred to him that his body might not take the alcohol abuse for too much longer. Many a time, his reason had told him that enough was enough but his need just wouldn't leave him alone and, once at home, his resolve would fade away. He would then succumb to the desire of opening another bottle, empty it in no time and slide off his seat into a drunken stupor till the next day. Sensing that life was gradually ebbing out of him, something inside of him would want to stop the nonsense. He would wish he could start with a clean slate and enjoy the rest of his days. Oh! So often he had thought of asking Martha or Jonathan, his trusted friend, to help him. He was sure they would if he came clean with them and really, but really, asked for their assistance. Yet he never found the opportunity to do so, mainly because he had to have a few drinks first, just to give himself that little bit of confidence to open up to them. He would then be off his brain before he could put together the first words of his pleading speech. By then, Martha or Jonathan would seem to be so far away, so out of his reach, to pay attention to him or to hear his desperate cry for help.

Peter went home that day feeling a bit run down and out of sorts. He was nauseous. He couldn't eat or drink, even if he had wanted to. He went straight to bed. The next morning his temperature was up. He asked Martha to phone the school and inform them of his sickness. For the next few days he battled the worst kind of flu. Martha took care of him and pampered him as she always did when he was ill. She couldn't help noticing that Peter's behaviour towards her was somehow different. He seemed to be more appreciative of whatever she did for him. Bringing him his medicine and a glass of water, she told him encouragingly, "It's time for your antibiotics dear and remember, you should take them till the course is finished. Hopefully, by then, you will feel well enough to go to Marcus's wedding."

"Martha dear, I wouldn't miss the wedding even if I was still burning with fever," he replied before swallowing his capsules.

The day before the wedding, when Marcus arrived home, after the final rehearsal for the wedding ceremony at the church, he saw Samuel backing his car out of his parent's driveway. Samuel stopped and came out of his car to say hello. They exchanged a few words over the shortish fence, "I hear congratulations are in order," Samuel said, visibly pleased to see his long-standing friend in his happy moments.

"You heard it right and thank you, I am also glad to hear that you can make it to the wedding. Mum told me you were away the last few weeks."

"I was, but I wouldn't miss going to your wedding for the world. I made sure to wrap up my assignment in time to fly back to Sydney. By the way, would it be all right if I brought a friend with me?" Samuel dared to ask, a bit sheepishly.

"Of course, especially if it's a girl friend," Marcus said jokingly, moving his eyebrows up and down.

"Indeed it is, thank you. We will be there and I wish you a long and happy life with your bride to be."

"I wish the same thing happens to you. This girlfriend, could she be the one?" Marcus asked, squinting his eyes to show his curiosity.

"I sure hope so," Samuel answered, a glint of excitement in his eyes.

"So it is serious, I am glad for you Samuel, you deserve to be as happy as I am right now."

"Thank you Marcus and good luck for your wedding day and the rest of your life."

"Thank you," Marcus said, before going inside his house.

On that late March evening, the weather was surprisingly agreeable. After the church ceremony that had left a lot of the attendants astounded, the stretch limousines began rolling towards the well-known reception hall. Peter and Martha were amongst the first few guests to enter the place. The hall had already taken the atmosphere of sheer happiness and joy. Every detail concerning the way the place was decorated was indicating that something wonderful was about to happen there. The bride and groom's relatives had gone overboard to make that night a night to remember in the years to come.

Adam, the best man, had a lot to be thanked for, of course. After discussing it with Marcus and Clara, he had organised a DJ for the western music and had put together a band that would play Assyrian and Persian music. He had taken care of the flower arrangements for both the church and the hall. He had hired the fancy cars and had paid for the impressive wedding cake. Adam had also helped with a lot more things that needed to be done. Not all of those were traditionally the duty of the best man but he was just eager to do as much as he could, for Jonathan's sake.

Finally the time came for the smiling bride and groom, a gaggle of bridesmaids, the men in the bridal party and the parents on both sides to make their entrance. Emotions running high, the packed hall exploded in cheers. Everyone stood up and clapped. As the music rose to a delightful crescendo, they welcomed the newlyweds with admiration. The pair and their entourage were then led to their special tables. Balancing their trays aloft, the waiters arrived with the drinks.

Wrapped in a froth of lace and tulle and still smiling, Clara made herself comfortable on her elegant chair before placing her dainty bouquet on the table. For a while she let her eyes rest on the tulips, delphiniums, hyacinths and daffodils in the tasteful arrangement then, lifting her head, she watched the guests getting ushered to their designated tables. Dazed by the surroundings, everything around her began suddenly to dissolve into a jumbled mixture of glitter and vibrant colours. In her mind, Clara came to wonder why she never experienced the much anticipated apprehension a bride was expected to feel at the threshold of her new life. She felt like laughing at the thought of it. Marrying Marcus meant the end of her loneliness. It was as if God had reached down and had touched her life by bringing her and Marcus together. She couldn't believe that her life could actually be going from a devastating sadness to such a magnificent and overwhelming joy.

The cameraman caught her as she smiled, remembering how excited and proud her brother looked before he began marching with her along the aisle to give her away. She was certain that Matthew had wished to see her hitched to a handsome, honest and all round good guy, and in his eyes, Marcus happened to fit the bill perfectly.

In a dreamlike state, Clara heard Jonathan welcoming the guests from behind the microphone. "I am not very good at speeches so I will be brief. In the south of Iran, there is a region inhabited by tribal people. The men in that place believe that, to be happy a man needs to have a good wife, a good horse and a good rifle. I agree with the part about a good wife and I have one, but for my second and third choices, I will say a good son or daughter and a good friend. I wasn't blessed to have a daughter but tonight I got one and to me she will be the daughter I never had." His eyes misting, Jonathan looked at Adam who was standing there waiting for his turn to talk. "I had and still have a lot of good friends, both back home and in here but Adam is the friend who was there for me almost all my life. Tonight, I am taking this opportunity to thank him from the bottom of my heart for being my trusted friend," Jonathan managed to say before wrapping his arms around Adam's shoulders. "And thank you for all your help Adam. Without you we wouldn't have been able to put all of this together," he added.

Adam began delivering his speech with, "I think I speak for everyone when I say..." Clara's mind wandered again. She thought of her parents and how wonderful it would have been if they were there to share her happiness. "And now the bride and groom will open the dance," she heard Adam conclude before, squeezing her hand, Marcus helped her off her chair. The two strolled onto the dance floor, relishing the first moments of their life as husband and wife.

The whisky and champagne stirring everyone's blood with wedding excitement, the guests paired off and gathered around to join the happy couple in their dance. Alice had also made her attempt at elegance. Clara watched her dancing with Matthew. Alice looked like she was enjoying herself but Clara couldn't help imagining the thought she was having at that precise moment. Knowing her, Alice was surely making plans on how to redecorate her empty room for her daughter.

Repeatedly glancing at the door, Martha was anxiously waiting for Samuel and his date to arrive. He had told his mother that they might be late, as his girlfriend, who was a model, had to come after a fashion parade.

Peter had not touched any alcoholic drink and wasn't about to start doing so, since he was still on antibiotics and still feeling crook. Martha couldn't be happier about this turn of events. She didn't have to be a genius to know how the evening could end if he was his old self. She dreaded to think about the worst case scenario. Lost in her thoughts, she suddenly heard Samuel's voice, "Mum, dad, this is Aurore," Samuel was saying.

"Glad to meet you Mr and Mrs Goddard," the attractive girl said, stretching her hand towards Samuel's parents.

Martha couldn't believe her eyes when she lifted her head and gazed at the most glamorous woman she had ever met. The shocked look on Peter's face didn't go unnoticed to her either.

After the introductions and a few brief banalities, Samuel whisked Aurore onto the dance floor, allowing her to show off the naked back of the black crêpe de chine dress she was wearing. A white rolled collar that was narrow around her neckline at the front was widening gradually as it went all the way down to a few inches below her waistline and rested nonchalantly on her buttock. A big black and white silk flower, matching the one pinned on her chignon, was casually placed at the centre back and barely covering the area under her waistline. A long strand of pearls, knotted just past the base of her neck was let to fall down her spine in a loop.

Raising a quizzical eyebrow, "Gosh! Good thing she had two of those flowers, otherwise we would be able to peer down her bum crack," Peter exclaimed.

"Shush! They can hear you," Martha tried to quieten him down.

On the dance floor, the soft tune stopped and more lively music filled the air. Led by Samuel, as Aurore swirled, her short skirt rose higher to reveal a glimpse of her well toned thighs. "She is a knockout, absolutely divine. Where did our son meet such a striking girl?" Martha ventured to say.

An odd expression crossed Peter's gaunt face that gave Martha an uneasy feeling. He nodded pensively then, "If you want my opinion, she is too sophisticated for Samuel, too wrong for him, if you know what I mean," he uttered in a chipped but decided voice as he took a long cooling sip of his orange juice.

"For heaven's sake, don't scoff at the girl, it's only a dress, a bit flash but only a dress. She was probably wearing it at the parade," Martha protested, trying to keep her voice down and steady.

"I am not talking about the dress or the makeup. A girl like that doesn't fit in with us. She is not from our world, our ordinary class," Peter said gloomily. Slipping another hors d'oeuvre between his pale lips, "She is champagne and caviar, we are simple beer and peanuts kind of people," he added.

Not particularly keen to sit through another one of her husband's irrational fault finding assaults, especially one in public, Martha decided to curtail the conversation by diverting his attention elsewhere.

The waiters kept hovering over the guests to make sure everyone's glasses were filled all the time and there were enough savouries on the tables. The music stopped and, as the dancers were returning to their seats, the master of ceremonies grabbed the microphone and starting with, "Ladies and gentlemen, may I have your attention," he said something about three dancers being united again after almost thirty years.

A sudden hush followed, then a group of people began applauding and chanting. "We want the terrific trio to dance," they repeatedly shouted. The Assyrian music throbbed out. A sense of expectation became visible among the guests. Some rose to their feet to see what was happening when they saw three men throw themselves onto the dance floor. "Jonathan is going to dance," Samuel blurted out, urging his parents to stand up and watch.

Emotions were at an all time high for those who knew the history of the three young friends and their special dance. They looked older and, in Adam's case, heavier than he used to be. Twirling a handkerchief, Adam took the lead and, tapping wildly, the trio began dancing with the same raw energy, the same passion and raised spirit they used to dance in their younger days. In all honesty, they performed with the same old clockwork precision and that made them so pleased with themselves and their joy so complete. Indeed it was another heartwarming event to make that glorious evening even more so.

Remembering her first meeting with Jonathan had Liuba exhilarated. Feeling her heart racing, without realising it, she was clapping her hands so vigorously that they ended up hurting. As soon as the dance finished, she got hold of Freeda's hand, tears in her eyes, "Weren't they remarkable? I believe they danced as well as they used to," she said.

"They were sensational," Freeda agreed with a smile. "It's good that Saul could come," she added.

A few hours later, while the bride was throwing her bouquet towards the single girls, Liuba cornered Freeda and asked her about the rumours concerning the break up of Violet and Ari. She also pressed her to tell about the brewing of a romance between Juliet and Israel. "Yes, unfortunately Violet and Ari are having some problems that are just irreconcilable. It's too long a story. We'll have to leave it for later. As for Juliet, it's too soon to tell, but there is something there. Israel will leave with his father but he is planning to return. Adam has offered him a job. We have to wait and see what the future has in store for them."

"I hope whatever is right for Juliet happens. Life is so much harder for youngsters nowadays, I feel sorry for them. In our days, things were a lot simpler," Liuba concluded philosophically.

The bride and groom had already left and the last guests were about to do the same. When the place was free at last, the waiters started to clear the tables. Liuba and Freeda were rounding up the things they had to take home. Adam and Jonathan packed their cars with the presents. The place was ready for the cleaners. Adam looked around then sat down for a bit of rest. The other members of the family joined in. "Well, we did it, and I am glad that the wedding went without a snag," Adam said.

"We did everything to make it an authentic Assyrian wedding but I am a bit disappointed. There were no flare-ups of ancient family feuds, not even one fistfight and nobody got excessively drunk and disorderly. How can we call this an Assyrian wedding?" Jonathan said jokingly and they all laughed.

"Jokes aside, we are all glad that there were no embarrassing moments to spoil the occasion," Matthew said, feeling euphoric with relief.

As soon as they were home alone, Jonathan hugged and kissed his wife and complimented her again on how beautiful she had looked at the wedding. They started getting ready to go to bed when he felt he had to let her in on uncle Malcolm's state of health. Remembering all the kind and considerate things he had done for them when they had first arrived in Australia as well as afterwards, Liuba couldn't help feeling deeply sorry for Malcolm. With a saddened voice, she suggested they go and visit him first thing in the morning. The next day, they met him in his family room as he was going over some papers with Adam. Malcolm looked surprisingly calm and greeted them in his usual friendly way. Liuba opened the subject of his illness and while she and Jonathan were wishing him well, they urged him not to lose faith, "Miracles do happen," she was telling him when the phone rang. Adam went to answer it and came back looking distraught. "The call was from Iran. It was mum. Dad is not well again," he blurted out, for a second forgetting about his uncle's sickness.

"Go, you have to go. You have to be with your mother," he heard his uncle utter, suppressing a cough with difficulty.

"But you?" Adam started to argue."

"Don't worry about me. Go, your mother needs you, otherwise she wouldn't have called."

"We will be here, don't worry about uncle, we will stay here until you come back," Jonathan said.

"Yes! I miss Liuba's cooking anyway, maybe that will be my miracle cure," Malcolm said, trying to convince Adam to go.

The next day, the Vardas arrived with a bag holding their essentials and saw Adam leave for the airport.

Jonathan and Liuba did their best to pamper Malcolm as well as take care of everything else in the house. Soon after Adam's departure, Freeda had to rush to Violet's house to comfort her and prevent her from being in contact with her husband. Violet had thrown Ari out of the house after discovering he had gambled his pay cheque away the previous night. Leaving her alone and distraught at home, he had decided to join his so-called mates for a poker game. "That was the straw that broke the camel's back," she had told her mother on the phone, fuming with anger. Nevertheless, Freeda feared that Ari could easily sweet-talk her daughter into giving him a second chance. She had to persuade Violet to move back home and file for divorce. "If only Adam didn't have to leave now," she told Liuba before leaving.

When Adam's plane landed at Mehrabad Airport in Tehran, he hired a car and went straight to the hospital. There, he was told that his father had suffered yet another heart attack, this time fatal, and was on his way to the morgue. Amid the chaos, Adam managed to locate his mother. He cursed himself for not being able to get there soon enough to see his father on his deathbed. He stayed by his mother's side throughout the whole funeral and mourning period. Eventually he was forced to tell her of his uncle's illness. The news made her cry a little more. She looked so lost, so helpless, Adam didn't really know how to console her.

Upon hearing of his brother's death, despite his own critical condition, Malcolm had made numerous phone calls to his nephew, insisting that Adam not leave his mother alone in Iran. "Do whatever you have to do but don't come back without her," he had told him firmly. Thank goodness the celebrations of the two thousand and five hundred years of kingdom in Iran were over and getting in and out of the country was easier again. Before and during that time, the government had to take some serious security precautions to ensure the safety of all the royalties and representatives of other countries that had come to take part in the events.

Carrying a big tray laden with a bowl of piping hot soup, some freshly squeezed orange juice and two lightly toasted slices of bread,

Liuba pushed the door and entered Malcolm's room. His eyes were shut. 'He must have dozed off,' she thought. She tiptoed to his side and gently placed the tray on the coffee table nearby. Malcolm moaned in his sleep and turned to his side. Liuba could swear she heard him say, "My beautiful, my darling Seraphima, I can't wait to see you again." At that moment, a piece of paper slid out of the man's fingers and fell to the floor. She bent down to pick it up. To her surprise, Liuba realised it was an old and worn out photograph of Adam's mother. Discretely she pushed the photo under Malcolm's pillow.

Liuba couldn't help remembering the day of Adam's graduation, all those years ago, when she had witnessed uncle Malcolm hugging and kissing Seraphima goodbye before leaving for Australia. Puzzled, she began debating on the subject and ended up with the startling conclusion that Malcolm had been and still was in love with his sister-in-law. Malcolm opened his eyes, "Oh, it's you," he said, as if he was expecting to see someone else.

"I brought you some soup," Liuba said calmly.

"Thank you Liuba and God bless you, you are so kind to me, I can't believe my luck."

"Don't mention it uncle, this is nothing compared to your kindness. We have a debt of gratitude for all the help you gave us when we needed it. Malcolm didn't answer, instead he fumbled under his pillow and, after a while, he looked relieved when his fingers touched the precious photo. His secret was still safe, he thought.

That night, in the guest bedroom, when she was alone with Jonathan, Liuba recounted the whole incident to her husband. Taken aback by the revelation, "The poor fellow! If this is true, he must have suffered hell seeing her marry his brother," Jonathan said, feeling genuinely sorry for the old man he admired so much.

"Yes."

"It seems that with all the money he raked in, he couldn't have the one thing that was most important to him," he added.

"As they say, money is not everything," Liuba quoted pensively. Jonathan answered her with an expressive nod.

Chapter 20

After months of secretly seeing each other behind Geneviève's back, Samuel had made yet another plan to meet Aurore after work. Since she had her car left in a garage for repairs, he picked her up and, after a furtive kiss he pulled out from the curb. "Where are we going?" she asked.

"You'll see," he only said, with a flicker of a smile on his lips and off he drove. He looked somewhat preoccupied. Aurore sat back in her seat and closed her eyes, trying to get a bit of rest. Relaxed and refreshed she opened them as Samuel turned into a car park area and stopped. Seconds later, the two entered the romantic seaside restaurant where Samuel had chosen and made reservations. A waiter directed them to the cosy corner by the window.

Almost an hour had gone by since their dinner had been served but their food was hardly touched. Overwhelmed by the mystical sounds that surrounded them, the two were sitting opposite each other, amorously holding hands over the small round table. It was a glorious early autumn night. As the harbour lights were pleasantly dancing on the still waters, Samuel's heart was beating just that little bit faster, with a sweet and tender anticipation of what the future would bring to them. Lifting his head, his eyes met with the emerald of hers. He smiled with delight. He had plenty to smile about. Aurore looked as flamboyant as she always did to him. He couldn't believe that they had come so far in their relationship.

While displaying her generous smile and pearly white teeth, Aurore gently pulled her hand out of his. One more time, she glanced at the tiny diamond on the ring that Samuel had presented her with, moments earlier. He had gone down on one knee and, holding a little velvety box in front of her, he had bashfully asked her to marry him. He knew she cared a great deal about him, yet her instant acceptance had taken him over the moon.

Chatting gaily, the two sat there a bit longer, totally heedless of all the astonishing colours and sights of the wondrously picturesque view that was spread in front of them. Aurore had accepted his marriage proposal but the things he had heard about her mother, mostly from Aurore herself, were disturbing his peace of mind. He had come to acknowledge that Geneviève was a strong-willed woman who would probably disagree with her daughter being involved, let alone wish to marry, a simple newspaper employee. Her future son-in-law had to be a lot more deserving than he was. He should be heir to a multimillion-dollar corporation or a self-made tycoon, for instance.

As if reading his mind, a slight frown appeared on Aurore's brow, "Samuel, I believe you know the kind of fight we are going to be up against, with mum and her unrealistic expectations," she said, trying to keep her fears at bay and not spoil the occasion.

"Yes, I know, but what can she do? I love you and you love me. She just has to accept the fact, and the sooner the better," he said, overcome by a surprising rush of optimism.

Deep inside though, Samuel was dreading the moment he had to put himself in proximity with the domineering lady.

A sudden breeze buffeted their bodies as they stepped outside the restaurant. Lovingly, Samuel wrapped his arm around her shoulders, as they walked towards his car. Unpredicted tears misting his eyes, Samuel ran the fingers of his free hand through the crazy mop of his blond hair then, turning to her, "You are going to be firm with her, won't you?" he asked worriedly.

"I'll surely try my best," she replied.

"And if she takes a stand against us?"

"Then we will just have to elope, won't we?" she answered his question with another question.

"Come to think of it, that may not be such a bad idea. I know I'll never measure up to the concept of the son-in-law your mother contemplates to have, therefore..."

"She can contemplate all she wants. She can even try to match-make me with every filthy rich eligible bachelor in the world. I don't care. You will still be the one I'll marry," she murmured, as she pressed her head against the comforting curve of his shoulder. After that, Samuel drove his sweetheart to her home and saw her to her door.

For the last hour and a half, Geneviève had been going back and forth to the window of her drawing room. She was anxiously waiting for her daughter to come back from wherever she was. Lately, she had noticed that Aurore was out more often and was returning home past her usual time. Occasionally, Geneviève had dropped a hint that it was imperative for a model to have enough sleep and look her best if she intended to continue with her short and demanding career. "Yes mum," Aurore had answered her every time, with that familiar 'tell me something new' kind of grin.

Geneviève had taken her daughter's attitude with a grain of salt, thinking it was normal for a young person to act that way, even though Aurore had already been through the teenage rebellious stage. Still pacing the room, Geneviève recalled bumping into an old acquaintance a few weeks ago. They were at one of those Wool Corporation presentations. The woman had casually asked Geneviève whether Aurore and her boyfriend were planning to tie the knot. "Aurore doesn't have a boyfriend. What makes you think that she has one?" Geneviève had asked.

"I saw her with a good looking man outside a theatre, they looked like they were an item but maybe I was wrong," the woman had said, trying to minimise the damage she might have caused.

"Aurore goes out with friends sometimes but I never heard her being interested in anyone in particular. I am sure she would tell me if there was something to tell," Geneviève had said to end the gossip.

Geneviève had not taken that incident seriously. Alarm bells had not gone off then, but with Aurore still not home, she was starting to become more and more alarmed. Her maternal instinct was about to take a life of its own. She paced the room some more until finally she caught sight of them on the footpath outside the gate. Recognising Samuel, her eyes glistened with a mixture of anger and apprehension. "Mon Dieu! It's that pesky journalist," she exclaimed then, she remembered his bright blue eyes, his radiant face and his athletic body. 'I will have a battle on my hand. The young man is too dangerously handsome. It will be hard to tell Aurore not to get too attached to such an Adonis,' she thought.

Aurore opened the front door with her key and tiptoed inside quietly. Believing her mother was fast asleep in the main bedroom, she intended to sneak to her own room when, on top of the stairs, she found herself face to face with Geneviève. "So, you are dating Pépe le Pew. How long has this been going on?" Geneviève asked, trying to keep her cool.

"Long enough. Isn't he gorgeous?" Aurore enquired excitedly, while taking her high heeled shoes off her feet.

"What do you mean by long enough? I hope you are not..."

"And what would be wrong with that, maman?"

"For starters, he is a bare arsed, insignificant journalist," Geneviève said, raising her voice slightly.

"I don't know the exact definition of bare arsed but I can easily guess what you mean mum. Samuel doesn't deserve to be subjected to that kind of discrimination just because he is not loaded," Aurore said, doing her best not to let her mother intimidate her.

"What I mean is that he is not the Mr Right I had in mind for you."

"Well mother, to me he is damn bloody close," Aurore replied, a bit flushed but prepared to stand her ground. She had promised Samuel that she would be strong.

"Darling, you may not have my drive to go after wealth, perhaps because you were never deprived of it, but money is the most important ingredient in a relationship. I tell you, men, if you scratch the surface they are all the same. You should enjoy their company for a while then let them go, like a butterfly that flies from one flower to another till it finds the best one to stay on. In other words, keep digging until you strike gold..."

"Before long and with a bit of luck, Samuel will be earning a lot of money, when he makes it to the top of his career," Aurore said, trying to convince herself more than her mother.

"Waiting for luck to happen is a luxury you cannot afford, darling. You need a solid reassurance before taking the plunge," Geneviève argued, in an attempt to reason with her daughter.

"I agree, money may be a dependable commodity maman, but it is not everything. I love Samuel. Do you know what am I saying? I appreciate your concern but I don't know how to deal with your inability to tolerate class differences. You have always been a relentless snob, I am sorry...."

"Not as sorry as you will be in a few years' time when you realise that you didn't make the best of decisions, and one more thing, I am not a snob. I just don't want you to ruin your life."

"It's my life mum and if you don't agree with my choice of a man, I can't do anything about it. By the way, tonight Samuel asked me to marry him and I said yes," Aurore interjected.

"You said what? The man doesn't have a bucket to piss in and you said yes to his ludicrous proposal. Are you out of your mind? Even after ten years, he will still be a nobody," Geneviève screeched, livid with contempt.

Realising it was futile to debate the issue any further with her closed minded mother and, remembering Samuel's advice to be firm with her, Aurore responded with a rasping voice, "Stop it, stop projecting your personal fantasies on to me, mother. I have my own mind. I have my own life to live. No disrespect to you but I believe I am entitled to make my own mistakes. Most importantly, mum, I love Samuel. I can't tell it any simpler."

"Love? Does that word still exist in the dictionary?"

"Mum, it seems to me that you have never been really in love, because if you had been you would have had some idea about it. Then again maybe it's asking too much from someone who..."

Holding a well manicured index in front of her daughter's face, Geneviève gave vent to her anger, unable to control herself any longer.

"Don't you dare use that tone with me, mademoiselle. How on earth did you become so arrogant? I would never know. I bent backwards to ensure your safety and comfort and you allow yourself to resent it and insult me for it? If this is your declaration of independence, you can have it."

The tension between the two women was so thick one could reach and touch it. Temples burning, Geneviève walked away and headed towards the living room, where she dropped her shaking body on the big couch. Breathing heavily, she tried to pinpoint exactly what Aurore had said that had hit a sensitive chord and made her lose her temper like that? Her question got answered when, like magic, a familiar name washed over her, "Farhad," she murmured with a sigh. Closing her eyes, she visualised his unique features and shuddered, astounded by the way her whole body had been reacting lately every time his name had invaded her thoughts, every time she had the opportunity to stand close to him or hear his voice as he talked to her. Blinking back her budding tears, 'I do know what love is, don't you worry about that my darling and I do know very well how it takes over your existence and how it hurts when you can't be with the only person you want to be with. What was I thinking, for heaven's sake? How could I be so insensitive to even consider standing in the way of you and your happiness when I am going through hell, trying to restore my sanity? You deserve to be happy my beautiful baby, even if it is for a short time, and I'll be damned if I let you suffer like I do at this moment,' she murmured.

Rising to her feet, she rushed back to find her daughter. Aurore was sitting on the floor, hugging her knees. Her face looked clearly distraught by her mother's hardheartedness. Geneviève sat next to her, silent at first then, caressing Aurore's shiny hair, she softly whispered, "Ma cherie, I only want your happiness." Then, holding her daughter's hand, "And if Samuel is capable of giving it to you, I will be glad to give you both my blessing. I never meant to be a pigheaded, scornful mother. You are all I have and I want us to stay friends as we have always been," she concluded, her voice trailing away.

Wondering what had turned the tide so suddenly, Aurore stared at her mother's tear stained face for a fraction of time then, throwing her arms around her, "Maman, I love you," she blurted out. Feeling an apology was in order, she began with, "Forgive me if I was rude..."

"As I said, I will not object to your marriage, in fact I will help you in any way I can. You don't have to worry about the wedding. I am going to take care of everything. One more thing though, you have to give me your word Aurore that you won't be getting pregnant, as long as you can stretch your modelling career."

"We can talk about these things later maman."

"Yes, we'd better go to bed now. We have a big day tomorrow."

Once in her bedroom, Geneviève's worries about her daughter's future resurfaced and kept her awake. Eventually she fell asleep, but only after she had some of the details of the big wedding planned in her mind.

A lot of time had gone by since Farhad and Geneviève had that quasi-intimate conversation about him and his wife not being able to have children. The last three weeks of it, he was on holiday. Farhad arrived at work that morning with a radiant face and a twinkle in his eyes. Minutes later, he walked towards the boss' office, two minded whether he should impart his good tidings with her and the whole world, for that matter, or wait a bit longer. He was going to be a father at last and he was feeling like shouting the news from the rooftop for everyone to hear. When he reached the door, he knocked and quietly stepped inside, "Good morning," he said merrily.

"Come in," she gestured with her hand, his familiar voice stopping her in her tracks. Sensing something was amiss in her demeanour, "If it's a bad time, I can come back later," he suggested.

"Sit down please," she said, showing him the chair across her desk.

"Is everything all right?" he asked, deciding to put his happy news on the back burner for the time being.

"Why do you ask?" she uttered, looking surprised that he had noticed the unsettled mood she was in. After a surreptitious glance at his gorgeous face, she asked, "You look like the cat that has swallowed the canary, what's up? Did you have a good vacation?"

"It was perfect, but you don't look a hundred percent. Am I right? Is something bothering you?"

"I am all right. Hell! I am not all right."

"Do you want to talk about it, I can be a good listener," he said with kindness.

"It's my daughter. It disturbs me to see her throw her life away," she reluctantly said.

"Throw her life away? Is she experimenting with drugs or something like that?" he asked.

Geneviève didn't answer straight away so he came up with another question. "Is she getting sucked into some kind of a bizarre cult, because a lot of that is going on these days?"

Geneviève shook her head, dismissing both of Farhad's guesses.

"No, no, she is getting sucked into a stupid marriage and, instead of stopping her from making a big mistake, I gave her my word that I will let her marry the fellow."

"Anything wrong with the guy? Criminal record, drug addiction, too old for her or perhaps you think he is after her money?"

"No, no, no and no. He is young, good-looking and pretty decent. I made some inquiries in that regard," she said, giving Farhad a 'you know what I mean' kind of smile. When she saw his eyes widen, she added, "He is still not right for her. He is fresh out of uni, wet behind the ears, he is a simple would-be journalist."

"And that is a problem?"

"Yes! Can you see her live on a journo's salary? I was looking, with a degree of favour, to this powerful businessman's son who keeps dropping hints that he is interested in her but no, she goes and falls in love with the son of an ordinary teacher."

"What do you have against teachers?"

"Nothing, except for the insignificant money that they make. Half of their lives, people like them, live in rented houses. If they are lucky, they manage to buy a small house in a godforsaken area and struggle the rest of their life paying it off."

"In what godforsaken area do they live?"

"He used to have a room near the university but now he is back with his parents in Crow's Nest."

"Crow's Nest? That's not a bad place. I was expecting to hear a name I hadn't heard of before," Farhad said with an amused air.

Putting her best frown on her face, Geneviève blurted out, "What I mean is that they are middle class people and Samuel, that's his name, with his poor prospects, will only be capable of giving Aurore nothing more than the same mediocre life him and his parents have lived. I am afraid Samuel is way beneath my lovely daughter. For heaven's sake, Aurore is pretty enough and refined enough to marry a prince."

"Marry a prince," Farhad repeated haughtily, creasing his fore-head. "My mother married a prince and she lived to regret it ever since. As far back as I can remember, she rued the day she set eyes on the so-and-so who caused her all that heartache," he added pensively.

A brief moment of silence passed between them. "Was this so-and-so your father?" Geneviève finally asked with a whispering voice and a sudden interest in the matter.

"Yes, my father was a prince."

"Oh! Now I see why Eddy called you prince that day. So it wasn't just a nickname or a figure of speech."

"No, my father was indeed a descendent from the last Iranian royal family, the Kajar dynasty, to be precise. When Reza Shah Pahlavi came to power in the year 1925, all the members of the last royal family were given the right to stay in their country, providing they kept a low profile. I am not sure but I think there were not supposed to do military service and were not allowed to start any kind of business. Anyway, most of them, including my grandfather, lived a quiet and comfortable life with the money they were left with."

Farhad stopped to catch his breath but her curiosity awakened, Geneviève couldn't let go of the subject. She pursued with her questioning.

"Are you going to tell me what happened to her, I mean your mother?"

"As I said, my father lived in a huge property with his father and a large group of servants, cooks, gardeners and chauffeurs. Anyway, when my grandfather died, being an only child, my father inherited the lot. That's when he met my mother and married her. Soon after their wedding, my mother realised she had married an idler, a boozer, an opium user and, to top it off, a compulsive gambler and a womaniser. Mother was from a well-off and respectable family who lived by their ethics and their moral standards."

"And she couldn't stomach all that," Geneviève interrupted.

"Of course, being married to a titled man, a woman is not supposed to complain but mother let her husband know that she wasn't happy with his behaviour and his lack of interest in her and her wellbeing. As time passed, his way of thinking and his condescending attitude towards her broke her heart."

"He didn't make any attempt to change, I gather."

"No, he didn't. That's when she decided to make a trip to America where her father was at the time. He had been transferred by his firm to represent them there."

"Oh, yes! You did come from America, as I recall."

"That's right. It was after her arrival that my mother found out she was pregnant, with me. She wrote letters to my father, telling him that if he didn't clean up his act, she would not return to him but she didn't mention a word about her pregnancy.

"This is getting interesting."

"Anyway, a few weeks later, mother received a telegram informing her that her husband had died in a car crash. She and my grandad rushed back home only to find out that, at the time of the accident, my father was dead drunk and that he was not alone in the car. A woman, one of his whores no doubt, had also been killed in the crash. Mum and grandad tried to claim her inheritance but my father's lawyers came up with papers of divorce my father had prepared to send to my mother, in order to end his union with her, by mail."

"Could he have done that?" Geneviève asked with indignation.

"Yes, don't look surprised. Men had the law on their side in those days. They had the authority to dispose of their spouses whenever they wished by just paying the previously agreed upon sum which was written on the marriage documents."

"How awful! Tell me, what happened then. Did your mother get anything from his estate eventually?"

"Mum and grandad exhausted all the legal avenues and won the case mainly because of me. You see I was born eight months after she had left Iran and that helped. I was nine years old when the legal battle was finally over. By that time, a lot of money had been wasted and when at last, my father's assets were liquidated, most of the money went to pay the lawyers and my father's gambling debts."

"What a shame. It would have been better if she never went back to Iran. How much longer did you stay in your country?"

332 Margaret A Youhana

"Well, grandad stayed in Iran but mother and I returned to America. Over there, she worked really hard to get her degree. Of course, grandad helped her financially."

"You mean she studied?"

"Yes, she was trying to become an interior decorator. We lived a lonely life until mother remarried and had a taste of happiness at last. By the way, Forouhar is my mother's maiden name. I had no desire to be called by my father's name or to carry his title. That's why I didn't like it when Eddy let the cat out of the bag and called me prince."

"I understand. Tell me, where did you meet your wife?"

"I met her in the university canteen. Some mutual friends introduced us to each other, mainly because her name was Shereen. It started as a joke but our corresponding names worked their magic."

"Why is that?"

"Well, because Farhad and Shereen are the equivalent of Romeo and Juliet in the Persian literature," he concluded with a smile.

"Isn't that interesting. Actually, I know a husband and wife in the rag trade. They have a business called Adam and Eve and their own names are, you guessed it, Adam and Eve."

"Oh! Fate must have put them together as it did with my wife and me. Now, back to your daughter. I don't have enough information about the guy's character to give a fair comment on the matter but I hope my mother's story gave you something to think about. What I am trying to say is that money and distinction are not necessarily fundamental for a good marriage. My wife and I started our life together with the bare essentials in a single bedroom condominium but that didn't stop us from being happy. I am sorry. I didn't mean to put my nose where it doesn't belong but if there's nothing worrisome about the young man, maybe it's better to leave your daughter to make her own decisions."

Hanging on to Farhad's every word, Geneviève nodded a few times before asking, "Is your mother still in America?"

"No! We all came to Australia. My stepfather is an Aussie. He told us so many good things about his country, we just had to come and see it for ourselves," Farhad said, smiling openly.

"I wouldn't mind meeting your family some day."

"Well, if you ever decide to visit Shereen in hospital, you may see everyone at the same time."

"In hospital? Is she going to have an op...?"

"A baby!" Farhad said grinning from ear to ear.

"A baby?" Geneviève cried aloud, stunned by the news.

"Yes, and it happened thanks to you and the good Doctor Abernethy. I can't tell you how grateful we are."

"Oh! I am so glad for you, congratulations. I am sure you will be a good father."

"I'll surely try. Hopefully everything will go well for Shereen and the baby..."

"We just have to think positively, don't we?"

"Thank you again," he said as he took a giftwrapped box out of his bulging pocket, "This is a small token of our appreciation," he added, handing it to her.

"You didn't have to..." she said.

Opening the box, Geneviève took out a delicate crystal flower vase. "Oh. A Lalique, it's beautiful, you really shouldn't have done this, it must have cost you a fortune."

"It's all right."

"Thank you," she said, admiringly placing the piece on her desk.

"Don't mention it. Now I have a few questions to ask you about this new account. I also don't seem to have a copy of David Jone's latest payment."

Shereen was not the only one who was expecting in those days. Clara also had some good news of her own to share with her family. Jonathan and Liuba were ecstatic with joy, so was Matthew. They couldn't wait for the baby to arrive so they could spoil it rotten.

The Varda's jubilation was unfortunately tainted a bit. They had to get ready to go and visit uncle Malcolm in hospital. Freeda had called earlier to tell them that the doctors had decided to remove part of his lungs. Adam was still in Iran, assisting his mother in whatever she had to do before getting on the plane that would take them both to Australia.

After dropping Aurore at her home on the night of the proposal, deliriously happy, Samuel drove towards Crow's Nest. Martha was still awake when she heard his car stop outside. She let her son in and asked him if he needed tea or something. Dragging his father out of bed, Samuel told both his parents all that had gone on that evening between him and the beautiful model they met at Marcus' wedding. "And now we are engaged to be married," he cried out at the end, joy transforming his features so much that the sight of his face brought tears to Martha's eyes.

Peter congratulated him but, to his wife's relief, he didn't say a word about his qualms. He managed to cover his lack of enthusiasm by rubbing his eyes and feigning a lengthy yawn. Still, in a fatherly way, on his way back to bed, he tapped Samuel on the shoulder and told him, "Well son, I wish you all the happiness that you deserve. We will talk about your plans for the future tomorrow. Good night for now. I need to go back to my beauty sleep."

"Good night dad, good night mum, I love you both."

"We have to invite Aurore and her family over soon," Martha suggested excitedly.

"We will talk about that too," Samuel said then, ambling to his room; he wondered if he could get any sleep at all, being so exhilarated by the way the evening had unfolded.

Martha was anxiously browsing through some cooking books to find suitable recipes to follow for the lunch party they were giving on Saturday. They had invited Aurore and her mother over to get a chance to know each other better. They also needed to talk about the details of the upcoming wedding. Frustrated, she closed the books and, scratching her head, "Oh, what am I going to do, she lamented then, remembering Liuba, she slipped her feet into her comfortable shoes and raced next door to discuss the problem with her friend. She found Liuba at her sewing machine busy making something for Clara's baby who was due in five months time. After commenting on the few already completed items from the layette, shyly Martha spoke about the party and her inability to decide what was more appropriate to serve the guests.

"Don't worry Martha. If you don't mind, I will help you prepare a presentable tray of hors d'oeuvres. Marcus and Clara are coming to visit and I intend to make vine leaf dolma for the weekend. I can double the ingredients and give you half of it. That will be another meal to put on the table, in addition to something traditional that you are so good at. We can whip up a cake as well, maybe a biscuit cake that doesn't need baking. You can serve it with ice cream."

"Oh, that will be perfect. I don't know how to thank you. I knew I could count on you. You always have the best ideas."

Since early morning, Martha had been running around, cooking, cleaning, setting the table and making sure that everything was as perfect as it could be. Samuel had already left to pick up his guests and bring them over. They were due to arrive in another twenty minutes, when suddenly an idea popped into Martha's mind. She called Peter, "I just thought of something. Could you please run to the florist and buy a small bunch of flowers. They will brighten the room and that vase looks kind of empty, sitting there."

Peter came to say, why don't we pick some from the garden but he though it best not to argue with his wife. She was nervous enough and that wasn't the right time to start a row. They already had one the night before when she asked him to go easy on the drink. He grabbed his keys and was on his way to Willoughby Road. Parking the car in a hurry, he rushed towards the florist. At the door he nearly bumped into a heavily perfumed and well dressed lady holding a splendid flower arrangement. She was getting out of the shop. For a while they seemed to be blocking the way for one another. Peter was about to apologise when he recognised her. For some peculiar reason Geneviève's face had stayed in his mind since he had seen her on that interview she had with the host of the midday show, some time ago. His sense of humour getting the best of him, making the gallant gesture of letting her pass, "Well, well, well, if it's not the town's trollop gracing us with her presence. To what do we owe this honour?" he gushed disparagingly.

Geneviève could have treated Peter's insulting remarks with the contempt they deserved but instead, she just threw the word "Jerk" at his face and walked past him, heading towards her Mercedes. Samuel and Aurore were at the newsagent next door buying the latest of the bridal magazines. Geneviève had made a last minute decision that the bottle of champagne she brought from home wasn't enough to give to Samuel's parents. She thought a bunch of flowers in her hands would make their entrance more decorous. She opened her car's door, placed the flowers on the back seat and waited for Samuel and Aurore to come out of the shop. 'How long does it take to buy a few magazines?' She thought, feeling slightly nervous.

Peter just finished fitting the flowers he bought into the vase when the doorbell chimed. "I'll get it," he yelled as he went and opened the door. He saw the happy couple first then, standing next to them, to his horror his eyes caught sight of the superb flower arrangement he had seen earlier in the hands of the woman he had learned to despise. 'Good Grace,' he thought.

Tongue-tied, Peter didn't say anything and just stared at them feeling hopelessly disconcerted. His eyes went from the flowers to the top part of Geneviève's face. "Aren't you going to invite us in," Geneviève's voice as well as her perfume filled the air. Samuel was busy twiddling a strand of Aurore's hair around his finger and didn't notice anything out of the ordinary going on.

"Come in please," Peter finally managed to utter, visibly agitated. "Welcome to our humble abode," he added, remembering how wealthy the famous fashion designer was.

As they all entered, Peter went on with his nervous prattle, "Did you have a nice ride coming over? Can I offer you a drink or something?"

Martha showed up in time to rescue the situation. Samuel began the introductions. "This is dad," he said pointing at his father, "and this is mum," he said, putting his arms around Martha's shoulders.

The words, "How do you do," and, "It's nice seeing you," were said a lot of times as they shook each other's hands. Trying to come to grips with his unsettled state of mind, "We have met before," Peter said, looking at Aurore then turning to Geneviève, "I kind of know you too, from an interview I saw on the telly," he added, staring into her eyes.

"Oh, yes, the midday show. Unfortunately I didn't see it, I was working that day," Aurore interjected.

"Sam has talked a lot about you but he never told me that you were as beautiful as your daughter, Mrs De La Lande," Martha said, addressing Geneviève.

"Oh, thank you, you are so kind and please call me Geneviève."

"You too, call me Martha and thank you for your champagne and these lovely flowers. You shouldn't have gone to so much trouble."

"Don't mention it," Geneviève murmured with a self-lauding smile as she finally realised the reason behind Peter's crude words at the florist's door. 'For Samuel and Aurore's sake, I will put up with you but, after the wedding, you'd better watch out. One word out of place and I will make you regret it for the rest of your miserable life,' she was muttering in her mind.

They had a lively conversation during the lunch as well as when they had dessert. Afterwards, Samuel invited Aurore to his room to show her his record collection. Martha took a tray laden with glasses to the kitchen. Geneviève could have offered to help her but instead she approached Peter and, with a voice that she tried to keep calm and low, she told him that she would forget the florist incident if he kept on being civil and not make waves.

"No worries love, Sam's peace of mind is my first priority," he answered her.

"And Aurore's is mine," Geneviève whispered, happy that the party had gone without an obvious hiccup.

Samuel and Aurore were supposed to go to one of her friend's birthday party in the evening so before leaving, Samuel changed into his party clothes. They all left to go to Geneviève's house. Aurore had to get dressed too and Samuel had left his car over there.

At the last minute that evening, Marcus had called to say that something had come up and they had to postpone their visit. The Vardas and the Goddards were therefore left with a lot of food on their hands. Martha went to return Liuba's two serving platters that she had borrowed. She was also itching to tell her how the party had gone. "Let's have dinner together," Jonathan proposed.

"I'll go and ask Peter," Martha said.

"Phone him, don't walk all the way there," Liuba suggested.

Martha dialled their number and told Peter to bring over the hors d'oeuvre tray and whatever else he could carry next door.

Since his meeting with the school principal, Peter had taken it easy with his alcohol consumption but he decided to ignore her warning on that occasion. Besides the hors d'oeuvres, Peter could only carry his chilled beers that were left untouched. He had a lot on his mind and was in great need for a good dose of pick-me-up. As soon as the food was laid on the table, he couldn't wait to guzzle a good amount of beer, while telling Jonathan the identity of Aurore's mother. As accurately as possible, he recounted her interview on the television, then, "I tell you mate, that woman is bad news," he said.

Jonathan tried to make light of what Peter was trying to imply but Peter couldn't let go of the idea that his son was making a big mistake by marrying Aurore.

Ever since Peter had seen Aurore that night, at Marcus's wedding, this small voice inside of him had been telling him that no good would come from Sam's relationship with the girl. Now that he had found out she was the rich bitch's daughter, that voice had risen to a deafening height.

"People are like water, they seek their own level. I tell you, these two sheilas are not on our level, they are not our kind of people," he said.

"They are not from a different planet, Peter. Sam and Aurore will surely find a common ground where they can be happy together. Love conquers all, you'll see," Jonathan argued, taking a slow sip from his watered down drink.

The others ate in silence, letting Peter drop a few words every now and then, his curt sentences gradually turning into a drunken babble. "If only I knew, if only I was told she was related to that... I tell you, that minx will be the death of me. She is evil. She is a devil in disguise. There is something about her that... I don't know, something that goes straight to my nerves."

"Aren't you exaggerating a bit," Liuba said, but Peter didn't hear her. He was already lost in a world of his own.

"As for her daughter, that's what I think, what is that saying Martha dear? An acorn doesn't fall far from its tree or something like that," he struggled to remember while wiping his mouth with the back of his hand, making Martha cringe with embarrassment.

"Come on, Peter. This is not always the case. People are not the carbon copy of their parents," Jonathan protested again.

"Mark my word, I can feel it here," Peter grumbled, pointing all his right hand's fingers to his heart.

Cutting through the character assassination that seemed to her a tad excessive and unfair, Martha intervened. "It's really up to Sam to keep his future wife in check, no matter how manipulative and evil you believe her mother is. He can shape Aurore into a good wife and a perfect mother for their children."

"Enjoy your delusions, Martha. I don't know why I even bother stating my opinion. Nobody will listen anyway. I used to take

5

people as I found them, leaving the judging for the Almighty but in this case, I can't help it, I am worried about Sam, truly worried."

Martha decided it was time to change the subject before Peter spoiled the evening any further. "How is your friend Malcolm now," she inquired.

"Oh, he is all right for the time being but who knows. Cancer is a cruel enemy, pitiless indeed. It seems that the illness advances at a steady rate for a while then accelerates towards the inevitable. He is getting closer to that stage, I am afraid. We are going to visit him tomorrow," Jonathan answered.

"I hope he can wait until Adam is back," Liuba said on her way to the kitchen to make tea for everyone. A bit later, the Goddards left. Peter stayed in his foul mood for the rest of the day. By bedtime, he was way over his limits and unfit to reason with. Martha busied herself in the kitchen and went to bed after he was sound asleep. The good thing was that Peter had all Sunday to sober up and be presentable on Monday.

The classiest reception hall was reserved for the wedding, so was the Catholic Church in Wahroonga. "Let's not make a big production of it," Samuel had suggested but Geneviève had chosen to ignore his plea and had gone ahead with her grandiose plans. In fact she had exercised all her power to get everything done the way she had wanted them to be. Aurore was used to following her mother's lead, therefore she didn't object to any of Geneviève's decisions. Disputing mother dear's wishes was futile anyway, she thought. In all honesty, the only thing Geneviève had consulted her daughter about was how she would like the neckline on her wedding dress to be. "Do you want a décolleté or would you prefer a high close fitting collar like this?" she had asked her, showing her a rough sketch of a high necked dress.

Aurore knew that Samuel didn't want a big, elaborate wedding, but she also knew what was best for both of them if they wanted their marriage to happen at all.

Geneviève had decided on Josephine style, bell bottomed pistachio green silk dresses for the bridesmaids. The dresses would each have a flat rectangular bow at the centre front with long tails hanging all the way down to the knee level. The groom, his best man, the father of the groom and the man who would give the bride away would be each wearing a mid-grey tailcoat ensemble. She had yet to decide on the colour of their bowties. The groomsmen would have pistachio green suits with darker green trimming around the wide lapels and white lace and pintucked shirts. Their bowties and cummerbunds were to be the same colour as the bridesmaid's dresses.

Everything seemed to be spot on, according to the latest fashion, but there were a few snags worth looking into. For example, who would be the man to give Aurore away and would Peter cooperate and comport as expected of him? How could Geneviève convince him to follow her plans and would Martha be dressed properly and not embarrass Geneviève in front of her important guests? All these questions not only made Geneviève's head turn, they also terrified her. She thought long and hard about all these problems but Peter appeared to be her biggest worry. Anguish seizing her, she put her pad down, 'I have to have a serious talk to Samuel,' she decided, while clenching and unclenching the pen she was using to put her ideas on paper.

When Geneviève had her talk with Samuel, she more like laid down the rules and stressed that his father should wear tails. She informed him too that she would send Martha a few outfits to choose from, "Something that would suit the occasion," she explained. Without mincing her words, she even told Samuel the number of guests he was allowed to invite. After all, she was paying the bills so she had every right to run the show her own way. Samuel had heard the lady speak her mind, loudly and clearly. No translation was needed. Knowing his options, he didn't have anything to say but to accept his future mother-in-law's demands. It was his turn then to go and talk to his parents and let them in on the dress code and Geneviève's proposal to provide Martha's outfit.

Without a word of complaint, Martha agreed with whatever she was offered to wear but when it came to Peter, things were not so easy. His initial resentment towards Geneviève and her outrageous bossiness swelled into aggravation when the subject of a formal costume came about. Even though he was trying to be cooperative, he categorically refused to dress up like a flaming gala, as he put it. "A dinner jacket and a bowtie, I don't mind, but nothing else," he declared in a huff then continued, "and a word of advice for you my son, today you let them dictate you one little bit, tomorrow they will see it fit to walk all over you. You know what they say, give them an inch and they will ask for a yard. Anyway, if you see that they are crossing the line, speak up and let them know who is the man in the house. Don't keep your feelings bottled up inside of you, these sorts of things can fester and poison your life. Stay in control at all times, don't let your guards down, if you know what I mean. Do you know what I mean son?"

"Yes dad," was all that Samuel said before leaving. Blinded by his love for Aurore, he didn't have the predisposition to absorb lectures. All that bile making Peter yearn for alcohol, he poured himself a glass of scotch and downed it in one go, savouring the feel as it went down his throat.

As soon as Sam walked out of the door, as usual, Peter took it out on Martha for not backing him up. "He has fallen in their trap, hook, line and sinker. They have got him snowed. They have him under a spell, Martha, and you don't seem to care," he blurted out, flinging a pointing finger at her.

This time, Peter's vehement words hit a very sensitive nerve. Her patience worn to a frazzle by his crass comments, Martha couldn't allow him to call her an uncaring mother. She finally snapped and, in a surprisingly angry voice, "Don't you dare, Peter, turn this around on me. If anyone cares it's me and I am sick and tired of you laying a guilt trip on me. Not everything that goes wrong in this household is my fault. If only you could listen for a change instead of going on and on about your personal belief system, maybe then you would come to your senses," she yelled, fuming with rage.

Martha got up to leave the room before things turned uglier between them but instantly reconsidered, thinking this was not the time to shy away from a possibly productive fight. It was time to bring Peter down from his high horses. She stayed, thinking that maybe she could reason with him and somehow make him see and understand the tricky situation they were in. Lowering her voice slightly, she began to talk, hoping against hope that they could come up with some sort of compromise together. "I know you don't like Aurore or her mother. For some reason or another, you have it in your mind that they are monsters. I am also aware that women in position of authority have always posed a problem for you but can't you make an effort, for Sam's sake. Can't you forget who Geneviève is or how she has made her money? I agree, she is bossy but she is also a mother looking after her daughter's best interest. She too wants to do the right thing by her child."

"So what am I supposed to do, woman?" Peter said, briskly brushing aside a mop of dishevelled hair from his face, "am I supposed to sit and watch her make a mug of me, as well as tearing my son's life apart? It's a fact of life the world over that water and oil don't mix. I am telling you, Aurore and Sam are not a good combination. I have nothing against Aurore but she is going to break his heart one way or another. He will end up hurt. He won't come out of this unscathed. I can feel it. We are going to lose him Martha, just like we lost Jeremy." Peter stopped abruptly after uttering Jeremy's name. It was such a long time since he had talked about their departed son. An eerie expression crossed his face that gave Martha a sickening feeling. She stared at him with awe then turned her face away. Peter continued with his plea, "Like a moth drawn to a flame, he will burn, Martha, and we won't be able to do a thing to prevent it."

"Maybe there is some truth in what you are saying but it's out of our hands. Sam is head over heels in love with the girl. All we can do now is to be there for him," she said as she kept wondering why Peter had brought up Jeremy's name in an already tense situation. What did Jeremy's death have to do with Sam marrying Aurore and where was the similarity?

Peter stood up to put away the bottle of scotch but he turned around and sat in front of his wife. With a softer voice, he began to speak in a way he used to when they had a normal relationship together. Purposefully avoiding his gaze, she just sat there and stared at the space beyond him.

"Martha dear, I am not talking about the problems every newlyweds are bound to come across. I am not worried about the few minor hurdles that Sam and Aurore may have to overcome in the course of their conjugal life. I just can't shake this feeling I have deep in my heart that this marriage is going to break our son in two," she could hear him say, squinting up at her.

Her hands resting limply on her lap, 'Oh, no, he is in his melodramatic stage again. I hate to know what he'll say next,' Martha was thinking, but to her bewilderment, she saw Peter drop himself to his knees before her, unconsciously still holding his half full bottle of scotch. He tried to look her in the eyes. "Where did it all start to go wrong for us, Martha. What came between us?" he suddenly asked with a trembling voice.

Martha remained silent. It took her a moment to register the words she had heard him say and work out the meaning of them. Finally, overcome by a strong desire to give him a piece of her mind, while she had the chance, she snatched the bottle from his hand and brandishing it, "This came between us, you did all the undoing," she yelled accusingly.

Martha was expecting Peter to lash out and reject her answer in the same tone, instead she heard him utter in a softer and saddened voice, "I know! I admit I didn't make life easy for us. I was not doing myself or anyone else, especially not you, a favour, being off this planet every night. I am sorry I caused you pain. I hate myself for it. I know I haven't been a model husband or a decent human being for

that matter, but Martha dear, after Jeremy, my brain wasn't operating on all cylinders. I was at my devastating low. I felt like sinking
deeper and deeper into despair. Way before that, I had already been
struggling with feelings of uselessness and trying to come to terms
with all the missed opportunities. When we lost Jeremy, I blamed
myself for what happened to him and I believed I didn't deserve to
stay alive. The thought occurred to me to end it all but I didn't even
have the guts to do that. By taking my self-destruction in small
dozes, in a way I had been punishing myself. If I hadn't turned to
alcohol it's possible that things would have been different between
us. We might have consoled each other," he kept saying under his
breath, in a gradually weakening tone.

Martha had endured a lot and for too long from her husband's
drinking and subsequent irrational temper. She was fed up being
constantly stung by his unwarranted and derogatory criticism. No
longer could she stand the brawls from which she always used to
come out drained and demoralised. She was not about to pin her
hopes on a few reassuring sentences that were spilling out of Peter's
whisky smelling mouth. She didn't feel like celebrating yet, not then
and certainly not seconds later, when she heard him declare, to no
one in particular, that he intended to go cold turkey.

"Martha, I have to do something about my drinking problem
before it gets out of hand and I become a certified alcoholic," he was
saying.

Martha was eager to show him how boring his empty promises
were. Sarcasm getting the best of her, she managed a wry grin, "Talk
is cheap. I'll believe it when I see it. Then again, pigs may fly one
day," she whispered through her teeth. Hearing her clearly, Peter
replied, "If I tell you I won't drink then I won't drink, Martha. This
is my pledge to you. I know it will be hard but I have to try because
I don't want to squander any more of the precious time that we can
still have together. With some disciplined effort and with your help
Martha dear, I may just get this monkey off my back."

Letting out a moan, Peter grabbed the bottle and scrambled to his feet. With a slight waddling gate, he walked to the kitchen, carrying his bottle.

Taken aback by her husband's admission of his drinking problem and his willingness to quit, Martha couldn't think straight for a while when the gurgling noise of a liquid going down the sink took her out of her daze. She jumped with the clinking sound the empty bottle made as it landed in the garbage bin. From the corner of her eye she saw Peter walk back towards her. He sat next to her on the footstool, "No one has said it will be easy but Martha, I am going to do it or die trying. As I said, I will definitively need your help. I am here, hat in hand, imploring you to help me, so what do you say, Martha? Can I count on you dear," he asked in a begging way.

Turning her head to face him, Martha noticed him helplessly looking at her through his doleful eyes. Helplessness! Wasn't that the very thing that had attracted her to Peter in the first place, when she had met him on that hospital bed all those years ago? Now, how come she couldn't stand it? Why was it that this aspect of his wasn't as endearing to her as it had been then? Still, half convinced that he was genuinely asking for her assistance, she felt like giving him the benefit of the doubt, "Of course I will, haven't I been doing that all along?" she started saying.

"You have and I am grateful to you, even though I didn't deserve it most of the times, but Martha Leigh, I have to tell you this, the pain has not lessened, it is as fierce as ever. I would give anything to have Jeremy back. The fact that I never verbalised these thoughts doesn't mean that I didn't feel them. I was hurting, hurting like you cannot imagine," Peter murmured in a sob.

"Sure I can, I was hurting too, remember? I mourned Jeremy's death in silence and yes, if alcohol hadn't been part of the equation, maybe we would have found solace in each other. We could have helped one another with our grief and heartbreak. Losing Jeremy was like a big part of me had died away but I had to go on living for Sam's sake, in case he needed me for something, someday. Now maybe the time has come for me, for us, to do just that. We have to keep an eye on him Peter and support him in his future life."

"I suppose you are right dear. I promise, I will do my part. I will have to stay sober from now on even if it kills me. I have to keep my eyes peeled in case his future wife or the dragon lady try to tighten their grip on him. Marrying the girl is one thing, staying married to her is another one. With all my being, I wish him luck, I truly do," he said wholeheartedly as he slid one arm around Martha's shoulders and wiped a tear or two from his eyes with the other.

A few minutes later, Martha persuaded her husband to go to bed. He didn't protest. As she was placing the cover over him, Peter grabbed her hand and bringing it to his lips, "Thank you my lovely Florence Nightingale," he said then, turning on his side, he closed his eyes and before long his loud snoring began filling the room. It seemed that the time had come for them to suspend their hostilities.

In the days that followed till the actual wedding day, Peter and Martha didn't breathe a word about what went on between them that night. They were both happy to have rediscovered the feelings they still had for one another and didn't see the need to broadcast it to all. As if the events of the last few years had never happened, the pair took up where they had left off, with the blissful life they once shared together. Despite his cravings for alcohol that, at times, were putting him through hell, Peter managed to stay on top of the situation. He was so affectionate, so understanding and so overly cooperative, it was as if someone had kidnapped him and replaced him with a look alike who had a much more agreeable nature.

Martha couldn't be more pleased. There were no more silent treatments, no coldshouldering each other. She had the Peter of the olden days back in her existence. Her outlook on life had changed considerably with the warmth that had begun to return into her heart. She was so overwhelmingly content that she welcomed Geneviève's parcel containing three outfits and matching accessories that was delivered to her. With Peter's help, she chose the one that fitted her best. Peter still persisted that it would be better if he'd hire his dinner suit and the things that went with it, "Only to remind Geneviève that I won't be ordered around and that she didn't win this round. And one more thing, don't forget to thank her and ask her to forward us her bill for your clothes, when you send the rest of her things back. We may like her taste in women's clothing but we are not a charity case," he stressed. Martha had a brief reflection on the matter then she nodded her consent. 'It's a start,' she thought.

Next door, the Vardas were also running around preparing themselves for Samuel's wedding and looking for the most suitable gifts to give the newlyweds. Even Clara went out of her way and bought herself a glittery maternity dress to wear on the night, as she would be almost twenty weeks into her pregnancy by then.

Chapter 21

The night before Adam and his mother's plane was due to land at Sydney Airport, Jonathan phoned Freeda to inquire about the exact time of their arrival.

"Twenty five past ten," Freeda said before reminding him that he and Liuba were expected for lunch.

"What is the flight number?" he asked holding a pen to write it down.

"You are not planning to go there, are you?"

"Yes, we are, we will be there to pick them up."

"No, that's a long way to drive. You don't have to do that. They can catch a taxi," she said.

"Nonsense, it's the least we can do. We will be there, don't worry. They may need help with the luggage and we don't want them to have to wait for a taxi."

"Thank you for your trouble," Freeda said appreciatively, since she had to stay home to look after Malcolm and get on with her cooking.

It had been over twenty years since the last time Jonathan and Liuba had seen Seraphima. When they spotted her coming through Customs with Adam, they noticed that, even though she had aged, she still had kept some of her charm and natural beauty. After a long drive from the airport, Jonathan steered his car in the driveway and parked in front of Malcolm's stately house. They were almost out of the car when they got sight of Adam's two frantic daughters who talked erratically and at the same time.

"Calm down, what's the matter?" Adam asked, suspecting the worst.

"They took uncle to hospital, mum said you go on without her. She meant have lunch. She phoned a while ago. She'll phone again to tell you what to do. I mean what to take to the hospital," the girls managed to say together.

"Why? What happened? Did uncle have a relapse?" Adam inquired, worried sick.

"Yes, mum was so scared. I called the ambulance. Uncle was a bit better, he was breathing easier, when they were taking him," Violet said excitedly.

Eventually the girls remembered to kiss and welcome their father and grandmother and help her get in the house. They all had lunch in a hurry, hardly exchanging a few words. They were anxiously waiting for the phone to ring. It rang finally and Freeda could give the necessary instructions to Adam, "And don't forget his navy robe and his slippers," she uttered before hanging up.

Adam and Jonathan left instantly for the hospital. Violet and Juliet took on the task of clearing the table and stacking the dishwasher. Liuba was helping Seraphima unpack and settle in her designated room. As the sunshine shooting through the open window was brightening the turquoise bedspread, Seraphima took the last of her clothing items off the bed and hung it in the wardrobe. She smoothed the bedspread then walked to the window and gazed in awe at the breathtaking sight and the magical beauty of the garden outside. Liuba asked her about the latest news in Iran and inquired about their mutual acquaintances. They sat there on a settee and talked some more. When unintentionally Liuba mentioned Shimoon's name, Seraphima's eyes filled with tears. Liuba thought it was better to give her a tour of the rest of the place, letting her recover from her grief as well as familiarise herself with the house she would be living in from then on. On her brief tour, Seraphima came to acknowledge that

Malcolm's magnificent house testified to his wealth, and the décor, his good taste. Back in the living room, they were having tea when Adam, Jonathan and Freeda came back.

"How is your uncle?" Seraphima asked caringly, looking at each of them in turn.

"Stable, he has to undergo another series of tests. They keep giving him drips and he uses an oxygen mask," Freeda said.

"I would like to go and see him some time, if it is possible," Seraphima let out, turning to her son for an answer.

"Of course mum, I'll take you tomorrow," Adam said.

Time and hardship had erased Seraphima's youth but that didn't stop the pale face of Malcolm lighting up unbelievably when he set eyes on her. He stared at her delicate face and her salt and pepper hair that were partly concealed beneath a black laced scarf. He stared long enough for Adam to notice the particular glint that had so magically transformed his uncle's features. Malcolm was holding Seraphima's hand with such devotion it was as if he was trying to draw warmth from it, or some mystical strength that would keep him alive. Puzzled, Adam left the room and went out to find the doctor and try to discuss his uncle's prognosis with him. Unable to erase the scene he had just witnessed, he wondered what to make of it. He got this feeling that the two might have had some issues that needed to be talked over.

Back in the room, Malcolm batted his eyelids as he tried hard to prop himself up a little, "Here, let me help you," Seraphima stood up to give him a hand.

"I am all right, thank you," he said, labouring for breath.

"Do you need another pillow behind your back?"

"No, don't worry. Sit down. Seraphima, I am very sorry about your loss. My brother was a good man. Pity I couldn't be there when he was sick. I intended to fly over but I got sick myself..." Malcolm stayed silent for a while then went on with a renewed energy. "I was not doing so badly. I don't know what triggered that attack I had yesterday. Maybe it was the excitement of meeting you again," he added with a faint smile that made him cough violently.

Seraphima asked him if he wanted some water. He said 'No' with a wave of his shaky hand. When he felt better he continued talking. "Seraphima, I care about you a lot, I always did. Did you know that?" he asked with an exceptionally warm voice.

"Yes, Malcolm, you have always been a very kind and caring person, to everyone especially to Adam. I will always be grateful..."

"No! I meant, I cared about you dear," he said, stressing on the last word. He coughed and gasped some more.

"Don't tire yourself, you need your rest Malcolm," Seraphima said, looking around to see if there was something she could do to help him.

"I don't have much time, I don't want to go before telling you this, I was in love with you, I mean before you went and married my brother, and I never stopped loving you. I couldn't stay in Tehran and watch you play happy family when I was feeling so miserable, that's why I went away. I needed to be by myself. I needed to lick my wounds in private, elsewhere. I still have the ring I wanted to give you that last Sunday before I heard about you and Shimoon's plans..."

"Oh! You never told me. You were so reserved, so quiet," she said. Then, "Actually, I suspected you of having some feelings for me, the night before you left for Australia. Over the years, I ended up believing it might have been nothing but the sadness of separation. I even blamed my imagination playing tricks on me," she added, smiling despite herself.

"It wasn't your imagination. I did and I still do love you. And I will continue loving you as long as I can draw breath. God willing, if I come out of here, we will talk some more about this."

Seraphima felt a rush of warmth in her chest. It rose to her face and made her blush. Malcolm ran his tongue across his parched lips and closed his eyes, exhausted by the effort he had put in expressing those few heartfelt sentences. At last he had managed to get those words off his chest and had let her know what she meant to him.

In a disquieting silence, Seraphima sat there motionless, clutching her handbag. She studied Malcolm's face with a mixture of awe and pity. Pity to see him in such a deplorable condition and perplexedly overwhelmed by the declaration of his undying love for her. Not in a million years could she have guessed the depth of the feelings her brother-in-law had for her.

When Adam came back, Seraphima was still slightly flushed. Dropping her head down, "He is resting. Did you see the doctor?" she whispered.

In an attempt to hide the inner turmoil that Malcolm's words had left her in, Seraphima rummaged in her handbag for a handkerchief she didn't need. Any eye contact with her son could reveal her state of mind and that wasn't what she wished to happen. It was best that she kept her discovery to herself.

"Yes!" Adam said, glancing at Malcolm. When he realised that his uncle's eyes were shut, he turned to his mother and shook his head from side to side letting her draw her own conclusion that Malcolm was not doing all that well.

Seraphima felt a tightening in her stomach. Silently, they left the room. Outside, she asked her son if there was something anyone could do to save Malcolm's life. "Unfortunately not. The cancer has invaded most of his lungs. At this stage, it seems that the cure rate is discouragingly small. I am afraid it may be the end for uncle. The doctor and his colleague said that eventually uncle would not be able to breathe on his own. When that happens, they said they will leave the choice to us, either prolong his life by keeping him hooked on the machines, or let him die in peace," Adam replied gloomily.

"Do you think it's time to call the priest, to give him his last rites, his last Holy Communion? He is still a believer, I hope. I remember he never missed going to church on Sundays, in the olden days..."

"Yes! He actually is," Adam confirmed.

"I think he deserves to die with dignity, don't you think so? Why prolong the agony if there's no hope left?"

"We will decide when the time comes. Now I just can't bring myself to accept that this is really happening. The man who could cast a mighty long shadow, reduced to this?" Adam said, visibly distraught by the thought of losing his much loved and esteemed uncle.

They were about to get back in when they saw Jonathan and Liuba come in through the glass door at the end of the corridor. Adam let his mother go back in alone. He walked towards the Vardas to answer the questions he knew they would have regarding his uncle. At the end of his report, Adam couldn't stop himself from telling them about the way his uncle had reacted earlier when he had come face to face with his mother. "Looks like he is still carrying a torch for her," Jonathan let slip.

"Jonathan!" Liuba chided her husband.

"What? What are you talking about?" Adam asked shocked by the casual way Jonathan talked about his mother and his uncle.

"Don't listen to him," Liuba said, trying to do some damage control but the cat was already out of the bag.

"Tell me the truth if there is something to tell, please. I have the right to know."

"We think, I mean Liuba had her suspicions that he may still be pining after her. Something had made Liuba believe that he might have had deep feelings towards your mum in his younger days. She has also seen a picture of your mother falling from under his pillow," Jonathan tried to explain with a touch of clumsiness.

"I'll be damned! Why is it that the person who is entitled to know something is the last one to be told about it," Adam exclaimed pensively.

"Please Adam, don't make an issue of it. It's not the right time. Your mother may not even be aware of this," Jonathan pleaded with his friend.

"Especially, try not to bring my name up, if possible," Liuba added.

Adam dropped his mother home and rushed to the office. He had a few papers to go over before the important meeting he had scheduled for later. Freeda and the girls were all out.

A different person than the one she had been the previous day when she first arrived, Seraphima stepped inside the house and closed the door. She walked to the kitchen and poured a glass of water, which she drank in one go. She placed the glass next to the big pile of dirty dishes sitting in and around the sink. Taking her eyes away from the mess, she looked through the window and gazed admiringly at a few beautiful statuettes. They were tastefully placed in a man-made miniature rainforest that Malcolm had the landscapers create in the far end of the backyard. Never in her life had she seen a scene so relaxing, so easy on the eyes. She opened the window and let the sweet scent of summer drift in through the flyscreen then took herself to the ample sofa in the family room. Sitting there, unconsciously her avid eyes began scanning the room and she realised that, without flaunting it, prosperity was evident in every piece of furniture, every item on display, every painting hanging on the walls around her.

Deep in thought, the images of the times long gone started to carry Seraphima away. What if Malcolm had revealed his feelings for her back in Iran, like weeks before she had agreed to marry his brother? She thought. Of course, Shimoon was a lot more mature and much better looking than Malcolm was at the time. Seraphima had believed he was more of a romantic type too but now, after hearing Malcolm admit his everlasting love for her, she couldn't decide which one of the two brothers would have tipped the scale in that regard.

Seraphima's thought took her to the times when Malcolm used to pay them a brief visit, whenever he had to be in Tehran for some reason or another. What if, on one of those rare visits, when her husband wasn't home, he had let her know what was in his heart? What if he had asked her to run away with him? Seraphima couldn't help herself from playing this insolent guessing game, neither could she stop recollecting how torturously boring her life had been, year after year. She had a lot of grey hair to prove the mental distress and the lacklustre of her existence. Unconsciously, she began to relive the last days of every month when she had to skimp and scrape to make ends meet. Her husband's inadequate salary could only be stretched so far. He had always been too proud or maybe too pig-headed to accept his younger brother's offer of help.

When Adam was still at home, he never really felt that his parents could have done with a boost in their income. In Australia, he was far too busy learning the ins and outs of his job to even remember how deprived he would have been in Iran if it weren't for his kind uncle's frequent presents to him. In her letters to Australia, Seraphima had kept her money worries to herself. Persistently, she had made Adam believe that they had everything they needed but that couldn't have been any further from the truth. It was an eye opener to Adam when, after years being away, he set foot in his parental house and saw mediocrity at its most blatant. He blamed himself for assuming that his parents lived reasonably well.

Soon after his father died, Adam let his mother sort out her belongings in order to get ready to fly to Australia. In no time Seraphima got rid of the few worn out pieces of furniture and the useless clutter in the drawers. It was then that she realised the only worthwhile items left were given to them by Malcolm and lately by Adam, as Christmas or birthday gifts. Over the years she had considered herself lucky for having a rich and generous brother-in-law. If things had been different, if she had married Malcolm instead of Shimoon, she would have been the benevolent relative who would look after Shimoon and his family whenever it pleased her, she couldn't help thinking.

Yesterday, after she arrived, she was given the tour of the house but she was too tired from her trip and too preoccupied by Malcolm's state of health to take notice of what she really saw. It felt as if she had been walking in a showroom of some sort. All she could remember from the tour was that the whole house had an air of enveloping comfort.

Automatically, like a curious little girl left alone with her mother's makeup kit, she got up and ambled to the formal lounge and dining room as well as every other room in the house and had a serious look at everything in them. "Spectacular will not begin to describe this," she said rather loudly. After feasting her eyes on all that opulence, bewitched by the grandeur of the place, in a trance like state, she went back to her spot on the sofa. Without batting her eyes, she stayed there for a while before recognising the empty feeling she had in the pit of her stomach.

Out of the blue, Seraphima recalled something she had heard people say many times. It was something like, 'What the eyes don't see, the heart won't miss.' Alas, her eyes had seen how her life would have been and her heart had begun grieving over it. Had she not rushed and married Shimoon, who could tell, maybe in a year or two, Malcolm would have been capable of warming his way to her heart.

In the early years of her marriage, Seraphima had considered herself to be a fairly happy woman. Today, she was questioning herself, 'Happy as opposed to whom, the battered, the betrayed or maybe the abandoned wives?' Today, the truth was staring at her. There was more to life than the dull existence she used to call living.

Seraphima's life might have been reasonably acceptable all the while she was busy taking care of Adam but, after he had left, her days had turned nauseatingly monotonous. And now it was too late, too late to turn back the clock and too late to alter the past. That opportunity had slipped out of her hands. She had missed the boat, big time. The saddest part was that she had no idea what her future would be like. After Malcolm, she was going to live in his house, cohabitating with her son's wife, a woman she hardly knew and her two granddaughters that she had met only a few hours earlier. She wondered if she would be welcomed there with open arms by every one of them or be regarded as an undesired outsider.

A car screeched outside, the noise jolted Seraphima out of her thoughts. She felt a bit ashamed for having them, ashamed for passing judgment before knowing for sure how the three women would be treating her. She also chided herself for turning into a shallow and so materialistic person, all of a sudden. It wasn't decent of her to let her mind wonder about Malcolm's feelings and his wealth, when her husband's body was, as they say, still warm in his grave. Yet, those pangs of conscience were short lived. She let a sigh slip out and once more the familiar emptiness engulfed her being. She couldn't help acknowledge that she had wasted a good chunk of her life tolerating Shimoon's fuddy-duddy ways when she could have been cherished and pampered by a man with such a high profile as Malcolm.

Remembering Malcolm, 'And to think that, at this very moment, the poor man is lying hopelessly on a hospital bed, fighting with forces that are marching against him,' she couldn't stop herself thinking. Those thoughts made her feel angry. She felt sorry for Malcolm. She felt sorry for herself. Listlessly, she rubbed her eyes and rose to her feet. She felt the need to pour her heart to someone, someone who would be interested to hear the story of her life. She thought of using Liuba as her confidante, but mulling the idea over for a bit, she decided to give it a miss. "Seraphima, you are certifiably insane if you believe that your boring little life story matters to the world," she muttered, sitting still on that soft sofa.

Seraphima's tired little life story was real unfortunately, and still continuing, and her world had been turned upside down since she had come back from the hospital. Her visit with Malcolm had left her reeling, her mind had been invaded by a whole lot of speculations and what ifs. It had made her feel numb and extremely vulnerable. She had always regarded Malcolm with a tremendous amount of respect. Love, between them, had never been a subject for her to ponder on.

Old time memories crowding her mind, Seraphima went on wrestling with her unrestrained thoughts. Suddenly, as though awakened from a deep sleep, she came to her senses and, jumping to her feet, she hurriedly smoothed her black gabardine skirt over her hips and blinked a few times to regain control of her faculties. Feeling thirsty again reminded her of the dirty dishes she had seen accumulated in the kitchen sink. Her sense of duty told her that it was only proper for her to go and take care of the mess. Still not over her jetlag, the task made her more tired and irritable. It was no wonder that the inevitable question popped in her head. She asked herself the reason behind her decision to leave Iran. Why did she consider moving to Australia without feeling the need to deliberate the pros and cons of her decision? And now that she was here, what was her role supposed to be in that big house, when everyone was out working or going about his or her daily routine?

Lunchtime was approaching and some members of the family were bound to come home, or would they? Nobody had bothered to tell Seraphima how to occupy herself for the rest of the day. She went to her room and lay down on her bed. Before long, she slipped into a much needed sleep. Around one-thirty in the afternoon, she woke up with the sound of the front door closing noisily, followed by the chatter of Freeda and the girls and the dropping of bags of grocery on the kitchen bench. Seraphima went to greet them, "Have you eaten something?" asked Freeda, still holding a bag of fresh French sticks against her chest.

"No, I was resting," she said, as she helped her daughter-in-law place the bag on the overcrowded bench. As quickly as they could, Freeda and the girls transferred a few things from the fridge to the dining table, cut the bread and began making sandwiches. Seraphima spread butter on her bread and topped it with some fig jam. She ate in silence. The rest devoured their sandwiches rather hurriedly. They had to go out again. As they explained, they had an appointment with a bridal shop. Juliet's wedding to Israel was in a few months and, because of Malcolm's sickness, they had fallen behind with their preparations.

The three women were out of the door as quickly as they had come in. Seraphima was left on her own again. She was left alone and depressed. They had gone without as much as a thank you for washing the dishes. Actually, there was another pile of them to be washed. Carrying the tray of crockery to the kitchen, Seraphima's scarf dropped to her shoulders, so did a few tears that rolled down her face. As she placed the tray next to the sink, she wiped her eyes wondering what her tears were for. Was she crying for her departed husband, for Malcolm who was nearing his end or for being treated like a maid by her son's family, commencing the second day after her arrival?

Too busy feeling sorry for herself, Seraphima had not spotted the electric dishwasher tucked under the bench in that ultra-modern kitchen.

Seraphima had been in Australia for a whole week and hadn't seen anything of it yet. That afternoon she was nonchalantly brushing her dull and greying hair, listening to the sound of the wind wreaking havoc in the trees outside her window. A summer storm was nearing. In the next room, Freeda was going through the rigmarole of filling forms for her medical benefit. Adam hadn't returned from the hospital yet. Sadness in her heart, Seraphima was convinced that nothing would ever happen to lift her spirit. Still grappling with the knowledge that Malcolm had always loved and wanted her, she didn't even know what to wish for. She heard the front door open and shut. When no one held any hope for Malcolm's recovery, suddenly good news arrived to change her mood. It seemed that the last treatment the doctors were trying on Malcolm had made a difference, Adam had come to inform them about it. They were all glad that he had responded favourably. They went as far as believing that he might actually conquer the illness or, at least, be well enough to attend the wedding.

Adam was the only one who was not so optimistic. For some reason he remembered an incident that had occurred in his childhood. It was something about an injured bird he had found on the street one day. Together with his father, they had tried to revive and bring it back to life. The bird had shown signs of recovery. It had flapped its wings, had struggled to fly away but eventually had dropped down, limp and lifeless. His father had told Adam that all creatures do that before they die. They gather every bit of their energy and make a last effort to live before giving up altogether. Deep in his heart, Adam felt that his uncle's cancer would return to finish what it had started, if what his father had said applied to humans too.

The next morning, on the doctor's request, the members of the family took turns to see Malcolm. They kept their visits short, in order not to tire him. When Seraphima went in, she sat by his side silently and stared at his emaciated face. "You are here," he said, turning his smiling face towards her. He tried to grab her hand. In a wave of tenderness, he held it for a while and squeezed it gently.

"I prayed for you," she said, noticing that his energy level had picked up since she last saw him. He looked like he was on the mend. 'Maybe there is hope for him to make it. Maybe he could really be restored to his former self,' she thought.

"In a few days, God willing, I might be well enough to go home. Should this happen, as my hope is..."

"Oh, Malcolm, you don't have to rush, make sure you are strong enough before you leave the hospital," Seraphima interrupted.

"I will be, trust me. I have a few things to take care of. I need to make a new will. A certain clause in the testament needs to be specified."

"Yes, but don't you go and tire yourself unnecessarily."

"Don't worry dear," he said with his once imposing and remarkable voice that had become so weak lately.

Outside the rain persisted and despite the humidity that was making her arthritic joints throb with pain, in Seraphima's heart, a soothing warmth had begun to manifest itself. The thought of all the words that Malcolm had left unsaid had restored her confidence that maybe not everything was lost for her. Maybe fate had stepped in to give her a little something that would take the edge off her sadness. Only, for the life of her, she didn't have the slightest clue as to what that something could be to brighten her days.

Chapter 22

I n Geneviève's spanking mansion, every light in every room was on. The beauticians were running around getting the bridesmaids dolled up. After fastening the long line of tiny buttons at the back of Aurore's shimmering silk chiffon dress, "c'est parfait, absolument parfait," Geneviève affirmed. As she fluffed the skirt that flowed about her daughter like a cloud of steam, choked up by mixed emotions, Geneviève tried hard to prevent herself from crying. She was also worried that tears could make her mascara run and she wouldn't have time to start her makeup all over again.

Elegant in its basic simplicity, the bridal gown was by all means the most enchanting wedding dress Aurore would have wished to wear, on her big day. Stepping back to view herself in the cheval mirror, she smiled. Her smile confirmed that she agreed with her mother. "It is really perfect mum, thank you," she whispered, gratitude bringing a warm glow in her beautiful eyes.

One of the bridesmaids helped Jule the hairdresser secure the diamante tiara and the veil on the bride's head. The makeup lady applied the ultimate touch-up to Aurore's face and she was ready. "My little darling, let me hold you one last time before you leave this house," her mother implored. And without waiting for a reply, Geneviève gave her daughter a careful hug and, her lips barely touching Aurore's face, she kissed her. "You are the most beautiful bride I have ever seen," she said, before she let go of her.

Finally when everyone was ready, Geneviève and the maid put most of the lights off and the house alarm on and they were all on their way out. Beaming with happiness, Aurore left the house she loved so much. The whole gang ambled towards the decorated limousines that were waiting at the door to take them to the church.

Followed by Geneviève and the bridesmaids, Aurore walked through a glare of flashing lights coming from the cameras of professional as well as amateur photographers. Dragging her long trail behind her, she passed through the church door as an organist struck the wedding march. Flanked by her overdressed mother and holding her head high, bouquet in hands, she inched her way along the aisle to get to the altar. As she got closer, mesmerised and finding it hard to believe his luck, Samuel couldn't take his eyes off her. "It is happening, it is actually happening," he whispered under his breath.

Geneviève had put her foot down to be the one who gives the bride away. "I raised her on my own, so I should have the privilege," she had argued. She couldn't even admit it to herself that the real reason behind this decision was her aspiration to shine alongside her daughter. It was her undying desire to be noticed by the only person she cared and was longing to be admired by. Even the fact that Farhad's wife was pregnant and that he had eyes for no other woman but her, couldn't stop Geneviève wanting his approval on how she was dressed and coiffed.

Struggling on her uncomfortable high-heeled shoes, Geneviève's legs went weak when she spotted Farhad standing at the edge of a pew. As always, one look at his sleekly dressed figure and the pit of her stomach churned. Once again his fascinating looks turned her heart over and the distressful realisation that she was still yearning for him made her feel ill. She could still see the reflection of her dreams in his eyes. He was still the light of her life, her raison d'être. It was a good thing that nobody could ban her from fantasising about him.

Geneviève stood one step behind the bride and waited for the others to assume their places. In the eyes of her mind, she saw herself twirling round and round in Farhad's arms. Sensing his tender grip, she was allowing herself to float around an imaginary dance floor, oblivious to the rest of the world. Her daydreaming got interrupted though, when she heard the priest ask, "Who is giving this woman away?"

"I am," she answered, blushing under her heavy makeup. A few minutes later she was listening attentively to the solemn exchanges of vows. Her maternal feelings kicking in, with a lump in her throat, she closed her eyes to savour the moment. So far, Geneviève had been cautiously optimistic about this union but, all of a sudden, she startled herself awake. When she least expected it, she began wondering whether this marriage was a mistake and if it was, how much was she to blame for letting it to get to that stage.

As they were leaving the church, Samuel and Aurore passed through a shower of confetti and rice. Later, at the reception hall, when the bride and groom and their entourage made their entry, an admiring murmur echoed from the guests who were already there. They were greeted and seated by uniformed ushers.

Once they had the formalities out of the way, the party began and was soon in full swing. The glittering array of friends and acquaintances were having a really good time. Well dressed waiters carrying authentic French Champagne in slender stemmed glasses kept making their way around the tables. After their initial opening dance, Samuel and Aurore were again amongst the many dancing couples. Their bodies in sync, they were graciously moving to the rhythm of the music. As they moved under the scintillating light of the huge crystal chandeliers, the diamante tiara on Aurore's head gleamed magnificently. Utterly happy, she couldn't stop herself humming the words of the song they were dancing to. Reassured that nothing could possibly spoil their night, Samuel gave his wife a peck on the cheek and, pressing her against his chest, he inwardly whispered, "Let the good times roll."

From the moment the Goddards sat at their table in the luxurious reception hall, overcome by conflicting emotions, Peter kept stuffing his face with scrumptious hors d'oeuvres. Every now and then he washed them down with juices that the waiters regularly brought to their table. As long as he wasn't making sarcastic remarks or going for the alcoholic stuff, it was all right with Martha. His eating was nothing that couldn't be remedied with some antacid, in case he suffered indigestion, she was thinking.

From across the big round table, Jonathan was doing his part in keeping an eye on Peter. Trying to take his neighbour's mind off the wedding, he kept talking about irrelevant incidents and spicing them up with little jokes. In detail, he also recounted how his own parents had eloped. "He was on his horse. She was waiting for him in her father's orchard holding a few of her clothes that she had stashed in the food basket she was supposed to be taking for the workers. Bending down, right in front of her stunned grandmother, he grabbed her by her waist and they fled to the chapel in the nearest village to theirs," he was saying, when Clara came back from her trip to the little girl's room. As soon as she sat down she declared that the other pregnant lady they had bumped into in the doorway was also from Iran, "Her name is Shereen, she told me."

The waiters arrived and started serving the dinner. Jonathan was convinced that, since Samuel and Aurore had already been married at the church, there was no point dwelling on the subject of whether their marriage would last or not. It was a done deal and they all had better enjoy themselves and worry about it later, if things were doomed to go astray between the two. After the lavish dinner the dance floor was once again filled with dancing couples.

Having knocked back a copious amount of food, soft drinks and juices, Peter felt the need to pay a visit to a certain establishment, as he liked to call it, so he made a dash to the hotel's lavatories. On his way back, his fatherly love gave him the urge to make a stop in front of the tastefully ornate bridal table. He wished to congratulate his son and exchange a few words with him, and maybe welcome his daughter-in-law in his family. He was halfway into the huge lobby when he found himself face to face with Geneviève. She was chatting with a guest while he was fiddling with his cumbersome camera. Begrudgingly, Peter thought he had to acknowledge her presence but, despite his determination to stay civil, the words just poured out of his mouth as he made the gesture of taking his hat off and saluting her. "Well, well, well, if it's not the bane of my life. My, oh my! Don't we look like mutton dressed up as a lamb?" he said with a snort, pretending he was trying to suppress his laughter.

Regarding him with pure venom, she scowled her dissatisfaction. "Tell me Peter, this unattractive stubbornness, does it come to you naturally or did you have to work hard at acquiring it? Sorry, I suppose it was presumptuous of me asking you to present yourself in a civilised way, just this once," she said through her teeth, ice dripping from every syllable.

Holding the bottom edge of his dinner jacket, Peter twisted around like a little girl and comically batted his eyes. "Actually, I thought I looked like a million dollars," he said. Then, making a sad face, he asked, "Don't you think that I look cute?"

"Not at all," she said, moving her hand in front of herself.

"Does that mean I am off your dance card your highness?" he asked.

Ignoring his question, she said, "It's your son's wedding, for heaven's sake. Was it so hard for you..."

"Oh! My mistake. I though it was your daughter's wedding. Come to think of it, I wondered why I was invited in the first place," he interrupted with a straight face.

"I wish you'd lose that sick sense of humour," Geneviève interjected, her voice rising with irritation.

"At least I have one, darling," he said, still keeping his calm.

Geneviève rolled her eyes in a mock horror and went on, "If only you had the courtesy to feel a little ashamed of yourself. Of course

I was aware of your lack of social grace but tell me, what did you think you would achieve by defying some simple rules?"

"For your information Ma'am, I live by my own rules and no one, you hear me, no one is going to dictate to me what I should or shouldn't do," he blurted out trying hard not to be excessively loud.

"Just who do you think you are?" she asked, squinting her eyes in disgust.

"Never mind who I am. I know what you are. You are nothing but a big mouth and a lot of hot air Mrs De La bloody Lande," he uttered through gritted teeth.

Had he stayed a little longer, Peter's emotions would probably boil over, therefore he turned around rather abruptly and began leaving. Bumping into a passing waiter on his way, he grabbed a glass of something from his tray and ceremoniously holding it between his fingers, he turned his head and looking at her with blazing eyes, he drowned the content in a gulp. With his bare hand, he then wiped his mouth that was twisted in an ironic wryness.

"So that's how much your son means to you?" he heard Geneviève say as he walked away.

In the hotel's lobby, except for a few members of the staff and a couple of waiters, not many other people witnessed that unpleasant encounter, still a bit of whispering followed Peter's retreat from the scene.

'How can such a swell looking man be so obnoxious,' Geneviève thought as she watched him zigzagging through the crowd.

'How dare she question my feelings for my son?' Peter was thinking when, a few steps further he spotted Jonathan and noticed the look of concern on his face. Geneviève's last comment was like rubbing salt in his open wound and the fact that she had the last word more than justified the fast mounting resentment Peter felt towards her.

Followed by Jonathan and blind to the eye-catching elegance of the surroundings, and ignoring the irritating general chatter of the guests, Peter hurried over to their table. Once there he sat sideways next to his wife and, caressing her done up silvery hair, he sedately stared into her eyes and, with a soft but firm tone, "We are going home, Martha Leigh," he declared.

Martha looked around perplexedly and was about to ask him why, when from behind Peter, Jonathan made her a sign that meant, 'It's best not to argue and just do as he says.' Sensing trouble, Martha grabbed her evening bag and nodding at everyone at their table, she got up and followed her husband without a second thought. They walked together towards the closest door of the hall then eased themselves out of the imposing entrance door. On the dance floor, their son and his new wife were gently swaying to the beat of their hearts and the music.

"We'd better follow them, I feel worried a bit, you know?" Jonathan said, addressing Marcus and Clara.

"It's a good idea dad, but it's best if Clara and I stayed until the end. It won't look good if we all vacate the table," Marcus suggested.

"Of course. I didn't mean you should leave too. You stay and enjoy yourselves but give us a call when you get home no matter how late it is. We need to know that you got home safely."

"We will dad."

Outside, the first drops of rain had started to fall. Martha pulled her shimmery shawl tightly around her shoulders and practically ran to keep pace with Peter. As soon as they got in the car, surprisingly with the first turn of the key, the engine sprang to life and Peter's old Ford Valiant screeched off the parking place. After a right turn, the car went to merge with the dwindling traffic.

Jonathan and Liuba also rushed to their car. "What did really happen back there? Did he have a fight with the mother?" Liuba asked.

"Yes! That woman is good at pushing buttons," he only said, visibly upset with the way things had turned out.

"God have mercy on Samuel," Liuba whispered, wiping a droplet of rain from her face.

At the reception hall, the music had stopped momentarily. With a tremulous excitement, Samuel was holding his bride's hand as they walked to their table. A small number of guests who couldn't stay to see the wedding cake being cut were waiting to wish them all the happiness of the world before leaving. Her intensely green eyes shining like a pair of emeralds, Geneviève was standing there too. She was shaking hands with the guests, utterly flattered by the compliments and praises that she believed were her due.

Meanwhile, in the Goddard's car the tension was palpable. Martha kept her quiet but she was sickeningly eager to know what had prompted Peter to act the way he did. What was so damn important that they had to leave before the night had ended? She could hear the sound of her heart, every beat stabbing her with an unexplained fear. For the life of her, she couldn't comprehend the hostility her husband was harbouring towards Geneviève. Granted they didn't see eye to eye on some matters but did he have to make such a big deal of it? She was thinking.

Martha was grateful though that they got out of there without Peter making a scene and publicly embarrassing their son. Judging by the way Peter had conducted himself in the last few weeks, she couldn't bring herself to blame him for any wrongdoing. She didn't even smell liquor on his breath. Anger building up inside her, inwardly she cursed Geneviève for stirring up trouble and making her miss the end of her son's wedding reception. Why couldn't she leave things well enough alone? Martha really wished she could see her son and his bride off to their honeymoon. She was counting on having a few photos taken with them as they were saying their goodbyes.

Peter was having a conversation with himself too and although he was driving responsibly, his irregular breathing was telling a lot about what was passing through his head. 'Oh, what I wouldn't give to be able to wipe that arrogant smirk off the bitch's face,' he was thinking.

The stormy clouds gathering on the horizon were also telling that the light rain would intensify any time now. Peter had entered the Crows Nest area and was cruising along Willoughby Road. He was still sulking. Martha was fuming. She couldn't take any more of that nerve wrecking silence. "Are you going to talk or not?" she finally asked Peter.

"Talk about what, dear?" he answered as he turned left into a long street that would take them to the street where they lived. Suddenly, from the opposite lane, a driver, trying to overtake the vehicle in front of him, moved in Peter's lane. Headlights glaring, his car was coming straight at Peter. Stunned, Peter swerved abruptly to the left to prevent a head-on collision. The other car sped past, narrowly missing Peter's taillight. A disaster could have been prevented if it wasn't for the signpost that was standing at the side of the road. Peter managed to dodge the offending car but he couldn't do the same with the obstacle. Simultaneously, Martha heard a bang and the sound of metal crushing. As in a nightmare, she heard herself screaming. A terrible pain tore through her body before she passed out.

It all happened so quickly. There was a big chance that the young drivers who had caused that catastrophe didn't even realise what they had done. The two cars driving behind Peter stopped, then the Varda's vehicle approached and did the same. There was a deafening sound of a horn blaring. Jonathan opened the door on his side and stepped out to find out what was happening and why people in front of him were leaving their cars, when he saw the wreckage. "Oh, my God, it's them," he shouted. "It's them," he repeated, turning to Liuba.

Her hand flying to her mouth and shaking uncontrollably, Liuba got out of the car too. They both rushed to the scene, hoping to see that their neighbours were all right. The first thing Jonathan saw was Peter's chest resting against the steering wheel and activating the horn.

A lady who was at her balcony rescuing her baby's blanket from getting rained on witnessed the whole thing and called the police. Minutes later the wailing sound of sirens filled the air. It took a while for the officers to free the occupants out of the mangled green Valiant and transfer them into the ambulance. Martha was still alive but the paramedics had pronounced Peter dead on impact.

Jonathan was helping the police with their inquiries by answering their questions regarding the victims of the car crash. He was allowed to go with them to the hospital. Farhad appeared out of nowhere and recognised them from the wedding. He volunteered his help. Feeling not in a good shape to drive, Liuba asked him if he could possibly park their car somewhere safe and drive her to her home.

"No problem, " Farhad said. Minutes later, he led her towards his car and drove her to her house. Before getting out of the car, Liuba thanked him and his wife for their kindness and, once inside her home, she phoned the wedding venue and asked for Marcus. Her voice still shaking with the dreadful shock, she told her son about the accident and gave him the unpleasant task of relaying it to Samuel. "Tell him they took them to the Royal North Shore Hospital," she mentioned again.

"I'll take Clara home and go there myself. If you want to go too, I'll come and pick you up."

"Yes please. I won't be able to sleep anyway and Martha may need me," she said, choked up by sadness.

Chatting away with a few of his co-workers, Samuel was beaming with joy when Marcus tapped him on the shoulder. He had a grave look on his face but Samuel was too busy being happy to take notice. "Samuel, I have something to tell you, it's important," he said. At that same time, Aurore called Samuel asking him to join her so they could pose for a photo with some of her friends from the modelling agency. Samuel was about to tell Marcus to wait a while but, Marcus insisted, "This can't wait my friend, it's about your parents."

"What about my parents? I need to take photos with them too. Where are they?" he asked, looking around to see them.

"Actually, they left a while ago," Marcus said and when he saw disappointment on Samuel's face he added, "I am sorry to tell you this Samuel, I am afraid your parents were involved in a car accident on their way home."

After a short period of confusion, the words registered in Samuel's mind. A weary look appeared in his eyes. "They are OK, aren't they?" he inquired, hoping that nothing major had happened to them.

"I don't exactly know all the details but I was told that you are needed at the Royal North Shore Hospital's emergency unit." Marcus blurted out in a gloomier tone.

Without preambles, Samuel whispered the news to Aurore and their entourage. He then ran out and ordered one of the limousine drivers to take him straight to the hospital. The maid of honour and her husband proposed to take Aurore to her new home. As they were beginning to make their retreat without attracting too many people's attention, Marcus grabbed the bride's arm and told her the truth about her in-law's accident. After they left, Geneviève asked the best man to kindly inform the guests that the party was over.

Outside, the rain came bucketing down. As she sat uncomfortably in the back of their car, Aurore was glad that her maid of honour and her husband couldn't see the indignation on her face. She was in no way ready to let her excitement die down. She had her heart set on that trip to the Caribbean that was given to them by no other than her dear mother as their wedding present. No way would she give up on that sort of honeymoon. 'First thing in the morning I have to call Giselle and ask her if she can cancel the tickets and reschedule for a later date,' she thought.

On his way to the hospital, Samuel couldn't stop himself wondering if his father had been drinking and if that had been the cause of the accident. The very thought of that made his blood boil with resentment. Upon his arrival in the emergency room, after introducing himself at the desk, he was given the horrific news that his father was already dead when he was brought in. "My mother, is she all right?" he asked with trepidation.

"She has suffered a fracture on her left thigh and her left arm is badly bruised. She has bumped her head somewhere too. She is still unconscious. The doctors are doing their best to stabilise her," a young doctor answered him.

"Can I see her?"

"Sure, I can take you there but not right now. At the moment, the doctors are with her. It's best to let them do their job. If you go down this corridor and turn left, you will find the waiting room. I'll come to get you when they are done."

Samuel went out and, after a few inquiries he finally got hold of the doctor who had checked his father. Badly shaken with grief and anxiety, Samuel didn't know what to say or ask the surgeon. "I am very sorry..." Doctor Boswell began to say then, looking at the way Samuel was dressed, he asked him if they had all been at a party.

"Yes, my wedding party," Samuel said.

"Oh that explains the clothes. I am really sorry. Losing your father is bad enough but losing him on your wedding night must be terrible. Please accept my condolences," the doctor said, caringly patting Samuel on the shoulder.

"Tell me doctor, was my father under the influence?" Samuel asked, unable to keep the burning question unanswered any longer.

Looking at the chart he was holding and in no uncertain terms, the doctor confirmed that the alcohol level in Peter's blood was nil. "Actually, we suspect that your father's death was mostly caused by a heart attack and not from the few superficial injuries that he had sustained. We are still running tests, trying to ascertain our finding. We will inform you of the results," he added before he was called away.

Pain and confusion set in his eyes, Samuel strode off too. On his way, unsure that they would let him see his mother, he stood in front of a window and looked out through the glass. He felt the need to have a peephole to the world beyond the hospital, hoping he would see a tranquil place, a place devoid of suffering, where he would be able to forget his problems just by imagining he was actually there. The only things he saw were the early morning lights and shadows that were eerily dancing on the wall of another one of the hospital's buildings. Dismayed, he left his unfriendly window and walked towards the intensive care unit to face his mother's medical crisis.

This time Samuel was allowed to enter. A rim of her silvery hair peeking from beneath the hospital head cover and, as pale as a ghost, Martha was on the bed, attached to all sorts of beeping machines. Blood and other liquids were dripping from hanging bags into her vein. "Mum, it's me Sam," he murmured, hoarse with worry and when he didn't hear any sound coming from her discoloured lips, he asked a nurse who was adjusting the drips, "What are her chances of survival and recovery?"

The nurse glanced at Samuel then signalled a doctor who was talking to another patient. The doctor excused himself and came closer to answer Samuel's question. "Your mother has lost a lot of blood. Her femur is badly broken. She has a hairline fracture on her upper arm and a concussion to the side of her head. At this time, her state is considered critical. We are keeping an eye on her heart and blood pressure and we are waiting for her to regain consciousness. In the next twenty-four hours, if she shows signs of improvement, there's a big chance she will pull through. It's only then that we would be able to concentrate on her injuries. She may need an operation or two to have her thighbone reconstructed. Even then, it will be a while before she can be anything near her old self again. Still, we are hopeful that she will soon come to. We just have to wait and see," the doctor added trying not to sound too pessimistic.

Looking at the shape his mother was in, in Samuel's mind, the word hopeful didn't have that ring of confidence about it. Worriedly shifting from one foot to the other, he stood by Martha's bedside, talking to her softly, hoping that if she could hear him she might fight harder and come back to him. After all, she was the only relative he had left in the world. A nurse brought him a chair. Samuel thanked her and moved it closer to the bed. He then took his tailcoat off, folded it under his arm and sat down. He gently grabbed his mother's limp hand and squeezing it in his, he continued with his monologue.

Samuel's eyes were burning. He blinked a few times and mercifully tears began oozing out from between his lashes and rolling down his face. He didn't bother wiping them but stopped talking. Crushed under the weight of his sorrow, he stayed in that same position until he felt a hand on his shoulder. It was Marcus who urged him to get out for a while. They walked through a long corridor and headed towards the waiting room where they both sank in the nearest armchairs. "I am sorry about your dad," Marcus said, trying hard to prevent tears from gathering in his eyes.

"Why Marcus, why did this have to happen tonight?" Samuel cried, then all of a sudden he turned to Marcus and asked him if he knew the reason why both of their parents had to leave so early. Marcus had no choice but to tell Samuel the little that he himself knew. "I think your dad had a tiff with your mother-in-law. My dad believes that she had started the argument."

Anger, raw and powerful taking hold of his whole body, Samuel blurted out, "So you are saying that the bossy boots killed him."

"I wouldn't go that far. She might have made him nervous enough to leave but..."

"You would if you knew that my father has died from a heart attack. She killed him as if she had plunged a knife in his heart. I will never forgive the heartless bitch," Samuel said, a bit louder than the hospital rules allow.

"I have reason to believe that it wasn't just her doing. Apparently your dad was caught in the middle of two drivers trying to overtake each other. It seems that there was a lady standing on a balcony who saw what happened. She was the one who called the police."

Looking Marcus in the eyes, Samuel said as he scrambled to his feet, "What am I going to do Marcus, what am I going to do? What if my mother doesn't regain consciousness? I'd better go back there."

"I'll go find dad. Mum is here too. She came to see if she could be of any help to your mum."

"You are all so nice, I can't thank you enough." Samuel said and went back to his mother's side. He sat by her bed again and talked to her. Over and over, he begged her not to leave him too. In between talks, he prayed for her as fervently as he could. Unexpectedly, Samuel felt the presence of his late brother by his side. Asking his help from beyond, he prayed some more. As if she heard his desperate plea, Martha opened and closed her eyes then a faint moaning sound came out of her throat. "She is coming to!" Samuel cried, waving his hand to the nurse who hurried to alert the doctor.

The doctor came and checked Martha's vital signs. After batting her eyelids a few times, Martha went back to the way she was before but the doctor was confident that she was going to be all right. The Vardas arrived and took turns to see her. A few hours later, seeing the state that Samuel was in, Liuba insisted on Marcus giving him a lift home. "We are both here, if something happens we will call you," she said firmly, signalling her son to take him.

"You need to go home to your bride who must be worried sick. Have a bit of rest if you can. We have a lot to do tomorrow, regarding your dad," Jonathan added with sadness.

"How about you, you are as tired as I am. You haven't had any sleep either."

"Don't worry about us, go," Liuba stressed.

Looking a bedraggled mess, Samuel turned his newly cut personal key in the lock and quietly opened, entered and shut the front door to the place he was to share with his new bride. It was a townhouse he and Aurore had bought and decorated together. Totally depleted of energy, he passed by the archway that led to the living room. He threw his tailcoat in the direction of the hatstand he had bought the previous weekend believing it was a must to have in his future home. Then, holding on to the ramp, he dragged his tired body up the carpeted stairs expecting to find his wife fast asleep in the bedroom. To his surprise, he heard her talking.

From the tone of her voice and the way she was conducting the conversation, Samuel deducted that Aurore was on the phone. The words she spoke were somewhat incomprehensible at first but, as he approached the landing, he distinctively heard her say, "And the idiot, it wasn't bad enough that he made a nuisance of himself at the reception and irritated my mother to tears, what with all the trouble she went through organising the lavish wedding, he had the gall to go and get himself killed. Talking of bad timing! It was as if he did it on purpose, just to spite us."

There was a pause. It seemed as though Aurore was listening to whatever the person on the other end of the line was saying then, she said, "Hardly a tragedy but yes, his death did ruin our chances, my chance to go and enjoy my honeymoon. I tell you, the stupid despicable drunkard truly messed up things for me."

As if he had stepped into the twilight zone, Samuel froze in his spot, unable to take another step. He stood there long enough to catch the last bit of the callous piece of gossip and found out what kind of an insensitive girl he was married to. Chagrin crossing his face, disillusioned and dismayed to breaking point, he turned his heels around and took the way down the stairs, each step taking him an eternity to descend.

After kicking away his jacket that had missed the hook on the hatstand, Samuel went to flop down heavily on the settee in the living room. It was only two nights ago that they had been sitting on that same settee. He remembered how, sealing it with the most passionate kiss, they both had pledged their eternal love for each other.

Elbows resting on his knees, temples throbbing, nerves in tatters, Samuel went on holding his aching head. Those few uncalled for words he had inadvertently overheard must have made a tremendous impact on his whole being. They had indeed blown him away. Samuel just couldn't believe this was happening to him. Without any warning he was shown the ugly side of his other half. The flawless image he had of his beloved Aurore in his mind had lost its lustre. It had been tarnished beyond repair in a matter of seconds. "Like mother, like daughter," he recalled hearing his father say once and he had refused to believe it.

Not only had Samuel lost his father, whom he loved and respected despite the few little imperfections in his character, he was likely to lose his mother as well. He didn't need any more heartache. His sleepless eyes filled with more tears, bitter tears that kept rolling down his face like a stream that spills down a hillside. Somewhere in his heart, he felt an invisible crack appear and gradually deepen. A wall started to go up between him and the woman he was supposed to live with until death did them part.

Samuel wiped his eyes with his bare hand when, out of the blue, a sentence popped into his mind. He had heard it from Jonathan's friend Adam. For some reason, Adam had quoted it from a textbook he had to study at school back in Iran. The book was originally written in the Sanskrit language. It said, as he vaguely recalled, "A rain of two hundreds years would not settle the troublesome dust that you have raised with your irresponsible words." How true he thought, because he couldn't see himself forgetting in a hurry those heartless comments that had come out of Aurore's mouth.

As if his inner turmoil wasn't bad enough, Samuel suddenly became aware of the dilemma he was faced with. He was now forced to choose between two evils. He could go upstairs and make his wife eat her words and apologise, even though in his book, what she had said was beyond forgiveness. He could also let go of the fury that had started to bubble inside of him and ignore the whole incident; ignore the pain she had caused him, stay put and make a semblance that he had just arrived home. Both of his options were easier said than done but he had to decide on one or the other.

Samuel believed that Aurore's nasty words would keep coming back to haunt him. He was sure they would mar his waking hours as well as disrupt his sleep, no matter how hard he would try to sugarcoat them. Nevertheless, he had to live with them should he wish to stay with her.

Samuel couldn't say how long he sat there weeping openly when he felt a hand caressing his head. "Darling, I didn't hear you come in. I am sorry for what has happened," he heard his wife say. Standing behind him, she waited a while then asked, "How is your mum?" When she didn't get any reply, she went on, "Is there's something I can do..." Her voice echoed in Samuel's mind like a call from far, far away. It took him a while to respond by shaking his head. Aurore got the hint that he didn't need her help. Unable to see how contempt had his face all screwed up, she persisted in keeping the communication lines open. "It's a bit chilly here, how about we go upstairs and get some sleep. You must be exhausted darling. Do you want me to run the bath for you, it will relax you?"

"Relax me? Do you think I can relax?" he blurted out suddenly. "My father is in the morgue and my mother could join him any minute and you think I can relax. This was supposed to be the happiest night of my life. Look at me," he cried with a desolate tone, pointing his open palms downward and gazing at his crumpled, dusty and blood stained wedding attire.

"I know this must be hard on you. I am really sorry. I wish your mother gets well soon," Aurore could only mutter.

After a long silence, without looking at her, Samuel brought himself to ask her, "You were talking to Giselle, weren't you? You were cancelling the...," the rest of the sentence hung in the air like a dark cloud.

Aurore's heart missed a beat. A cold shiver rippled down her spine. "Yes!" she answered, trying hard to conceal her panic, and quickly changed the subject. She kept playing the attentive wife who cares for her husband's wellbeing while, in her head, the question, 'How much did he hear?' wreaked havoc with her nerves.

"Go back to sleep. I need some time to myself," Samuel almost ordered her. Aurore thought it was wiser to make herself scarce and not have to answer any more questions, in case he had heard a lot more than she would have wanted him to. On her way upstairs, 'What wouldn't I do at this moment if I could take back every unpleasant word I had let myself utter,' she thought.

Worriedly Aurore began weighing the consequences of her nasty and unthoughtful faux pas. 'Whatever possessed me to talk the way I did? Those repulsive things I said will hang over my head forever. They are bound to draw a wedge between us. They might have already changed his perception of me. What am I going to do?' she kept wondering. She had all the questions but not one answer to reassure her, to show her a way out of the mess she had created. Arms crossed she was sitting on the bed, biting her lips and silently chiding herself for having spoken her mind loud enough for him to hear.

The early birds had not picked the scattered rice off the church's stairs yet, when Aurore felt the silent progress of the first crack in her marriage.

After a while, feeling cold in her flimsy nightgown, she slid under the covers. A long time went by. She was about to fall asleep when she sensed the bed move. Aurore pretended to be in deep sleep when she felt Samuel's arms grabbing her. Without a word, he hastily rolled her on her back and pulled her to the middle of the bed. Momentarily confused, Aurore blinked and let out a sleepy moan to make him believe she was just waking up. 'Seize the moment girl, this could be the answer to your problem,' she thought.

"What am I supposed to do Aurore, what am I supposed to do? I need you, I need you," Samuel cried as his hands travelled below her waistline, reaching hungrily for her velvety soft and warm hips.

Was that a moment of strength or one of weakness? Samuel would have the rest of his days to figure that out. 'He says he needs me and I'll be damned if I try to stop him now,' Aurore went on thinking, her mind filled with a deliciously tingling anticipation of heated moments of love. Using her silken voice, she purred and arched her back. "Oh Samuel," she whispered when, to her surprise, she realised Samuel was in the process of having his way with her. Caught off-guard, Aurore lay there unable to make a move to participate or to stop him. Contrary to her wild expectations, there were no words of love, no fiery kisses and certainly none of the intimacy that normally comes before the actual lovemaking act. The whole event ended as quickly as it had begun and, as soon as it was over, Samuel dropped onto his side of the bed and drifted into an agitated but much needed sleep.

Unable to make sense of whatever had transpired between her and her husband, feeling neglected, used and tossed aside, Aurore stayed awake for quite a while. Eventually, as she wriggled to find a comfortable position to sleep, eyes shut, she sarcastically murmured through her teeth, "And they lived happily ever after."

Samuel woke several times during the three hours he intended to sleep. He had to meet with Jonathan. Together they had to go and talk with the manager of a funeral parlour.

Aurore got up a bit before midday and found herself alone in their bed. She had a splitting headache. Streaming through the window, the sun was straight in her face. Moving away from the sunny spot, the incident of the night before came back to her. 'Did that really happen or is this a figment of my imagination?' she wondered, baffled by Samuel's strange behaviour. Thinking some more about the subject, it dawned on her that Samuel seemed to be transformed into a totally different person from the one she had known before. As a matter of fact, he was nothing like the man who had made love to her only two nights ago.

Eyes closed, Aurore tried to relive those few glorious hours they had shared on that very same bed, the day it was delivered to them. Together they had put the satin bed sheets on. They had put the covers on the new pillows, had fluffed them and when everything else was in place, instead of leaving, Samuel had scooped her off the floor and had placed her gently on the bed. She could still hear his soft and caressing voice as he told her over and over how much he loved her.

Aurore could still feel Samuel's warm lips impatiently going for hers and kissing them so very enchantingly, so unrestrainedly, she was left out of breath. His kisses were followed by incredible moments of complete and utter euphoria. The captivating memories of his passionate embrace and the way his touch had made her groan with pleasure were all there. Comparing them with those of a few hours ago, they were telling her that things might never be the same again. Thinking about the events of the previous night, straight after Marcus had given them the tragic news, aggravated her headache. It was undeniable that Aurore had started her conjugal life under less than ideal circumstances and that realisation made her suddenly feel cheated and very angry at the world.

After finalising everything with the undertakers, utterly dispirited Samuel went to see his mother. He found two doctors standing by her bed discussing her case. They were worried about her. Her heart was a bit weak but they believed they couldn't wait much longer if they wished to fix her broken bone. After they left, Samuel sat by her side and caressed her hand then he began talking to her, "Promise me you won't jump ship on me too mum, because I need you. You can't imagine how much I need you. You have to fight harder mum, for yourself and for me. Mum, I desperately need you now." In her semi-unconscious mind, his words sounded like they were coming from miles away, like a call on the wind. Martha finally came to and mumbled a few words. Two hours later, they hurriedly prepared her for her operation.